THE SHINING BADGE

BOOKS BY GILBERT MORRIS

THE HOUSE OF WINSLOW SERIES

1. The Honorable Imposter
2. The Captive Bride
3. The Indentured Heart
4. The Gentle Rebel
5. The Saintly Buccaneer
6. The Holy Warrior
7. The Reluctant Bridegroom
8. The Last Confederate
9. The Dixie Widow
10. The Wounded Yankee
11. The Union Belle
12. The Final Adversary
13. The Crossed Sabres
14. The Valiant Gunman
15. The Gallant Outlaw
16. The Jeweled Spur
17. The Yukon Queen
18. The Rough Rider
19. The Iron Lady
20. The Silver Star
21. The Shadow Portrait
22. The White Hunter
23. The Flying Cavalier
24. The Glorious Prodigal
25. The Amazon Quest
26. The Golden Angel
27. The Heavenly Fugitive
28. The Fiery Ring
29. The Pilgrim Song
30. The Beloved Enemy
31. The Shining Badge

CHENEY DUVALL, M.D.[1]

1. The Stars for a Light
2. Shadow of the Mountains
3. A City Not Forsaken
4. Toward the Sunrising
5. Secret Place of Thunder
6. In the Twilight, in the Evening
7. Island of the Innocent
8. Driven With the Wind

CHENEY AND SHILOH: THE INHERITANCE[1]

1. Where Two Seas Met
2. The Moon by Night

THE SPIRIT OF APPALACHIA[2]

1. Over the Misty Mountains
2. Beyond the Quiet Hills
3. Among the King's Soldiers
4. Beneath the Mockingbird's Wings
5. Around the River's Bend

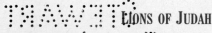

LIONS OF JUDAH

1. Heart of a Lion
2. No Woman So Fair
3. The Gate of Heaven

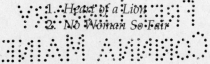

[1]with Lynn Morris   [2]with Aaron McCarver

GILBERT MORRIS

the SHINING BADGE

BETHANYHOUSE
Minneapolis, Minnesota

The Shining Badge
Copyright © 2004
Gilbert Morris

Cover illustration by Bill Graff
Cover design by Danielle White

Published by Bethany House Publishers
11400 Hampshire Avenue South
Bloomington, Minnesota 55438
www.bethanyhouse.com

Bethany House Publishers is a Division of
Baker Book House Company, Grand Rapids, Michigan.

Printed in the United States of America

Library of Congress Cataloging-in-Publication Data

Morris, Gilbert.
    The shining badge / by Gilbert Morris.
    p.   cm.
    ISBN 0-7642-2743-2 (pbk.)
    1. Winslow family (Fictitious characters)—Fiction. 2. Women in politics—Fiction. 3. Women—Georgia—Fiction. 4. Sheriffs—Fiction. 5. Georgia—Fiction. I. Title.
    PS3563.O8742S497   2004
    813'.54—dc22   2003023571

TO NANCI ANDEREGG—

When I was a child I was taught to sing a little chorus
that contained the words "Brighten the corner where you
are." Since those days I have been aware of a few
individuals who exemplified the words of that song—
and you, Nanci, are not the least of these!
Thanks, and thanks, and ever thanks for
brightening the days of me and my family.

GILBERT MORRIS spent ten years as a pastor before becoming Professor of English at Ouachita Baptist University in Arkansas and earning a Ph.D. at the University of Arkansas. A prolific writer, he has had over 25 scholarly articles and 200 poems published in various periodicals, and over the past years has had more than 180 novels published. His family includes three grown children, and he and his wife live in Gulf Shores, Alabama.

Contents

PART FOUR
New Beginnings

THE HOUSE OF WINSLOW

★ ★ ★ ★

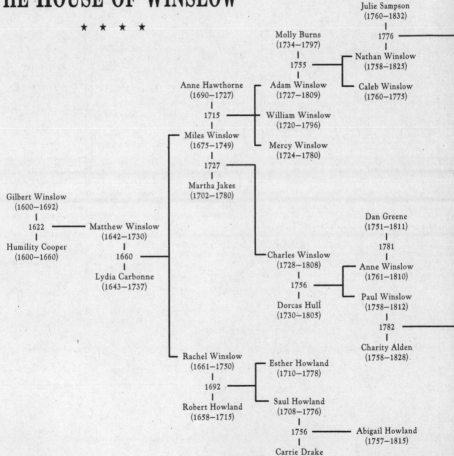

Julie Sampson
(1760–1832)
|
1776 ————

Molly Burns
(1734–1797)
|
1755
|
Adam Winslow
(1727–1809)

Nathan Winslow
(1758–1825)

Caleb Winslow
(1760–1775)

Anne Hawthorne
(1690–1727)
|
1715 ————
|
Miles Winslow
(1675–1749)
|
1727
|
Martha Jakes
(1702–1780)

William Winslow
(1720–1796)

Mercy Winslow
(1724–1780)

Gilbert Winslow
(1600–1692)
|
1622 ———— Matthew Winslow
(1642–1730)
|
Humility Cooper   1660 ————
(1600–1660)
|
Lydia Carbonne
(1643–1737)

Charles Winslow
(1728–1808)
|
1756
|
Dorcas Hull
(1730–1805)

Dan Greene
(1751–1811)
|
1781
|
Anne Winslow
(1761–1810)

Paul Winslow
(1758–1812)
|
1782 ————
|
Charity Alden
(1758–1828)

Rachel Winslow
(1661–1750)
|
1692
|
Robert Howland
(1658–1715)

Esther Howland
(1710–1778)

Saul Howland
(1708–1776)
|
1756 ———— Abigail Howland
(1757–1815)
|
Carrie Drake
(1720–1785)

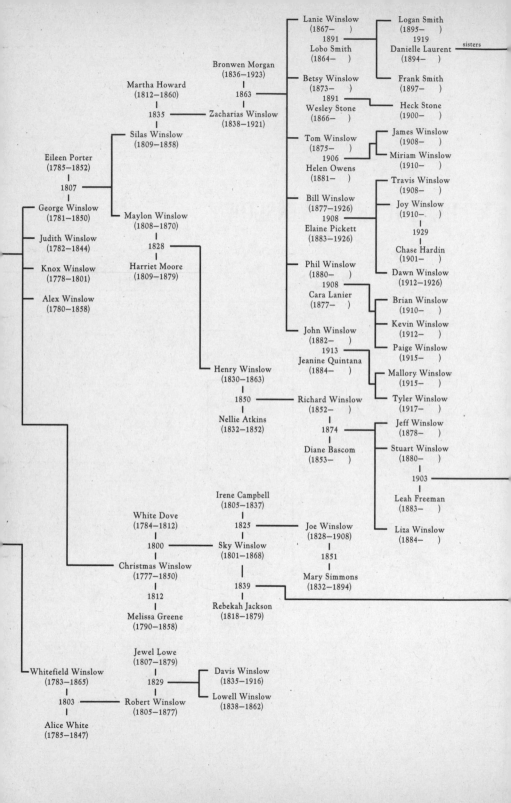

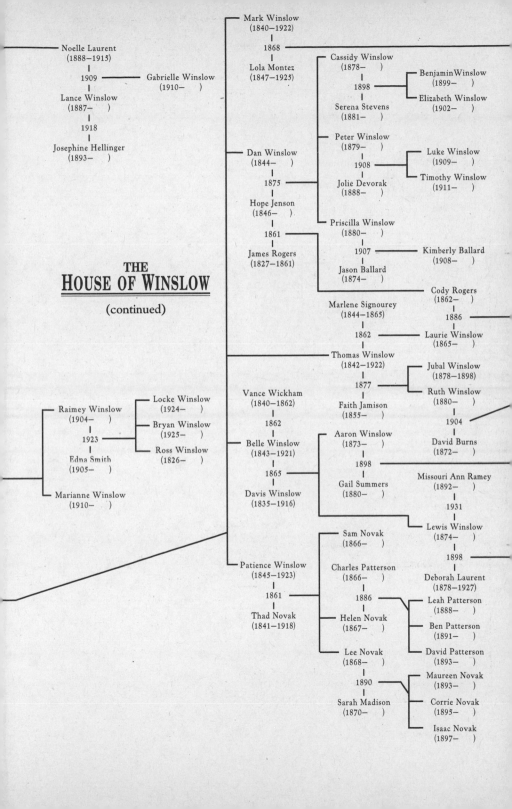

Noelle Laurent
(1888—1915)
|
1909 ———— Gabrielle Winslow
| (1910—   )
Lance Winslow
(1887—   )
|
1918
|
Josephine Hellinger
(1893—   )

THE
HOUSE OF WINSLOW
(continued)

Mark Winslow
(1840—1922)
|
1868
|
Lola Montez
(1847—1925)

Cassidy Winslow
(1878—   )
|
1898 ———— BenjaminWinslow
| (1899—   )
Serena Stevens   Elizabeth Winslow
(1881—   )   (1902—   )

Dan Winslow
(1844—   )
|
1875
|
Hope Jenson
(1846—   )

Peter Winslow
(1879—   )
|
1908 ———— Luke Winslow
| (1909—   )
Jolie Devorak   Timothy Winslow
(1888—   )   (1911—   )

Priscilla Winslow
(1880—   )
|
1907 ———— Kimberly Ballard
| (1908—   )
Jason Ballard
(1874—   )

James Rogers
(1827—1861)
|
1861
|

Marlene Signourey
(1844—1865)
|
1862
|
Thomas Winslow
(1842—1922)
|
1877
|
Faith Jamison
(1855—   )

Cody Rogers
(1862—   )
|
1886
|
Laurie Winslow
(1865—   )

Jubal Winslow
(1878—1898)
Ruth Winslow
(1880—   )
|
1904
|
David Burns
(1872—   )

Raimey Winslow
(1904—   )
|
1923
|
Edna Smith
(1905—   )
|
Marianne Winslow
(1910—   )

Locke Winslow
(1924—   )
Bryan Winslow
(1925—   )
Ross Winslow
(1826—   )

Vance Wickham
(1840—1862)
|
1862
|
Belle Winslow
(1843—1921)
|
1865
|
Davis Winslow
(1835—1916)

Aaron Winslow
(1873—   )
|
1898
|
Gail Summers
(1880—   )

Missouri Ann Ramey
(1892—   )
|
1931
|
Lewis Winslow
(1874—   )
|
1898
|
Deborah Laurent
(1878—1927)

Patience Winslow
(1845—1923)
|
1861
|
Thad Novak
(1841—1918)

Sam Novak
(1866—   )
Charles Patterson
(1866—   )
|
1886
|
Helen Novak
(1867—   )

Leah Patterson
(1888—   )
Ben Patterson
(1891—   )

Lee Novak
(1868—   )
|
1890
|
Sarah Madison
(1870—   )

David Patterson
(1893—   )
Maureen Novak
(1893—   )
Corrie Novak
(1895—   )
Isaac Novak
(1897—   )

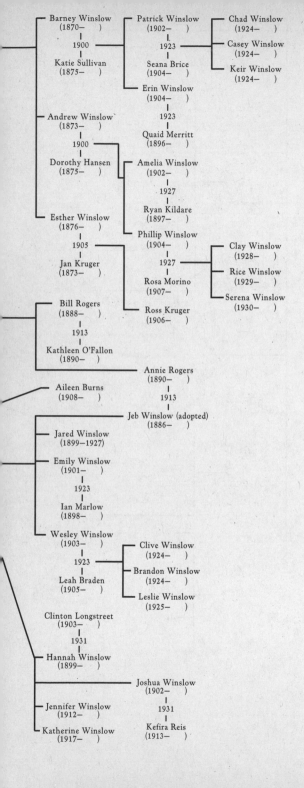

Barney Winslow
(1870–   )
|
1900
|
Katie Sullivan
(1875–   )

Patrick Winslow
(1902–   )
|
1923
|
Seana Brice
(1904–   )

Chad Winslow
(1924–   )

Casey Winslow
(1924–   )

Keir Winslow
(1924–   )

Erin Winslow
(1904–   )
|
1923
|
Quaid Merritt
(1896–   )

Andrew Winslow
(1873–   )
|
1900
|
Dorothy Hansen
(1875–   )

Amelia Winslow
(1902–   )
|
1927
|
Ryan Kildare
(1897–   )

Esther Winslow
(1876–   )
|
1905
|
Jan Kruger
(1873–   )

Phillip Winslow
(1904–   )
|
1927
|
Rosa Morino
(1907–   )

Clay Winslow
(1928–   )

Rice Winslow
(1929–   )

Serena Winslow
(1930–   )

Ross Kruger
(1906–   )

Bill Rogers
(1888–   )
|
1913
|
Kathleen O'Fallon
(1890–   )

Annie Rogers
(1890–   )
|
1913
|
Jeb Winslow (adopted)
(1886–   )

Aileen Burns
(1908–   )

Jared Winslow
(1899–1927)

Emily Winslow
(1901–   )
|
1923
|
Ian Marlow
(1898–   )

Wesley Winslow
(1903–   )
|
1923
|
Leah Braden
(1905–   )

Clive Winslow
(1924–   )

Brandon Winslow
(1924–   )

Leslie Winslow
(1925–   )

Clinton Longstreet
(1903–   )
|
1931
|
Hannah Winslow
(1899–   )

Joshua Winslow
(1902–   )
|
1931
|
Kefira Reis
(1913–   )

Jennifer Winslow
(1912–   )

Katherine Winslow
(1917–   )

PART ONE

Jenny

★　★　★

CHAPTER ONE

GHOSTS

★ ★ ★

The ancient Studebaker truck shivered violently, then came to an abrupt halt as Lewis Winslow jammed his foot down on the brake. As soon as the truck stopped, steam boiled out from under the hood like a miniature geyser. Shaking his head angrily, he beat his fists against the steering wheel. "Worn-out piece of junk! I'd like to dump you in an automobile graveyard, wherever that is!"

Knowing little about cars or engines, Lewis sat there tensely, halfway expecting the engine to blow up. He'd had a difficult trip nursing the truck to town, and now as he sat waiting as the steam slowly subsided, he thought back to the time when he and his family had left New York in this very vehicle. He'd lost every dime he possessed in the stock market crash. After having enjoyed a life of affluence, the Lewis Winslow family had been forced to move south in this pickup truck, carrying little besides the clothes on their backs. Raw memories brushed across Lewis's mind, but he suddenly leaned back and stroked his chin thoughtfully. "I shouldn't be angry at you, old girl," he said patting the seat as if it were a faithful dog. "If it hadn't been for you and Clint, we'd probably be in the poorhouse back in New York right now."

When Lewis opened the door, its creaking squeal raked across his nerves, and he thought back to the expensive cars he had owned when he had been a wealthy stockbroker. He had given his family everything they wanted, but in October of '29 when the market crashed, he'd become a pauper. He remembered clearly the desperation that had seized him then and how relieved he had been when his daughter Hannah had discovered the title deed to a farm that had belonged to his first wife's family in northern Georgia. Now, gathering his packages from the seat, Lewis felt a moment of intense gratitude and said aloud, "Thank you, Lord, for pulling my family up and giving us this beautiful place to live." Slamming the door, he turned toward the house, but as he did, he was struck in the legs by a huge dog that suddenly reared up on him and licked his face.

"Get down, Stonewall!" Lewis protested. He tried to shove the animal away, but nothing pleased Stonewall more than to sit on someone's feet. For some reason the animal delighted in it, and now he put all one hundred and sixty of his pounds on Lewis's feet and looked up adoringly.

"Get off of my feet, you monster!" Since Stonewall weighed almost as much as Lewis himself, it was all he could do to shove the animal away with his knees. Stonewall stared at him reproachfully, then at once reared up on him again.

"Stop that!" Lewis commanded and then shoved him away with his hip. He started toward the house, and Stonewall persisted in getting right in front of him, making progress almost impossible. "Why in the world did you take up with us?" Lewis moaned. The dog had simply showed up one day, battle scarred and fearful to look at. Kat had discovered him and claimed him for her own. Despite all protests from Lewis and his wife, Missouri Ann, Kat had begged and pleaded until finally the dog had been allowed to stay. He was as strong as a bull and would try to fetch anything, including a six-foot fence post. He also loved to swim, but most of all he loved to sit on people's feet. He was tremendously loyal toward all of the Winslow clan, but strangers were often taken aback at the sight of the huge dog facing them with fangs bared when they approached one of the family.

Lewis turned to follow the beaten path that led to the back door into the kitchen. As he passed by the chicken pen, he heard a sound and stopped quickly. Foxes had been known to get into the chicken house, but that did not seem likely in broad daylight, not with Stonewall roaming loose. He waited for a moment, heard a cry again, and this time he recognized it as the voice of his wife. Dropping the groceries, heedless as they spilled out on the yard, he ran toward the fenced yard and opened the gate. The door to the hen house was open, and as he stepped from the brilliant sunlight into the dim light of the hen house, he paused for his eyes to adjust. His eyesight cleared, and with a start he saw his wife on the floor.

"Help me, Lewis, I'm stuck here!"

Missouri Ann Ramey Winslow had been Lewis's wife for just over a year, and she was eight months pregnant. She was a large woman, strong and active, but now one leg was doubled under her and the other disappeared in a hole in the floor.

"What happened?" Lewis demanded as he moved toward her and knelt at her side.

"Oh, I come out to gather the eggs, and this foolish board broke. I can't get out." Missouri Ann spoke calmly and showed no sign of strain. She was a woman of great faith and said, "Don't worry, now. Just go get Clint, and you two can hoist me up."

Lewis felt a flicker of fear. Missouri Ann was thirty-nine years old, older than most women care to have a baby. He had grown to love her dearly, and despite his shock at becoming a father at the age of fifty-seven he had found himself more and more grateful for Missouri Ann and for the child that was to come. Ignoring her protests, he reached down and snapped off the rotten board, enlarging the hole. Then, moving around behind her, he put his hand under her arms and said, "Come on. Up you go." He heaved, and Missouri Ann pushed with her free foot, and her leg suddenly appeared.

She laughed and turned around to face him. "Well, you didn't carry me over the threshold, but I guess this is about the same thing. I'm big as a house anyway. Thank you, dear."

Lewis took her kiss, but he was still concerned. "You've got some scratches on that leg. We've got to go get it taken care of. I'll get the wheelbarrow and wheel you inside."

Missouri Ann laughed. She was not a beautiful woman, but she was striking. Her hair was jet black except for an inch-wide silver streak that began at her brow and went to the tips of her long tresses. The silver track was so startling that everyone's eyes always went to it first. She had large, expressive blue-gray eyes and well-formed lips. She was a large woman at five-eleven, one inch taller than Lewis, and had been shapely before the child had ballooned her out. Now she reached out and touched Lewis's face affectionately. "Well, don't be silly. I'm not riding in any old wheelbarrow. I can walk."

Lewis ushered her out of the hen house, and when they passed out of the fenced chicken yard, he looked up to see Stonewall eating the bologna Lewis had brought back from the store. "Let that alone, you no-count mangy hound!"

Stonewall came at once and tried again to sit on his feet, but Lewis shoved him away. He quickly gathered up the groceries scattered about the yard and carried them into the house. As they entered through the back door, his daughter Hannah turned from the kitchen and cried at once, "What happened, Ma?"

"Oh, I'm so big I broke through the floor in the hen house."

"Her leg's all scratched up, Hannah. Put something on it, will you?"

Hannah Winslow Longstreet, little more than a bride herself, came at once. She had brown eyes and auburn hair pulled back in a simple knot. "You sit down here, Ma, and I'll take care of you."

"You go on about your business, Lewis," Missouri Ann said. "Hannah can take care of this. I'm all right."

Lewis put the groceries down, commenting sourly, "Stonewall ate the bologna."

"That's all right. You go along, Dad." Hannah smiled. She watched as Lewis left and then turned to her stepmother.

"That's the last time you get out of the house until this baby comes," she said firmly.

"Reckon you're right about that, Hannah. I didn't tell Lewis, but it scared me a little. Not for myself but for the baby."

While her stepmother recounted the incident, Hannah cleaned the scratches and applied iodine, which caused Missouri Ann to open her eyes and exclaim, "Ouch, that burns!"

"You gave Dad a fright. He's scared enough about becoming a father at his age. He's afraid people are laughing at him."

"Why would they laugh? He's a good, strong man, and fifty-seven—why, that's not old at all. My grandpa, he lived to be ninety-three and was hale right up to the very end." Her eyes grew soft, and she reached out and touched Hannah's hair. "God's been right good to give me a family. I thought I was done with havin' young'uns, and then one day the Lord just told me that He would bring me a husband and we'd have children."

Hannah smiled, remembering how Missouri Ann had, on her first meeting with Hannah's father, announced, "God sent you to be my husband." Later she had announced that they would have children together as well.

"Dad is happier than I've seen him in years. He never really was himself after Mother died, but you've come to fill a place in his heart." She hugged the older woman and whispered, "I'm so happy for both of you!"

★ ★ ★

". . . and now let's see what's going on down in Pine Ridge."

Lewis sat in his chair staring at the wall across from him, listening as Lum and Abner carried on their usual hijinks. He had grown fond of the radio program, for the two rural characters had captivated America almost as much as Amos and Andy had.

Lewis was only half listening, however. He was still

shaken over the accident suffered by Missouri Ann. He got up nervously now and walked around the room, conscious of a touch of pride, for it was a beautiful room indeed. He remembered how abysmal it had been the first time he had walked into it on arriving from New York. A group of squatters had settled in and had even allowed pigs and chickens inside, but the Winslows had worked tirelessly to clean the house. Now he admired, as always, the beautiful job of wallpapering that he and Hannah had done.

He stopped for a moment, his eyes fixed on the framed medal that occupied a space over the fireplace. It was the Congressional Medal of Honor he had won in the Spanish-American War. He thought for a moment of the violent action of that day and how he and his brother Aaron had fought as fiercely as men can fight. It all seemed long ago now, but the medal was there to remind him, and it gave him a feeling of pride. He never spoke of his war exploits to anyone, but they were vividly embossed in his memory.

He moved over and studied the picture of Deborah, his first wife. The picture was taken when she was only a girl, but he had always liked it. She had grown up in this old house before moving to New York City, where he had met her, and he felt, as always, a tug of sadness. But the awful, searing agony of loss had faded now, and he thought of her often as being happy and joyous in heaven. He moved to the other pictures on the wall, one of a wedding picture of Hannah and her husband, Clint, and once again he felt a surge of gratitude. Hannah had been a recluse for many years, never leaving the house. She had been molested as a young woman and had been unable to recover. But Clint Longstreet had appeared from nowhere, it seemed, and had won Hannah's love, and now the two were happily married.

The next picture was of his daughter Jennifer, the prettiest of all the girls, he had to admit. She smiled out at him through the photograph, and he shook his head, wondering at how far she had come. Jenny had been a spoiled socialite in New York, and he could never have dreamed that she would have survived a move to the hills of rural Georgia, but she had.

The picture next to hers was of Katherine, who was called

Kat. It was a relatively new picture, and although it was in black and white, his mind filled in the missing colors, the same gray-green eyes and tawny hair as Josh, his older son. Kat was a tomboy who loved hunting and fishing and anything out-of-doors, but there was a hint of real beauty in her expression. She looked a great deal like his first wife, Deborah, as well as Josh. Then, for a long moment, Lewis studied the portrait of Joshua, his son, whose poor choices in life had almost destroyed him. He had been a hard drinker and had served a month in the penitentiary, but now he had found success working as an archeologist in Egypt. He was so far away, and yet at times Lewis felt that he was here with them.

He came then to the picture of himself and Missouri Ann as they stood in the church, Missouri wearing a lovely white wedding dress and he himself wearing a beautifully tailored gray suit. He could not get over the marvel of finding a woman to stand beside him and give him comfort at his ancient age (as he thought of himself). He had long ago given up on such thoughts, but Missouri Ann had brought a new joy in his life that equaled, at least, that which he had known when he had married his first wife. She certainly was nothing like Deborah had been, for Missouri was rural Georgian to the bone, and her language revealed her country upbringing. Having become a member of the Winslow family, Missouri Ann was now embarrassed by her speech and was taking lessons from the whole family on how to speak properly—to become "genteel," as she called it.

Lewis reached out and touched the photograph and then whispered, "Thank you, Lord, for my family. You've been good to all of us."

"What in the world are you doing, Dad?"

Jenny had entered the room and saw her father standing there staring at his wedding picture. "Are you admiring yourself?" she teased.

"Oh no," Lewis said hurriedly, "I'm just a little upset. You see, Missouri Ann—"

"Oh, I know. She's fine, Dad." Jenny came over and reached up and brushed a lock of Lewis's hair back. "She's fine. Just a few scratches."

"I'll tell you it scared me, Jenny. Made my knees weak."

"It didn't make you very weak. Ma told me that you reached down and picked her up like she weighed nothing." Jenny's eyes danced as she spoke, for she loved to tease her father. She did not know what an attractive picture she made for him at that moment. Her laughing eyes were a brilliant green, and her hair was not auburn but a bright red. "Come on and sit down," she said, "I'll get you some tea."

"No, I don't want any." Lewis walked across the room and sat down, and as soon as Jenny sat down beside him, he said, "It scared me witless. Mostly about the baby."

Jenny reached over and took her father's hand and held it and patted it. "The baby's all right." She laughed. "You didn't waste any time. Married just over a year and you're almost a father again."

"I don't know how I got into this," Lewis said ruefully. "Sometimes I think it's all a dream."

"God did it. That's what your dear wife says."

"She never had any doubt, did she?" Lewis grimaced. "I never will forget when I woke up in her house delirious with a broken leg, and almost the first thing she said was, 'God sent you to be my husband.'"

"Well, she was right about that, and she's right about the baby too. She always said that you and she would have children."

"I've forgotten everything I ever knew about babies. What will I do, Jenny?"

"You'll do just what you did when Josh was born. You'll learn how to change diapers."

"Great Caesar! At my age!"

Missouri entered at that moment and was not even limping. "I'm all bandaged up and as good as new."

"Well, sit down here and try to tell Dad that, Ma." Jenny smiled. "He's always been a worrywart."

Jenny rose and Missouri took her seat. "You look like you've been into something sour, husband," she said. "Come on, now. Let's have a smile."

Lewis tried to frown, but his face broke. "Woman, you are unusual! That's the kindest thing I can say."

Jenny found pleasure in watching the couple but now said, "I'll leave you two lovebirds alone. Kat and I are going to town."

"I just got back from town. That old truck is on its last leg."

"No, it's not. Clint's going to keep it running," Jenny said cheerfully.

"Well, put some water in the radiator before you go."

"All right." Jenny left the room, and as soon as she did, Lewis slipped his arms around Missouri Ann and held her. "I'm quite an armful, especially now," she whispered.

Lewis stroked her hair and kissed her on the cheek. "I couldn't bear it if anything happened to you, sweetheart," he whispered.

Missouri Ann could not answer, for her throat seemed to close and tears burned her eyes. She had yearned for affection and love for so long! Her first husband had been quiet and distant, and she had never known what it was to be appreciated. Joining the Winslow family had brought new life to her, and now she put her head on Lewis's shoulder and just thanked God as her beloved husband held her tightly.

He started to say something else when a loud voice broke into their private moment. "The old Townsend place, it's haunted!" Startled, both Lewis and Missouri Ann turned to see Kat barreling into the room. Her gray eyes were wide open, and her overalls were tattered and filthy from the straps down to the frayed cuffs. Her tawny hair was uncombed, but this was seldom a matter of concern for Kat Winslow. At fourteen she was just beginning to develop a girlish figure, but this was hidden beneath the shapeless overalls. "Dallas says he's seen lights there at night."

"Oh, don't be foolish!" Lewis said. "There's no such thing as ghosts."

"Yes, there is too!" Kat argued.

As Lewis had often remarked, she would argue with a tree. All Winslows displayed a characteristic stubbornness, but with Kat it was absolutely unrestrained.

"No," Lewis said, "the lights Dallas saw must have a logical explanation."

Kat began to argue that there were indeed such things as haunts and ghosts, but Jenny appeared in the door, saying, "If you're going with me, Kat, you'd better get cleaned up. You've got ten minutes."

"I'll get my swimsuit too. We can go swimming on the way back!" Kat whirled and raced for the door but paused long enough to nod firmly. "Dallas says they were spooky lights bobbing up and down. And Dallas don't lie."

"Doesn't lie," Jenny corrected, and the two girls disappeared up the stairs.

Lewis sighed. "I'm not sure I like the ideas that boy is putting into her head," he said, referring to Dallas Sharp, one of the neighbor boys and Kat's good friend. "And every day she spends with him, the worse her speech gets too!"

"Well, most people around here believe in haunted houses and such things, but I don't. As for her speech, she's just tryin' to fit in down here. She'll grow out of that and be her own person one of these days."

"You think she'll ever throw those filthy overalls away and put on a dress like a normal girl?"

"Of course she will," Missouri Ann asserted, nodding firmly. "She'll come out of it before you know it and be a beautiful young lady—just like Jenny and Hannah."

"And you, sweetheart." Lewis knew that his new wife was starved for expressions of love, and he was rewarded for his kindness with a winning smile and a kiss.

★ ★ ★

As Jenny brought the Studebaker to a halt in front of the Huntington General Store, the afternoon sun was already waning. "We've got to hurry, Kat. I want to get home before dark."

"Aw, I wanta go see a movie!"

"We're not going to see any movie."

"But they got one of them cartoons on—Mickey Mouse."

"*Those* cartoons, Kat! And I'm sorry, but money's just too tight. We'll save up and maybe go next time we're in town."

The girls stepped out of the truck and entered the general store, where the owner, H. G. Huntington, stocked everything from mule harnesses to oatmeal. Next to bolts of cloth for ladies' dresses sat barrels of pickles, their sour smell mixing with the fragrance of cinnamon.

"I've got to get some spices for Ma," Jenny said as she sniffed the cinnamon. "She's been hankering for pumpkin pie."

"I'm gonna look at the knives," Kat announced and strode over to peer into the case of knives she always admired when they visited the general store.

Jenny quickly found the spices she needed, then turned and walked back toward the counter. She had been aware of a loud voice, and now she saw a man in the uniform of the county sheriff's office standing in front of a huge black man. She stopped and watched Mr. Huntington, who stood behind the counter looking helpless. His eyes met Jenny's for a moment, and then he shook his head ruefully. Aloud he said, "It's probably my error, Deputy."

Deputy Max Conroy was six feet tall and lean as a snake. Beneath his wide-brimmed cap with its peaked crown, he stared coldly at the owner and said, "This buck here tried to steal some groceries. That's what you told me."

"I . . . I made a mistake. He's a good boy. He was on his way to pay for it."

Deputy Conroy shook his head. "You done made charges, Mr. Huntington. I'll have to take him in."

"I won't press the charges," Huntington said quickly.

Jenny could see Conroy's cold green eyes, but her gaze turned quickly to the man who stood before him. He was a huge black man, tall as well as broad, and the thought came to her, *You could split Max Conroy in two.* She did not like Deputy Conroy, for he had pressed himself on her several times trying to convince her to go out with him. Now she heard Conroy say, "All right, Noah, get yourself out of here. But I got my eye on you. I'm gonna have you back doin' time again. They let you out too soon is what I say. Now, get on outta here!"

The black man turned and walked away swiftly. Jenny had

heard Missouri Ann talk about Noah Valentine. He had grown up with a widowed mother and a number of younger brothers and sisters. According to Missouri, Noah had gotten in trouble and been sent to the state penitentiary for the crime of selling moonshine. Perhaps because her stepson, Joshua, had been sentenced for the same charge, Missouri felt compassion for Noah. Jenny remembered how Missouri Ann had said, *"Noah got saved while he was in the penitentiary just like Josh, and when he came home he started in workin' hard, takin' care of his mother and all those brothers and sisters. He never misses a Sunday at church, and he's even preached there several times. But people won't give him a chance around here. Once a man's been in the pen, that black mark never goes away. But Noah Valentine's a good man, I don't care what they say!"*

Jenny had turned to watch the big man leave when suddenly she felt her arm seized and turned around quickly to face Deputy Max Conroy. He was smiling at her now, and his grip was somehow intimidating. "That's mighty sweet perfume you got on there, Jenny."

Jenny tried to remove her arm, but he held fast. "Let go, Max."

"My, you're a regular touch-me-not! Look, I'm not such a bad fella. They're havin' a dance over at Cedar Mount tomorrow night. Let's me and you go show 'em how it's done."

"I'd rather not."

Conroy's grip tightened. He was a strong man despite being so lean, and the smile on his lips did not reach his eyes. "You New York girls are pretty stuck up, but you'll find out it's different down here in Georgia."

"Let me go!"

Jenny tried to pull her arm away, but Conroy only laughed. "You'll have to do better than that," he said. "Now, about that dance—"

"Let her go, Max."

Conroy whirled quickly to see the bulky form of Noel Beauchamp, the sheriff. Beauchamp was a thickset man, with a deep chest and steady brown eyes. "You got nothin' to do but annoy customers here at the store, Max? Maybe you need some time off."

"Oh, Noel, I was just havin' a little fun."

"Go have your fun somewhere else."

"Sure, Sheriff."

Conroy turned and left, but his back was stiff with suppressed anger.

Jenny watched him go. "You made him mad, Sheriff Beauchamp."

"Max is always mad. If he gives you any trouble, you let me know."

"He was picking on Noah Valentine again, Sheriff," Huntington said.

"I don't think Max has enough work to do. I'll keep an eye on him."

Jenny said, "Stop by and see us sometime, Sheriff."

"I'll do that, Miss Jenny. Your family all right?"

"All doing fine."

Beauchamp smiled, wrinkles appearing around the corners of his eyes. "Your father's going to be a daddy again. That'll be quite a switch for him, won't it?"

"He's real nervous about it, Sheriff, but he'll do fine."

"I know he will."

Jenny found Kat still staring at the knife case, and the two left the store. Kat babbled all the way home about the ghosts at the Townsend place.

Then switching the subject, she said, "Let's go to the swimming hole. There's still time."

"No, it's too late now."

"But we've got a whole hour yet. That's plenty of time."

Although Jenny was in a hurry to get home, she was also hot and sweaty and the idea of a swim appealed to her. "All right, but we can't stay long." She pulled off the highway and followed an old logging road down to the river. Jenny had been delighted to find this private spot for swimming, where the river made a bend and was thickly bordered by first-growth timber, completely sheltered from the highway.

She parked the truck and the two changed into their suits behind some thick fir trees, then ran laughing into the river. For half an hour they sputtered and laughed, reveling in the coolness of the water. Finally Jenny decided, "Come on, we've got to get home."

Kat protested, but ten minutes later they were dressed and Jenny was pulling the truck back onto the highway. Just as she turned, Kat suddenly cried, "See there? I told you the house was haunted!"

Jenny slowed the truck to a stop and turned to peer out the window. "Where?" she said.

"There!" It was almost dark now, but far away Jenny could see a light bobbing up and down in front of a house that was partly sheltered by tall trees. "That's the Townsend place, and that's a ghost!"

"It's not a ghost. It's somebody carrying a lantern."

Jenny put the truck back in gear, and as they started off, she scolded Kat. "Stop talking about silly things like ghosts! That's probably just some coon hunter starting in early."

"It's no coon hunter. It's a ghost!" Kat said firmly. "You'll see when it comes over to haunt our place!"

CHAPTER TWO

JENNY MAKES A CALL

★ ★ ★

"Get away, Stonewall. Dogs don't eat worms!"

Kat shoved at the huge dog, who had joined her as she dug for angle worms under the eaves of the house. She had discovered that the leaves gathered there made a rich black soil that made finding fishing bait much easier. Stonewall crowded in closer. He plumped himself down on her feet, and Kat shook her head with disgust. "How do you 'spect me to dig bait when you're sittin' on my feet? Get away!"

With some effort she shoved the big dog away, which was quite a task, since he weighed more than she did. He backed up the minimal distance and stood watching as she drove the spade into the ground, turned over a shovelful of the loose soil and then began grabbing the worms as they wiggled and squirmed to get away. With satisfaction she dumped them into a large can half filled with leaf mold and watched as they quickly disappeared. "You can hide down there if you want to," Kat said with satisfaction, "but after a while you'll be in the belly of a fish."

The sun was dipping westward, and for a moment Kat watched with pleasure as it touched the ragged rim of hills to the west. The sun seemed to break like the yolk of an egg, spilling out and outlining the edges of the low-lying mountains before disappearing completely. She stood for a time absolutely still, which was unusual for her, and thought with satisfaction how much better her life was since they had moved from New York to the hills of Georgia. The adults had had more difficulty adjusting, but she had loved the rural life from the day they had arrived. Now as the day's heat came out of the earth, she waited until long streaks of light broke against the fading sky, and the shadows began to grow purplish against the mountains in the distance. A movement caught her eye, and she turned to see Clint coming from the barn. Throwing the spade down, she raced across the yard, driving straight through a flock of guineas that screamed their peculiar call as she scattered them. "Clint!" she cried. "Clint, it's time for Little Orphan Annie!"

Clint Longstreet stopped and grinned down at the young girl, a smile lifting the corners of his lips. He was a tall, lanky man with gray-green eyes, sandy hair, and a face somewhat the worse for wear. His nose had been broken once in some forgotten battle, and a scar ran along the jawline on the right side of his face. He reached up to shove his straw hat back, revealing that the tip of his right little finger was missing. "Little Orphan Annie," he said. "I don't think I recollect promisin' to listen to that program with you."

Kat came at once and grabbed Clint's arm and began tugging at him. "Yes, you did, Clint! Last night at supper you said you'd listen to it with me."

Longstreet allowed himself to be pulled up the steps, remarking only, "Ma'll kill you if you go takin' those muddy shoes in the house."

Kat kicked off the shoes, then said, "Hurry up, we'll miss it! It's almost time!"

The two entered the house. The front door opened down a spacious hallway, and Clint allowed himself to be tugged into the parlor. For once no one was in the room, and Clint settled down into a cane-bottom rocker cushioned with a garish orange cushion. He watched as Kat went over and turned on the radio, then remarked, "I'm glad we've got electricity and don't have to fool with one of them battery radios. They always went out just when you wanted to hear a ball game the worst."

"Be quiet, Clint, it's starting!" Kat commanded. She came over and plopped down on the floor next to him, resting her head against his leg. The girl's affection toward him was pleasing to Clint. He had been a bachelor until just recently, when he had married Hannah, and he had never had much to do with children. While he had helped take over the affairs of the Winslows after their lives had come crashing down, he had come to love Kat Winslow. He laid his hand on her shoulder as she listened and thought, *Maybe Hannah and me will have a little girl. Wouldn't that be something!*

As the radio gradually warmed up, a warbly tenor voice began to emerge from the speaker, singing,

> *"Who's that little chatterbox?*
> *The one with the pretty auburn locks?*
> *Who-oo can it be?*
> *Cute little she.*
> *It's Little Orphan Annie!"*

Little Orphan Annie mania had swept across the country. Everyone was aware of the dramatic adventures of the small girl who shouted "Leapin' lizards!" on the least provocation. The earliest episodes had been lifted directly from newspaper story lines, and the plots were relatively simple, Annie foiling the schemes of foreign agents and criminals of all sorts. Annie, along with her dog, Sandy, had captivated America's children—and not a few of the adults.

Finally the announcer said, "Now for the secret message. Only Annie's friends will be able to decode this. If you don't have your Little Orphan Annie secret decoder ring, you're missing out, kids. So send in those Ovaltine coupons."

"Clint, come on!"

"Where we going now?" Clint protested as Kat pulled him to his feet.

"We're going to drink some Ovaltine."

"Ovaltine! I hate that stuff!"

"It's good for you. It says so right on the box. Come on."

Kat went over, turned the radio off, and again took Clint

by the hand, tugging him toward the kitchen. "You've got to drink more Ovaltine if I'm ever going to get my Secret Decoder ring."

"I'd rather pay cash money than drink that stuff."

"It's good. I like it."

Missouri Ann was sitting on a stool at the kitchen table when the two entered, the ingredients for a pie out in front of her. Jenny, who had on a white apron over her dress, looked up and smiled. "What have you two been up to?"

"Clint wants an Ovaltine," Kat announced. "A lot of it in a big glass."

"No, I don't," Clint protested, but his protests were ignored. Kat went to the larder and pulled out a box, then fetched the largest glass in the kitchen. Pouring it full of fresh, sweet milk, she added two liberal spoonfuls of Ovaltine and stirred it. "Now, you drink all this, Clint."

Clint made a face but managed to down the Ovaltine. "There, that ought to make you happy," he said.

"You sure you don't want some more?"

"No, I feel like that stuff's in my blood."

"I'm going to have some too." The three adults watched as Kat fixed herself a glass of milk liberally laced with Ovaltine and drank it down, having to force the last few swallows.

"You're going to pop," Jenny warned.

"No, I'm not. And as soon as I get that Secret Decoder ring, you'll see something. Come on, Clint, you can go help me dig some more worms. And then maybe later tonight we'll go over to the old Townsend place and see the ghosts."

"What ghosts?"

"The ones at the old Townsend place. It's haunted. Dallas told me he seen some of 'em."

"He *saw* some of them," Jenny said quickly, "and don't be foolish. There's no such things as ghosts."

"There are too. Dallas saw them—and so did you!"

"I think we'd better go dig worms," Clint said, grinning. He turned, and the two left the room, Kat protesting loudly that there were *too* such things as ghosts.

"That child would argue with anything," Missouri Ann said mildly.

"She's certainly foolish about Clint."

"Well, she ought to be. He's nothing but a big toy for her." Missouri Ann turned and looked fondly at Jenny. She had formed a real bond with all of her stepchildren, and she and Jenny had become very close indeed. She studied the girl now, admiring her fair, clear skin, for Jenny had the most beautiful complexion Missouri had ever seen. Jenny also had a trim, feminine figure, which was the object of male admiration everywhere she went. Suddenly Missouri asked, "Whatever happened to Clyde Bailey? He was coming around pretty often."

"I wasn't interested."

"And Dennie Fulton—he came courting you for a time."

"Wasn't interested."

Missouri Ann studied the young woman for a moment and said, "I think a pretty girl like you would be interested in gentleman callers. There's lots of them around here if you'd just shake the tree."

Jenny laughed. "I'd have no man that I'd have to shake out of a tree like he was a coon or a possum. Here, you're going to teach me how to make this pie." She looked at the ingredients on the table and shook her head. "I never heard of such a thing as a squash pie."

Missouri Ann laughed, "Well, that's because probably no one ever made one except me. I invented this myself."

"Those big crook-neck squashes sure don't look like they'd make a good pie."

"Buttermilk doesn't sound like it'd make a good pie either, but nothin' better than good buttermilk pie." The two women laughed a great deal, for Jenny knew almost nothing about cooking. She insisted on writing down every step, especially the ingredients. "You never say how much you use of anything. You say 'pinch of this' and 'a dab of that' and 'a little bit of something else.' That's all right for you, but I have to write it all down."

"Well, write it down, then," Missouri Ann said. "It takes two cups of milk, two cups of sugar, three eggs, and two cups of cooked, mashed squash—oh yes, you add a mite of ground cinnamon and ginger and nutmeg. Oh, I don't know how much! A teaspoon of each, I guess. Then put in a little flour to thicken it."

Jenny insisted on writing down the exact measurements. Then, under Missouri Ann's directions, she combined all the ingredients. Finally she poured the filling into unbaked pie shells and baked them for fifteen minutes at a hot temperature, which was a little hard to judge in a wood stove. Then Missouri Ann said, "You'll have to let it bake for about forty-five minutes more."

"How will I know when it's done?"

Missouri Ann was surprised at the question. "Why, you stick a knife in it. When it comes out clean, it's all did."

"You mean it's all done, Missouri Ann."

Missouri Ann laughed. "That's right. I'll never learn to talk good."

"Well, you teach me how to bake, and I'll teach you how to talk."

"I don't want your pa or any of you to be ashamed of me."

Jenny went over and put her arm around the large woman. "We could never be that," she said gently. "You've brought such joy into Dad's life and into this house."

Missouri Ann hugged the girl and said, "It'll be noisy around here when the little one comes. I hope it doesn't bother anybody."

"A new Winslow come into the world," Jenny said, her eyes sparkling. "It'll be exciting."

"It'll be that." Missouri Ann leaned back and placed her hands on her stomach. "I'm reckonin' it's a boy. He rides high." A thought came to her then, and she said, "All that foolishness Kat keeps spoutin' about haunts and spooks and ghosts over at the old Townsend place, there's nothin' to that."

"You think it was just tramps?"

"No, Dolly Cannon told me that the bank rented the old place out. It was just settin' vacant, and nobody's got the money to buy it. So, they rented it out to somebody or other."

"Who was it?"

"Dolly didn't know. I'll tell you what, though. You probably didn't do this in the big city, but here in the country when a new family moves in, it's considered fittin' to take somethin' to eat as sort of a welcomin' into the neighborhood. You know, I was thinkin' we could bake another one of these squash pies. We've got plenty of squash left. I'm too big and awkward to go, but maybe you could do it."

"I can do that," Jenny said. "I'm going to take the truck and go to town to get some feed for the cows. I'll stop on the way and meet them. I hope they're nice people."

"They probably are. We'll believe so, anyhow, until they prove different."

★   ★   ★

The next day, after helping Hannah with the housework all morning, Jenny went outside and drew rainwater from the barrel. The water from the well was rather hard, so Clint had taught them the trick of collecting rain through a series of gutters into a barrel. He had warned them that you had to use it up or it would breed mosquitoes.

Jenny washed her hair with rainwater and allowed it to dry in the sun, using a series of clean, soft towels. Finally she brushed it until it shone with brilliant red tints in the sunlight, and she thought about how kids had teased her when she was a girl.

Redheaded peckerwood sittin' on a fence,
Tryin' to make a dollar out of fifteen cents.

Another old memory brushed across her mind. She remembered how she had fallen madly in love with Harold Horton at the age of eleven. He had won her heart by telling her he loved red hair, and although Harold himself was fairly homely, he was her first real attachment. A smile touched her broad lips as she remembered how she had fallen out of love with him when she discovered that he was six months younger than she was.

"I wonder where Harold is now," she murmured. She went inside and took a leisurely bath. Afterward, she put on fresh underwear and the green dress that matched her eyes.

Then she went downstairs. "I'm going to town now, Dad," she said, finding Lewis in the kitchen talking with Missouri Ann. The two were drinking tea as they usually did several times during the day.

"Don't forget the pie," Missouri Ann said.

"What pie is that?" Lewis inquired.

"Jenny's taking a squash pie over to the new folks that moved into the Townsend place."

"What's their name?"

"I don't know," Jenny said.

"Dolly didn't know either. She just said the bank had rented it out to some folks."

"I'll find out all about them." Jenny smiled. She went over and kissed her father on the cheek, then gave Missouri Ann a hug. "You be careful with that Winslow, now. I'm expecting a spectacular brother."

"Maybe it'll be a girl," Lewis suggested.

"No, it'll be a boy," Missouri Ann said firmly.

Lewis laughed aloud. "I wish I was as certain about any *one* thing as you are about *everything*. Did the Lord tell you it'd be a boy?"

"Don't be foolish! I can tell from the way he rides. High and in the middle."

"Well, we'll know pretty soon, won't we?" Jenny left the house and started up the old Studebaker. It had many thousands of miles on it, and she was always amazed when it started. Clint, however, was a first-class mechanic, and through his tinkering, somehow the ancient truck always responded.

It was a beautiful May afternoon, and Jenny felt a sense of exuberance. She had never paid all that much attention to the out-of-doors. Growing up in the city she had been more interested in ballrooms and department stores. But since moving to Georgia, she had become aware of the world she inhabited in a way that startled her. She had found a particular pleasure in seeing the first emerald spears of grass pierce the colorless earth and form a gentle green carpet. The branches of the trees, which had been barren and naked, had suddenly turned pale gold and then the tiny tender buds had developed into the most delicate leaves imaginable. She had smelled the freshness of the earth in a way she never had in the city, and the colors here seemed to be almost violent after the gray city streets she was accustomed to.

As the ancient truck rumbled along the rutted roads, she passed farmers out plowing their fields, some with tractors but still plenty with mules and horses. She had known few of her neighbors in New York City, but now being baptized into the life of the community, she could call out the names of many of those she passed. The road grew broader and more firmly packed and finally turned into a paved surface. She followed it into town and pulled up in front of the Huntington General Store.

As she got out and went inside, she had an unpleasant memory of Max Conroy and his persecution of Noah Valentine. She had an instinctive dislike of Max Conroy, irrational except for the fact that she had seen fear in the eyes of many as he passed. The black people especially grew tight and fell silent when the tall deputy walked by. Jenny was not overly wise in the ways of the world, but she knew that when people were afraid, there was usually a cause. She picked up the thread Hannah had requested and a sack of candy for Kat, then waited until Bud McKeeley, the hired man at the store, loaded the feed into the back of the truck. She gave him a smile, and he flushed and mumbled, "Weren't nothin', Miss Jenny."

Jenny knew he had a crush on her and did not want to encourage it. She was used to such things but somehow had grown more sensitive to them during recent months. *Perhaps losing everything wasn't all that bad,* she thought as the truck rumbled back toward the west. *I would never have paid any attention to an adolescent boy with a crush on me, not back in New York, but now a young boy in love somehow seems poignant to me. I wonder why that is.*

Without knowing it, Jenny had become more sensitive to the world around her, not only the natural world of trees and grass and birds but of people too. In all truth, she had been a selfish young woman given over to pleasures purchased by her father's money. She had been, she realized now, a tremendous snob. She had even disliked Clint when he had first arrived to work for her father. But losing everything had changed Jenny's entire way of thinking. She had developed a sensitive spirit and a genuine compassion for the plights of others.

Finally she came to herself with a start and turned off the road that led to the old Townsend place. She pulled up in front of the house and studied it before she got out. It was an old house, once painted white but now faded. It looked a great deal as their own place had before they had started renovating it. The house was two stories tall with three gables, and a porch ran along the front of it. Some of the windows had been broken and the panes replaced with old newspapers and what appeared to be cardboard. Behind the house was a barn with faded red paint, and between the house and the barn stood an outhouse. A movement caught her eye, and she saw a line stretched between an enormous walnut tree and the end of the house. Clothes were stirring as the warm afternoon breezes rippled them gently.

For a moment Jenny hesitated, feeling out of place. She had not grown up in this sort of world where you called on neighbors, but this was her home now, and she was determined to become a part of it. Walking up the steps, she saw that the door was open and she could see down the hallway that went the length of the house. The screen door was patched and blocked her vision, but she knocked loudly and then waited. From far away she heard the sound of a radio and thought, *There must be somebody home.* She knocked louder, but still there was no answer. For a moment she stood there, balancing the pie in her left hand, and then walked back down the steps. She started for the truck, then thought that perhaps someone might be in the kitchen, as was often true in her own home. Going around the house, she saw an orange-striped cat staring at her arrogantly.

"Hello, kitty," she said, but he merely kept his half-lidded eyes fixed on her. When she reached the rear of the house, she found a pair of steps leading up to a screened-in back porch. The screen was punctured in several places and badly needed repair. Standing on the steps, she looked in and could partially see into the kitchen. She could hear the radio clearly now. It was playing a song that had become very popular the past year, called, "Life Is Just a Bowl of Cherries." It was a rather ironic song, she thought, considering how many in the country were without a paycheck and had little or no food. By leaning forward, she could see a man sitting at the table, his head close to the radio. She called, "Hello," but he did not move.

Ordinarily Jenny would not have thought of doing such a thing, but she wanted to carry out her mission. Stepping inside on the porch, she walked toward the door that led to the kitchen and said, "Excuse me, but—" She had no chance to say anything else, for the man moved so quickly she could not take it in. One instant he was sitting at the table, and the next he flew to his feet so fast he was a mere blur—and she saw with a cold shock that he had a gun in his hand. She stood absolutely still, not knowing what to do. He was not a large man, no more than five-ten she judged, and wore a pair of khaki jeans and a white dress shirt, open at the collar. His hair was a tawny, golden brown, and he had the most penetrating blue eyes she had ever seen.

"Who are you?" he asked roughly. "What are you doing here?" He put the gun back down on the table, and Jenny gasped with relief.

"My name is Jenny Winslow."

"Why didn't you knock?"

"I did knock!" Jenny said indignantly. "I knocked at the front door, but you couldn't hear, I suppose, because of the radio, so I came around to the back."

The brilliant blue eyes took her in, and Jenny thought he had one of the most masculine faces she had ever seen. His face was wedge-shaped and not deeply tanned, which made her suspect he was not a native. His mouth was wide and drawn up into a tight line, and, although he had laid down the gun, Jenny felt some fear of him. After all, they were alone in the house, as far as she knew. "My family asked me to come by and welcome you to the neighborhood," she said frostily.

A deep sigh went through the man who stood opposite

her, and he seemed to relax. "I'm not used to visitors. You startled me a bit."

"Do you always pull a gun on people that startle you?"

For a moment the man did not answer, and when he did, he did not speak of the gun. "My name's Varek," he said. "Clay Varek. It's a pretty good idea, Miss Winslow, not to go into houses uninvited."

"It's a pretty good idea not to point a gun at people who come to welcome you into the community either!"

A small smile tugged at the corners of Clay Varek's lips. "I expect you're right," he said. "Sorry about that. I'd been cleaning my gun, and I wasn't expecting company, like I said."

Jenny had rarely felt so ill at ease. "I shouldn't have come in," she admitted grudgingly, "but anyway here's the pie."

Varek stepped closer and saw alarm flicker in the young woman's eyes. He said quietly, "Thanks a lot. I'm not much of a cook." Taking the pie, he lifted the cover and turned his head. "What kind is it?"

"It's squash pie."

"That'll be a switch. I never heard of squash pie. Thank you."

Jenny nodded curtly. "You're very welcome," she said. She turned and, without another word, left the house. She was relieved to be out of there. Clay Varek's actions had frightened her more than she wanted to admit. She was not accustomed to guns except for the rifle Clint kept at the house for hunting, and she still remembered the flash of blue fire from Clay's eyes when he had suddenly whirled around to point his gun at her. As she walked toward the truck, she felt angry with herself for what had happened. "I should never have gone into the house," she muttered. "You can believe I won't be coming back, Mr. Clay Varek!"

She got into the truck, started the engine, and engaged the gears, but when the truck began to roll, she heard a thump, thump, thump from the rear tires.

"Oh no. A flat!" Shutting the engine off, she got out and walked to the back where, sure enough, the right tire was absolutely flat. She stood there helplessly, not knowing what to do.

For a moment she considered how long it would take her to walk back. She knew she was at least three miles from her own house, and she dreaded the walk.

"A little trouble?"

Jenny turned and saw that Varek had come out of the house so quietly she had not heard him.

"I've got a flat."

"So I see. Well, why don't you go sit on the porch. I'll fix it for you."

"That . . . that would be very nice of you."

Jenny showed Varek where the tire tubes were, and he found the spare and looked at it critically. It was thin with almost no tread. "You can almost see through it, but maybe it'll get you home."

At that moment a faint cry came from the house, and Varek turned to look in that direction. "I'll be right back," he said.

Jenny watched as he moved quickly toward the house. It sounded like a child crying, but she had seen no sign of a woman, and she wondered where the man's wife was.

She had waited only a few seconds when Varek came back outside. He was holding a little girl in his arms, and she was clinging to him with both arms around his neck. "This is Jamie. Jamie, this is Miss Winslow."

"Hello, Jamie," Jenny said, smiling at the girl. She had blond hair and light blue eyes and her face was dirty. Her hair needed washing too, Jenny noted, and she wore only a pair of dingy white panties.

"She's a little bit shy with strangers, but she'll get used to you."

Jenny thought of the sack of candy she had bought in the store, and she said, "I've got something you might like." She moved to the front of the truck, opened the door, and picked out the sack.

"Can she have candy, Mr. Varek?"

"She loves it."

"Look, Jamie, would you like some of this?"

The child stared at Jenny with round eyes and then smiled. "Candy," she said and nodded.

"Yes. Why don't you and I sit over here, and we'll watch your daddy fix the truck."

"Candy!"

Jenny reached out and took the child, who came to her at once. She moved over to a bench by the picket fence and sat down on it, holding the child in her lap. She unwrapped one of the pieces of candy and gave it to Jamie, who popped it right into her mouth.

Clay Varek was watching the two carefully, and then finally he nodded as if satisfied and began to jack up the truck.

Jenny soon found that the child was not at all shy once she had assured herself that all was well. Between taking pieces of candy, Jenny asked her questions, and she answered freely enough.

"How old are you, Jamie?"

The little girl held up two grimy fingers.

"Two? What a big girl." Then, feeling guilty even as she formed the question, Jenny asked, "Is your mama inside?"

Varek, by this time, had let the truck down and had heard the question. "She doesn't have one," he said gruffly.

"Oh," Jenny said. "I'm sorry! I didn't mean to be nosy."

"Didn't you?"

Jenny rose at once and handed the rest of the sack of candy to Varek. "There, Mr. Varek, give these to Jamie."

"I'm sure she'll find a use for 'em."

"And thanks for fixing my truck."

"No trouble." Varek looked down at the ground for a moment and was silent. Jenny wondered what he was thinking, and finally he lifted his head and met her eyes. "I was wrong about the gun. Sorry about that, Miss Winslow."

"It's all right," Jenny said. "I shouldn't have come into the house." She turned and climbed into the truck, then started the engine and drove away. When she looked back, Jamie waved at her, but the man did not move. He simply stood there holding the child.

★ ★ ★

"There's no woman there as far as I can tell," Jenny said. She had been cornered at once by Kat and Hannah, and she had explained her visit. She had left out the incident about the gun, but for some reason Kat was suspicious.

"He's probably a criminal and kidnapped that baby. Every baby has a mama!"

"Not always," Hannah said gently.

"Well, I'll spy on them!"

"No, you won't!" Hannah said sharply.

The door opened at this point, and Clint walked in. "What's happening?" he asked, then listened as Jenny told him about her encounter with Clay Varek. "Sounds a little odd. A man and a baby and no woman. But I've got some bad news."

"Bad news? What is it?" Jenny asked quickly.

"It's Sheriff Beauchamp."

"What's happened to him?" Hannah said.

"He was with some of his officers over in the north part of the county. They were raidin' a still and there was shootin'. The sheriff was killed. Got him right in the heart."

"How awful!" Jenny said. "He was such a nice man."

"Yes, he was."

"Well, who'll be sheriff now?" Kat said. She accepted death, at least in theory, more readily than the adults, who were all shaken by the news.

"That's right. There'll have to be a new sheriff."

"There's an election in two months, but the county commissioners have temporarily appointed Max Conroy."

Jenny blinked with surprise. "That man? Why, he's awful!"

Clint stared at her thoughtfully. "Yes, he is, but he's the sheriff at least until the next election—and he's pretty sure to be elected."

CHAPTER THREE

A TIME TO BE BORN

★　★　★

Lewis Winslow sat rigidly upright in the cane-bottom rocker, staring at the paper in front of him. He had been trying to put his problems out of his mind by reading the newspaper, but there seemed to be no comfort there.

The headline on the front page declared that the body of the kidnapped son of Charles and Anne Lindberg had been found in the woods only a few miles from the Lindberg home. Lewis lowered his head and murmured a prayer for the Lindberg family. Then he turned the page and read that Al Capone had entered a federal penitentiary in Atlanta the week before. The organized crime leader would serve eleven years for income tax evasion. Lewis shook his head, thinking, *All the evil that man has done, and all they get him on is tax evasion? And why in the world did they have to send him down to our state?* Sighing, Lewis turned the page again and read an article about the nation's desperate economy. The Depression, which held America in a grip of iron, seemed to get worse every day. As the nation headed toward the summer of 1932, the Depression had reached its lowest point yet. Twelve million people were unemployed and eighteen million were on relief. It was a Presidential election year and few had any doubt about

Hoover's chances of winning another term. Will Rogers summed up the mood of a nation: "If someone bit an apple and found a worm in it," he joked, "Hoover would get the blame." Lewis had seen a hitchhiker on the road, dressed practically in rags and holding up a sign that said, "Give me a lift or I'll vote for Hoover."

Hoover's name had actually become synonymous with the word *Depression*. His name had entered the language in a rather dark fashion. *Hoovervilles* were the shantytowns of the poor and dispossessed. Hobos and tramps sleeping under bridges covered themselves with *Hoover blankets*, which were nothing but yellowed newspaper. *Hoover hogs* were wild rabbits consumed as food, while shoes with holes in them were *Hoover shoes*, and broken-down shells of automobiles pulled along by mules were called *Hoover cars*.

Disgusted with his president and deeply concerned about the plight of his country, Lewis folded the paper and laid it in his lap, leaning his head back to put the country's problems out of his mind and concentrate on his own. He had not been sleeping well of late, being very concerned about the approaching birth of the baby. All of his other children had been born under prosperous circumstances. There had been doctors from prestigious medical schools, the most modern hospitals, and every medical advantage. Things were very different here. Yes, there were country doctors, and even a small old-fashioned hospital in town, but Lewis would have felt better if he could provide Missouri with the best possible care. Not that she would have wanted it. She planned to have Doc Peturis deliver the baby right here in her own home.

"Lewis. . . ?" Missouri Ann had come into the room wearing soft shoes, making an entrance so quiet Lewis hadn't heard her. He got up at once and started to speak, but she beat him to it. "I think, Lewis," she said calmly, "you'd better go for Dr. Peturis."

Lewis started, and when he spoke his voice was constricted by the tightness of his throat. "You mean . . . you mean the baby's coming?"

"I think it is." There was a calmness in Missouri Ann completely lacking in her husband. She smiled and came over to stand beside him, moving carefully as if she carried something infinitely precious. "I think it would be best if you send Jenny to get him."

"Here, sit down. How do you feel? Are you hurting?" Lewis shot the questions at Missouri so quickly that she laughed. "I'm fine, but I'd feel better if Doc Peturis was on his way."

"Here, you sit right down and don't move!" Lewis steered Missouri Ann's bulky form to the rocker, sat her down in it, then brushed his hand across his face in a nervous gesture. "I'll send her right now," he said, then turned and literally dashed out of the room.

★ ★ ★

Jenny was staking beans, using green cane pulled from beside the river. It was a hot day late in May, and sweat had soaked through her clothing. She stopped, pulled a handkerchief out of the pocket of her apron and mopped her face with it. For a moment she stared at her hands and then smiled, thinking of how work had hardened them since she had left New York. She was rather proud of herself, having discovered that she could stand up to the hard, physical work—she who had never done anything more strenuous than attend a ball or, perhaps, play a game of tennis.

Something suddenly struck her in the legs, and she looked down to see Stonewall, who had stayed with her all morning. He plopped himself down on her feet and looked up, his tongue lolling as if he were grinning at her.

"Get off of my feet, you monster. You must weigh two hundred pounds!" Jenny shoved the huge dog away. Then she picked another cane that had been trimmed to the right height and, stooping over, pushed it into the soil next to the emerald green seedling. As she worked steadily down the row, she thought of Clay Varek. He had been on her mind often since her encounter with him, and for some reason, she felt a great curiosity. All of the other people in her world had little niches that they fit neatly into, but Varek was different.

Something about him puzzled her, and she thought of the gun that had appeared almost magically in his hand. His quickness to draw his gun disturbed her, but then she remembered the child and how protective he had been. This was a puzzle, and she said to herself, "Where's his wife, I wonder, if he has one. There's something wrong about a man raising a baby alone. . . ."

"Jenny—Jenny!"

Hearing her name, Jenny turned to see her father running awkwardly toward her. His hair was blowing in the slight breeze, and his eyes were wide. "It's Missouri! The baby's coming!"

Jenny immediately dropped the cane she had in her hand and went to meet Lewis. "Did she say it was for sure?"

"I don't know. She just said to get the doctor. I want you to go get Peturis."

"Now, calm down, Dad. Hannah's here, and you two can take care of Missouri."

"I know, but I want you to hurry." Lewis ran both hands through his hair and gripped it, as if he were trying to lift himself off the ground by pulling it. His eyes were wide, and Jenny had never seen him look so disturbed. She knew at that moment how very much in love Lewis was with Missouri Ann, and she felt glad for it. Patting his shoulder, she said, "You go back to her. I'll change clothes."

"He may not be at his office."

"If he's not at his office, he's gone to visit a patient. I'll find out where he is, and I'll bring him back." She gave her father a slight push, saying, "Now, you go back to Ma. She needs you."

★   ★   ★

Jenny saw the steam rising out from underneath the hood of the truck and muttered, "Blast! I'll have to get some water!" The old Studebaker was reliable for a truck of its ancient lineage, but the radiator was a problem. Usually whoever drove it carried a gallon of water along, but Jenny had forgotten that in her hurry. When she reached down beside her, she saw that the jug was empty and remembered she had forgotten to fill it up.

"Come on, truck, you can't quit now!"

She glanced along the side of the road, hoping for a creek or a pond left over from the spring rains, but the spring had been hot, with fewer rains than usual, and she saw nothing. Finally, up ahead, she saw a shack off to one side of the road. She knew the Valentine family lived there. She remembered how Noah Valentine had been abused by Max Conroy in the general store.

The house was not painted, but the yard was clear, and Jenny saw Noah's huge form working in a garden out to the side. She pulled in, and when he came up to the window, she said, "The truck overheated. Can I get some water?"

Noah nodded and smiled. "Yes, ma'am. The well's around back. I'll fill it for you."

She drove the truck around behind the house, which was a long, low structure of two sections with a passage between, all covered under one roof. It was called a dogtrot house, Jenny had learned, because the dogs usually stayed under the shade of the roofed passageway during the hot summers. Jenny shut off the engine and got out as Noah lifted the hood. He reached out and touched the radiator cap, then jerked his hand back. "She mighty hot, miss. Better let it cool down for a mite 'fore I pour the water in."

"I'm in a big hurry," she said, then added, "My name's Jenny Winslow, by the way."

"Yes, ma'am, I knows that. I'm Noah Valentine."

Jenny smiled and said, "I'm glad to know you, Noah." She looked at the truck and asked, "Why can't we pour the water right in?"

"'Cause that might bust the engine. When it's hot like that you need to let it cool off just a little bit. You in a mighty big hurry?"

"Yes, I'm going for the doctor. My stepmother's having a baby."

"Is that right!" Noah said, "Well, I tell you what we do. We'll pour in just a little bit of water at a time." He reached in the hip pocket of his faded overalls, pulled out a crimson bandana, and removed the radiator cap. He went over to the well, pulled up a bucketful of water, and picked up a gourd that had been carved into a drinking vessel. "Here," he said, "we give it just a little bit. Not much." Carefully he let a thin stream of water down into the radiator, and the steam boiled up. "She mighty hot," he said, "but we'll get you on your way pretty soon."

Jenny knew little about black people. She had been afforded little contact with them in New York, mostly with servants in one form or another. Now as she stood there dwarfed by the huge black man, she thought of how the sheriff had vilified him in public. Noah Valentine was big enough and obviously strong enough to crush most men, including Conroy, but he had simply stood there helplessly. A quick pity ran through Jenny at the thought of what it must be like to be at the mercy of others. "How are the crops coming along?" she asked.

"Just fine, ma'am. The cotton's gonna do real good this year. I notice you ain't put none in."

"No, we don't know enough about farming to do that. My brother-in-law, Clint Longstreet, knows how, but we thought this year we'd just put in some sorghum and a huge garden so we'll have plenty to eat this winter."

"That might be best. Ain't gonna get much for cotton this year the way things is."

The two stood there talking, and Jenny was impressed with the gentleness of the man despite his awesome size and obvious strength. She lifted her head and turned, saying, "Someone's come, I think."

"I'll just go see who it is, Miss Winslow. You keep pourin' this water in there just a little bit at a time. It's coolin' down right nice, but we don't want to bust that engine."

Jenny took the gourd and obeyed Noah's instruction, pouring in a little at a time. She was glad he had been there, for she would probably have filled it up with cold water and perhaps ruined the engine. As she poured the water, she heard voices but could not make out the words. She saw that the steam was not rushing out of the engine now, so she quickly filled the radiator, then replaced the cap. The impulse to thank Noah came to her, and after she put the hood down she stepped around the side of the house. She saw a police car out in front with *Sheriff's Department* printed in white letters on the side. She did not step out in view but for some reason kept herself concealed. Glancing back, she saw that the truck was hidden behind the house and something of what was happening before her set off an alarm in her head.

The two uniformed deputies were flanking Noah, and each of them had a nightstick in his hand. She had seen the deputies before but did not know their names. One of them was a large man with his belly hanging over his belt and tow-colored hair. The other was a much smaller man. His hat was pushed back on his head revealing black hair, and there was a sneer on his face as he stared at Noah Valentine.

"Come on, nig, we know you robbed that store. You might as well 'fess up to it."

"No, suh, I ain't robbed no store," Noah protested, shaking his head vigorously. "I was here all night last night. You can ask my mama if it ain't so."

The big deputy laughed, a raucous, cruel sound. "Well, how 'bout that, Arlie? His mama will tell us he was here all night. Now, ain't that sweet!"

The smaller deputy named Arlie grinned with a sharklike expression. "I guess we'll just have to take her word for it, won't we, Merle?"

Jenny somehow knew what was coming, but it happened so fast she was unable to respond.

The grin faded from the smaller man's face. "You gonna confess to holdin' up the store?" he asked. "You might as well, 'cause we'll get it out of you one way or another."

"No, suh, I ain't held up no store, Deputy Pender."

Arlie Pender, like many small men, felt the need to prove himself to those who were larger. "You callin' me a liar?" he snapped.

"No, suh, I ain't."

"He called me a liar, Merle. I ain't standin' for that!"

In a swift move, the small deputy lifted his nightstick and brought it down hard on Noah's skull. Jenny gasped, the sound of the sharp blow nearly making her sick. It sounded like someone striking a watermelon with a blunt instrument. She saw Noah go down on one knee, his hands covering his head. The rich, red blood was coursing down his face when suddenly the large man raised his stick too and struck at him. Noah was covering his head, so the stick struck his thick arm, but then both the men began to rain down blows, cursing and shouting.

Afterward Jenny did not remember making any conscious decision to interfere. She simply found herself running toward the trio and heard herself shouting, "You stop that, you hear me!" She came to stand before the two men, and Noah, who was now lying on his stomach trying to cover his head, rolled over and looked up at her, blood streaming down his face. He struggled to his feet, his eyes half glazed from the force of the terrific blows he had taken.

"You're interfering with a police action here, lady," Pender said.

"That's right," Merle Arp said. "He was resisting arrest."

"No, he wasn't," Jenny said. She looked up at the big man fearlessly, her eyes were flashing, her face pale. "You hit him without any provocation!"

The small deputy laughed. "You must be a Yankee. I can tell from the way you talk."

"Doesn't matter how I talk! You two struck this man without any cause."

"Well, now, that's just your word against ours," Merle Arp said. His eyes went over Jenny in a suggestive manner, and he said, "You ain't bad lookin' for a Yankee girl. Me and you might step out some night."

"But now just step back, miss. We're takin' this man in."

A movement caught Jenny's eyes, and she turned to see a tall black woman wearing a faded brown dress come outside. She was holding a small child no more than three or four by the hand, and several other children gathered behind her. "He wasn't doin' nothin' to you. I seen it all. You hit him for nothin'!" she said.

"Get back in the house, Mama!" Noah said. He wiped the

blood from his face and turned to the two men. "I didn't rob no store."

"You'll have your chance to prove that. Put the cuffs on him, Merle."

Jenny watched helplessly as they put the cuffs on the big man and forced him into the backseat of the car. Deputy Merle Arp stopped long enough to run his eyes up and down her figure and said, "I'll be seein' you, sweetie. I think you and me would go pretty well together."

"You'll see me all right, but it'll be in court! I'll be there to testify to what you two did."

The two deputies grinned at each other, and then Arlie Pender winked at her. "You just do all you want to, Yankee lady."

The car pulled out, and Jenny turned to the black woman. "I saw it all," she said. "I'll go see the sheriff about it. My name's Jenny Winslow. I live down the road."

"I'm Hattie. Noah's mama." A deep sadness revealed itself in the woman's large brown eyes. She was a strong woman but bowed by time and trouble. "It won't do no good. That sheriff, he hates my boy just 'cause he got in trouble one time."

"What did he do?"

"He sold some moonshine whiskey, and he had to go to the pen, but he found the good Lord while he was there. He served his time, and ever since he's been helpin' me raise these chil'uns. They daddy's dead."

"It'll be all right, Hattie. They can't do anything to him because I saw it all."

"You don't know this place, Miss Winslow. A black man ain't got no defense against a white man's word."

Jenny, at that moment, felt a surge of rage such as she had rarely experienced. Her life before the stock market crash had been smooth and relatively uneventful. She had not experienced things like this in New York City, but now standing in front of the pitiful shack with the sorrowing mother in front of her, a resolution formed itself. She nodded and said, "I'll go see the sheriff right away, Hattie. Don't worry about it. The Lord will take care of you."

"The good Lord will have to because there ain't nobody else. But I thank you, miss, for your kindness."

Jenny went back, got into the truck, and left. As she pulled out onto the highway, she took one glance and saw Hattie Valentine staring at her, the children gathered about her. They made a sad tableau to her, and the resolution to help Noah Valentine grew into something stronger than she had ever known before.

★   ★   ★

Dr. Harrison Peturis was enjoying a rare moment of rest. He was one of the few doctors in the county that would go outside the city limits to treat patients, and as a result he kept a busy schedule. He leaned back in his chair reading from his favorite book, *Paradise Lost*. He always read the book aloud, and his voice rolled as he seemed to chew on the words and brought them out in full-throated tones:

> *"At certain revolutions all the damned*
> *Are brought; and feel by turns the bitter change*
> *Of fierce extremes, extremes by change more fierce,*
> *From beds of raging fire to starve in ice*
> *Their soft ethereal warmth, and there to pine*
> *Immovable, infixed, and frozen round*
> *Periods of time, thence hurried back to fire."*

"Now *there's* a punishment for you." Peturis got up and read the lines again, filling his office with the sound of his powerful voice. He was a big man, built like a huge stump. Everything about him was thick—his arms, his legs, his body, his neck. He had coarse salt-and-pepper hair, a clipped black beard, and snapping brown eyes. As he continued to read from the poem with obvious enjoyment, he stopped only to puff on the thin cheroot that he kept clamped between his jaws like a bulldog. White ash from the cigar covered the front of his vest, and some flakes even showed in the blackness of his beard.

The door opened, and Peturis looked up to see his nurse,

Geraldine Sweeting, enter. She was tall and rail thin, with a voice surprisingly deep for a woman. "Doctor, Jenny Winslow's here."

Tossing the book on his desk, Peturis turned and nodded. "Must be time for that baby." He walked out of the office and found Jenny standing in the waiting room. Without preamble, Jenny said, "You've got to come, Dr. Peturis. It's my stepmother. The baby's on the way."

"How's she doing?"

Jenny shook her head. "She seems all right to me, but I don't know anything about babies."

"All right. I'll come right away. No patients here. Geraldine, you'd better come along with me. At her age it's liable to be a troublesome delivery."

"Would you hurry please, Doctor," Jenny urged. "I think my father's worried."

Peturis puffed on the cigar rapidly, then pulled it from his lips and grinned. "He ought to know all about having babies. He had you, didn't he?"

"This is different. He's older now. Please hurry, Doctor."

"All right. All right. I'm on my way."

"I've got one errand to run, and then I'll be right home."

Jenny left the doctor's office and went at once to the sheriff's office. She walked in and found the new sheriff, Max Conroy, standing with his two deputies. The three grinned at her when she entered.

"Well, I've been expecting you," Max said. "I understand there's a little difference of opinion here about this business."

"Noah Valentine didn't do a thing, Sheriff. These two just started hitting him for nothing."

Conroy shrugged and said, "I have to take my deputies' word for it. Noah's been in fights before. As a matter of fact, he once beat up a fellow so bad he almost didn't make it."

"But that was then and this is now!"

Jenny stood there arguing, but she saw that the men were toying with her. A fourth man was in the room, but he said nothing. He was standing against the wall, not tall but well built, and bearing the uniform of the sheriff's office. Jenny did not notice him at first, but when she turned she saw him standing there and surmised that he was an Indian. He had copper cheeks and eyes black as obsidian, and his face was absolutely expressionless, so she had no hope of his helping her.

"You boys leave here, and I'll settle this with Miss Winslow," Conroy said. The two deputies, Arp and Pender, laughed and then disappeared into the back, where there was evidently an extension of the office. The copper-faced man said nothing but went out the front door. As soon as the door was closed, Conroy walked over to stand by Jenny. He was no more than thirty-five, tall, lean, and wiry. He had sandy hair, and his green eyes were as cold as she remembered them from the store. There was something suggestive in his manner that made Jenny's stomach turn. "You just don't understand these niggers," he said with a half smile. "You got to crack down hard on 'em. Why, half of 'em are cutting the other half to bits with razors on Saturday night."

"Sheriff, I admit I'm new to this country, but if I had seen what I witnessed this afternoon in New York, I would have come to the same conclusion. Your deputies attacked Noah Valentine for no reason."

"That's not what they say."

Jenny felt a sense of hopelessness, but something about the bland expression of the deputies and the sheriff infuriated her. "Why would I lie?"

"Now look, Jenny, when you get to know me better you'll understand that this is a tough job. We have to be hard. Maybe the boys get a little over-anxious sometimes, but they put their lives on the line every day." He reached out and put his hand on her arm and squeezed it. "Look, why don't you and I go out tonight? We can talk about this."

Jenny wrenched her arm away. "I'm not going out with you, not ever," she said, "and you haven't heard the last of this!" She turned away and heard Conroy's laughter follow her. She slammed the door and started blindly down the street but quickly collided with a man.

"Excuse me," she muttered. Looking up, she saw it was the deputy who hadn't said anything.

"My name's Billy Moon, Miss Winslow."

The voice seemed to come from deep within the man's chest. He was more muscular than most men, extremely strong looking, and although his face was expressionless, she saw something in his eyes that caused her to feel he was a different sort of man than the sheriff and the other two deputies.

"It's not fair, Deputy Moon," she said.

Moon studied her for a moment, then said, "If I were you, I'd go see Luke Dixon."

"Luke Dixon? Who's he?"

"He's a lawyer. Trying to be, anyway. He does surveying on the side to make a living."

"Why should I go see him?"

"He's a pretty good man, and he sometimes takes on cases other lawyers won't handle. He's got a bad name with some of the local leadership around here because he won't play their game."

"I don't have any money for a lawyer."

"Go see him anyway," Moon said quietly. He hesitated, then said, "If you do go, you might tell him I heard Merle and Arlie brag on how they beat Noah up."

"You'd testify to that?"

"Yes." The answer came quickly, and Moon said, "We had a pretty good department here as long as Sheriff Beauchamp was around."

"It must be hard for you."

"I don't think I'll be around long. Conroy's trying to figure out a way to get rid of me. He will after the next election."

"I'll go see Dixon."

"Drive down Main Street, turn to your right at the next corner. You'll probably find him there. He's between jobs at the moment."

"Thank you, Deputy."

"You're welcome, miss."

Moving quickly along the street, Jenny found the office of Luke Dixon without any trouble. The sign outside his door read *Luke Dixon, Attorney at Law*. She entered and at once was greeted by a lanky man with a head full of blond hair and pale blue eyes. "Can I help you, miss?"

"My name's Jennifer Winslow, and I need help."

"Have a seat," Dixon said. His eyes took her in quickly, and he sat back and listened as she explained why she was there.

"And what would you like for me to do?"

"I'd like for you to defend him. He doesn't have any help at all. His mother and his brothers and sisters saw what happened."

"Their word won't mean much in court. It'll have to be up to you. Are you ready to testify?"

"Yes."

"All right. I'll see what I can do." He hesitated, then said, "I heard about your folks. Your dad won the Congressional Medal of Honor, didn't he?"

"Yes, in the Spanish-American War."

Dixon did not comment, but Jenny could see that this meant something to him.

"All right," he finally said. "I'll go down and see Noah. I always liked the man. He was a rough one in his early days, but he's been straight since he got back. Straight as the law will let him."

"I . . . I don't have any money," Jenny said simply.

"Neither do I." Dixon grinned suddenly. "Maybe you can make me a chocolate pie. We'll call it square."

Jenny smiled at him and made a pretty picture in his eyes, though she did not know it. "I can only make squash pie."

"Squash pie? I never heard of it, but you do it. That'll be payment enough."

★ ★ ★

Lewis had not stopped pacing the floor for what seemed like hours. Clint had tried several times to get him to sit down, but it never lasted. Finally Clint said, "You might as well calm down, Lewis. This may take a long time."

Lewis, ordinarily the mildest of men and very fond of Clint, suddenly struck out. "Wait until you're in a mess like this! We'll see how you handle it!"

Jenny came to stand beside her father. She patted his arm and said, "It's not a mess. It's a baby. Now, you sit down. I'll bring some coffee."

Jenny left, and the two men sat down in the living room, Lewis twisting anxiously in his seat. Hannah came in once and tried to calm her father, but it seemed impossible. Jenny came back and, glancing at the clock, saw that she had been back for two hours. Dr. Peturis had come out twice, each time saying that things were going "pretty well." On the last time he had said, "She's a little older than most mothers, but she's strong."

Jenny sat down beside her father and tried to take his mind off of Missouri Ann. She related what she had seen at Noah Valentine's and then went on to tell of her visit at the sheriff's office.

"Those three are pretty sorry," Clint said. "There's going to be an election in a few weeks, but no one's running against Conroy. One man started to run, but then he dropped out. My guess is Conroy's cronies threatened him."

"Maybe someone else will run," Jenny offered.

"I doubt it. Nobody can beat Conroy."

"Why not, Clint?" Hannah asked.

"Because there's money behind him. Nobody really knows what's going on, but the big money in this county is all behind Conroy. The men I talk to think it's got somethin' to do with bootleggin' in the county. They know Conroy will wink at it. There's big money to be had."

"I didn't know there was that much money in this county," Lewis said, making an effort to concentrate.

"The way I hear it the moonshine operation has gotten big here. A lot of booze going up north, and if Conroy gets in office, it'll be bigger yet."

At that instant Dr. Peturis came out. Lewis jumped to his feet and cried, "How is she, Doctor?"

"You've got a boy, Mr. Winslow. A fine boy."

"How's my wife?"

"She's doing well. She had a hard time, but—"

At that moment the door opened, and Nurse Sweeting said, "Doctor, come quick!"

Peturis whirled and rushed back down the hall and into the bedroom, and Lewis would have followed him, but Clint held his arm. "Hang on, Lewis."

"Well, what could be wrong?"

Jenny and Hannah tried to calm him, but Lewis was pale and sat down as if his legs would no longer support him.

The waiting seemed intolerable. The clock ticking on the mantel was the loudest sound in the room.

Finally Peturis came out again, and leaping up, Lewis ran to him as if he would grab him. "What is it? What's wrong?"

"Nothing's wrong."

"Is my wife all right?"

"She's fine. Doing wonderfully well."

"And how's the baby?"

Peturis reached into his pocket and pulled out a cheroot. Everyone watched as he extracted a kitchen match, struck it on his fingernail, and lit it. When he had it glowing comfortably, he blew a smoke ring and then grinned broadly. "They're fine."

"They!" Lewis blinked with shock and glanced wildly around at the others. "They? You mean they're twins? There are two of them?"

"No," Peturis looked at his cigar and chuckled deep in his chest. "There's *three* of them. Three fine boys. Congratulations, Winslow." The laugh grew broader, and he shook his head. "Looks like you're not going to have a great deal of spare time in the future."

Lewis stood there and could not speak for a moment. Finally he swallowed hard and said, "Three of them?"

"That's right. You'd better start thinking up some new names," Peturis said, grinning. Then he took Lewis's arm. "Come on. You can go see these new boys of yours."

CHAPTER FOUR

THREE ARE BETTER THAN ONE

★ ★ ★

The end of May had come, and as Jenny took down diapers from the clothesline, she wondered what life had been like before the onslaught of babies had struck the Winslow home. The breeze filled the diapers, puffing them up into rounded shapes, and they flapped like white flags along the line strung from the house to the towering walnut tree in the front yard. Jenny filled the clothesbasket and turned to see Hannah, who had come out with another load of wet diapers.

"There's no end to it, is there?" Hannah shook her head ruefully.

"I think having one baby would be easier after seeing how hard three are."

"Even naming them was hard," Hannah replied as she removed a clothespin from her mouth and pinned one corner of a diaper to the line. As she clipped the other one, she added, "They had struggled so hard to choose one name for a boy and then all of a sudden they had to pick two more."

Indeed, this had been one of the many problems the triplets had brought. Lewis and Missouri had settled on the name Michael if the baby was a boy, but when they were suddenly faced with naming two others, they chose Samuel, Missouri's father's name, for one but were stumped for a third name. Then, the day after their birth, Hannah had a dream in which she proclaimed the Lord had given her a name for the boy. "His name is Temple."

"Temple?" Lewis said. "I never heard of a man called Temple."

"Well, I have," Missouri said. "Sam Houston had a son, and his name was Temple. Temple Houston. I think it's a beautiful name."

Lewis stared at the three boys lined up on the bed and laughed. "Michael, Samuel, and Temple. Michael, I suppose, will always be the oldest by about thirty minutes."

"God is going to use these boys. I just know He is," Missouri Ann had sighed.

Now Hannah and Jenny finished hanging the laundry and then went back inside. Missouri was sitting in the rocking chair, nursing Temple. She looked up and frowned. "I need to be doing some of the work."

"You're doing exactly the kind of work you're supposed to do. You nurse those babies, and we'll take care of the diapers," Jenny said, smiling.

Missouri cuddled the infant in her arms and stroked his hair, which was a beautiful auburn color. "I've always been embarrassed by being so big, but God knew what He was doing. Only a giantess could nurse all three of these fellows."

Hannah laughed and began to fold diapers as Missouri continued to speak. "It's a miracle. Every time I think about it, I just can hardly keep from crying. Here a year ago I was living by myself out in that old house, no husband, my two children grown and gone, and now look at me. Right in the middle of the finest family in the world." She hugged Temple and whispered endearments to him, then suddenly looked over and said, "Hannah, you'll be having your own baby."

The words struck against Hannah with almost a physical force. Her face grew slightly pale, and she whispered, "How could you know that?"

"The Lord just whispered to me that you're going to have a boy, and he's going to be a great servant of God."

"Is that right, Hannah?" Jenny asked with astonishment. "You're really expecting?"

"I . . . I haven't been sure, but I think so."

"You can be sure of it. The Lord don't make no mistakes," Missouri said, smiling. "Have you told Clint yet?"

"No, I wanted to wait until I was absolutely sure."

"Well, I think if Missouri says it's so, why don't you go tell him?" Jenny grinned.

"All right, I will." Hannah got up but stopped as she reached the doorway. Turning around, with wonder in her eyes, she whispered, "After what I went through in New York, I never thought I'd have a husband, much less a child, but God is good."

She turned and left the room, and Jenny said, "She'll be a wonderful mother—just like you, Ma."

★   ★   ★

"Hand me that screwdriver, would you, Lewis?"

"This one?" Lewis picked up a screwdriver and handed it to Clint. The two of them were putting new rings in the truck. Kat was hovering over them offering her help but was actually more in the way than anything else. She wore the usual ragged overalls and was barefooted, and a smudge of black grease marked her forehead.

"You've got grease all over your head," Lewis said. "Come here." Pulling a handkerchief out of his pocket, he carefully wiped the girl's forehead, then squeezed her and gave her a kiss.

Kat was a youngster who held nothing back, saying anything that came to her mind. Lewis knew this, but still he was shocked when she looked at him directly with her gray-green eyes and asked, "Daddy, are you going to love me any less with all those boys around?"

"What a question! Of course not."

"But if you've got more children to love, you'll have to divide your love up," Kat said. "It's like a pie. If you got one pie, and you've got four people to eat it, you cut four slices.

But if there are five or six, you have to make the slices smaller. So you can't love me as much because you have to give some of your love to Temple and Sam and Michael."

"What an idea!" Lewis said. He reached over and pulled the girl into his arms, knowing her desire for affection. He thought for a moment, trying to find a way to put it that would assure her of the very deep love he had for this youngest daughter of his. "Love isn't like a pie. It's just the opposite. True enough with a pie you've only got so much to give away, but with love the more you give away, the more you have."

"Is that right?"

"It's absolutely right, and I want you to always give it away. For if you keep it, it spoils and goes bad, like milk that's not used."

Kat pondered this for what seemed like a long time. Both of the men were watching her, fascinated by the processes of her mind. She was the brightest and most inquisitive youngster either of them had ever seen, and finally she sighed and smiled brilliantly. "I'm glad you told me, Daddy. Now I won't have to worry about that."

"Why, of course not. We all have those boys to love, and you're going to have a fine time helping raise them."

"I will too! Ma's going to let me change a diaper pretty soon."

"That's quite an honor." Lewis made a face at Clint.

"Come on, Daddy, let's go hunting. You promised me you'd take me."

"I've got to help Clint with this."

Clint said quickly. "I'm about finished up here. You might as well take her while it's daylight, Lewis."

"All right. We'll do it. Come along, Kat."

The two left and Clint watched them go, conscious, as always, of the miracle of family. He had been alone for so long in his own life that he had known nothing of family love, but the Winslows had shown him the wonder of it. And after he had married Hannah, he felt closer to the Winslows than ever.

He watched for a moment as father and daughter left the house, the dog bounding along at their heels. Lewis was carrying the shotgun, and Clint could hear Kat begging to be allowed to carry it and Lewis denying her the privilege.

"Where are those two going?"

Clint turned, surprised, and saw that Hannah had come out.

"They're going out to scare squirrels. I think they're pretty safe, though. I've never figured out how Lewis could be a war hero when he can't hit the side of a barn except with a shotgun." He stood up, stretched, and asked, "How's Missouri?"

"She's doing fine."

"She's a wonderful woman. I've never known anybody quite like her."

"She's not the woman I would've thought Daddy would have fallen in love with, but they make a perfect match."

Clint reached over, pulled the rag out, and wiped the grease from his hand, then came over to pull her into his arms. "No more perfect than we are," he smiled. He kissed her and then shook his head. "Every day I wake up thinking the dream will be over and I'll be back on the road or in a jail somewhere. And here I am with the prettiest wife in the whole world and the sweetest."

Hannah had done without male appreciation most of her life. As a young woman, she had had a bad experience with a man and then had lived the life of a recluse, avoiding all men for years. But she had always longed for such words as this, and now life seemed to glow within her, and she reached up and put her hand on his cheek. "I've got something to tell you."

"What is it?"

"We're going to have a baby, Clint."

Clint stood staring at her and shook his head as if he hadn't heard, and then he saw the smile on her face. He let out a whoop. "A baby! Well, glory to God!" He put his arms around her but very gently instead of roughly as he usually did.

He hugged her, and then he stepped back and took her hands. "I hope it's a girl just like you."

Humor bubbled up and mixed with joy in Hannah, and she laughed aloud. "Maybe it'll be triplets."

"Wait a minute, now," Clint said, pretending to be

alarmed. "That's too much of a good thing. Tell you what. Let's start out slow and just have one little girl. Then if we like her, we'll have a boy. And come to think of it, I have three young ones to practice on now. So by the time our baby gets here, I'll know all about it."

Hannah leaned into his arms again, laid her face against his chest, and hugged him fiercely. She felt a joy that only a woman can know who has long been hungry for love and has finally found it.

★   ★   ★

Clay Varek looked up from the floor he was mopping, sniffed, and with a groan, wheeled and ran to the stove. The stew was boiling over, and when he touched the pot handle, he burned his hand. Quickly he grabbed a towel and picked up the pot. The stew dribbled onto the stove and sent an odor of burned meat throughout the kitchen.

"Blast it!" He put it down on the tile trivet and began to clean up the mess, scraping the excess from the top of the cook stove. The smell permeated the kitchen, and wiping his hands with disgust, he picked up the coffeepot and poured some coffee into a white cup with a missing handle. Sitting down, he stared across the room and thought for a moment about how much better the place looked. He had taken the house without seeing it because the rent had been cheap, but when he had seen it, he understood why. It had been un-inhabited for years and had a terrible odor. It had been used and misused by visiting tramps, and most of the windows were broken out and animals had taken up residence inside.

Varek well knew that housekeeping was not his strong point, but he had plunged in with a vigor that marked every-thing he did. He had attacked the house in sections, cleaning out one bedroom and setting it up for himself with a bed for Jamie in the same room. Then he had launched the main cru-sade, which was to clean up the kitchen. He was thankful enough that there was some indoor plumbing, although he'd had to replace the well pump, and having electricity brought to the house had been a major expense.

As he sat there thinking of chores to do, he realized that he was weary. He was a strong man, but he had not known how hard housekeeping was until it all fell on him. The cooking, the washing, what ironing was done, cleaning the house inside and making repairs outside kept him busy from early morning until night.

A sudden creaking sound startled him, and he whirled quickly, his hand going to his belt. The gun was not there as he was accustomed to, and when he saw that it was merely the screen door moved by the wind, he relaxed and took a sip of coffee. "You've gotta stop being so edgy." He spoke the words aloud, and the sound of his own voice seemed to startle him. He forced himself to be still, and then as he finished his coffee, he heard Jamie crying. He got up and went to the bedroom, moving over to the half bed he had fixed for her. Her face was flushed, he saw, and when he put his hand on her forehead, he was startled at how high her fever was.

"I don't feel good," Jamie whimpered.

Varek made up his mind immediately. "I expect we'd better take you to see the doctor." She was wearing few clothes, for she had been hot, and there was no fan in the room. He put a dress on her, slipped her shoes on, and then left the house. He put her inside the used Chevrolet, but when he tried to start it, he found the battery was dead.

He sat there frustrated, then shook his head. "Come on, Jamie, we'll have to walk."

"All the way?" the child asked. Her face was very flushed, and fear touched Clay. He knew little about children, especially about childhood diseases. "It'll be all right," he said. "Somebody will pick us up. Come along, now." Picking up the child, he stepped out of the car and started down the road. It was a good six miles to town, but traffic was fairly common, and he was hopeful someone would pick them up quickly. But there was a natural glumness in Clay Varek as if he always expected the worse and was rarely disappointed. In the back of his mind he was already planning to make the entire walk, and grimly he set himself to the task.

Jenny saw the pair as she drove along the highway. She

recognized Varek and the child and pulled up behind them. She watched as he turned, and when he came to stand outside her window, she said, "Where are you going?"

"I've got to go to the doctor. Jamie's sick."

"Well, get in. I'll take you there." She saw him hesitate and knew that he was not a man who took favors easily, but he nodded and said curtly, "Thanks." He went around and got in, and once the truck was moving, she asked, "When did she get sick?"

"Just yesterday. Just a little fever, but it's higher today, I think. I don't have any way to take it."

"Which doctor do you want to go to?"

"I don't know any of them."

"We use Dr. Peturis. He's a little bit rough, but he's a kind man. I've heard he's good with children."

"Take me there if you don't mind." He hesitated, then said, "Sorry to be such trouble."

"You're not from around here, are you, Mr. Varek?"

"No, you can tell from my voice, I guess."

"Yes, we're from New York, so we all have northern accents. It makes it a bit hard."

As she drove along, Jenny offered a little of her history, and then finally she said, "I'd take Jamie to my stepmother. She's very good with anyone who's sick, but she just had some babies herself."

"Babies?"

"Yes, triplets."

Clay suddenly smiled, and as Jenny watched him, she saw it made him look much younger. "One is all I can handle." He hesitated, then said, "It's hard on a man raising a child without a woman."

Jamie looked up, though her face was flushed. "You do fine, Daddy."

Varek hugged the child and laughed shortly. "Well, it would be better if you had a mama."

Jenny kept waiting for him to say more about his wife, but he seemed to steer away from anything so personal. He did say finally, "That was a good squash pie."

Jenny laughed. "It's the only kind I know how to cook. I'm

having to learn how to live in the country. I've always been a city girl."

"I'll have to learn too. I'm from Chicago."

"You lived there all your life?"

"Quite a bit of it. Including the last ten years." He said no more, and the conversation was rather bland until Jenny pulled up in front of Dr. Peturis's office. "There's the doctor's office. Why don't you take Jamie in? I'll do my errand, then run you home again."

Varek shook his head. "I hate to be a burden to anybody."

"Don't be silly. That's what neighbors are for." She reached over and brushed the hair back from Jamie's face. "You go on in with your daddy now, and I'll be back. And you'll be well soon."

Jenny waited until Varek and the child were inside; then she drove to Luke Dixon's office. She entered and found that Dixon was engaged in conversation with a tall, rawboned farmer. She waited in the outside room until the farmer left, and Dixon said, "Come on in, Miss Winslow."

"You can call me Jenny."

"Fine, and I'm Luke."

"What about Noah?"

Dixon shook his head. "They're going to charge him with assaulting an officer and resisting arrest."

"What will that mean if he's found guilty?"

"It'll mean going back to prison, maybe for as much as five years."

"But he didn't do it!"

Luke Dixon studied the young woman before him, noting the richness of her lips, which were now pressed together almost willfully. Her hair was thick and red with golden lights that gleamed under the overhead lights. He was conscious of the full, soft lines of her body within her dress. Her face was a mirror, he noted, that changed as her feelings changed, the features reflecting the swift changes of her mind.

"Can you help him, Luke?"

"I can try, but you'll have to testify that he didn't start the trouble. I can tell you right now that won't make you very popular, challenging a white man's word. Two white men, as a matter of fact, over the fate of a black man."

"What about you?"

"I'm not popular anyway," he laughed. He smiled then, and she admired the strong bone structure of his face. "Why are you helping him?"

"I just like lost causes. I've got the scars to show for it." Luke suddenly said, "You're not married, are you?"

"No."

"Got a steady boyfriend who'd beat me up if I asked you out?"

The question obviously amused Jenny, and she laughed in a way he found very attractive, her chin tilting up and her lips curving in pretty lines. "No boyfriend at all."

"That's good. I'll pick you up at seven."

"You're pretty sure of yourself, aren't you?"

"Actually I'm pretty shy, and I have to put on this act to make people think I'm outgoing."

Luke could almost see a curtain of reserve fall away, and a teasing expression of gaiety lit her eyes. Luke decided at that moment that Jenny Winslow was a complex and striking woman.

"All right, pick me up at seven," she said. "You'll have to come in and meet the family. There's quite a bunch of us."

"I'll wear my graduation suit," he smiled. "We'll talk about the case tonight."

"All right, Luke . . . and thanks." She put out her hand, and he looked at it for a moment, then took it. He squeezed it firmly but not hard as he nodded.

"Seven o'clock it is."

Jenny left the office feeling pleased. She had not given romance much thought since leaving New York. There it had been her chief topic of conversation and the center of her thoughts, but it had only rarely entered her mind since moving to Georgia. But she liked Luke Dixon and was looking forward to the evening.

Going back to the doctor's office, she walked into the waiting room and, seeing no sign of Varek and Jamie, figured they were in with the doctor. There was no nurse to ask, and three other patients were waiting, so she simply sat and waited with them. After a short time Varek came out carrying Jamie. He had a slip of paper in his hand, and his eyes sought hers at once.

"What is it, Clay?"

He did not answer but nodded at the door. She went outside, and as soon as they were clear of the office, he said, "It's the flu, but the doctor doesn't think it's dangerous." Relief flooded his face, and she saw how tense he had been.

"Is that a prescription?"

"Yes. You know where the drugstore is?"

"Sure. Come on."

She took Varek to the drugstore and stayed with Jamie while he went inside. She found the child, despite her discomfort, was bright and very intelligent. Jenny was tempted to ask about her mother, but she clamped down on that impulse with restraint.

Varek came out, got into the truck, and nodded. She started the engine, and neither of them spoke until they were out of town. As the Studebaker rumbled over the road, he turned and faced her. "I've been hearing talk about you."

"What kind of talk?"

"That you're taking on the powers that be."

"Oh, you mean about Noah Valentine."

"Yes. Why are you doing it?"

She did not answer for a time, and then she turned and looked at him, removing her eyes from the road for a moment. "Because it's the right thing to do," she said firmly.

Varek watched her as she drove along, admiring her profile and thinking, *She is the kind of woman who won't back down from a just fight.* It was a way he had of summing up people, and he always respected those with enormous certainty and a positive will. There was fire in this girl that made her lovely, and he found himself drawn to her.

She turned to face him and said, "Do you think it's wrong? You think I shouldn't do it?"

"That's up to you." He got out of the truck then, took Jamie, and leaned over and for a moment studied Jenny's face. "But you can get hurt doing the right thing—I can tell you that from experience. Thanks for the ride."

"I'll come by and see how Jamie's doing tomorrow," she called out after him. Jamie waved over his shoulder, and Jenny waved back, then started the truck. As she drove toward home, she thought about what Varek had said: *"A person can get hurt doing the right thing."* A stubbornness rose in her, and she said, "I may get hurt, but I'm going to do what I think is right!"

CHAPTER FIVE

PROMISE TO A MOTHER

★ ★ ★

Glancing up at the calendar that hung from her bedroom wall, Jenny noted that it was the first day of June. She also noted the year, 1932, and said under her breath, "I despise that calendar!"

"What's wrong with it?" Kat asked. She had come in to watch Jenny dress for her date with Luke Dixon. She sat flat on the floor with her arms around Stonewall, who occasionally turned to lick her face. "I think it's pretty."

"It belongs in a garage somewhere. It's a girlie calendar. The only reason it's here is because it was free." The calendar pictured a shapely young woman who was trying to climb over a fence and in the process was exposing more than was appropriate of her lovely legs.

"Why doesn't she just jump over the fence?" Kat asked, pulling at Stonewall's ears. "It'd be easier than gettin' all caught up on it."

"Oh, it's just a silly calendar. I'm going to get a good one someday. One with a little more decorum."

"What's decorum?"

Jenny was finishing the process of dressing and said impatiently, "Don't you ever get tired of asking questions, Kat?"

"How am I going to learn if I don't ask questions?"

"Well, decorum means that a thing fits right in its place. Like you wouldn't wear a swimming suit to church. That wouldn't be the proper decorum."

"And you wouldn't wear that dress you got on to go swimming." Kat found this picture hilarious and laughed, rolling on the floor and pulling the dog down with her.

Jenny could not help but smile at the pair. Then she stood before the mirror and examined herself critically. Most of her city clothing had been sold to raise money to leave New York, and she had not bought a dress since. She had saved only a few of her nicer dresses, and now she examined the one she was wearing, wondering if it would do for Summerdale, Georgia. The aqua dress was actually a two-piece outfit made up of a matching skirt and jacket. The skirt had an embroidered front and inverted pleats. The loose-fitting jacket had elbow-length sleeves and a low neckline, which revealed the ivory blouse underneath. The black patent-leather shoes she wore were mildly scuffed and seemed too dark to go with such a light-colored dress. She sighed. "It will have to do."

Kat said, "You look real pretty, Jenny."

"Why, thank you, Kat." Walking over to Kat, she kissed her on the cheek, ruffled her hair, and then said quickly to the dog, "Get away from me, Stonewall. I don't want you shedding on my dress."

"Jenny, what's Luke Dixon like?"

"He's like a lawyer."

"I know that, but what does he look like?"

"Oh, he's tall, about six feet, and he's got blond hair and light blue eyes."

"Is he handsome like Doug Fairbanks Jr.?"

"No, not at all."

Kat continued to pepper her with questions concerning her date, and finally she said, "Are you going to let him kiss you good-night when he brings you home?"

Jenny laughed aloud and shook her head. "I don't think so. It's not proper to let a man kiss you on your first date."

"Can he kiss you on the second date, then?"

"I don't know if there's going to be a second date," Jenny

said. She suddenly heard the sound of a car coming down the driveway and ran over to the window. Kat accompanied her, and Stonewall reared up and put his huge paws on the windowsill, staring out with the two women. "It's him," Kat said.

"I guess it is," Jenny agreed.

"I'll go down and let him in while you finish dressing."

Jenny had no time to protest, for Kat sailed out the door followed by the huge dog, who sounded like a horse galloping across the floor. Jenny smiled and shook her head. "Those two are a pair." She picked up the cloche hat and pulled it down over her hair. Then she stepped in front of the mirror again, giving her appearance a final check. She used very few cosmetics, but she had tinted her lips slightly. "My mouth's too big," she muttered. "And my hair's too red. Well, Counselor, you'll just have to put up with it." She turned and walked down the steps and found Kat standing in front of Dixon, asking rather impertinent questions. As Jenny approached, Kat turned and said, "I already told him he couldn't kiss you on the first date."

Jenny flushed and could not speak for a moment.

Luke Dixon grinned broadly and said, "I told your sister here that I promised my mother I would never kiss a young lady on the first date."

"Well, that's all settled, then," Jenny said.

"But you can kiss her on the second date," Kat piped up and nodded sagely. "She's already told me that."

"I did not tell you that!" Jenny objected. She knew her skin was so fair that when she blushed it was very obvious, and she hated that fact. She was saved from further embarrassment when Lewis came in carrying a baby. "This is my father, Lewis Winslow. Dad, this is Luke Dixon."

"Glad to know you, Luke," Lewis said, nodding. "And this is Michael."

"I heard about your good fortune." Dixon smiled, then turned as Missouri came in and was introduced, with a baby in her arms as well. "And which one is this?" Dixon asked.

"This is Sam," Missouri said. Dixon admired the two babies, and then Clint and Hannah came out, Hannah with Temple in her arms. After they were introduced, Dixon said,

"Well, three babies all at once. That's quite an undertaking."

"And that ain't all," Kat said. "Hannah's got another one right inside there." She pointed to Hannah's stomach, and Hannah flushed scarlet. Clint, however, was delighted and shook his head. "You'll have to forgive Kat. She doesn't believe in keeping any secrets."

"I think we'd better go, Luke, unless you've changed your mind after being subjected to this crowd," Jenny said.

"Not at all. It's been a pleasure. Congratulations to you both." He smiled at Lewis and Missouri, then turning to Clint, he asked, "Are you expecting three as well?"

"Not this time," Clint said quickly. "We're just going to start out kind of easy."

Jenny turned and Luke nodded, then followed her outside. "That's quite a family you have there."

He opened the door to the Oldsmobile. When she got in, he shut it carefully, then walked around and got in behind the wheel. He had left the engine running, and now he said, "This thing doesn't always start right, so I don't turn if off until I'm sure of where I'm going."

"And where are we going?"

"You like barbecue?"

"Barbecue? I don't know as I've ever had any."

"You've never had barbecue?" Luke stared at her with surprise. "Well, you're in for a treat. Hang on to your hat, lady."

★   ★   ★

Luke opened the door, and Jenny got out of the car. "I didn't have a chance to tell you how nice you look."

"You look nice too. I guess lawyers have to dress in suits all the time."

"Not really. I just wanted to impress you." Luke was wearing a gray herringbone suit, with a double-breasted jacket and close-fitting trousers with turned-up cuffs. "Well, if I drop dead, they won't have to do too much to me," he said.

Jenny laughed and then turned to look at the building. "They don't go much for decor, do they?"

"Nope, you have to go somewhere else for that, but I guarantee you they have the best barbecued ribs in the world." He hesitated and said, "We could have gone to a fancier place, but I'm just a poor, struggling lawyer."

"Well, I'm poor and struggling too, so this looks fine."

The two stepped inside, and Jenny surveyed the large room with tables covered in red-and-white-checked cloths. The place was half full, and a short, muscular man came over and said, "Ah, it's good to see you, Mr. Dixon. I got a good table for you."

"This is Miss Jennifer Winslow, Hank. She's never eaten barbecue before, so I've given you a good recommendation."

"Never eaten barbecue!" Hank rolled his eyes and said, "Where you been that your education has been so neglected?"

"New York," Jenny smiled, "but I'm expecting great things from what Luke's told me."

The proprietor hustled them over to a table, sat them down, and Luke said quickly, "Just bring us the barbecued ribs. What would you like to drink, Jenny?"

"Iced tea would be fine."

"Make that two."

After the proprietor left, Luke leaned back in his chair and said, "Well, I've been giving Noah's case a lot of thought."

"Do you think you can get him off?"

"It's not going to be easy, and it's going to be a pretty nasty fight. It always is when there's a black involved with a white. Especially if those whites happen to wear uniforms."

They talked about the case until a pretty black girl wearing a red-and-white uniform came over carrying two enormous platters. She set one down in front of each of them and smiled shyly. "How are you, Mr. Dixon?"

"I'm just fine, Emma." The girl started to turn away, but Luke said, "This is Miss Jennifer Winslow, Emma. She's going to help your brother. As a matter of fact, she's the one who got me involved." The girl turned back quickly. She had creamy, chocolate-colored skin, and large liquid brown eyes. "Oh, I thank you, Miss Winslow! Noah ain't done nothin' wrong. Them police just been after him since he once got in trouble."

"I hear you've been having some trouble yourself with those deputies," Luke said.

"Deputy Arp, he's been after me," Emma said, dropping her eyes. "It ain't right, and when my brother Noah caught him tryin' to put his hands on me, he grabbed him and pushed him away. I thought that policeman was going to shoot him."

"Well, maybe we can do something about that too, Emma."

The young woman turned her eyes on Dixon and smiled shyly. "Thank you, Mr. Dixon. Ain't many people would go out of their way to help folks like us."

After the waitress left, Dixon said, "Well, I'd guess you ask blessings at your house over food."

"Yes, we do."

"Do you want to do it or shall I?"

"You go ahead, Luke."

Luke bowed his head, and Jenny followed suit. Luke said simply, "Thank you, Lord, for the food, for every good blessing you've given us. All good things come from you, and we thank you for them in Jesus' name. Amen. Now," he said, "let's start eating."

Jenny looked at the huge slab of ribs. "But . . . how do you eat them?"

"Watch me." Taking a knife, he sliced off one rib, picked it up with his fingers, and began eating it like corn on the cob. "You're gonna get yourself greasy, but it's the only way to eat ribs."

Following Dixon's method, Jenny sliced off one of the ribs and took a bite. Her eyes flew open wide. "It's delicious!"

"Here, put some of this barbecue sauce on it. It'll make it even better."

The two ate with enjoyment, Jenny delighted by the food. Emma brought them a plate of fresh-baked corn bread, which Luke insisted Jenny butter liberally. She also brought them some collards with pepper sauce, and Jenny laughed at herself, grease dripping all over her hands and her face. Luke had to order extra napkins so they could clean themselves up, but finally they sat back and drank coffee and nibbled at the blackberry cobbler Emma had brought them.

"You intend to be a successful lawyer, I suppose, Luke," Jenny said, tasting the delicious cobbler.

"Oh, sure," Luke shrugged. "I'm going into politics when I get a little steam. No reason why I can't be governor one day, and then after that, there's always the senate."

Jenny stared at him. "Are you serious?"

"I'm as serious as a man ever got. But I don't have any money or any powerful friends. The only way I can make it is to get myself a reputation. I guess that's one reason why I'm helping Noah. To get a reputation as a fighting lawyer taking on lost causes. I'll have to win the common people's votes."

Jenny said, "Well, in any case, I'm very grateful to you for helping Noah."

"I'll warn you again," Luke said, shaking his head. "You're going to be a target if you testify in favor of a black man against a white man."

Jenny smiled at him. "You'll take care of me, Luke."

He leaned forward and took her hand. "I'll do my best, lady. Now, we're going to go to the movies."

"What's on?"

"I'm not going to tell you." He left a liberal tip for Emma, told her what a good job she had done, and then the two left. Fortunately the Oldsmobile started, and he drove them to the Palace Theater. When they stepped up in front of the marquis, Jenny stopped suddenly. "Why, this is that horrible monster movie!"

"Sure. Frankenstein. Everybody's talking about it."

"I'm not going to see a thing like that."

"You mean after I filled you full of good ribs and blackberry cobbler, I can't get you in to see a little movie? Come on, be a sport. It's only make-believe."

Kat had actually begged their father to take her to this movie months ago, and he had refused, saying it was depraved. Clint had finally volunteered to take her, saying, "I'll put my hands over her eyes so she can't see the bad parts." Then he had grinned and said to Hannah, "And you can put your hands over mine." Remembering this, Jenny laughed and said, "All right, I can stand it if you can."

Luke bought the tickets, went inside, and found two seats halfway down. The lights went out soon, and soon the two of them were entranced by the problems of the monster, portrayed by Boris Karloff. Jenny was very much aware of Luke's shoulder pressing against hers, and once he put his arm around the seat back and then laid his hand gently on her shoulder. She stiffened, but when she glanced at him, she saw that he was really more interested in the monster than he was in her.

Finally the movie ended, and they left. After they got into the car, Jenny said, "It's late. You'd better take me home."

"All right. How'd you like the movie?"

"It was scary."

"Next time I'll take you to see Dr. Jekyll and Mr. Hyde, or Dracula. That one's even worse."

"No thank you! That's enough monsters for me. What did you think about that movie?"

"Well, to tell the truth, I liked the monster."

Jenny turned and laughed at him shortly. "You liked the monster?"

"Sure."

"Why in the world would you like him? He killed that little girl."

"He didn't mean to. He was just looking for companionship. Think about it, Jenny. Here he is the only one of his kind. Where is he going to find a lady monster? So he's doomed to a life of loneliness, and every time anybody sees him, they start screaming. That'd be a horrible way to live. No, I'm in favor of the monster. He was lonely."

They talked lightly about the movie until they reached the house, and he left the engine running while he escorted her up to the porch. She turned to him and said, "I had a wonderful time, Luke."

Luke was standing in front of her with a strange light in his eyes and a smile twitching at the corners of his mouth. "I've got a confession to make."

"A confession? What is it?"

"Well, I'm a pretty good fellow, but I do lie sometimes."

"Well, so do I, I suppose," she admitted.

"But," he grinned, "you wouldn't lie to your own mother, would you?"

Suddenly Jenny saw where he was heading, but she found him so charming she could not help but smile. "Let me guess. You're about to break your promise to your mother about never kissing a girl on a first date?"

"Got it right!" They stood facing each other, and Luke waited to see if she would turn away. She did not but seemed deeply engrossed in studying his face. He studied hers as well and was drawn to the beauty and goodness he saw in her. Something strong and vivid ran between them, and Luke Dixon pulled her into his arms. He kissed her then, and she responded. He sensed something soft and shining in her, her strength and loyalty, and when he lifted his lips, he found himself more shaken than she.

"Well," Jenny chuckled, her eyes bright, "I guess now I know how much I can trust you."

"Remember what Kat said. I can have a kiss on the second date." He smiled, then grew serious, "I'll see you in court tomorrow. Have your father there."

"I will. Good night, Luke. It was fun."

"Good night."

Going inside the house, Jenny went to her room at once. She undressed, put on a gown, and then slipped under the sheet. It was a warm night, and she did not pull her blanket up. She lay for a long time thinking of the evening. She had been kissed before, but she found herself liking Luke Dixon tremendously. She admired him for his willingness to take on an unpopular cause, but she knew that as a man he interested her greatly. Her last thought was, *How in the world will I explain that kiss to Kat in the morning? She'll be sure to ask!*

★ ★ ★

Jenny and Lewis found that Luke Dixon had reserved a place for them on the front row in the courtroom. Jenny felt as uncomfortable as she ever had in her life, for she knew nothing about courts and lawyers and judges. She glanced around nervously, looking up at the big ceiling fans that turned slowly, stirring up the hot air more than anything else, then turned her attention to where Luke sat beside Noah Valentine, the big man dwarfing the lawyer. Luke was wearing a white shirt and a maroon tie and looked calm and collected. Noah, on the other hand, was sweating profusely, and as he held his hands in front of him, Jenny could see that he was clasping them tightly, perhaps to keep them from trembling. There were no blacks in the courtroom that she could see, not even Noah's family. Turning her glance, she saw the district attorney, Alex DeRosa. Luke had pointed him out to her and informed her, "Alex and I are both ambitious. We fight it out in a courtroom, but so far he's a client or two ahead of me. Of course, he's got even more ambitions than I have."

Jenny turned to her father and said, "I wish all this had never come up, Dad."

Lewis turned and shook his head. "Things like this always come up, but you've done the right thing, Jenny. Are you nervous?"

"Yes, I am a little."

"Don't be. It'll come out all right."

Jenny wished she could take her father's advice, but all through the preliminaries she sat there tensely, often pulling out her handkerchief and mopping her face with it.

Finally the judge, a big man with a bulldog look named O. C. Pender, got the trial under way, and the prosecution at once began. Alex DeRosa was a small wiry man with black hair and pale gray eyes. He was meticulously dressed, and his voice carried clearly throughout the courtroom. "This trial will not take long, Your Honor."

Pender stared at him and said, "That depends on more than you can control, Mr. DeRosa."

DeRosa laughed and nodded. "I stand corrected, Your Honor, but the prosecutions case will not take long. I have only two witnesses. I call Deputy Arlie Pender to the stand."

Pender, wearing his uniform, swaggered to the stand. He took the oath, and DeRosa said, "Deputy, you were on duty on May the twentieth, I believe?"

"Yes, sir, that's right. Me and Deputy Arp was workin' together."

"And on that day you had occasion to stop at the Valentine house?"

"Yes, we did."

"Why did you stop there?"

"We had evidence that Noah Valentine had robbed a store, and—"

"Objection! Calling for a conclusion!"

"Objection sustained."

"Very well, Your Honor, but you did find the suspect at home?"

"Yes, we did."

"Tell us in your own words, Deputy, what happened."

"He come out of the house," Pender said, obviously enjoying his moment in the spotlight, "and we began to question him. He looked guilty—"

"Objection!"

"Objection sustained. The witness will not draw conclusions."

"I'm sorry, Your Honor. Continue, Deputy."

"Well, there wasn't much to it. We started askin' him questions just as easy as I'm talkin' now, but all of a sudden he got mad, and he took a swing at me."

"Let me get this clear. He struck at you first?"

"He sure did!"

"And what did you do?"

"Well, I had my night stick in my hand, so I hit him with it."

"And then what happened?"

"Well, he jumped on both of us, and me and Merle didn't have no chance at all, so we had to subdue him."

"But he did strike the first blow?"

"Yes, sir."

"I have no more questions," DeRosa said. "Your witness, Counselor."

Luke Dixon rose to his feet and ambled over to where the deputy watched him cautiously. "You say my client struck you first?"

"That's right. He did," Pender said aggressively.

"Where did he hit you?"

"Right in the face."

"How much do you weigh, Deputy?"

Pender stared at him, and DeRosa at once said, "I object, Your Honor. That has no bearing."

"I think I can show that it does."

"Objection overruled, but be careful with this, Mr. Dixon."

"Of course, Your Honor. How much do you weigh?"

"About a hundred and forty."

Luke turned and looked at Noah. "My client there weighs two hundred and sixty pounds and is very strong. I assume when he hit you in the face, he broke your nose?"

"Well, no, he didn't."

"But surely he loosened your teeth."

"No, he didn't."

"You mean to tell me that a man that big and strong hit you with his fist and left no mark at all?"

Pender glared at Dixon. "That's right," he said defiantly.

"No further questions. I think the jury can draw the conclusions necessary."

Lewis leaned over and whispered to Jenny, "That's one smart boyfriend you got there."

"Do you think the jury can see that the deputy was lying?" Jenny whispered back.

"I could see it. Surely they're as smart as I am."

Lewis and Jenny turned their attention back to the next witness approaching the stand—Deputy Merle Arp. He looked big and bulky as he moved across the room. He sat down and gave substantially the same testimony as his fellow deputy. When DeRosa turned the witness over to the defense, Luke sat where he was for a moment, letting the silence run on. Finally Judge Pender said, "Do you intend to question this witness, Mr. Dixon?"

"Yes, sir, I do." Getting to his feet, Luke came to take his position directly in front of Arp. "Deputy Arp, did you ever have any trouble with the defendant prior to May the twentieth?"

"Objection, that has no bearing!"

"I will allow it, Mr. DeRosa. Where are you going with this, Mr. Dixon?"

"Both deputies had preconceived prejudice against my client."

"Do it then and be quick about it."

"Had you had trouble with my client before?"

"I guess so."

"You guess so! You have so much trouble with people you can't remember for sure!" Dixon grew sharp, and Arp began to squirm in the chair. "Did you ever have any physical contact? Was there a time when you two came to blows?"

"I guess so. Once."

"Would you care to tell us about that?"

"He jumped on me when I wasn't lookin'."

"Why would he do that, Deputy?"

"I don't know."

Dixon suddenly said sharply, "It was because you had been payin' attention to his sister! Is that true?"

"Me after a nigger girl? I reckon not!"

"You deny, then, trying to force yourself on Emma Valentine."

"I wasn't doin' nothin' to her. Just talkin'."

DeRosa began to object, and Dixon at once said, "No more questions for this witness, but I reserve the right to recall him. One more question. Are you aware of the penalty for perjury, Deputy?"

"Objection!" DeRosa shouted. "He's badgering the witness!"

"No more questions, Your Honor," Dixon said.

That concluded the prosecution's case, and immediately, as soon as the judge instructed Dixon to begin the defense, Dixon called three witnesses, all white, who had witnessed the trouble between Noah Valentine and Deputy Merle Arp. They all testified to the same thing, that Arp had put his hands on Emma, and she had protested, whereupon Noah had come and grabbed the deputy and ejected him from the restaurant where the incident had taken place.

During all this testimony, DeRosa protested and objected constantly, but Jenny could see that the jury was looking at

Arp with rather sharp eyes. She knew that if anything would sway a jury, it was for a white man to pay attention to a black woman.

"I call Miss Jennifer Winslow to the stand."

Jenny took a deep breath and got up. She felt all eyes upon her as she took the oath and then sat down. "Your name is Jennifer Winslow?"

"Yes, sir, it is."

"And on May the twentieth you were at the home of my client?"

"Yes, sir, I was."

"What were you doing there?"

Jenny related how her truck had overheated, and she had driven it around to the back, where Noah Valentine had helped her fill the radiator with water.

Under careful questioning from Dixon, she related that Noah had gone to the front of the house and that when she had later filled the truck and had gone to thank him, she had seen Noah Valentine in between two officers.

"The two officers that have just testified, Deputy Arp and Deputy Pender?"

"Yes, sir."

"You've heard the testimony of these two officers. Would you tell us what you saw."

"I saw it all very clearly." Jenny lifted her head, and her voice resounded throughout the courtroom. "They were cursing him and accusing him of robbing a store, and he kept saying that he didn't do it. Then suddenly that one there, the little one, just raised his stick and hit him on the head."

"Just a moment. You've heard the testimony of Deputy Arlie Pender that Noah Valentine struck the first blow. That was not what happened?"

"It was not! Noah was just standing there, and that little man raised his club and hit him. It knocked him to his knees."

"And what did the other man do?"

"He began hitting him with his club too."

"And what did you do?"

"I ran out there and told them to stop."

"And what did they say?"

"They laughed at me and made fun of me, but I told them that I would testify in court that they struck the first blow. And they did!" Jenny stared at the two deputies. "Noah never raised his hands. He never hit anyone. He just put his hands over his head while they were beating him." She heard a buzz go through the courtroom, and then she heard Dixon say, "Thank you, Miss Winslow. Your witness, Mr. DeRosa."

DeRosa got up from his seat and came to stand directly in front of Jenny. "Now, Miss Winslow, you must be very careful here."

"I am very careful."

"Is your eyesight good?"

Jenny looked at DeRosa, who seemed to be making fun of her. She pointed at a bulletin just inside the front door of the courtroom. "I can read the print on that bulletin." She read out the first line and said, "Can you read it, Mr. DeRosa?"

DeRosa grew angry. "I will ask the questions here! Your Honor, will you please instruct the witness that all she needs to do is answer the questions."

"Yes, I will instruct her. And I will instruct you. Get on with your cross-examination."

"Are you a native of this county?"

"I'm a resident, yes."

"But this is not your home."

"Objection!" Dixon said. "Miss Winslow's residence is not in question here."

"Sustained."

"Your Honor," DeRosa said quickly, "I intend to show that this lady does not understand the way we live in this part of the world."

There was some argument between the two attorneys, but finally Judge Pender said, "You'd better get on with this, Mr. DeRosa, and you'd better be going somewhere with it."

"You're from New York, aren't you?"

"Yes, sir, I am." DeRosa made a long speech then, indicating that people from the North could not possibly understand southern problems and finally turned to Jenny, saying, "You will agree that things are different in New York and Georgia."

"Some things are different, but I don't think the law is

different in the North and the South—or it shouldn't be."

"My point is that people from the North have a different mind-set. They can't understand the problems of the South. Your people probably were in the Union Army."

"My people fought for the Confederacy! My grandfather and his brothers served under General Robert E. Lee. They all stacked their muskets at Appomattox. My grandmother was a spy for the Confederacy. We only moved to New York in recent years. Until then almost all the Winslows came from Virginia."

Lewis was chuckling to himself, admiring his daughter and thinking, *I hope he keeps at her. The more he tries to get her, the more the jury goes against him.*

DeRosa began to talk about the difficulty of law enforcement, and finally he turned to Jenny and said, "The sheriff of this county has a hard job."

Jenny was angry at the man and spoke before she thought. "I could be a better sheriff than the man who wears that badge! He's tarnished it, Mr. DeRosa."

"Your Honor, I ask for a mistrial. This witness—"

"Objection overruled."

DeRosa wiped his forehead, then said, "I beg for a recess, Your Honor."

"Very well. We'll take a thirty-minute recess."

Dixon nodded to Jenny, motioning to her, and she came to accompany him and Noah to the back of the courthouse, where they found themselves in a room with a long table and chairs surrounding it.

"How are we doing, Luke?"

Luke looked at her, then turned his eyes on Noah. "Well, we've got twelve southern white men on the jury, and this is the South. Plus, the defendant is black. No matter what the facts are, there's always danger." He started to say more, but suddenly the door opened, and the district attorney came in. "Luke, I need to talk to you."

"Talk away, Alex."

"Not here. Alone."

"You can say anything before my friends that you could say alone."

DeRosa hesitated and ran his hand over his hair. A worried light clouded his eyes, and he said, "This thing's gettin' out of hand."

"Are you ready to dismiss charges?"

DeRosa said, "We'll change the charge to resisting arrest."

Instantly Luke said, "All right, but there'll be no jail time. Probation—and there'll be no fine."

Alex DeRosa stared at Dixon, then smiled. "You win this time, but no perjury charges against the deputies."

"All right."

DeRosa left the room, and Jenny turned to Luke angrily. "That wasn't right!"

"It's better than getting five to ten years in the penitentiary, Jenny. We win."

"What does it mean, Mr. Dixon?" Noah asked.

"There'll be a lot of talk about it. You'll be under probation, and that means you'll have to report to somebody that the judge appoints once a week or something like that. But you won't go to jail."

"That sounds good to me. Thank you so much, both of you."

The three went outside, and Jenny took her seat next to her father. She did not have time to explain what had happened, for the judge came back at once. He had evidently had a meeting with the district attorney, for he said, "The district attorney has recommended that all charges be dropped except resisting arrest. Will the defendant rise."

Noah got to his feet, towering over Luke, and the judge said, "I sentence you to six months' probation. You will report to Chief of Police Thomas Matson. You understand, Noah?"

"Yes, sir, I do."

"Case dismissed!" the judge said and banged his gavel on the table.

Before Jenny could move, a bulky man wearing a white shirt and a rather frayed black tie came to her. "I'm Raymond Dent, editor of *The Record*."

"I'm glad to know you, Mr. Dent."

Dent nodded with admiration. "You did fine and so did Luke Dixon. It gives me hope that there could be somethin'

better than what we've got in the way of law around here."
He cocked his head to one side and said, "You mean what you
said about being a better sheriff than Max Conroy?"

"I was angry."

"I think you could beat him in the election."

Jenny stared at the editor and then laughed. "Why, that
couldn't be! I'm a woman. Didn't you notice?"

Raymond Dent chewed his lower lip, and his eyelids narrowed as he studied her. "You know how many women vote
in this county? You'd get every one of those votes and lots of
the men too."

"Well, I would like to see Max Conroy and his goons out
of office."

"Be careful, Jenny," Lewis said, winking at her. "Mr. Dent
here is a persuasive man. I've read his editorials. I'm glad to
know you, sir. I'm Lewis Winslow."

"I'm real happy to meet you, Mr. Winslow. I know your
record. We're glad to have you in the community." He stared
at Jenny and said, "I never thought I'd recommend a woman
to run, but I'd be willin' to vote for you myself, Miss Jenny, if
you'd do it."

Luke Dixon had come up to listen to the conversation,
Noah looming behind him, and he said now, "You know,
Jenny, it could work. The Lord knows this county needs more
honest law."

"I don't know anything about legal things, Luke."

"I do. I could teach you."

Jenny laughed. It was a joke to her. "All right. I'll be the
sheriff, and you can be the power behind the throne."

Raymond Dent stared at her, nodded, and said, "Good to
meet you both."

Jenny said, "That's the silliest thing I ever heard of. No one
would vote for a woman Yankee for sheriff of this county!"

★　★　★

Jenny stared at the paper in disbelief. "I can't believe this!"
she cried. Luke Dixon had brought her a fresh copy of *The*

Record, and the lead story said blatantly, "A New Candidate For Sheriff." She shook her head as she read the story, which stated that she would be a candidate for the office of sheriff in the coming election.

"This is crazy!"

"I don't think it is," Luke said. "Sit down. I want to talk to you."

The conversation that followed was long and sometimes heated. Jenny had thought at first it was just a joke, but the editor of *The Record* did not think so. He had gone to great lengths to explain how experience was not as important as honesty, and how he was violently opposed to Max Conroy. He pointed out that one good man had started to run but had been forced out by threats of physical violence.

Finally Jenny said, "I won't do it, and that's all there is to it. It's silly."

Luke stared at her and said, "I think it's the only chance this county's got. I know you don't know anything about being a sheriff, but you could hire good men. What we need is somebody that's honest. Honesty is more important than packing a big gun. We've found that out the hard way. Think about it, will you, Jenny?"

"No, I won't. It's ridiculous."

★ ★ ★

Dixon opened the door to his office and was nearly bowled over as Jenny came storming in. Her eyes were blazing, and she said, "Did you mean everything you said about my running for sheriff?"

"Why, sure I did. What's wrong?"

Jenny turned to him. Her lips were twitching, and he could see that she was terribly disturbed. "What is it, Jenny?" he said quickly.

"Somebody burned a cross out in front of our house last night. There were hooded riders out there, and they were shouting, 'You won't live if you run for sheriff, woman.'"

"The Klan. I thought they had sort of faded away," Dixon

said, his lips growing thin. He studied the young woman in front of him and said, "I'm sorry this had to happen. It's a bad part of the world down here. It's going away slowly, but it's still with us."

Jenny had not slept a wink. She turned now, and her face was lined with fatigue. "I'm going to run for sheriff, Luke, if you'll help me."

"Are you sure you want to do this? Those clansmen can play pretty rough."

"I think it's what God would have me do. Maybe I can help people like Noah."

"There are plenty like him around, and not all of them are black. Look, Jenny, this county's going down the drain. There's some big tie-in between racketeers in the North wanting bootleg liquor and local enforcement officers, and those people play for keeps. You could be putting your life on the line."

"I'll do it if you'll help me."

Luke Dixon felt an admiration for Jennifer Winslow stronger than he had for any woman he had ever met. "All right, Jenny, we'll do it. Your slogan will be, 'A shining badge. We'll get rid of those tarnished badges and start all over again!'"

CHAPTER SIX

CAMPAIGN

★ ★ ★

Luke Dixon took his eyes off the road long enough to turn to his right and study his passenger. A slight smile tugged at the corners of his lips as he watched Jenny staring straight ahead, her lips moving. She was, he knew, rehearsing her speech, and suddenly he reached over and put his hand on her shoulder. "You don't have to worry about your speech. It'll be great."

Startled out of her own little world, Jenny turned and stared at Dixon. He had his left hand loosely on the steering wheel, and his right was squeezing her shoulder. They had been on a total of three dates, and she had grown very fond of the blond-haired lawyer. At this moment, however, she was not thinking of dates but of arriving at the dedication of the George Paxton Bridge. It was to be her first political speech, and she had slept hardly a wink the previous night. Now, in the late afternoon with the sun going down, she suddenly cried out, "Luke, we must have all lost our minds! There's no way I could ever be elected even as a . . . a *dogcatcher* in this county!"

Luke dodged a pothole skillfully and let his hand remain resting on her shoulder. "You're going to do just fine, and you look nice too."

"Do you really think so?"

"I sure do. That dress has character."

The dedication of a bridge was one of the social events that people in the county loved. The Depression offered few free recreations, and at an event such as this there was sure to be a crowd. There would be free food, soft drinks, ice cream—and a great many political speeches. Looking down at her outfit, Jenny shook her head. "I don't know whether this is the right thing to wear or not. It looks too . . . too feminine for a politician."

The dress she had chosen was not new. She had worn it back in New York, and it did seem a little dressy. It was a black dress of crepe de chine, and along the bottom of the skirt were two rows of pleated flounces, and she had chosen to wear beige stockings and a pair of black sandals. She had a single row of pearls, artificial of course, around her neck, and a black felt hat with a bright ribbon around the edge. She grinned ruefully. "None of the other speakers will be wearing a dress like this. I think I should have worn something more mannish."

"There'll be plenty of men there, but you're a woman and a good-looking one and there's no getting around it." Luke laughed and patted her shoulder in an assuring fashion. "It's too late to uglify you. Sorry about that."

Jenny felt a rush of affection for Luke. She reached up and pressed his hand. "You got me into all this. Now you're going to have to get me out."

Luke was conscious of the warmth of her hand on his, and for a moment wondered where his relationship with her was going. At the age of thirty he had never been married, although he had had plenty of chances. The mothers of the county had driven themselves into a frenzy trying to get him to propose to one of their daughters, but Luke was struggling to get his fledgling practice off the ground. He knew Jenny was nervous, and he set out to reassure her.

"Just look at all that's been done. Look at the money we've raised. In times like these it's almost impossible, but it's come in. Some of it in nickels and dimes from schoolchildren, some of it in old crumpled dollar bills, but it has come. And look at the churches. I think every church in this county, including the Catholic church, has gotten behind you. They know what will happen if Conroy gets elected."

"That has been good, hasn't it?" As a matter of fact, this was not Jenny's first political speech. She had begun at Luke's advice by going to the pastor of every church in the county, from Pentecost to Episcopalian, asking for their support. Almost without exception, the pastors had been supportive. She had been emboldened to ask them for help, and now she said, "The Presbyterian church is paying for the barbecue at this meeting. I thought that was nice of them, since I'm not a Presbyterian."

"It was nice, and you can count on the good pastors in this county. I think what you ought to do next is go persuade every one of them to preach a sermon on good, honest government."

"Oh no, I'm not telling preachers what to preach."

"I guess not," Luke said thoughtfully. "But you don't really have to tell them. The church folks are stirred up. You'll carry ninety percent of them, I think. The black folks around here are most anxious to see you get elected too. Noah and his family, I think, have been working full-time handing out leaflets and putting up posters. They want to see someone in place who can help them for a change. This election has been good for this county."

Jenny felt a warm glow of satisfaction. "That has been good," she murmured again. "And it was good of Mr. Dent to do all of our printing for nothing."

"I think Dent would mortgage *The Record* and his own house too. He hates crookedness in government, and he sees you as the only chance for some honest administration."

"I brought a lot of leaflets to hand out, but I suppose all the politicians will be handing them out."

"You can bet on that." A rueful expression crossed Luke's face. "There's big money behind Conroy. It's hard to find a telephone pole without his ugly face on it. They spent hundreds of dollars on advertising."

The thought intimidated Jenny, and she sat there looking out at the fields as they sped down the highway. Finally she turned back to Luke and said, "It'll have to be the Lord that gets me into office. There's no way it can happen otherwise."

"That's probably what David said when he went out to face Goliath. All he had were five smooth stones."

"That's right, isn't it?" Jenny smiled. She trusted Luke Dixon, who was a fervent Christian and knew the Bible well. "And there was Gideon, who had only a handful of soldiers. He managed pretty well against the Midianites, didn't he?"

"Sure. We've got the Lord on our side. How can we lose?"

They chatted as Luke sped down the road, noticing all the traffic was headed toward the bridge. When they finally reached the George Paxton Bridge, the traffic grew heavier. Finally they had to pull off the road, and Luke remarked, "It's still half a mile to the bridge. This'll be the biggest crowd in the county except for the state fair. Can you walk it?"

"Yes, of course. Let me get these leaflets."

The two got out of the car and began walking. Jenny was amazed at how many people greeted her with a smile, and every time someone did, she shook their hand and gave them a flier stating her policy. She also gave them a smile and said, "I'd appreciate your vote next week."

Almost all of them responded well, although a few Conroy voters gave her hard looks and a few even harder words. They passed a group that all stared at her. There were three men wearing overalls and straw hats and one provocatively dressed young woman.

"Those are the Skinners," Luke said. "They were the ones that got your brother involved in moonshining."

Jenny stiffened. She had seen the Skinners at the trial and knew that Dora had succeeded in bringing her brother down. Joshua had survived, but he had spent a month in the penitentiary for selling illegal liquor. Now a stubborn look came to her, and before Luke could stop her, she walked right up to the big man who hadn't shaved recently, whom she knew to be the leader, Simon Skinner. "Hello, Mr. Skinner, how are you?" She put out her hand, and the man stared at her. Awkwardly he took her hand, and she smiled at him. "I'd appreciate your vote."

"I ain't votin' for no woman. It ain't fittin'."

Jenny did not lose her smile. She nodded to the other two sons of Skinner, then turned to Dora and stared at her. Dora Skinner was wearing a tight, revealing dress. She laughed and said, "How's Joshua getting along? When you write him, tell him I'm waiting for him to come back."

"You haven't heard? He's married now. He married a fine woman and is doing well."

"Well, he was always a bit too saintly for me anyway," Dora said, laughing. Then she turned her head to one side. "Whatever made you think you could be sheriff of this county? You're not tough enough for that."

"I think the Lord will help me," Jenny said quietly.

Dora's face changed, and her lip curled up. "You'd better have God on your side, 'cause you're gonna need 'im. Come on, Pa, let's go."

The Skinners hurried down the highway, and Luke said, "You did just fine." His smile was wide, and he said, "You put her in her place and old man Skinner too. They're into bootlegging up to their ears. You'll have to handle them when you're the sheriff."

The thought of "handling" people such as the Skinners frightened Jenny. She did not say anything, but Luke saw that she had been intimidated by the meeting. "They're a rough crowd, and there are others like them, but as you told them, the Lord's on our side. Come on. You're doing fine."

They reached the bridge, which was crowded, and a country band was already playing, sending lively music up over the crowd with guitars and mandolins and a big bass fiddle. There was an area for dancing too, but only a few couples were doing so. Most people were circulating along the tables that were piled high with food. Behind each table was a banner proclaiming the generosity of the most obvious donor, Max Conroy.

"Conroy had everything catered, and that's not very smart. Look at our table," Luke said proudly.

A long line was in front of the table marked "Jennifer Winslow, An Honest Sheriff." Beneath it, Hank and several helpers were passing out barbecue as fast as they could. One of the servers was Noah and another was his sister Emma.

They were placing barbecue sandwiches and ribs on paper plates while another was scooping out fried potatoes. Jenny walked up at once and spoke to the owner of the barbecue place. "Are the ribs going to hold out, Hank?"

"You bet they are. That Presbyterian preacher, he really done his self proud. I think we could feed half the county from this booth alone."

"That's good. How are you, Emma?"

"I'm mighty fine, Miss Jenny. Mighty fine. I'm tellin' everybody to vote for you."

Jenny smiled at the girl, then shook hands with Noah, and they turned and began going down the line, shaking hands with everybody waiting. She circulated for over an hour, stopping only to eat a sandwich quickly, and one time she passed Conroy's booth. The sheriff was standing there, and when he saw her, he made a remark that she could barely hear—a rude remark about women. The men around him laughed, and Jenny remembered Luke's admonition. She walked right over to him and stuck out her hand.

"Hello, Sheriff, it's good to see you. I thought I might try some of the free food you're handing out."

Conroy was somewhat taken aback. He scowled for a moment and then smiled broadly. "Well, you might as well get somethin' out of this. Here, fix the lady a plate."

People gathered around quickly, for the two candidates had not met at a public event. They made quite a contrast— Max Conroy in his freshly pressed uniform was an impressive-looking man. He was tall and masculine and looked every inch the perfect lawman. He wore cowboy boots, as he always did, which gave him three extra inches of height, and Jenny felt somewhat like a small child, but she did not let this show.

Conroy kept jabbing at her, asking questions such as, "Suppose a criminal runs into a man's rest room. Are you going in to get him?"

"I'd do the same thing you'd do if a female criminal ran into a woman's rest room, Sheriff."

A laugh went up, and Conroy's grin disappeared. It came back quickly, and he said loudly enough for everyone to hear.

"You're a nice-lookin' filly, Miss Jenny. You ought to do what women are supposed to do. Find you a man and have kids."

"I intend to do that one day, but first I'm going to see that there's honest government in this county, Sheriff." She turned and walked away, ignoring the catcalls that came after her.

"That was fine, Jenny." She turned to see her brother-in-law, Clint Longstreet, standing beside her along with Hannah.

"I was scared to death, Clint," Jenny confessed.

"Well, you didn't look it," Hannah said, smiling. "You looked right into his eyes. I was proud of you."

"But I've got to make a speech, and I've never made a speech in my life."

"No time like now to begin," Clint said. "I'll be right out there cheerin' for you and so will a lot of other folks. I'm right proud of you, sister-in-law."

Jenny had always admired Clint. He was a tough man in his own right, and she knew it would take men like him to stand by her if she ever did, by some miracle, get elected.

★ ★ ★

Jenny heard Luke Dixon speaking, but he seemed very far away. She heard him mention her name more than once but was so frightened she could not put the words together. Finally she heard him say loudly, "And now I give you the next sheriff of this fine county, Miss Jennifer Winslow. Let's hear it for the little lady."

Jenny found herself standing upright, seemingly supported by some power other than her own, and she moved stiff legged across the platform. She was the last speaker and was almost petrified. Max Conroy was a good speaker. He had a rough sense of humor that appealed to a large part of the crowd, was a native of the county, and had a great deal of experience in law enforcement. As Jenny listened to him and watched the crowd, her heart sank. *I can never beat him, and if I did, I wouldn't know what to do.* But now as she came to stand before the microphone, she breathed a quick prayer. *Lord, I'm*

*as bad off as David. Give me some smooth stones and don't let me
faint.*

She spoke up then with her first sentence. "There are no
women sheriffs in this state!" Cries went up from her oppo-
nents, and she waited until they died down. "If there were a
good man running against my opponent, I would not even
think of making this effort. I would support him. But no good
men have stepped forward, though I know there are many
strong men, some of them standing on this bridge, that would
do a fine job. But they didn't step into the gap."

A silence had fallen over the crowd, and more than one
man dropped his head with something like shame, for the
words were true enough. There were plenty of good men, but
none of them had been willing to face the machinery that
stood behind Max Conroy. It was dangerous, ill-paid work,
and usually thankless.

"I've never shot a gun in my life," she said, her voice ringing clearly, "but there are some things more important than
shooting guns—and being fair and honest is the first! I'm sure
my opponent can hit a target with that pistol of his much better than I could, but if I'm elected, I'll have men standing
beside me who are equally good shots. Of course, I could
never stand up to a man in a rough-and-tumble fight, but I
believe there are men who would stand beside anyone who
would offer a fair and equitable government to the people of
this county."

Clint then yelled, "You bet your sweet life, and I'm one of
them!"

A laugh went up and boos from the Conroy crowd, but
Jenny felt much better and an ease came to her. She began
speaking about Conroy's record, making it as objective as possible. She heard rumblings from those who supported the
sheriff, but she did not pause.

"I will learn to shoot a gun. My father will teach me. I'd
like to introduce my father. Would you stand up, Dad?" She
saw her father stand up, looking ill at ease. "He doesn't like
attention, and now I'm going to embarrass him. You need to
know what kind of a family I come from. This is my father,
Lewis Winslow. He's the best man I know." She paused for

one moment and said, "When this country was at war at the turn of this century, my father was beside Teddy Roosevelt going up San Juan Hill in Cuba. He won the Congressional Medal of Honor for his action there that day. He doesn't like me to talk about it, but every time I pass the fireplace at our house, I look up at that medal on the mantel that so few men have earned, and I'm thankful there are men like this in this county. I'm proud to be a Winslow," she said. "I know heritage means a great deal to southerners. I've lived for most of my life in New York, but my home is here. My great-uncle, Mark Winslow, fought with Robert E. Lee along with his brothers Thomas and Daniel. My grand-aunt, Lola Winslow, served the Confederacy as an agent. If you want to read a story of courage, read the story of Lola Winslow. They fought for states' rights, not for slavery. None of my people ever owned slaves." She paused and looked around and saw the black people that were on the edge of the crowd.

"If you elect me sheriff," she said clearly, "I will treat all people equally. That means if you are poor, I will give you exactly the same treatment I'd give a rich man. A woman will be heard exactly the same as a man. Black people or people of Mexico, people of any race or religion can come to me without fear. I know this will not please all of you, but I'm not here to please the crowd. I stand on one fact—the law must be the same for all people."

Clint let out a ringing yell and stood and began clapping. All over the bridge voices rang out, and the sound swept against Jenny. At that moment she knew she had done exactly the right thing. *I may lose this election, Lord, but these people deserve good government.*

"Now," she said, "my opponent did not ask for questions, but I will take them if you will give them clearly one at a time."

Simon Skinner was near the front of the crowd. He called out roughly, "What are you going to do, missy, when a man comes at you and takes that little gun away from you that you claim you're gonna carry?"

Jenny, for a moment, could not answer, but suddenly a man that towered over Skinner grabbed him by the back of his collar. It was the blacksmith Jude Tanner, and he squeezed and lifted Skinner until the tall, lanky man cried out and struggled, but he was like a child in the grip of the blacksmith.

"I will hire good, honest men such as Jude Tanner to handle that question, Mr. Skinner."

Applause and laughter went up, and Jenny knew she had won the point.

The questions went on for some time, and to her amazement, Jenny found that most of them were good questions from people friendly to her. She was not afraid to say, "I don't know," and she said it often. "I will have to be educated," she said finally before stepping aside. "But as I've said before, I don't think brute force or a vast knowledge of the law is what this county needs. We need justice for all people, and I might as well be honest with you. There are forces outside this county moving in. Racketeers from the North intend to use Georgia and other southern states as a source for their bootleg whiskey." She hesitated and then lifted her hand and said, "I pledge to you they will not use our land for their evil purposes."

The applause began then, and Jenny turned and went back to her seat. Her face was flushed, and her knees felt weak. The applause went on for a long time, and finally the lieutenant-governor came to the microphone. He was a Conroy supporter, but he was too wise a politician to attack a woman who had received an ovation. "We're grateful for our candidates, and we ask that you all come out and vote on election day. It's your chance to speak up for what you want."

Luke leaned over and touched Jenny's arm. "You did fine, Jenny," he said. "You couldn't have done better."

"Thank you, Luke. Do you think we have a chance?"

"Yes, I think you'll be the next sheriff. And then you'll really need prayer."

★   ★   ★

The day had been long, and Jenny had spent it as she had every other day since starting her campaign. She had made it a point to go to every small town in the county, going to every business she possibly could. She could not argue politics, for she was not well enough versed, although Luke Dixon was bringing her along in that matter, educating her until late at night on the issues of the day and the way the county machinery ran.

By now Jenny was almost blind with exhaustion as she drove the truck along the highway and thought of what a tough campaign it had been. She had received threatening phone calls, for she'd had to have a phone installed at Luke's insistence. Some of the calls had been obscene. She had simply hung up, but they had troubled her.

Now the election was only two days away, and her mind was swept as if by a hurricane.

She had gone home but had been so disturbed she had to get away for a while. She had remembered promising Jamie Varek to bring her a doll, and she had picked one that she had brought from New York with her, a treasured relic of her childhood. Now as she pulled up in front of Varek's house, she noted with approval that he was making progress on the house. It was looking better all the time. It was painted now, and the yard was cleaned up and even a few flowers were planted under the windows.

She picked up the paper sack containing the doll and went up the walkway. Jamie came bursting out the screen door to greet her, followed by Clay.

"Hello, sweetheart," Jenny said.

"Did you bring me a doll?"

"She gets right to the heart of it," Clay said, smiling. He came down the steps and nodded. "I hear you've been busy."

"Pretty busy." Jenny handed the sack to Jamie and watched the girl strip it away, then hold up the doll. It was a beautifully made doll with blond hair and blue eyes, and when you squeezed it, it made a sound vaguely resembling a baby's cry. "Squeeze it, and she'll cry for you, Jamie."

Jamie squeezed the doll and cried out in delight. "I'm going to name her Jemima."

"She loves Aunt Jemima's pancakes, which is about the best of my cooking, I reckon. So I guess Jemima's a good name," Clay said. "Come and sit on the porch for a while."

Jenny went up and sat down in one of the rockers, and Clay took another. Jamie crawled up in his lap, cuddling her doll and stroking its hair. She was astonished to find that the eyes closed when you laid the doll back and opened when you sat her up.

"You couldn't have brought her anything that would have made her happier," Clay said quietly. He was studying Jenny's face and said, "You look exhausted. Campaigning is pretty hard work, isn't it?"

"The hardest thing I've ever done," Jenny admitted. She laid her head back against the chair and rocked slowly. There was the smell of honeysuckle in the air, and the quietness fell on her like ointment. She had talked so much and listened so much and traveled so much, and now just to sit here in the quietness was a luxury.

The two sat there listening and smiling as Jamie played with the doll, and finally she ran off, saying, "I'm gonna put her on my bed and sing her to sleep."

"You're about played out," Clay observed once Jamie had gone.

"I don't know what makes me think I can do it. I think I've lost my mind. I let Luke Dixon talk me into it and a few others."

"Do you want to do it, Jennifer?"

Jenny looked up and studied Clay Varek. He made an arresting figure as he sat there, his white shirt fitted snugly against his shoulders and chest. He smiled at her then, and the smile took the rough edges from his face. He bent over and put his elbows on his knees, his shoulders loose. His tawny hair made a line across his forehead, and his mouth was wide and firm. The chin below was rather sharp, and there was something almost wolfish about him, Jenny noticed for the first time.

"I think you're doing a good thing," he said unexpectedly.

"You do?" Jenny was amazed, for he had never commented one way or the other on her campaign.

"Yes, and I guess I haven't been quick enough to tell you that. But I was in law enforcement for a long time, and it's a bad situation in this county."

"You were a sheriff?"

"I was a detective on the Chicago Police Force for eight years."

Jenny stared at Clay in shock. He had never spoken of his past, and now she knew that he was breaking some rule he had made for himself. "Why did you quit, Clay? Didn't you like it?"

"I liked some of it, but there's a lot of corruption out there. A man has to fight it all the time. People shoving money at him and wanting him to do the wrong thing." He hesitated, then passed his hand in front of his face in a helpless gesture. "But that wasn't why I quit." He sat still for a moment and then clasped his hands together, and his voice was summer soft on the air. "I had a good friend, Jennifer. His name was John Summers. He was my partner. He had a wife who gave him a child and then died, and he was trying to raise her. The two of us got caught in a shoot-out. We went down an alley together, and a gunman from a second-story window was about to shoot me. John leaped in front and took the bullet. I got the man who fired it, but Johnny was bleeding to death. I knew he was a goner." Clay Varek hesitated, and his voice seemed to break. "He asked me to look out for his little girl."

"And so you took Jamie to raise?"

"Yes. She had no kin, so I adopted her legally. But I couldn't stay on the force and take care of her. Besides, I couldn't face it after John died. I sold everything I had, which wasn't much, and came down here to try to start over again and give her a good home."

Jenny felt compassion for this strong man and a great admiration. "Not many men would do that, Clay."

Clay looked down at his hands. "John would have done it for me."

Jenny resisted the urge to reach over and put a hand on his shoulder, to try to comfort him somehow. Instead, she stood up, and Clay rose to stand beside her. "Thanks for the doll. It means a lot to Jamie."

"She's a wonderful child. I know you're very proud of her."

Clay's eyes clouded for a moment. "A man makes a sorry mother."

"Why don't you bring her over to our house sometime? My sister Kat would love to play with her. Kat may seem sort of wild, but she's very responsible."

"All right. I'll do that. And thanks, Jennifer."

★ ★ ★

On election day, Jenny looked up and saw Clay Varek walk into campaign headquarters. She greeted him at once, then asked, "Where's Jamie?"

"I left her with your folks. She's having a great time. I can't tell you how much I appreciate your putting me on to that. She had gotten lonesome, and I hadn't recognized it."

Jenny was very pleased that Clay had taken her up on her invitation. "I'm glad to help." She looked up at the clock and the wall and sighed, "Well, it will all be over by midnight."

"I think you'll win, Jennifer." Clay had insisted on calling her Jennifer, which pleased Jenny quite a bit. It didn't sound formal when he said it, and he was the only one who did. But she liked it.

"You mind if I make a suggestion? I've been around quite a few elections."

Luke Dixon had come up to hear him say this. "We need all the help we can get, Clay."

"Well, I think you need to put one of your people at every polling spot, and I think they ought to accompany that box of votes all the way back to headquarters, where they'll be counted."

Jenny stared at him. "You think they would try to steal the votes?"

"It's been done before."

"That's a good idea!" Luke exclaimed. "I hadn't thought of that. There's one box way out in the county right in the heart of moonshining country."

"You'd better go to that one yourself, Jenny. I'll go with you if you'd like."

"That's a good idea," Luke said quickly. "I'll assign someone to go to every box. It's going to be a close race."

★ ★ ★

The day went slowly for Jenny, and the boxes were counted from the county seat of Summerdale, where they were easily accessible, and the count was very close. "It could go either way," Luke said, a worried expression on his face. "It all depends on the outlying stations. You'd better go see about that box of votes over by Cartersville."

Jenny nodded. "Clay said he'd go with me."

"Not a bad idea. That's rough country around there. We've assigned an older couple to watch the box. I'm not sure they're able."

Jenny went at once and found Clay, and the two of them got into his car. By the time they made the trip, darkness had fallen, and when they reached the polling place, they saw that there were crowds still milling around in front. When they got out, there were catcalls and some rather obscene shouts directed toward Jenny. "What's the matter? You afraid you'll lose a vote? Well, you won't get any around here! Get your skirt out of here!"

The speaker was a fat, red-faced man who had obviously been drinking. Clay Varek stepped in front of him and said, "Shut your mouth!"

Clay's tone was soft, and the big man blinked at him and started to speak. But something he saw in Varek's eyes stopped him. He stared a moment longer at Clay and then turned and walked away unsteadily, muttering under his breath.

"Come on, Jenny, it's almost time to take the box in."

They entered the schoolhouse where the election was being held, and Jenny looked around. "The Parsons were supposed to be here watching the box."

"Mrs. Parson got sick," a hard-eyed woman said. "But we

didn't need 'em anyway. Her husband took her home."

"That's right." A short, muscular man with a droopy mustache moved over toward the box. "We'll take the box in."

Jenny saw several of the men moving toward the stubby man and did not know what to say. Varek stepped forward and said, "That's fine. You can hold the box, and we'll go right along with you."

"We don't need your help!"

Clay swept back his coat and revealed the pistol stuck in his belt. "We'll go with you," he said softly. "You don't mind, do you?"

The muscular man stared at the gun and then lifted his eyes to Clay. "I guess it'll be all right," he muttered.

"You can ride in our car. Bring anybody you want," Clay said.

Jenny's heart was beating fast as she looked around and saw that there were some hard-looking men there. But Clay stood firm, and although he did not pull out the revolver stuck in his belt, there was something about him that kept their strict attention.

"Let's go," Clay said.

Jenny felt weak-kneed, but she got into the car in the front seat with Clay. The muscular man got in the back holding the box, along with one of his friends. "You didn't need to come all the way out here for this," he said weakly.

Clay turned and smiled at him. "We appreciate your help. You just hang on to that box, buddy."

After they returned, the vote counting went on for over an hour as they waited for all the outlying districts to report in. Jenny was standing outside along with a host of others, including Max Conroy. A silence had fallen over the crowd, and Jenny had never felt so helpless in her life. Finally Gerald Thackery, the clerk who was in charge of the count, stepped outside. It was his moment of triumph. He was a small man, with thinning blond hair, and he held a paper in his hand. Deliberately he stopped, and somebody hollered, "Well, what is it, Gerald? Spit it out!"

"The new sheriff, according to the full vote, is . . ." He paused dramatically and said, "Miss Jennifer Winslow!"

A howl of anger went up from many, but there were riotous cheers as well. Jenny felt people around her patting her shoulder and shaking her hand, but she looked over the crowd and saw Max Conroy glaring at her. If she ever saw hatred in a human face, it was written on his, and she knew that the election might be over, but that the job was just beginning. He came forward and smiled, but when he leaned toward her he said in a voice so low that only she could hear, "You won, but you'll wish you lost before it's over."

Dixon appeared and hugged Jenny, saying, "Well, you're the sheriff, but we've got a lot to do."

And Jenny knew then that somehow her life could never be the same. She felt totally inadequate and whispered a quick prayer. "Lord, you'll have to help me because I can't do this alone!"

PART TWO

Sheriff Winslow

★ ★ ★

CHAPTER SEVEN

SHERIFF WINSLOW'S FIRST DAY

★ ★ ★

Standing in front of the narrow full-length mirror fastened to the wall of her bedroom, Jenny stared fixedly at her image. The first rays of the early sun slanted in through the window, throwing pale rays of light on the turkey-red carpet beside her bed, and reflected on the red of her hair as she stood staring at herself.

"I never thought I'd be putting on a thing like this," she muttered and shook her head in utter disbelief. There had been no uniforms designed for women, for all of the deputies in the sheriff's department were male. Jenny had worried over the problem for some time, and finally she and Missouri had come up with what seemed to be the best solution. She wore a light khaki tailored shirt with a straight skirt to match that fell just below her knees. A wide belt circled her waist, and a narrow leather belt crossed her chest from her waist to her right shoulder, fastening in the back. She wore calf-high dark brown boots, and at her side, in a polished brown holster, was the thirty-eight she had been issued. Turning to the bed, she picked up the fawn-colored felt hat with a stiff brim and a low crown, settled it squarely on her head, and then let her hands fall to her side.

For a long moment she stood completely still, staring at herself. *I feel ridiculous, and I hate the way I look, but there's no help for it. Lord, I don't know why you put me in this place. It's going to be harder than anything I've ever known, and I can't do it without you. So, I ask you to keep me safe and to let me be a blessing to the people in this county.* She took one more look at herself, then had to smile. She had always been a young woman with a keen sense of humor, and now somehow she seemed like a comic character in a very bad play.

Suddenly the door flew open, and Kat came bursting in. "Hey, you look great!" Kat said, staring with admiration. Her eyes went to the holster on Jenny's right side, and she said, "Can I hold the gun, Jenny?"

"No, you can't hold the gun."

"You gotta let me shoot it sometime. I ain't never shot a pistol."

"You *have* never shot a pistol! And you're not shooting this one. Come on, let's go downstairs."

The two went downstairs, and when they reached the dining room they found Lewis and Clint seated, with Hannah and Missouri serving the meal.

"Well, look at you!" Clint grinned. "I've never seen such a pretty policeman."

"I wish I were in China!" Jenny said vehemently. She went to her chair and plopped down. She put her hat down on the floor beside her and waited until Lewis asked the blessing.

Afterward, Lewis smiled at his daughter. "You look fine, Jenny. Are you excited about your first day in office?"

"I'm scared green."

Clint laughed then as he took a huge mouthful of scrambled eggs and asked, "Is that gun loaded?"

"I don't know."

Clint swallowed back a grin with a mouthful of egg, got up, and walked around to where Jenny sat. He slipped the thirty-eight out of the holster and glanced at it. "Nope. Where are the bullets?"

"I think I left them upstairs on my bedroom table."

"I'll go get them for you and load it."

As Clint left, Jenny muttered, "I feel like a fool in this out-fit."

"You look very nice," Hannah said. "We're all very proud of you."

Suddenly the sound of high-pitched squalling came to them. Lewis put down his fork and shook his head. "I think they're all wired together or something. It's never *one* of them that needs to be fed or changed. All three of them come due at exactly the same time."

Everyone left the table and went into the parlor, where the three babies were lying together in a crib. Hannah, Lewis, and Missouri at once began changing a baby apiece, and Lewis grinned. "I wish some of my associates back at my old office could see me now."

"Proud of yourself, aren't you?" Missouri laughed. She reached over and tugged a lock of his hair and said, "Well, I'm proud of you too." She turned then to Jenny, who was watching, and said, "I've gotta feed these babies. You go back and eat, Jenny, but I've been praying for you."

"What did you pray, Ma?"

"I prayed that you'd survive. That's what all of us have to do."

All except Missouri went back to the table and finished breakfast. Clint came back and handed the revolver to Jenny. "Be careful. It's ready to shoot."

Gingerly Jenny put the revolver back in the holster. It hung there, an unaccustomed weight at her side, and Clint was very much aware of her discomfort. "Are they gonna give you a police car?"

"That's what the county commissioner said."

"Well, I'll drive you in."

The two finished breakfast quickly, and then went out and climbed into the truck. Jenny said little during the trip, for she was apprehensive in a way that she never had been in her whole life. From time to time Clint looked over at her and saw the strain etched on her features. Finally he said, "The first time's always the worst."

"I don't think so. I think every day will be the worst."

"That's what I thought too until I swallowed my first lizard."

Jenny looked at Clint in surprise. He always had tall tales to tell her, and now she stared at him, expecting some sign of laughter, but he seemed perfectly serious. "What are you talking about—swallowing a lizard?"

"I never told you about that?" Clint said. He shrugged and swiveled the wheel to dodge a pothole. "It happened when I was just a young buck anxious to prove how tough I was. I went around tryin' to get people to bet that I wouldn't do some outrageous thing. One day down at the general store a tiny lizard no more than three inches long popped out to sun himself, and I scooped him up. I looked around at the rest of the fellers on the porch there, almost as wild as I was, and tried to get 'em to bet that I wouldn't swallow it whole."

Jenny laughed. "Did you really do that, Clint?"

"Sure did. And that ain't the point of it. I held that critter up by the tail and turned my head back and dangled him over my mouth. I just started to say, 'Come on, you fellas, what'll you bet I won't swallow him?' Of course, I didn't have any idea in the world of swallowin' that thing, but you know how lizards are. Suddenly his tail broke off, and he fell right down my throat. Before I knew what was happenin' he was halfway down my gullet, and I swallowed kind of without meanin' to."

Jenny laughed aloud. "What'd it feel like, Clint?"

"Well, I could feel its claws scratchin' all the way down, and then I kind of felt it runnin' around in my stomach."

"What in the world did you do?"

"One of the fellas had a jug of white lightnin' there, moonshine don't you know, and I was a drinkin' man in those days, and so he gave it to me, and I drank down as much as I could hold. Must have been a full pint."

Jenny found this to be terribly amusing and said, "Did it make you drunk?"

"Drunk! I reckon it did!" Clint grinned at her then. "And I guess it made the lizard drunk too, 'cause he quieted down. The boys kept pouring moonshine down me until I fell over. I didn't know nothin' about it until the next day."

"Did you really do that, Clint, or are you just making it up?"

"Well, I tell some tall tales, but that really happened." He dodged another pothole and said, "I guess the moral of that is don't count your lizards if you're holdin' them by the tail." He reached over then with his free hand and patted her shoulder affectionately. "I guess the other moral is I only had to swallow a lizard for the first time once!"

"The way I feel, Clint, I'd rather swallow a dozen lizards than face everybody today."

"I think you're looking at it wrong, Jenny. I've got a feelin' God's in this."

"I hope so. I prayed this morning that I'd be a blessing to somebody in this job."

"Well, there's plenty of room for that. The poor folks in this county have been stomped down, ignored by the law. You can make a difference, and you got the Christian people in this whole county praying for you. You remember that story in the Bible where Israel was attacked and one of the prophet Elisha's helpers got scared, and the prophet prayed? He prayed that that young fellow would see the truth, and when the young fellow looked up, he saw angels all over the place. And Elisha told him, 'There are more for us than there are against us, so don't worry.'"

Jenny reached up and captured Clint's hand and squeezed it. "I declare you are a comfort, Clint Longstreet."

Jenny felt more relaxed, and when Clint let her out in front of the county offices, she slammed the door, then leaned over and straightened her hat. "Do I look all right?"

"You look downright official. Go on and swallow your lizard, Jenny."

Jenny laughed and found that the tension had mostly flowed out of her. She mounted the steps to the county offices and saw two loafers in overalls leaning against the wall. One of them was whittling, and both of them were spitting tobacco juice. One said something under his breath to the other, who laughed, and Jenny was tempted to turn aside and challenge them, but she knew that this was the wrong way to go about it. She would wait until a more opportune time when something could really be done.

Turning into the county commissioner's office, she found Trevor Gaines sitting behind his desk writing furiously. He looked up, smiled, and got to his feet. "Well, good morning. First day on the job, eh?"

"Yes, sir."

"Well, let's get you sworn in." Gaines was not a big man, but he had a big lawyer's voice. This was his first term as county commissioner, and he was anxious to make a good record. He found the Bible and brought it around the desk and said, "All right, you'll put your hand on that. I'll give you the oath," he said.

The oath was very brief, simply stating that she would serve the county as sheriff faithfully and execute all her duties so help her God, and when it was finished Gaines put out his hand and took hers. "Congratulations, Sheriff. I want you to know that my office stands behind you."

"Thank you, sir. I need all the help I can get."

"Well, I wish you well. It's going to be tough. We've never had a woman sheriff before. I don't know any county in Georgia that does." Gaines scratched his head thoughtfully and added, "Let me just give you a little bit of advice, Sheriff. Don't try to save the world today. That's what new people do when they want to do well in their jobs. Just let things go easy. You've got a lot to learn, a new job like this. It's a hard job too and dangerous."

"I think that's good advice, sir." She hesitated, then said, "I don't even know what the procedure is. Do I keep all the deputies that I inherited, or am I free to get new ones?"

The question seemed to trouble Gaines. "Technically, I suppose, you could clean house, but if I was you, I'd wait a while. I know you're not too impressed with Merle Arp and Arlie Pender, but they know their jobs and for a while, at least, you're going to need people who know what they're doing. You'll just have to keep your eye on them. And you've got a good man in Billy Moon. I suggest you make Billy your official assistant sheriff. Listen to him. He's tough, and he knows what to do."

Jenny felt a warmth at Gaines's advice. "Thank you, sir. I

may be coming to you for advice from time to time."

The remark pleased Gaines. "Anytime, Jenny," he said informally. "Look on me as a friend."

Jenny left the commissioner's office and walked out the front entrance of the building, then turned down the street toward the county jail, which also housed the sheriff's office. It was a two-story red-brick structure with a steep-pitched metal roof. She glanced up at it, thinking how noisy it must be on the second floor when it rained. The long-term prisoners were housed there, she knew. The lower part of the structure was divided into holding cells for short-term prisoners and the jailer and the kitchen, where the food was prepared and taken to the cells. Her new office was also on the first floor and as she stepped inside, Jenny was struck by the fetid odor. It was the odor of a building that received little care, and she thought, *It doesn't have to stink like this. Somebody hasn't been doing their job. At least I can take care of that!*

She opened a door that read SHERIFF and stepped inside the large room, which was flanked on her left by a high counter running the length of the room. The room was crowded, and everyone's eyes were on her as she quickly surveyed the group. Some she already knew—Merle Arp, Arlie Pender, Billy Moon—and there were two older men there in uniform whom she had not met.

Billy Moon spoke up. "Let me introduce you, Sheriff. This is Frank Eddings and Kermit Bing. This is our new sheriff, deputies."

Eddings was a retired city policeman and Bing was a retired deputy. Both, she learned, now worked part-time for the sheriff's office as needed. She went around and shook hands with each of the deputies, including Pender and Arp.

"And this is our clerk, Ruby French," Moon said, motioning toward the woman who had come up to stand with the others.

"I'm glad to know you, Sheriff." Ruby French was a sleek brunette with large brown eyes and better dressed than most. There was a sensuous air about her that Jenny recognized instantly, but she only smiled and nodded. "I'll be depending on you, Ruby, to keep me out of trouble. I've got a lot to learn."

"I'll be glad to do what I can, Sheriff."

"And this is Harold Porter. We just call him Legs. And this is his wife, Mattie. They take care of the jail and do the cooking."

Jenny was not impressed by the couple. They were both carelessly dressed in clothes that were not the cleanest, and Legs had not shaved in at least two days. He nodded and muttered a fair greeting, and his wife did no more than stare at her.

Jenny knew it was time for her to present herself, and she remembered the commissioner's advice. "I don't have to tell any of you how inexperienced I am. I've never had any idea I would be in a position like this. But now that I am here, I want to tell you I'm going to do the best I can, and I'll expect each of you to do the same." She then looked directly at Arp and shifted her eyes to Pender. She distrusted both men, but she said evenly, "We'll scratch out all the past and start at a new beginning. As far as I'm concerned, I'll form my opinions of you and your work from what you do from this day forward—not by what's gone on in the past."

Billy Moon grinned and said, "That's fine, Sheriff. I wouldn't want you to know about all my bad habits. You'll learn them quick enough."

Jenny felt secure with Moon and said, "Why don't you show me through the system, Billy. Start treating me just as if I didn't know anything—which is pretty well true."

Moon nodded, and Jenny said, "All right, this will be school day."

Billy Moon was a soft-spoken man, but he knew the sheriff's office well. He showed her through the armory, and Jenny was dazed by the variety of guns, including rifles, long-barreled shotguns, sawed-off shotguns, and pistols of various caliber.

"Have you done much shooting, Sheriff?"

"None at all."

Billy's eyes showed humor. "Then I'd better take you out this afternoon, and we'll start breaking you in."

"That'll be fine," Jenny said, although she dreaded the thought of it.

For two hours she went over the routines, Billy exhibiting the work schedules for the various deputies, and then she spent an hour with Ruby, going over accounts and office procedures. Ruby showed no animosity toward her but, on the other hand, was not overly friendly.

Finally Jenny said, "I've had about all I can absorb for one morning."

"You want to take a look at the jail and meet some of the prisoners?" Moon asked.

"I think that would be good."

The two left the sheriff's office, and as they did, she noticed that the floor was crusted with dirt. "Who's the janitor here?"

"Well, we don't have one right now. Sheriff Conroy paid Mattie to do some cleaning up." He shook his head, adding, "She didn't earn it, though. Pretty bad, isn't it?"

"We'll have to do better than this. There's no excuse for dirt."

Billy suddenly laughed. "You think the sheriff's office is dirty? Wait until you see the jail."

They entered the west wing of the building, which included the living quarters for Legs and Mattie and the kitchen. Jenny had nothing to say about their living quarters, but the kitchen was a disaster. She was accustomed to cleanliness all her life, and the filth in the kitchen was abominable. Mattie, a slovenly, overweight woman, whined, "I ain't had time to clean up much."

"Didn't you know I was coming, Mattie?" Jenny asked evenly.

"Well, I reckon I did."

"I'll expect this place to be cleaned up."

"Well, I ain't got much time."

Jenny stared at her but did not answer. She followed Billy upstairs, and the stench was overwhelming.

"We got eight cells here for men and four for women," Billy said. "And we got this one room that we use for a mess hall, and if they behave, we let 'em out to write letters at the tables. There's a radio in there too, for good behavior."

Jenny was disgusted as she walked down the hall between the cells where the men were kept. There had been no attempt at all at cleaning, and when she looked into the men's bathroom and got a whiff of it, her stomach retched. She turned away quickly, and her eyes met those of Billy Moon. He said nothing, and Jenny said, "Let's see what the women's section looks like." The women's section was no better, and the inmates stared at her. She spoke to each one of them, and some of them muttered a greeting in return.

"It's about noon, isn't it, Billy?"

Billy glanced at his wristwatch. "Yep. Lunch is due up right now."

Jenny's expression did not change, but a light danced in her eyes. "I think you and I, and the jailer and his wife, will have lunch with the prisoners today."

Billy was taken aback. "Why, you can't eat that mess they bring up here!"

Jenny said firmly, "I think I'll get acquainted with some of the inmates. You go down and tell Mattie and Legs that the four of us will be eating with the prisoners today. Make sure they understand they don't have any choice."

Billy's obsidian eyes glinted with humor. "Yes, ma'am, Sheriff. I'll see to it they're here."

Jenny spent the next thirty minutes getting acquainted with the prisoners. Most of the women were in for minor infractions and only two of the men were long-term. She was aware of Legs and his wife laboring up the stairs carrying the food but ignored them. Finally Billy came and said, "Time to eat. I hope you're real hungry." His lips twitched at the corners and said, "I expect you ate in some nice places in New York."

"Very nice."

"Well, try to think of that."

The prisoners were released, and all of them were directed by Billy into the chow hall. Two long tables were there, and they sat down at once. Legs and Mattie were standing nervously by, and Mattie whined, "This ain't the way we do it here, Sheriff."

"We may do it this way a lot. I'm sure you prepared a fine meal for the inmates."

One of the inmates, a small mousy-looking man sniggered but said nothing.

The meal consisted of a plate of white beans, practically unseasoned and so undercooked that they were hard to chew. The corn bread was stale and tough as hardtack. The vegetables consisted of a huge pot of greens. Mattie went by and filled everybody's plate up except hers and Legs'. "My stomach's a might tender today," she grunted.

"Mine too. I'm a little bit off my feed," Legs said.

Jenny stared at the two and said, "Fill up your plates. I insist. I want you to eat what you cooked."

Jenny took one bite of the beans and knew it would be her last. The greens were bitter, and the corn bread was inedible. She saw that the inmates were all watching her carefully, and she turned her gaze on the Porters. "This food's not fit to eat."

"I do the best I can," Legs whined. "I ain't got no budget for fancy food."

"I don't think beans are that expensive—even *if* you cook them. I don't expect fancy food," she said firmly, "but I do expect fresh, wholesome, thoroughly cooked meals." She turned to Billy and said, "Billy, go down to the Elite Café and order a good lunch, whatever the special is, for these inmates." She looked back at Legs and Mattie and added, "Take whatever the cost is out of the jailer's salary."

"Why, you can't do that!" Legs shouted angrily.

"I believe I can." Jenny's voice was controlled but hard-edged, and she was not smiling. She was angry to the bone and knew without being told that this was not the worst meal these inmates had been served. "Now," she instructed the jailers, "go feed this mess to the pigs if they'll have it." Then she turned to the prisoners and announced, "Your lunches will be a little late today, but they should be good."

One of the women said, "Thank you, ma'am. It's been awful hard eating that slop these two have been serving."

"They won't be serving slop anymore." Jenny said, "Porter, you and Mattie come with me. We're going to have a meeting. Billy, I want you to listen to this."

The four left the jail, and when they got downstairs, Jenny said, "You've been paid to clean up the sheriff's office. It's filthy. What you do in your own quarters is your business, but this kitchen's going to be spotless, and the cells upstairs are going to be clean. I'll be making an inspection the first thing in the morning. You can take your choice. You're going to either start delivering, or you can go look for other employment."

Jenny turned and walked away, and Billy Moon followed her. As soon as they were in the corridor separating the two sections, he said, "They won't stay long, not if there's real work involved."

"Good. Surely there's somebody better than those two."

Moon chewed his lip thoughtfully. "Trouble is they're kin to Dwight Hightower, the county judge."

"What difference does that make?"

"Well, Sheriff Beauchamp tried to fire them when he was in office, but Hightower blocked it."

Jenny said quietly, "I don't know anything about procedure, but I know a good job of cleaning and cooking when I see it. And this may be a test case, Billy. I don't know how much power the judge has, but I'll go toe to toe with him on this."

Billy Moon studied the young woman in front of him. He saw the courage in her but at the same time was aware that she was beyond her depth in politics. "It's going to be like walking through a mine field, Sheriff, but I'm glad you're here. As for Judge Hightower, I've been waiting to see somebody take him down for quite a while."

"I'm depending on you, Billy." Jenny put out her hand, and it was enclosed quickly by the deputy's big paw. "You'll have to help me."

"I reckon I'll do that, Sheriff."

★ ★ ★

The room reeked of alcohol and was filled with smoke from the cigars that all four card players had in hand. The room was richly furnished, decorated in the best of taste, everything expensive, including the thick drapes that covered the windows and the Persian rug underfoot. Judge Dwight Hightower, at the age of fifty, looked like an aging Hollywood movie star. He had silver hair and rather patrician features. He looked around the table at the other three men, including Millington Wheeler, Max Conroy, whom he knew well, and a man called Vito Canelli, whom he did not know at all. All he knew was that Canelli was involved in organized crime in Chicago. Canelli didn't refer to his boss by name, but since Al Capone was serving time in an Atlanta penitentiary, Hightower guessed he worked for Capone's successor, rumored to be a man named Frank "The Enforcer" Nitti. There was something dangerous about Canelli, but Hightower felt confident to handle him.

The four had been playing poker for only about an hour, and now Hightower looked over toward Conroy and said, "Too bad about losing that election."

"Next time we'll do better." Conroy had been drinking heavily, and there was a dissatisfaction about him as he muttered, "That woman won't last. It's a tough job. She'll quit before too long."

Canelli was silent as the talk went on between the other three men about the election. Finally he said, "We have to know what's going on with the local law."

Conroy quickly said, "I'll know what's happening, Mr. Canelli. I've got some men inside the sheriff's office. We'll know every move they make before they make it."

Canelli puffed at his cigar, and his almost black eyes took in the tall form of Conroy. "I'll be depending on that."

Conroy was flushed and had lost more money than he could afford. Hightower said, "Why don't you go check on what's going on with Jack and that crew over in the south of the county, Max."

"Sure, I'll do that, Judge."

As soon as Conroy left, Canelli stared at the two men across from him. He threw his cards down as if bored with them. "I'm not sure we can do business."

"Now, wait a minute, Mr. Canelli!" Judge Hightower said quickly. "We can handle it here."

"You lost the election. That means you don't have enough support."

"It was a jumped-up thing. All the preachers got into it. Next time we'll know what to look for," the judge said. "But Conroy was right about one thing. That woman sheriff won't last. It's too rough a job for a woman, and we can make it even rougher."

"I'm not sure," Canelli said. "As long as the law was in your pocket, it was a sure thing. If we're going to keep doing business, the men making the booze are going to have to be protected."

"That won't be hard. The woman doesn't know the first thing about being a sheriff, and as Conroy said, we've got two deputies that'll let us know what's happening."

Canelli got to his feet. "My boss wants a steady flow of product. We've got to be sure of delivery. Expense is no object, but the stuff has got to get through."

Millington Wheeler was a strange addition to this party. He was probably the leading citizen in Summerdale, and at the age of forty-eight, was in his prime. He was a chairman of the board of deacons in the Baptist church, and with his wife, Helen, ruled society, such as it was, in the county. He had long been involved with Judge Hightower, the two of them finding ways to make money off of county contracts, but what people did not know was that Wheeler had lost most of his money with the fall of the stock market. He had kept it covered up, but he had overextended himself. Now he had a burning desire to recoup. He hated himself sometimes for what he was doing. He used to take pride in his honesty, but he had convinced himself that making and selling bootleg whiskey was not the sin the preachers made it out to be. He had subscribed to Al Capone's ideas, who had said, "I'm just a businessman." Of course, Wheeler shuddered now, thinking about where that had landed him.

Leaning forward, Wheeler said, "This thing has got to work, Judge."

"Yes, it does, but you know it could be dangerous." Judge Hightower put his cigar down and picked up the glass. He sipped from the amber-colored liquid, then said, "These mob types think nothing of human life. If we cross them, we're dead."

"Look, it's just a business, Dwight. Prohibition is going to be repealed soon. We both know that. It hasn't worked. This is the last chance we've got to really put ourselves in good shape."

The two spoke quietly for a time, and then Wheeler said, "What about Conroy?"

"I'll put him on the county payroll. Assistant to the super-intendent of the highway department. But his real job will be twofold. One is to make sure that our suppliers don't get arrested, and two—to get rid of that woman." Hightower stared at Wheeler. "Just make it rough, Wheeler. And there's no turning back. Once we start, we're in for good."

"We can do it. Look, Dwight," he said, and his voice was quietly desperate. "Nobody but you knows about the financial pocket I'm in, but this will get me out of it. Then I'll retire and let you run the show. But I've got to get out of this hole I'm in."

The two men stared at each other, and then Wheeler rose, saying, "I'll call you tomorrow." He left, and Hightower sat there for a time thinking hard. Finally he rose and went to the second floor of his mansion. He knocked on Canelli's door, and when a voice bid him enter, he stepped inside. Vito Canelli was standing facing him, his hand in the pocket of his suit. Hightower knew it was on a gun, but he ignored it. "It'll be all right, Vito. We can make it work."

"What about Wheeler? He seems like a weak sister to me."

"He's been rich all his life, and he was hard hit by the stock market. He tried to make it up by gambling on horses."

"He's a weak sister, Judge. I hear he's religious, and that ain't good."

Judge Hightower let contempt show in his expression. "He's a hypocrite. He likes to make a show, but his religion don't keep his hands clean."

Vito stood there and thought hard for a moment. He took his hand out of his pocket and nodded. "All right, we'll do it. Get him tied into it, Judge. We can't have any problems here. I'll tell you right now, the boss don't like excuses."

CHAPTER EIGHT

A VEILED THREAT

★ ★ ★

"I can't stand these blasted flies!"

The heat in the sheriff's office was oppressive, and a faulty screen had admitted a number of large black flies, which seemed determined to land on Jenny's hair. She swiped at one of them ineffectually, then took out her handkerchief from her hip pocket and wiped her forehead. "Why can't we get that screen fixed, Ruby?"

Ruby French was sitting alongside Jenny. The two women had been seated for over two hours at a long, scarred wooden table covered with papers, documents, and records of various sizes and shapes and age. It had been a difficult time for Jenny, for she was totally ignorant of politics on a county level, and it seemed that whoever had originally organized the bookkeeping system had delighted in making it as mysterious and obscure as possible.

Ruby drummed with a pencil on the table and found a smile. "The budget's pretty tight around here, Sheriff."

"Look, why don't you just call me Jenny when we're not in a formal situation."

"That's fine with me. Anyway, it would probably cost ten dollars to go around and repair all the screens that need fixing. Maybe twenty. If we spend the money for that, we'll have to take it away from something else."

"Well, take it out of my salary. These flies are going to drive me crazy!" Suddenly Jenny laughed aloud. "Here I am with problems as big as Mount Olympus, and I'm worried about flies. Don't pay any attention to me, Ruby. You're doing a great job. I'm just thickheaded."

"No, you're not. This bookkeeping was designed by Noah after he got off the ark, I think. What it needs is a complete renovation."

"Why don't we do it, then?"

"Once again, it would take money."

"Well, I think it ought to be modernized. Could you do it?"

"I suppose I could. It would mean a lot of extra work."

"Well, do it. I'll get the money from somewhere."

Ruby French put the pencil down and said, "Let's have some iced tea. Maybe that'll cool you off a little bit." She rose and went to the back of the office where an icebox was wedged into a corner. Opening the door, she took an ice pick and chipped away at the block of ice that had been put in earlier in the day. "Someday we'll get us one of those new electric ice boxes, and we won't have to have the iceman coming by." She chipped off enough slivers to fill two glasses, shut the door, then filled them with tea from a covered pitcher. The two women put sugar and lemon in and then sat back, and as Jenny sipped the tea gratefully, she said, "What about you, Ruby?"

"What do you mean, what about me?"

"I mean, do you have a family? Are you married? I don't know anything about you at all."

Ruby lifted the glass and carefully traced the watery ring with her forefinger. She did not answer for some time. When she finally looked up, there was an aura of sadness in her eyes. At the same time there was a mixture of anger and regret. "I was married once. I thought it was the romance of a lifetime, but that only lasted until the first time he beat me up."

"He beat you?"

"Yes, and I put up with it for three years. Finally he ran

off with a dancer in a cooch show."

"What's a cooch show?"

"Dancers in a carnival. Kind of a striptease act."

"I'm sorry, Ruby."

"Well, we all have to eat our peck of dirt, and I guess Kenneth was mine. No more men for me."

"Not ever?"

"I do what I want to now. I don't have to put up with a sorry man."

From outside the building came the sound of a harmonica playing a merry tune. The two women listened to it for a moment, and then Jenny turned to the woman beside her. "What am I going to do with Legs and Mattie? They're absolutely worthless. I thought making them eat with the inmates would cause them to do a better job, but it didn't. And they're not fulfilling their job to clean the office either."

"Not much you can do about them. Like Billy told you, they're distant relatives to Judge Hightower. He's not proud of them, but he pressured Sheriff Beauchamp into putting them on. The sheriff tried every way he could to get rid of them, but the judge can squeeze pretty hard. Have you met him yet?"

"Just once. He seemed very nice."

"Oh, he's a handsome guy all right and pretty smooth—but a rattlesnake is pretty according to some people. Don't let him box you in a corner. Don't give him a handle on you in any way."

"But we can't put up with this any longer. Those people are stealing. They take the food budget, stick half of it in their pocket, and buy the cheapest things they can find. While the inmates are half starved, those two are running around with county money in their pockets."

Ruby studied the young woman before her. She had been highly skeptical of the whole concept of a female sheriff, and she still was as far as results were concerned. But she had to admit that Jennifer Winslow was a good woman. *A little bit innocent*, she had said to Billy Moon, *which is going to get her hurt*. Now as she took in the rich shine of Jenny's red hair and the wide pleasant lips and the fine coloring, she said briefly,

"That's life, Jenny. There's crookedness in this world and meanness, and you're not going to take it out. You're not gonna be able to stop it all."

Jenny stared at Ruby, and her lips grew firm. "I'm going to do something about that pair!"

"Watch your back," Ruby warned. "The judge has a dozen ways to get at you, and he doesn't mind using them."

"I'm going up to see if they've cleaned the cells yet. My head's tired with all this anyhow. Thanks for the lesson."

"You're doing fine. It just takes a while to get accustomed to it."

Leaving the sheriff's office, Jenny moved into the corridor, then up the stairs that led to the cells on the second floor. She had learned to call out as she entered, "Woman in the hall!" for sometimes the inmates were not dressed. She waited for time to let her warning take effect and then stepped inside. She went at once to the bathroom, and she saw that it was filthy—disgustingly so. Her lips tightened, and she stepped outside and moved down the row of cells. She stopped at one where a small man with a wild head of black hair was grinning up at her. "Hello, Jimmy. How's it going today?"

"Finer than silk, Sheriff."

Jimmy Duo had become a fixture at the jail. He was the leading contender for the office of town drunk, and the jail had become almost a home to him. He came over now and stood up and, being no taller than Jenny, looked her directly in the eyes. "It's gonna be a fine day."

Jenny stared at Duo, wondering how anyone in his situation could consider any day fine. Duo's eyes were red rimmed, his cheeks were sunk in, and his hands were shaking. He would be released at noon after the meal, and she knew he would immediately go searching for whiskey. "Jimmy, don't you ever get tired of the way you live?"

"I'm tired of it all the time, Sheriff." Duo grinned broadly. He was a cheerful fellow, at least outwardly, but there was a look in his eyes that belied his cheerful demeanor.

"There's a better way to live than this. Why don't you give the Lord a chance to do something with you?"

"The Lord gave up on me a long time ago, I reckon. I ain't

given Him no encouragement, don't you see?"

"No, I don't see. The Lord God is always ready. When you get out of here, let's have a talk, just you and me."

"Well, you can talk to me all you want to, Sheriff Winslow. I've been talked to a lot, but somehow I always come out on the short end of it. I always wanted to be a Christian man, but when I start thataway, I wind up drunk in an alley."

Jenny's heart went out to the small man. He was no more than thirty, but he looked fifty. She had heard his story from Moon, how he had been a fine young fellow, a shining example of a scholar in his early days in school. But he had fallen prey to alcohol and had been in the gutter ever since. "We'll talk about it, Jimmy," she said. Then she turned, for she heard the steel door opening at the end of the hall. "Must be lunchtime."

"We'll probably have T-bones and baked potatoes today." Jimmy winked at her, and those listening mocked him with groans.

Jenny stood watching as Legs and Mattie Porter brought in the food. She had tried for a week to make them eat their own cooking, and apparently nothing was too bad for them to gag down. She stared in dismay at this day's offering, which consisted of a runny stew of limp vegetables that reeked of hot sauce, evidently to cover up the real smell. Both Legs and Mattie stared at her, daring her to say something. She knew they felt secure with Judge Hightower's backing, and for a moment she was tempted to fire them on the spot. Instead, she simply turned and left, but anger was stirring in her. She went out the front door, calling out, "I'm going down to the café. Can I bring you something back, Ruby?"

"No, not this time."

As she strode down the street, Jenny was aware of the scrutiny of those she passed. The sight of a woman in the sheriff's uniform had not sunk in yet, and she had become, more or less, accustomed to the curious stares. She had grown flustered once when a young boy no more than four had said loudly to his mother, "Mama, why's that policeman wearing a skirt?"

As she walked down Main Street, she was suddenly struck

with how the small town of Summerdale had more or less become the center of her world. After living in New York City most of her life, the thought occurred to her, *Why, you could put this whole town in one little section of New York, and it would be hard to find!* Still, something about the town had become part of her. She passed by Henry's Pool Hall and noted that the usual supply of acne-ridden young men were there, some of them standing on the front porch, watching her as she went by. She nodded, and one of them mumbled, "Hello, Sheriff." Across the street was the garage and blacksmith shop, and she waved at Jude Tanner, who was working on a car outside the building. He waved at her and called out, "Hi, Sheriff!"

"Hello, Jude!"

"You comin' to the box supper?"

"I guess so."

"Well, I'll make a bid on your box. Put somethin' good in it."

She liked Jude a great deal. He was a giant in form but had the gentleness of a child, which she found very attractive. She passed Taylor's Barbershop, where the endless checker game went on out in front on a wooden table surrounded by loafers. Then she turned into the Elite Café.

"Over here, Sheriff. Just in time to buy my lunch."

Jenny walked over to where Luke Dixon was seated. He got up as she came to the table and pulled out her chair, and the two sat down.

"My treat today, Sheriff."

"Why, thank you, Luke." The two sat down and at once the owner of the Elite, Maisy Hayes, came over to take their order. "Afternoon, Sheriff."

"Hello, Maisy. What's good today?"

"We got fried chicken or salmon croquettes—and we got okra, tomatoes, and corn."

"That all sounds good to me," Luke said cheerfully. "Bring us a big plateful of everything and some tea for the sheriff."

"What have you got for dessert?" Jenny asked.

"Cherry cobbler."

"Good, I'll have some of that when we're finished."

Maisy nodded and left. She called in the order through a

window, then brought another glass of iced tea for Jenny. She refilled Dixon's glass and said, "Enjoy your dinner."

Dixon watched as Jenny thirstily drained her glass of tea, then asked, "You know how I know this is a good café?"

"No. How?"

"Look there. Maisy's got four calendars over there. You can always tell how good a café is by how many calendars it has on its walls. If it doesn't have any, forget it. One, it's not too good. Two, better than average. Three is real good. But a *four*-calendar café, now that means something."

Jenny always enjoyed Dixon's rather wild thinking. She found him an attractive man, and now as he sat there entertaining her with his light patter, she was glad she had someone like him to trust.

"I've got a problem with Legs and Mattie, the jailer and his wife." She went on to explain how pitiful their work was. "I'd fire them in a minute. There's bound to be somebody who could do the work better than they do it, but Ruby and Billy have both warned me that they are some distant kin to Judge Hightower. They said Sheriff Beauchamp tried to fire them, and Hightower somehow put pressure on him. Isn't there something I can do, Luke?"

"Well, a dirty jail and bad meals might be less of a problem than locking horns with Hightower." Luke's green eyes grew thoughtful, and he sipped the tea, thinking hard. "Maybe you'd better hold off for a while."

"But they feed the inmates nothing but swill, and the place is filthy."

Luke listened as Jenny spoke passionately and finally said, "I knew you'd be running into things like this, but it's a little soon to take action on the Porters. Let me feel out the situation. Maybe there's a way I can help."

"Will you, Luke? That's sweet of you."

With a swift move, Jenny slapped at a fly that had lit on her cheek. To her surprise she hit it, and she uttered a disgusted, "Ugh!" then grabbed her napkin and began scrubbing at her cheek. "I've got to go wash my hands," she said. She went to the rest room, washed thoroughly, and then came back and sat down. "I wish I could kill every fly in this county, Luke."

"Why, the Lord made all those flies for some purpose, don't you suppose?"

"What purpose would a fly have, or a mosquito?"

"No idea," Luke said. At that moment the food came, and when Maisy left, Luke said, "Why don't you bless this food." The two bowed their heads, and Jenny asked a quick blessing, and when Jenny bit into the fried chicken, she said, "This is delicious!"

Luke had attacked one of the salmon croquettes first, and his eyes opened with surprise. "And this salmon croquette, why, it's the best I ever had! And look how fresh the vegetables look."

"I wonder who the cook is."

"A woman named Sadie, but she's outdone herself this time. You know," he went on, "that fly you killed. I've been thinking about it."

Jenny stared at him and then laughed. "Your mind's like a butterfly jumping around! What about that fly?"

"Did you know there's a religion in India called Jainism that practices what they call *ahimsa*. The whole religion is based on the idea that killing any living thing is wrong."

"You mean they can't kill a cow and eat it?"

"Certainly not! Why, they can't even burn candles or lights if there's danger a moth might fly into them. And they cover their mouth and nose with cloth masks so they won't inhale any gnats."

"You're making it all up."

"I am not! I read it in a book. It said the Jainists won't plow fields for fear of cutting up worms. They won't work as a carpenter because it might kill something."

"Must be a pretty hard life. I'd hate to do without fried chicken."

"Me either, but there's all kinds of peculiar things in the world. That's in a country where ten thousand humans die every year from snake bites, but they won't kill a snake."

"You know more useless stuff than any man I ever met," Jenny said. She went on listening to Luke as he regaled her, and then finally, when they had finished the cherry cobbler, which was excellent, they both rose. Jenny waited while Luke paid Maisy, and she said, "I'd like to give my compliments to the chef."

"Sure."

"All right if I step back and tell Sadie how good the food was?"

"Sadie's been off for a week now. Got a substitute. Go on back if you want to."

The two went through the swinging door, and as Jenny entered, she saw a huge man wearing tan trousers and a white shirt. When he turned, she exclaimed, "Why, Noah, it's you!"

"Hello, Sheriff." Noah Valentine grinned. "Good to see you."

"I didn't know you were a cook, Noah."

"I always done most of the cookin' for Mama for the kids, so when the job came up here I took it."

"Well, you did a fine job, Noah. I never had better fried chicken in my life, and that cobbler. Did you make that from scratch?"

"I even picked the cherries. Glad you liked it, Sheriff Winslow."

The two congratulated Noah warmly, and as they left the café, an idea began fermenting. "Why couldn't Noah be the jailer, Luke? Did you see that kitchen? It was clean as a pin. Why, you could eat off the floor."

"You'd have some problems there. Not just with the judge."

"What do you mean?"

"Well, Noah's got two strikes against him. He's black, and he's been in trouble with the law. You've got those two deputies, Arp and Pender, who hate him, and they'd all be under the same roof."

Jenny walked slowly down the sidewalk thinking on what Luke had said, and finally when they reached his office, she turned and said, "Thanks for the lunch."

He stared at her seriously. "I know what you're thinking, and my advice is, don't do it."

"I'm not thinking anything."

"Yes you are. You're thinking of firing that pair of incompetents and hiring Noah Valentine as jailer and cook."

"I didn't know you were a mind reader."

"You're not all that hard to read, Jenny. You've got that kind of face. I'm not saying it's not a good idea. As a matter of fact, it might be a great idea." He paused for a moment and said, "If you can face up to the judge on the small things, that might be better than getting hit with a big problem. If you decide to try it, I'll be with you. We might even get Raymond Dent to do a story on it. Human-interest stuff. How good it is to help men who have been in trouble to do honest work."

Jenny's eyes brightened, and she said, "I've got to start someplace. Sooner or later I'm going to lock horns with the judge, so I might as well get started. Thanks, Luke."

Luke Dixon watched Jennifer Winslow as she walked with determined strides toward the office. "I hope I told her the right thing," he said. "But that woman's got a streak of stubbornness in her that I didn't dream possible in any female that pretty."

* * *

Jenny took no action about replacing Legs and his wife. The one rule she had formulated before going into this office was to pray about everything. For two days she kept a close watch on the Porters and knew that nothing she could say would make them improve. She did not plan to talk to the judge, but she did talk to Maisy Hayes about her regular cook and discovered that Sadie would be back on the job at the beginning of the next week. "I've got that long to think about it. I may be making a bad mistake, but I've got to do something."

That was on Thursday. Jenny had spent almost all her time inside going over the books with Ruby and trying to learn the procedures, but she spoke to Billy that afternoon and said, "I want to get out some, Billy. I'll go with you on your run today."

"Fine, Sheriff! It's a good day for it. Nice and hot."

Indeed, the early July weather had been blisteringly hot. The Fourth, two days earlier, had been thoroughly celebrated, and as Billy drove her down the county roads, he said, "Not much happening. It seems like a holiday always takes the meanness out of people."

"Well, there were enough drunks in jail after the Fourth. Plenty of fines coming in. Maybe we can afford a raise for the deputies soon."

"I wouldn't count on it. The county commission has to approve all those things, and Judge Hightower's pretty tight with the nickel, at least as far as the sheriff's office is concerned."

"Tell me all about the politics of the county. Who do I need to be hard on? Who do I need to be careful of?" Jenny asked. Then she sat back, and as the two cruised slowly down the roads, stopping a speeder now and then and giving them a ticket, Luke went over the history and the personnel of the county. He knew everybody and everything as far as Jenny could tell, and she soaked it up, knowing she would need it. Finally he said, "The judge doesn't like to be challenged. He's got big ideas. Sooner or later you'll butt heads with him. Don't back down. He'll respect you if you stand up to him, but he'll give you a hard time."

They called back in periodically, and then at four o'clock, they got a report. Billy called and came back to the car, saying, "There's a fight at the Black Diamond." He got in the car and left with a screeching of tires.

"What's the Black Diamond?"

"It's a tavern, a saloon—whatever. It's against the law to sell liquor, but it's there all the time. Pretty bad fight from what Ruby said."

The Black Diamond was a wooden-framed structure denuded of all paint except long strips that hung destitute in the rays of the evening sun. Dilapidated cars and two wagons decorated the parking lot, and as they got out, Billy said, "This is going to be pretty rough. Let me handle any rough stuff. You can do the talking, though, Sheriff."

The two walked in through the door, and by the dim light

of the naked bulbs hanging from wires overhead, Jenny took in the scene. It was a large room with two doors that led to other parts of the building, perhaps bathrooms and dwelling quarters. Along one wall was a bar and behind it a cracked mirror. The walls were covered with pictures of bathing beauties, and there were almost a dozen men in the room and two or three women. One man was lying on the floor, his face bloody; another was sitting in a chair, his head back, apparently only half conscious. His features were battered, and he nursed one arm as if it were broken.

"What's goin' on, Tal?"

Tal Holbert, the owner of the Black Diamond, shrugged his beefy shoulders. "Nothin' much, Billy. Just a little brawl." He appeared nervous, and he turned to look at three big men all wearing overalls and whose faces were scarred with signs of battle.

Billy Moon said, "Sheriff, this is Bart Cundiff. These are his boys Perry and Ace. Fellas, this is Sheriff Winslow." Jenny recognized the men as the squatters who had been living in their house when they had first arrived in Georgia. They were crude, filthy people, and only the threat of Clint's shotgun had persuaded them to leave. Swearing and grumbling, they had left, leaving a reeking mess behind them. Jenny remembered the Cundiffs only too well, but they didn't seem to remember her, at least not at the moment.

The three men were obviously drunk, and they all looked dangerous. Jenny had absolutely no idea what to do, but she stepped forward and said, "You three will have to come with us. You're under arrest. We'll take these other two to the doctor."

"I ain't bein' arrested by no woman," Bart Cundiff said. He was a hulking man with green eyes and unkempt hair, and his sons bore him a strong resemblance.

Moon stepped up beside her and removed his nightstick from his belt. He tapped it into his palm, saying, "You're going in one way or another, Bart. Easy or hard. Your choice."

Jenny knew a cold touch of fear as Cundiff's wild eyes stared at her, but she determined to show nothing. "Come along," she said. She walked up and took Cundiff by the arm, intending to lead him from the room. She never saw the blow he threw at her. All she knew was that something struck her in the side of the face, and she remembered falling, but she did not feel the floor when she struck it.

Consciousness came back, and she found herself sitting in a chair. Moon was kneeling beside her with a damp cloth in his hand. "Take it easy now, Jenny. You're gonna be all right."

A terrible pain struck Jenny, and she reached up and touched her eye.

"You're gonna have a wicked shiner there, boss."

Memory came flooding back, and she looked at Billy's bronzed face and then shifted to see that the room was empty now, except for the three Cundiffs. They were all wearing cuffs, and Bart Cundiff was bleeding over one eyebrow. Then she turned back to Billy and saw that his lip was swollen, and he had a bruise on his left cheek. She whispered, "Thank you, Billy."

He leaned forward and whispered, "Be tough, boss. Tell 'em they're goin' where the sun won't shine on 'em."

Jenny got up and, ignoring the pain, said, "You three are goin' where the sun won't shine on you! Now, get out in that car!" She pulled the nightstick from her belt and stepped forward, and Ace Cundiff flinched as she lifted it. "All right—all right, we're goin'! You don't hafta hit me again!"

The three were herded out and crammed into the backseat. "You drive, Sheriff, and I'll keep an eye on these bad characters."

Jenny drove back to the jail, where the three were booked and put in cells, all three protesting loudly.

"They'll pay their fines and get out tomorrow. We really don't have anything on 'em, Sheriff," Moon said. "Did me good to bust their heads a little bit, though." He leaned forward and examined her. "You'd better get somethin' cold on that or you're gonna have a whale of a shiner. Gonna be all kinds of people askin' you what happened. Tell them you busted all three of the Cundiffs. It'll make you into a hero!"

★ ★ ★

When Jenny eased out of bed the next morning, she still had a headache. She went to the mirror and saw that the bruise was a glorious mixture of black and purple and green and yellow. *I didn't know skin could turn so many colors,* she thought. She considered putting a bandage over the eye, which was half shut, but stubbornly determined she would wear it like a badge of honor. When she went downstairs, Kat took one look at Jenny's face and said, "You look awful, Jenny."

Jenny tried to smile. "I think it looks worse than it really is."

"Well, you sure do *look* awful," Kat repeated.

"We're not going to talk about that at the table," Lewis said quickly.

"Why not?" Kat protested. "You're always saying the family needs to talk things over. Well, that's what I'm trying to do."

Jenny said quickly, "It was part of my job. Billy Moon and I got involved with some men who had been drinking."

Kat, in her usual straightforward manner, demanded the rest of the story, and Jenny told it.

"Did you shoot any of 'em?" Kat asked, grinning.

"No."

"I should have been there," Clint said, shaking his head remorsefully.

"Billy took care of them pretty well."

"Moon's a tough fellow and a good guy," Clint said.

"Did Billy shoot 'em?" Kat asked.

"No, he didn't," Lewis spoke up loudly, "and that's enough talk about that."

Lewis said little after that, but when he walked Jenny out to the car, he put his arm around her. "I'm worried about you. This job is dangerous."

"Not as long as I have Billy with me. Don't worry, Dad. I'll be all right."

She got into the car and drove down to the jail, and as soon as she went in, she found Billy and Ruby talking together. Moon said, "Well, the Cundiffs are out already."

"How'd they get out so quick?"

"Max Conroy came by and paid their fines. He claims they're workin' for him on the road crew."

"It'll be the first honest work they ever did," Ruby said. "That's an awful-lookin' eye you got there. Why don't you take the day off?"

"No, I don't . . ." She turned and fell silent as Judge Hightower came in. He walked over to her and nodded pleasantly. "Good morning, Sheriff. How are you, Billy and Ruby?"

They all responded to the judge, and finally he said, "I heard about the fight. Good thing you were there, Billy."

"Yes, it was," Jenny said shortly. She knew the judge had implied that she would not have been able to handle the Cundiffs on her own, and worse than that, she knew he was right.

"Come back to my office, Judge."

She led the judge back to the tiny cubicle, no more than ten feet square, with room enough only for a desk and a filing cabinet and two chairs. The judge sat down and said, "I came by to talk to you about Harold Porter and Mattie. They're distant relatives of mine, you know."

"So I understand, Judge."

"They're not top-drawer material, but I'm going to have a talk with them and see that they do their work better."

"That won't be necessary, Judge."

Hightower lifted his eyebrows. "Oh, you've already talked to them?"

"I'm firing them."

Surprising Judge Dwight Hightower was not an easy thing to do, but Jenny saw that she had succeeded. A slight shock registered in his eyes, but he covered it quickly and regarded her intently. He was a handsome man filled with determination and had a reputation for being absolutely ruthless when it came to getting his own way.

"I'm sorry to hear that, Sheriff. I think you're making a mistake."

"Would you care to have lunch with us today? You'd get to sample some of their cooking."

"You won't reconsider?"

"No, I won't," Jenny said firmly. "They're a drain on the taxpayer, and I've already decided on the new jailer."

"And who might that be?"

"Noah Valentine."

Once again Jenny saw with pleasure that she had shaken the judge. "Well, you may have a little problem there."

"I don't think so, Judge. He's a good man, a fine cook, and he knows how to clean a place."

For a moment it seemed as though Hightower would allow anger to get the best of him, and Jenny hoped that he would. His face grew flushed, and his lips grew tight, and she saw the anger dancing in his eyes. She was disappointed when he looked down for a moment and then looked up and smiled pleasantly. "Well, you're the sheriff. It's your decision." He rose and started for the door. When he reached it, he turned and said, "Oh, by the way. We're having a commissioners' meeting tonight. I'm afraid it's going to be necessary to cut your budget a little."

"Unless I keep the Porters on?"

"Why, there's no connection." Hightower smiled pleasantly. "You and I ought to get along together, Sheriff. We don't need dissension in county government. Think about it." He turned and left, and Jenny felt a tinge of cold anger such as she had rarely felt. She knew there was evil in this man, and she knew that he was going to do everything in his power to hurt her. But she refused to give in to his threats.

The sun was setting by the time Jenny reached her favorite spot in the woods near the secluded bend of the river. She was hot and sweaty, and the thought of a swim seemed enticing. Without stopping to consider it, she took the trail that led deep into the timber. The road was an old logging road, but since the country had been logged out, the weeds had grown up again. When she pulled up within fifteen feet of the shallow part of the river that formed an excellent swimming hole, she shut the engine off and sat for a moment, just enjoying the silence. Getting out of the car then, she reached into the backseat and pulled out the paper bag. She had promised Kat to take her swimming the previous day but had not been able to do it because of the affair with the Cundiffs. Now she fished out her swimming suit, changed quickly, and simply draped her clothes over the hood of the car. She followed the small, narrow path to the river's edge. The river had a sandy bottom at this point, and she waded out, then settled down. The water was deliciously cool, and she put her head under and swam strongly out away from the shore. The river's bend formed a small bay, and for a time she simply floated, enjoying the silence as the sun went down. The moon was becoming visible, and she stared up at the silver orb, thinking about the day and mostly about the threat of Judge Dwight Hightower.

She was suddenly alarmed when she heard the sound of a car. It was coming close, and fear ran through her. Her first thought, as irrational as it was, was of the Cundiffs or someone like them. Quickly, with strong strokes, she swam toward the bank. As she waded out of the water, car lights came on and she moved quickly toward the unfamiliar vehicle, not knowing who she might find.

As Jenny emerged from the path into the open spot, she was blinded by a flashing light. A voice cried out, "That was a great shot, Sheriff! Be sure you get a copy of *The Daily Standard*. You'll be on the front page tomorrow."

Jenny was almost totally blinded by what she knew was a flashbulb. Several more flashes went off, and there was the sound of raucous male laughter and crude remarks. Then she heard another car start up and recognized it as her squad car. She had time only to see the dust rise as the squad car pulled away. She cried out futilely, "Come back!" but both cars were gone. She heard them as they reached the highway and turned and then the sound faded.

Standing there in the darkness, Jennifer Winslow had never felt so vulnerable. She looked around, hoping her clothes were left, but the vandals had taken them too. Her mind began to function, and she thought, *They followed me from town. I don't know what for, but they got pictures of me—and they stole the car. It'll be all over the county tomorrow.*

The moon shone down on Jenny, and she suddenly felt tears well up in her eyes. She wanted to cry and wail out loud, but fiercely she rubbed the heels of her hands into her eyes and then settled down. "They won't beat me! I won't let them!" She lifted her head, pressed the water out of her hair, and started walking. It was in her mind to walk all the way home, a distance of five miles at least, but as she reached the highway she saw lights on the other side and realized it was Clay Varek's house. Humiliation filled her, but she knew she had to have help. The highway was empty, no cars were coming, so she walked down the side road.

When she got near to the house, she stood in the shadows of the yard and called out, "Clay! Clay Varek!"

Almost at once Clay opened the front door. She could make him out in the bright moonlight, pistol in hand. "Who's there?"

"It's me, Jenny Winslow."

He stepped out onto the front porch and started down the stairs toward her. Jenny said, "I need help, Clay. Can you get me a blanket, please?"

Clay Varek stopped, stared at her, then said, "Come on in." He turned back toward the house and entered ahead of her, and by the time she reached the door he was there with a blanket. She wrapped it around herself, and he said, "Come on in. Jamie's asleep."

He led her into the kitchen, pulled out a chair for her, and poured her a cup of coffee. He did not ask a single question until he brought the coffee and said, "You want sugar?"

"No, just black is fine." Her hands were unsteady, and she could not conceal it. Then she looked up, the misery clearly written on her face. "I stopped for a swim, Clay. It was so hot, and while I was there a car drove up. When I got out of the water, someone took pictures of me. A man called out to me that they'd be in *The Daily Standard*." Jenny recognized the name of the competing newspaper from a nearby township.

"Did you recognize their voices?"

"No, but they must have followed me. Nobody could find that swimming hole accidentally—especially when it was almost dark."

Clay poured himself a cup of coffee and sat down. He did not look at her directly but stared down into the cup, swirling the black liquid. "Well, it's come quicker than I thought."

"What, Clay?"

Varek lifted his eyes. "I knew Max Conroy and his crowd

wouldn't let it alone. Obviously they've been following you, and that rag *The Daily Standard* will print anything."

"I'll have to resign."

"No, you won't."

Jenny stared at him. "But what can I do?"

"You just keep on. You've got enemies, and now you know it. But don't quit. That would be a mistake." He got up suddenly and said, "I'll get you some of my clothes. They'll be too big, but better than that wet suit."

Fifteen minutes later, Jenny, wearing Varek's old clothes, sat in the front seat of his car holding Jamie. The child had awakened but had gone back to sleep again when they had gotten into the car.

As they drove along, Clay said, "You'll have to put out a call about your car. It's not going to look good."

"No, I'll look like an utter fool—which I am!"

"You're not a fool, Jenny. You're just not used to dealing with scum. Don't let them run you off. You told me once you thought God put you in this place. Well, if God put you there, He can keep you there."

Jenny did not speak. In her misery, the warmth of Clay's words soothed her. She looked over to him and held the child tightly to her breast. "Thank you, Clay," she whispered.

CHAPTER NINE

THE FRONT PAGE

★ ★ ★

Lying flat on her back, Jenny stared up at the ceiling. The first gray lights of dawn filtered through her window, throwing a ghostly illumination over the high ceiling. Putting her hands up over her head and locking her arms together, she discovered that she was stiff and tense—as she had been most of the night. Her sleep had been broken by fantastic dreams almost like visions, and as she lay there trying to relax, she went over and over the events of the previous night. They seemed to come involuntarily, and she could not help watching them in her mind's eye.

Suddenly she sat up and threw her legs over the side of the bed. She stared across the room but without seeing the gaily-colored wallpaper she had labored so hard to paste up. From somewhere far away came the mournful sound of a dog howling, as if to announce the coming of the new day—and on the heels of that, a rooster announcing that the night was over. "Get up—get up!" his crowing seemed to say. It was a sound Jenny ordinarily loved, but now she hardly noticed it. She tried to pray but discovered it was one of those times that the heavens seemed to be made of brass.

Getting slowly out of bed, she turned on the lamp,

blinking at the brightness of the light, then looked up into the mirror. She had forgotten how terrible a black eye could look, and now she saw that the flesh surrounding her eye was still a rainbow coalition of red, orange, sickly yellow, and brilliant purple. Tenderly she touched it, winced, then resolutely turned away.

Dressing quickly, she sat down, pulled out her Bible, and began to read. She was reading through the Old Testament and had reached the Third Psalm. Her lips moved as she whispered the words aloud:

> "Lord, how are they increased that trouble me! Many are they that rise up against me.
> Many there be which say of my soul, there is no help for him in God."

She closed her eyes and tried to frame some sort of petition but was overwhelmed with a sense of self-pity. She shook her head angrily, muttering "This won't do!" She began to read again and slowly the words began to sink into her spirit:

> "But thou, O Lord, art a shield for me; my glory, and the lifter up of mine head.
> I cried unto the Lord with my voice, and he heard me out of his holy hill.
> I laid me down and slept—"

Suddenly Jenny felt the presence of the Lord in the room. She remembered the setting of the psalm, how David's son Absalom, the dearest child he had, had raised a rebellion and was determined to kill his father. With a broken heart David had begun the psalm, but Jenny read again verse five: "I laid me down and slept . . ."

For a long time she sat there, her head bowed, thinking and meditating on the ancient king with his heart broken— yet he laid down and slept. She closed the Bible and prayed, "Lord, you'll have to take care of me. Just let me make it through this day. In Jesus' name."

She rose, picked up her hat, then noticed Clay's clothes she had worn the previous evening. Quickly she gathered them together, found a paper sack, and put them inside.

She went downstairs quickly and heard the sound of voices in the dining room. She hesitated for only a moment, dreading to go in but knowing that she had to. Putting the sack down in the hall, she went inside, and everyone turned to her. "Good morning," she said brightly. "Sorry to be late."

"We're just ready to start eating, daughter," Missouri said. She had one of the babies tucked under her arm. Jenny could not tell which one, for they were as alike as three coins. She went over and kissed the baby, who drooled at her and grinned toothlessly. "Which one is this one?"

"This is Temple."

Jenny sat down and noted that Hannah was holding one of the triplets and her father another. Lewis bowed his head, and they all followed suit. After he asked the blessing and they began eating, Jenny was very much aware that everyone was quiet, trying not to look at her, but exchanging concerned looks among themselves. Missouri sat down and applied herself to the food, which included fried eggs, fried ham, biscuits, and red-eye gravy with blackberry and plum jam to sweeten it up. "The revival's going to start next week," Missouri said. "I've heard a lot about that evangelist. I want us all to go every night."

Kat turned to Jenny and blurted out, "I can't believe you let some fellers steal your car. Did you shoot at 'em? Or didn't ya wanna shoot at your own car?"

"I wasn't exactly wearing my holster at the time."

"Did the guy taking the pictures steal it? Or was it someone with him?"

"I don't know."

"Leave your sister be, Kat," Lewis commanded in a quiet but firm voice.

Clint said, "I'll run you into your office this morning after breakfast."

"Thank you, Clint."

The meal proceeded, but suddenly the sound of a car pulling up attracted their attention. Kat got up and raced to the window. "It's Billy Moon in your car."

Kat ran to open the door, and Moon entered the dining room. As usual he was immaculately dressed. He was a strong-looking, powerful man, and his shirt fit him like a second skin. "We found the car. It was abandoned. No harm done to it. I thought you might need a ride in."

"Thanks, Billy. That's a relief. I was afraid they'd trash it."

Billy had a newspaper in his hand, and he tapped it against his leg. Jenny knew instantly what it was. "Is that *The Standard*?"

"I thought you might like to see it. It's pretty bad."

"Let me see it." Jenny took the paper, opened it, and saw an enlarged picture of herself. She was wearing her one-piece white bathing suit and was staring directly into the camera. Her hair was wet and down, and she looked as startled as a deer.

"What does it say, Jenny? Read it to us," Kat demanded.

"No, I don't think so." Jenny skimmed the story and then handed it over to Lewis. "Come on, Billy. I'm through here." She left the room, and as soon as the car started up, Lewis began to read the story. The picture itself was not bad, but the headline said, "Yankee Sheriff Fighting Crime." Al Deighton, the editor of *The Daily Standard* was close to Judge Hightower and a poker-playing friend of Max Conroy, the ex-sheriff.

"Is it bad, Lewis?"

"It's bad enough." He looked around and then shrugged. "You'll all read it anyhow. 'The county sheriff, Jennifer Winslow, has begun her career as a law-enforcement officer by taking swims in the river. This paper would have thought that there was plenty to do to keep a law-enforcement official busy, but apparently Sheriff Winslow is a lady of leisure. Of course, the sheriff is a New Yorker, and no doubt there the enforcement of the law is quite different from this part of the world.'"

Lewis read on and finally threw the paper down. "It's malicious and cruel and stupid!"

"It'll pass away," Missouri said, coming over to lay her hand on Lewis's shoulder.

Clint said, "I might pay that editor a little visit."

"No, you stay out of it," Hannah said quickly. "You're not supposed to take up the offenses of others."

"That's right," Missouri said. She moved the baby to her

other arm and said quietly, "The Bible says we're to pray for those that despitefully use us. When we do that, it puts coals of fire on their head."

Kat's eyes opened. "Well, then, I'll pray for that old newspaper guy, and I hope the coals burn his brains out!"

★ ★ ★

Merle Arp and Arlie Pender had derived a great deal of satisfaction out of the story on the front page of *The Daily Standard*. They read it aloud in the sheriff's office to Ruby French, who retorted angrily, "I don't think that's funny!"

"You don't? Well, look at this picture. Say, the sheriff's got a pretty nice-lookin' body on her there."

Arlie Pender laughed shrilly. "Ain't many sheriffs look that good in a bathing suit."

"She won't be able to stay around after this," Merle Arp said. He feasted his eyes on the picture and laughed coarsely. "The quicker she's gone the better."

Both deputies turned as the door opened, and Jenny walked through it with Billy Moon at her side. "Mornin', Sheriff." Pender grinned and made no attempt to hide the paper in his hand.

Jenny came to stand before him and knew she had to challenge him. "Did you check out the report on that still on the Donaldson place?"

Pender cast a quick glance at Merle Arp and spoke up. "Wasn't anything there, Sheriff."

"How do you know?" Jenny said, and her eyes were cold as polar ice.

"Why, we looked everywhere, and we couldn't find it."

"The mileage on your car shows you drove twelve miles yesterday. It's sixteen miles to the Donaldson place. My arithmetic tells me that's thirty-two miles at least."

Arp's mouth dropped opened, and then he said quickly, "Well, we used my car."

"To save the county gas money?" Moon said. "First time I ever heard of you doin' a thing like that."

The two deputies could not meet the eyes of Jenny or Moon, and Jenny said, "I told you the first day I came here we were starting over—that nothing in the past counted. But you don't seem to want that. If you two can't do your jobs, I'll find somebody else who can. Now, get out of here. Billy, give them something to do and see that they do it."

Both Arp and Pender gave her poisonous glances, but they left without saying another word.

After they left, Ruby said, "Good for you, Sheriff. Those two are worthless." Then she said, "I got a phone call this morning. The meeting of the finance committee was bad news. They cut our budget by ten percent." She shook her head, a worried look in her eyes. "I don't know how we're going to make those cuts, Jenny. We're working on a razor's edge now."

Jenny stood there for one moment. She felt humiliated, yet there was a flash of anger in her eyes as she said, "I know where we can cut. We're paying two salaries, one to Legs and one to Mattie. I can cut that in two and hire one person."

"Be careful. You'll make an enemy of the judge."

"He's already my enemy. This won't change anything."

★　★　★

Noah was humming to himself as he mended the fence that ran around the chicken yard. From time to time the chickens would gather, and he would say, "Shoo away, you chickens! You go get fat so I can have you for supper."

The sound of a car caught his attention, and he turned to see the sheriff's car pull up. At once a worried frown wrinkled his forehead, but then he saw Jennifer Winslow get out. He went to meet her at once. "Good mornin', Miss Jenny. You're out early this mornin'."

"Doing a little fence mending, Noah?"

"Yes, ma'am, I am. A fox done got into this and et two of our chickens last night."

"Noah, I want you to come to work for the sheriff's office."

If Jenny had announced to Noah that she wanted him to

jump over the house, Noah could not have been more surprised. He doubted his own hearing for a moment, and he said, "You can't mean that, Sheriff!"

"Yes, I do. Are you still working at the Elite Café?"

"No, ma'am, the cook, she came back yesterday."

"Then you don't have any job right now."

"No, ma'am, just part-time things I get when I can."

"All right, you're the new jailer. You'll be taking the places of two people, and you'll have to do the work of two people." She named the salary and saw his eyes open wide. "Will you do it?"

"You shore you want me to do this, Miss Jenny?" And suddenly he smiled. "Ain't you noticed that I'm black?"

"I noticed that. What about it?"

"For a black man to take white folks' jobs, it ain't gonna set well."

"You just be on the job early tomorrow morning, and I'll take care of any trouble. Your job will be to clean up the jail and the sheriff's office and to cook."

"I'll do my best, Miss Jenny, I shorely will!"

"Good! I'll see you tomorrow."

★ ★ ★

Raymond Dent had been rousted out of his office by Jennifer Winslow. She had insisted he bring his camera, and when they went into the jail he said, "Why did you want me to bring my camera?"

"I want you to take pictures of this horrible mess." At that moment Legs and Mattie came down the hall, and Jenny said, "You two are fired. Have your things cleared out of here in an hour. You can pick up your check from Ruby."

Legs stared at her. "You can't fire us. We're kin to the judge!"

"The judge is not running this office! I am! You heard what I said. Mr. Dent, start taking pictures."

Dent listened as the two screamed obscenities at Jennifer Winslow, but finally she cut them off and told them if they needed help to get out, she would call Billy Moon.

Dent watched the couple disappear, both cursing violently. He turned back to Jenny and said, "You're not going to win the judge's favor."

"That's what everybody says."

"Who are you going to get to be the new jailer?"

"I've already got him. It's Noah Valentine."

Dent's eyes opened wide, and he laughed. "Well, I'll say this for you, Sheriff Jennifer Winslow, there's never a dull moment around the sheriff's office when you're in charge." He laughed and said, "Let me get some pictures of this hog wallow."

CHAPTER TEN

HUMMINGBIRD CAKE

★ ★ ★

The oil lamp sitting on the table beside the mirror cast a golden corona over the features of Noah Valentine. Carefully he drew the straight razor down the side of his cheek, wiped it against a towel to remove the shaving cream, then folded the razor and placed it carefully in the paper sack along with a few other small items. A thoughtfulness came to the big man then as he stared into the mirror, and he shook his head as if in doubt. *Don't know if this is gonna work. I just don't know.* Pushing the thought away, he picked up the paper sack, walked over and placed it into a larger bag, which contained his clothes. Taking one look around the small room, he hesitated, then said quietly, "Lord, if this thing works out, you gotta get involved in it, 'cause you know how folks are."

Passing through the door, he stepped into the largest room of the house—combination kitchen, dining room, and living area. His glance ran over the youngsters sitting around the table, who all turned to look at him as he entered. He walked over to his mother and kissed her on the cheek. "Breakfast smells good, Mama."

"You set down and eat."

"I don't reckon I'll have time. The sheriff said for me to be there a little bit early so she could show me around."

"You gonna be a policeman?"

Noah turned and looked at the bright-eyed girl with skin like chocolate who was staring at him with enormous eyes. Noah shook his head and laughed shortly. "No, Euphonia, I ain't gonna be *in* the jail. I'll be taking care of the people what is, cooking for 'em and stuff like that."

"You sit down and have a cup of coffee," Hattie Valentine said. "You got time for that."

Noah took his seat and looked around at the four children, ranging in age from six to fourteen. He gave thanks quickly for the help he had been able to give his mother. Since the death of George Valentine, it had been Noah who had been the strong right arm of his mother, Hattie. Now as she hovered over him, touching him once on the shoulder as if to reassure herself somehow, he knew she was troubled. Finishing the coffee, he rose from the table and picked up his sack. "You chil'uns be good and mind Mama, you hear me?" He nodded at the chorus of agreement, then walked outside. His mother followed him, and when he turned he saw the fear in her eyes. "You worried about this, ain't you, Mama?"

"Yes, I am."

"It's gonna be all right. You done met Miss Winslow. You knows what a good woman she is. She doin' this to help us as much as to help herself. She got a hard job, Mama. You gotta pray for her. Both of us do every day."

"But people ain't gonna like it hiring a black man to take white folks' place."

"That's probably so," Noah said calmly. He reached out, pulled her forward, and held her tightly. She seemed very small and frail against his massive strength, and he whispered, "It's gonna be all right. The good Lord will be with us." He straightened up, stepped back, and said, "I'll be gettin' a regular salary now, so we'll be able to buy the young'uns clothes, and I'll be bringin' groceries out every Saturday. If you need anything, you let me know, you hear, Mama?"

"I hear."

Noah smiled briefly, then turned and left. He plunged down the road, and as he walked rapidly toward town, some of the trouble he saw in his mother seemed to descend upon him. It was not going to be easy, this job that had come to him seemingly out of heaven. He thought back over his life and, as always, wished that he had been a better man, but then he shook his head and said aloud, "Lord, I done repented of all my past sins. You said they are buried in the sea as far as the east is from the west. So, Lord, you will just have to look out for me, 'cause I ain't got nobody else who will." He walked rapidly for a hundred paces and then added, "Except for Sheriff Winslow. Lord, that is a good woman, but she is in for big trouble. So I'm askin' you to take care of her. Bless her in every way, for she needs all the help she can get."

Five minutes after Noah prayed, a truck came along, and when it stopped Jesse Cannon stuck his head out. "You goin' to town, Noah?"

"Yes, sir, Mr. Cannon, I is."

"Get in. It's a long walk."

"Thank you, suh." Noah opened the door, got in, and the truck sagged with his weight. "Appreciate the ride, Mr. Cannon."

"No charge, Noah. How's your family?" he asked as he put the truck into motion again.

"Mighty fine, suh."

Jesse Cannon was a tall, lean man with silver hair. He was a Civil War veteran, but his eyes were still clear, and he had the strength that some old men have late in life. "I heard about your new job. Think you'll like it?"

"I 'spect I will, Mr. Cannon." Noah turned and studied the features of the old man, who had always been kind to him. "Miss Winslow's mighty nice takin' care of me like this."

"Fine woman. Comes from a fine family."

The two talked amiably for, indeed, Jesse Cannon and his wife, Dolly, were two people with white skin whom Noah trusted implicitly. He felt comfortable and spoke his heart to Cannon until they pulled up in front of the jail. Noah got out, picked up his sack, and nodded. "I thank you, suh, for the ride. It was mighty nice."

"You're welcome. Hope it goes well, Noah."

Noah Valentine turned and walked up the steps leading

into the county offices. His eyes picked up Merle Arp, who stood just outside the door watching him. Arp's hat was pulled down over his brow, and his eyes gleamed balefully.

"Morning, Deputy Arp."

"You're makin' a mistake, nigger." Arp's mouth twisted in a sneer. "You won't last long. You might as well quit. Turn around and go back right now."

Noah had lived in a white man's world for all of his life. He had learned to put on a completely blank mask when cursed by white men, and he did so now. Without another word he passed in through the door, leaving Arp glaring after him. He turned once to his right, and as he entered the sheriff's office, he saw the sheriff behind the long desk working with Ruby French.

"Mornin', Sheriff."

"Noah, you're here early."

"Yes, ma'am. I guess I am a little bit."

"Well, that's fine. Come along. We'll go over your duties."

Noah followed Jenny Winslow as she stepped into the corridor, and then the two of them passed into the living quarters.

"Oh no!"

Noah came to stand beside Jenny and looked around. The room looked as if a tornado had swept through it. Trash was everywhere. The bedclothes were scattered. In the kitchen filthy dishes were scattered across the cabinets, and Noah stood there silently.

"They did this deliberately!" Jenny exclaimed.

"Don't you worry, Sheriff. I can clean it up."

The two moved into the pantry, and a quick examination revealed that the Porters had taken every item of food except for what they had emptied and strewn on the floor.

"You'll have to start all over again with the groceries, Noah. Look, go down to the general store and get what you need to make breakfast for the inmates. Come back as quick as you can, cook something up, and feed them. Mr. Huntington knows you'll be coming, so he'll charge it for you."

Jenny shook her head in disgust. She reached to her belt

and removed a ring full of keys and handed them to Noah. "Here are all the keys you'll need, Noah. You can figure which ones fit the locks."

Noah reached out slowly and took the keys. Somehow he felt a fear that he could not keep bottled. He held the keys in his huge hand, staring at them as if they had some strange power. For a black man to have the authority over white men was unheard of in this part of the world. He looked up, met Jenny's eyes, and saw she was watching him intently. The two stood there silently, almost like two different species outwardly—Noah over six feet, six inches tall, weighing two hundred sixty pounds, his skin black as ebony, and Jennifer Winslow a foot shorter, with red hair and creamy complexion. She had known money, wealth, and influence, and Noah had known nothing but poverty and hard times. Still, they were both struggling to fit into a white *man's* world, and this connected the two somehow. Jenny suddenly reached up to pat Noah's shoulder. "Don't you worry," she said quietly. "It's going to be fine."

Noah blinked, then summoned up a smile. "I'll do my very best for you, Sheriff. You see if I don't! I'll go fetch them groceries now."

★ ★ ★

As Noah entered the Huntington General Store, he saw the owner standing beside the meat counter. Huntington was a tall man of forty, thin with hazel eyes and blond hair. Noah went at once to stand before him. Looking down, he said, "The sheriff, she axed me to pick up a few groceries, Mr. Huntington. I'se the new jailer."

"I heard about it, Noah. Well, you're all cleared. Take what you want, and I'll write it down for you."

"Thank you, suh. I'll just get a few things now to fix breakfast with, then I'll come back and stock up."

Noah moved quickly down the aisle to collect a few items: two dozen eggs, three pounds of bacon, bread, butter, salt and pepper. Huntington wrote it up and put the items in a sack.

"Where'd you learn how to cook, Noah?"

"My mama taught me, I reckon. When my daddy died, me and Mama had to make out as best we could. She was sick a lot, so I had to be cook and everything else."

"Well, I think you'll do a better job than what the prisoners have been used to. Good luck to you."

"Thank you, Mistuh Huntington. I'll be back right soon."

Noah returned to the jail and quickly prepared breakfast. Putting it on trays, he ascended the stairs and unlocked the steel door. When he went inside he had a moment's hesitation but then shook it away. "Breakfast time!" he called. As he walked down the hall toward the rec room, he saw the prisoners all staring at him. "I's the new jailer. My name's Noah Valentine. Let me set this down, then you'uns kin eat."

Noah quickly set the tray down, then went to unlock all the doors. There were seven male prisoners and three female, and when they filed into the dining area, Noah was aware of their scrutiny. He had become an expert in studying people's faces, and two of the male prisoners were staring at him with naked antagonism in their eyes. He thought, *They don't like black people, but I bet they'll like some good food.*

"Didn't have time to fix a lot, but there's plenty of scrambled eggs and bacon and toast with jam."

"How come we have to have a nigger jailer?" The speaker was a small, rat-faced man, who had not shaved in at least a week. He glared at Noah, his fists tightened and his back stiff as a board.

"That's just the way it is," Noah said quietly. "I'll do the best I kin to feed you right and to keep this place clean."

"Aw, Fred, you'd complain if they hung you with a new well rope!" Jimmy Duo laughed and nodded at Noah. "That smells mighty good, Noah. Let's have it."

The prisoners all took their plates and passed by, loading them down with the bacon and eggs. Noah had put the toast on a big platter, and the slices disappeared quickly. "I'll be makin' biscuits in the mornin'," Noah said. "I'll go down and fetch the coffee."

As he left, Noah heard the murmur of voices, some protesting and others pleased. Going downstairs, he simply picked up the huge coffee urn by the two handles and walked back upstairs with it. He filled the cups and passed them out to the inmates, making the sugar and condensed milk available to them. When they were all eating, he ran his eyes around the faces of the prisoners. It was a sad sight to him. Since he had been in jail himself, he knew the hopelessness that could exist there.

"Hey, these eggs are cooked good!"

Jimmy Duo was the speaker, and he raised his fork in a gesture of triumph. "It's great to have a hot meal for once."

"It *is* good," one of the women said. She had a hard face and stared at Noah for a moment, as if weighing him, then nodded. "I hope you can cook something besides bacon and eggs."

"I'll do my best, ma'am," Noah said.

Finally, when the meal was over, Noah looked over the group, who sat there drinking coffee, several of them still munching on the buttered toast layered with blackberry jam. "It's my job to clean dis place too," Noah said, his eyes running around to meet the faces that were watching him intently. "It's my job to clean it, but it be real nice if you folks would help me keep it clean."

"I ain't doin' none of your work!"

Jimmy Duo said, "Oh, shut up, Fred! I'll help Noah. Since this is just about my home full-time, I want to keep it nice. We'll start out on them bathrooms. They ain't been cleaned since Adam was born."

Noah said, "We do that as soon as I take care of these dishes, and I 'spect your sheets need launderin', don't they?"

"They ain't been washed in a coon's age," a short, fat man with a round, red face said. "And the bugs are terrible."

Noah said quietly, "I'm right sorry you have to be here. Some of you knows I've been in jail myself. I knows whut it's like. I'll do the bes' I can to make it as good as it can be."

When Noah left, Jimmy Duo said with satisfaction, "Well, if he can cook dinner and supper as good as he can breakfast, we're gonna be all right."

The inmate named Fred opened his mouth. "I don't want no—"

"Shut up, Fred!" Jimmy said amiably. "The worst part of bein' in this jail is listenin' to your gripin'. We got a good thing here. Now, you just keep your mouth shut!"

★ ★ ★

The clock in the tower of the city hall spoke with a metallic voice, rapping out five strokes. Judge Dwight Hightower pulled his watch from his vest pocket, stared at it for a moment, then said, "Clock's four minutes late." Snapping the face of the watch shut, he replaced it, then continued his walk down Main Street. He spoke to everyone he passed, and when he got to the county jail, the building that housed the sheriff's office, he hesitated for a moment.

A cold anger had been seething in him ever since Jennifer Winslow had fired the Porters. In all truth, Judge Hightower despised the Porters. They were an embarrassment to him, nothing but white trash, dishonest and dirty and lazy. But their jobs in the county as jailers had kept them from pestering him for handouts, and now that was over. He had found work for them in a small town twenty miles away, but he had been forced to offer a favor to one of the politicians there. He hated to be under any obligation to other politicians, and now as he stared at the door that read SHERIFF, he shook off those thoughts and opened the door. Inside he found Billy Moon and Jennifer Winslow in a conversation, which broke off as soon as he entered. "I don't mean to interrupt, Sheriff."

"It's all right, Judge. Come into my office and sit down."

"Hello, Deputy Moon."

"Good afternoon, Judge," Billy Moon said, his tone cold. No doubt Moon knew he and Max Conroy had planned to get rid of him as quickly as possible. Moon stared at him expressionlessly and then nodded at Jenny. "I'll talk to you later, Sheriff."

"All right, Deputy."

The sheriff examined Hightower with a bland expression. "Glad to have you come around for a visit, Judge."

Hightower studied the young woman before him. He had

been quite a ladies' man in his youth and still had an eye for an attractive woman. He had also become a keen judge of character, and as he took her in, he saw innocence but also a great deal of stubbornness.

"I'm sorry we had to cut the budget for your department, Sheriff, but we had to cut somewhere."

Jenny smiled and said, "Oh, don't worry about it, Judge. As a matter of fact, I've been talking to some of the other members of the council—especially the commissioner. I believe he's had some second thoughts about the budget cuts. He says the action will be reversed if he can swing it."

A fresh anger coursed through Hightower, for he knew that Trevor Gaines swung considerable influence. Nevertheless, he smiled as if highly pleased. "Well, that's good, Sheriff."

"I'm sure you'll support him, won't you?"

"Why, yes, of course." Hightower was angry, but he never let such things show.

"Maybe you'd like to see the changes we've made in the jail."

"Of course."

Hightower followed Jenny into the jailer's quarters, and she said, "We've completely redecorated it. It needed it pretty badly."

The judge had seen his relatives' quarters before, and now as he stared around at the newly renovated quarters, he was forced to say, "It looks very good."

"A couple of the inmates were grateful for the dinner they got, and the breakfast, so they helped Noah. By the way, Noah just carried the evening meal up. Let's go see what kind of a cook he is." Without waiting for an answer, Jenny turned and went upstairs. The judge followed reluctantly.

When they stepped into the dining area, the inmates were all seated around the table, and Noah was standing at one end pouring iced tea into glasses.

"Well, it smells delicious, Noah."

"It's great, Sheriff," Jimmy Duo said. "We got us a *real* cook now!"

The judge felt the eyes of everyone on him and forced

himself to smile. "It does smell delicious . . . and these look like new plates."

"Mr. Huntington donated some old stock. What is it you've cooked up here, Noah?"

"Well, we got some of my uncle Bubb's barbecued ribs. We got cracklin' corn bread, corn on the cob, and fried okra."

"It's the best meal I've had since I've been here." The speaker was a tall, husky man with dark brown eyes. "You couldn't buy a meal this good at a café."

"And we got dessert too, Sheriff."

"What kind of dessert?"

"This here is hummin'bird cake." Noah lifted a round plate with a large cake coated with white icing.

"I ain't never et no hummingbirds," Jimmy Duo said doubtfully. "An' I never heard of no cake made out of 'em."

"They ain't no hummin'birds in it, Jimmy," Noah said, smiling. "It's my grandma's recipe. She called it hummin'bird cake 'cause it's jes' enough to feed a hundred hummin'birds."

"Well, Judge, it looks fine, doesn't it?" Jenny smiled at Hightower. "Would you care to sample some of it?"

"No, I must be going. Thank you for taking me on the tour."

Jenny escorted the judge downstairs, and when they reached the corridor, he turned and said rather sternly, "We can't pamper these people, Sheriff."

"You're right, we can't, but I'll tell you what. After Noah's been on duty for one month, we'll compare the amount that's been spent on groceries with the amount the Porters spent for that same period of time." A smile crept to Jenny's lips, and she said sweetly, "It'll be interesting to find out where the money's been going, won't it, Judge?"

Judge Dwight Hightower knew he had been out-maneuvered, and he hated it. He glared at Jenny, and she saw then the man beneath the smooth exterior. He was a carnivore, and she had made an enemy out of him. She already knew that, however, and said, "Come back anytime, Judge. We never close."

CHAPTER ELEVEN

"HOW LONG DOES LOVE LAST?"

★ ★ ★

"Red Rover! Red Rover! Send somebody over!"

Recess, as always, was a noisy, active affair at James Miller Public School. One of the favorite games had been Red Rover, and now Kat clasped her right hand around the wrist of Dallas Sharp, and he in turn squeezed her wrist. With her other hand she held tightly to Maybelle Simmons's hand. Her face was flushed with the heat, for August had been a scorching month. Now the line of youngsters all linked together, looked across the open space, and waited for a challenger. Red Rover consisted of one side linking hands and challenging the other side to send somebody over and try to break the link. If they failed, they had to join with that side.

"Come on over, Georgie Porgie, you big sissy!" Kat called out. "You couldn't break a daisy chain!"

George Deighton, a sturdy fourteen-year-old, glared across at Kat. "I'm gonna break your arm, Kat Winslow! Get ready!"

Deighton lowered his head and ran full tilt across toward the other line. "Hang on, Dallas, don't let him through," Kat whispered fiercely.

"Why'd you have to make him mad? He's the biggest one they got," Dallas complained. He was fourteen, the same age as

Kat, and gritted his teeth as George plunged straight ahead.

"Remember what I told you. We'll get him," Kat muttered, her eyes bright and her lips tense with effort.

Deighton gave a great yell as he reached them and threw himself toward the arms of Kat and Dallas.

But those two had a plan. Just as he lunged forward they both suddenly squatted and brought their arms down to the level of George's knees. As he struck their arms and tripped, they rose up, causing the boy to turn a complete flip. He landed on his back and expelled a loud *Whoosh!* as he hit the ground.

"You didn't break the line, Georgie Porgie!" Kat yelled triumphantly.

George Deighton lay for a moment dazed, then crawled to his feet. He was struggling for breath, but his eyes glittered with anger. He stood there speechless, aware of the laughter that broke the air. He tried to think of the worst thing he could say to Kat Winslow, and finally he blurted out, "Your sister ain't nothin' but a tramp! She goes around sleeping with every man in the county!"

The charge brought a bright flush to Kat Winslow's cheeks. Without hesitation she flung herself at George, striking him in the nose with her fist and pummeling him as he fell over backward. He hit the ground, and although he was much larger, George could not stop the rain of blows that fell upon him. For a moment it was all he could do to defend himself. Then he struck out and caught Kat in the forehead with his fist. The blow unsettled her, and with a roar he came to his feet and struck out at her again. But even as he did, he was caught from behind and flung sprawling. Dallas had grabbed George by the shoulders and simply flung him away, and now he stepped up, saying, "You're so tough you have to fight girls. Is that it, George?"

George scrambled to his feet and flung himself at Dallas, and when Kat joined in the fray, Johnny Satterfield, one of George's best friends, threw himself into the fight.

The battle was sharp and furious, and Kat was screaming at the top of her lungs as she fought with all her strength, but suddenly Mrs. Williamson, the sixth-grade teacher, was there shouting at them. "You stop that this minute! You act like a bunch of maniacs! All four of you now are going to the principal's office."

Blood was streaming from Kat's nose and had stained the front of her white blouse. She wiped the blood from her upper lip and glared at George Deighton. "You ever say anything like that about my sister again, I'll hit you with a baseball bat!"

"You be quiet, Katherine," Mrs. Williamson said. "Now, all of you to the principal's office!"

★   ★   ★

"Lewis, what in the world are you doing?"

Looking up with a rather shame-faced expression, Lewis laughed. "I'm examining my sons. What do you think?" He felt a little foolish, for he had put all three babies in a semicircle in the parlor and had seated himself cross-legged and had been watching them for the past twenty minutes. "Nothing wrong with a man admiring his sons, is there?"

"Not a thing." Missouri came over and knelt down, holding on to Lewis's shoulder. He put his arm around her, and she smiled. "They are beautiful, aren't they?"

"Well, they are now, but when I first saw them they looked like about five pounds of raw hamburger apiece."

"Lewis Winslow! What an awful thing to say."

Lewis laughed and said, "I know better than to insult a new mother by saying bad things about her babies. But I will admit that they have improved a lot. Good-looking chaps all of them." He squeezed her warmly and added, "They get their good looks from the Winslow side of the family, don't you think?"

"Well, if you aren't the most conceited. . . !"

"But they get their stubbornness from you, so I guess that'll make them the most stubborn, best-lookin' men who ever lived."

"They really *do* look like you, Lewis."

"How can you tell under all that baby fat?"

"Well, just look at them. They've got your chin and your cheekbones too." She reached over and pulled on Temple's toe, and he kicked mightily. "They're strong, healthy babies, and they're going to be strong, godly men."

Lewis squeezed her shoulder and said, "You know, I'm happier than I ever thought I would be, Missouri, but—"

"But what? What is it?" Missouri interrupted.

"Well, I think about how old I am. I'm fifty-seven. When the boys are twenty, I'll be seventy-seven . . . if I live that long. I may not get to see them grow up."

"Yes, you will." Missouri's voice was fierce, and she turned and took him by the shirt. Shaking him, she insisted, "You're going to be around for a long time and see each of your boys grow up to be as good a man as you are."

"Better than that, I hope." They both jumped as the phone made a cacophonous jangle. "Who can that be?" Lewis muttered. He got to his feet, helped Missouri up, and went to the phone. Lifting the receiver, he said, "Hello?"

Missouri watched as he listened to the caller. She saw his eyes grow wide and then heard him exclaim, "I'll be there as quick as I can make it." He slammed the receiver down and turned to face her. "It's Kat. She's in some kind of trouble at school."

"What kind of trouble?"

"She got into a fight. I'll tell you about it when I get back. Here, I'll put the boys back in their bed so you won't have to pick 'em up." He snatched up the babies with alacrity and plunked them down in their crib. Dashing out of the house, he threw himself into the truck and drove out of the yard, leaving a cloud of dust behind.

He drove at the top rate of the old Studebaker's capacity and fifteen minutes later pulled up in front of the school. Shutting the engine off, he piled out and walked rapidly toward the building. When he went inside, he turned left and strode down to the principal's office. When he entered the reception area, he ignored the secretary and walked right into the office and saw four youngsters, including Kat and Dallas Sharp standing in front of Mr. Latimer, the principal. Latimer was a small man with blond hair and glasses. He tugged at his tie nervously and nodded. "Hello, Mr. Winslow."

"What's this all about, Mr. Latimer?"

"We have a problem with some of the students."

"I'll say we have a problem," another man in the room said. "That girl of your needs to be whipped!"

Lewis turned at once and faced Albert Deighton. "What's the trouble, Mr. Deighton?"

Deighton, a small-boned man with a pair of close-set brown eyes and a wide mouth, had a voice like a bullfrog. He was the editor of *The Daily Standard*, the newspaper that had printed that scandalous photograph of Jenny. Lewis knew Deighton had done all he could to get Jenny defeated in her race for sheriff. He was one of Hightower's cronies, and Lewis did not care for him at all. Ignoring him, Lewis turned back to the principal. "Tell me what happened, Mr. Latimer."

The principal began to explain and finally said, "I would have handled it myself, but George there called his father. Mr. Deighton wants your child expelled."

"I didn't start it, Daddy," Kat said at once.

"Did you hit him first?"

"Yes, I did!" Kat said defiantly. "And I'm not sorry."

"Why did you hit him?"

"It doesn't make any difference!" Albert Deighton said sharply. "She started the fight—she's the one that ought to take the responsibility."

"If you don't mind, Al, I'd like to know the reason for this," Mr. Latimer said. "Now, why did you hit him, Kat?"

He listened carefully as Kat told about the game and how Deighton had failed to break the line at Red Rover, and then her face grew pink with indignation. "He got mad, and he said that Jenny was a tramp and slept with men all over the county."

A cold fury seized Lewis Winslow. He was ordinarily a mild-mannered man, but this accusation touched off some sort of volcanic action in him. He turned quickly and faced Al Deighton, and polar ice was never colder than his eyes. "Al, if a man said that, I'd flatten him with anything handy—even a baseball bat."

Al Deighton opened his mouth to shout a reply. He was a bully, but something in the face of Lewis Winslow caused a warning to go off somewhere deep within him. He stood staring at Lewis and remembered that this was the man who had charged up San Juan Hill and showed enough grit and courage to win the Congressional Medal of Honor. His mouth clamped shut, and he swallowed hard. He saw that Winslow was waiting for him to make a remark and suddenly dropped his eyes.

Mr. Latimer said quickly, "I think we've heard about enough of this. I'll leave the discipline of your son for making such a remark up to you, Mr. Deighton—and you ought to make it rough on him. All four of you will write an essay on why peace is better than war, and the spelling and the grammar and the content will have to be acceptable to me or you'll keep writing it as long as you are in this school."

"Fair enough," Lewis said. He turned to Kat and smiled. "Good for you, daughter."

"Dallas helped me. We would've whipped both of 'em too if Miss Williamson hadn't stopped us."

"Always fight for your people, Kat." He turned and faced Al Deighton, and the silence seemed to grow heavy in the room. "If you ever say anything detrimental about my daughter again, Al, we'll have trouble."

Deighton did not say a word as Winslow turned and left the room. He glared at George and said, "We'll talk about this when you get home, George," then turned and left the room without another word.

★   ★   ★

"I'm gettin' a little long in the tooth for this sort of business, Sheriff."

Jenny was blinking, for she had walked straight into a vine and her smarting eye was now watering profusely. She stopped and wiped it with her handkerchief. The sun was almost down, but the day had been hot enough to fry eggs on the sidewalk in town. Even in the woods shaded by the towering oak trees there was not a breath of air stirring, and Jenny felt she had to exert extra effort to breathe. Giving her eye an extra wipe, she stuck the handkerchief in her pocket and blinked to clear her vision. "We needed you on this one, Kermit."

Kermit Bing was a large man, overweight and out of condition. He was in his late sixties and had spent most of his life as a deputy for the county. He had technically retired several years earlier but still worked part-time whenever there was need for extra help. Jenny had grown fond of Kermit, for he was a good man. He taught Sunday school classes at his church and had been a scout master for years, but since he had lost his wife two years earlier, he was not as cheerful, according to reports.

"I hope we get these fellows," Kermit gasped. They had been walking up a hill, dodging briars and vines and saplings that impeded their progress. Kermit peered ahead and said, "Are you sure they'll be there, Sheriff? Them Cundiffs is sneaky fellers."

"Billy's been spying them out," Jenny said. She was holding a rifle in her right hand, but it felt out of place. Billy Moon had been giving her shooting lessons with the side arm and with the rifle, but she still felt awkward and ill at ease. The idea of pointing a gun at a human being and pulling the trigger was repugnant to her, but now she grimly nodded. "They need to be put out of business."

"They're meaner than snakes," Kermit agreed.

The two struggled through the dense woods, crossing down through a steep gully. When they had scrambled to the top, they were both gasping for breath.

"Let's rest a minute," Jenny said, more for Kermit's sake than for her own. She did not like the look of his face, and he had mentioned once that he had had a mild heart attack a year back. As they sat down, she said, "How are those grandsons of yours?"

"They're doin' better than snuff." Kermit smiled, despite his heaving chest. He wiped his steaming brow as he gave her reports of his two grandsons, of whom he was inordinately proud. Finally he said, "You need a younger man on this kind of thing. I was pretty good in my younger days, but I'm too old now."

Secretly Jenny agreed, but she said cheerfully, "Well, Billy and Frank are coming up on the other side. We've got them trapped here."

"I've got to say, Miss Jenny, you've done a good job as

sheriff. I know it was hard for a woman with no experience, but you've got a good heart and you're honest. Back when Sheriff Beauchamp was running the show, it was pretty good, but after he passed, I didn't keer much about puttin' on my badge. I felt like Conroy sort of tarnished it, if you know what I mean."

"That's exactly what I said when I testified against Arp and Pender!" Jenny exclaimed. Then she reached over and patted the old man on the shoulder. "Well, if you're up to it, let's get this done."

"I'm fine, Sheriff."

The two rose and crept slowly toward the designated spot. Billy had identified the location, and now Jenny exclaimed, "There it is! And look, there comes Billy and Frank down that hill. We'd better move in with them."

The two moved forward, but when they reached the other two officers, Billy shook his head in disgust. "They've flown the coop and moved all the equipment. It was all here yesterday, but look at these tracks. There's been a truck in here that hauled it all off."

Jenny felt angry and frustrated. "How could they have known we were coming? Nobody knew outside the office."

Billy stared at her and cocked one eyebrow but said only, "We'll have to try again, Sheriff."

Jenny waited until Billy and Frank Eddings went to get the cars, and she was disgusted because she had been certain that they could make an arrest. Now she said to Bing, "Something's wrong, Kermit. How could they possibly find out what we were doing?"

Kermit Bing said quietly, "The next time we won't say a word at the office. Just me and you and Frank and Billy."

Suddenly Jenny stared at the deputy. "You don't trust people at the office?"

"Not saying a word 'cause I've got no proof. But next time it'll be just us four, Sheriff."

Jenny nodded and then said quietly, "You may be right, Kermit."

The air was still, and Kermit Bing looked up. "I've been on

this old earth a long time. It's not the same as it was when I had Helen with me."

"How long were you married, Kermit?"

"Forty-nine years. She was the best woman I ever knew," he said simply. "All those years I loved her more every day."

"That's so sweet," Jenny whispered. Her eyes grew misty at the thought of this old man. He was old now, but once he had been a young man full of blood and ambition. She tried to think of him as a young man of twenty courting his Helen. The years had come and gone, but they had stuck together. Kermit had often spoken of his love for his wife. He did it so simply. Most men, Jenny knew, were reticent about saying things like that aloud, but Kermit Bing had no reservations. Now he closed his eyes and leaned his head back against a tree. "The best woman I ever knew, and I had her for all those years," he murmured.

★ ★ ★

"I think you're some kind of a pervert, Luke Dixon."

Dixon had walked Jenny up to the porch. A single light bulb glowed faintly, dispelling the darkness. He pulled her down to sit on the steps beside him and said, "Well, I've been called lots of things but never that." He put his arm around her and said, "Maybe you'd better tell me all about it."

"You don't have to hug me so hard," Jenny smiled but did not attempt to pull away. "It's the movies you want to see. First it was Frankenstein and tonight that horrible Dracula film. Ugh, I don't even want to think about it. I suppose you feel sorry for that old vampire."

"Well, I do in a way."

"Why do you always feel sorry for monsters? He was evil."

"No, he wasn't evil. He didn't make himself into a vampire. Another vampire bit him, and he didn't have any choice."

Luke Dixon loved to argue. That was the lawyer in him, and for a while he sat there defending Count Dracula. Jenny was always amused at Luke, and finally she said, "Oh, shush! I don't want to hear about any vampires." She looked up at the moon, a huge silver medallion in the sky, and grew still for a moment.

"What are you thinking about, Jenny?"

"I was thinking about Kermit Bing."

"A good man."

"You know, he really is. I don't suppose he's ever had his name in the paper. Never done anything much except be a great husband and now a wonderful grandfather to his grandsons. There needs to be more people like him in the world."

"He's not been the same since his wife died. You should have known him before, Jenny. He was always full of practical jokes and laughing, but he's grown pretty quiet since then. He misses her a lot, I know."

"He talked about her today when we were out in the woods. He's like a man who's lost an arm—or something even more important."

"That's right. A man can lose an arm and get by, but when he loses his woman, he's like a ship without his rudder." Luke suddenly leaned over and kissed her cheek. "You smell good," he said.

"Thank you. Now, you behave yourself, Luke."

Luke saw that Jenny was in a pensive mood. He studied her profile, admiring the smooth curve of her cheek and the strength of her face, then asked, "What do you think about marriage?"

Surprised, Jenny turned to face him. He was, she saw, watching her curiously, and she was startled by his question. "Why, I think it's forever."

"No matter what?"

"No matter what. Someday I'll get married, and the minister will say 'as long as you both shall live.' That's the way it should be."

"It's a noble ambition. A little bit hard to achieve, though. Lots of couples don't make it."

"You know, I admire geese. Canadian geese, I mean."

"You're a funny girl," Luke said, laughing. "What do geese

have to do with what we're talking about?"

"Why, they mate forever. Don't you know that?"

"No, I didn't."

"Well, they do," Jenny said. "I read a book about them once. It was pretty dull, except when it got to the way they mate. It told about what a hard life they had struggling just to stay alive. The book said geese just can't afford to philander. They need one another all the time."

"Why more than other birds?"

"I think it's because they travel so far. And then I remember it said that they have inefficient digestive systems. They can't digest cellulose."

"What does that have to do with it?"

"Well, you see they have to fly, and they can't fly with a huge belly. The book said a meal of grass will digest in only two hours, so they have to stop and eat a lot. And then the female goose," Jenny said meditatively, "gives away her own energy resources through the laying of her eggs. Then for a month she has to sit on those eggs and can't leave to grab even one daily meal. Sometimes a female will starve to death right on the nest. Then the eggs won't hatch or the hatchlings will die."

"Why do you remember all this?"

"I don't know. It just makes me think about how awful it is that geese can be more faithful in love than human beings."

"What else did that book say?"

"Well, it said they have to work together full-time to raise a brood of goslings. While the female sits on the nest, the male has to stand watch. If a predator comes, he warns her by honking, and they fly to safety. Or else she hunkers down on the nest, and he flies alone, trying to lead the danger away. Even after the eggs hatch, they continue to do this because the goslings are flightless. So they need each other."

"You know, I think you're right. It would be good if all married couples were as faithful as geese." He shifted his arm and took out his billfold. "I found this the other day in a bunch of clippings I'd saved. I don't even know what it's from now. I forgot to mark the location, but I liked it." He held it up to the light and read:

"Fidelity, enforced and unto death, is the price you pay for the kind of love you never want to give up, for someone you want to hold forever, tighter and tighter, whether he's close or far away, someone who becomes dearer to you the more you sacrifice for his sake."

Luke fell silent, holding the paper in his hand. For a time the two of them sat, and then finally she rose. She turned to face him as he stood before her, and when he leaned to kiss her, her lips were ready. He held her tightly, and she felt a sense of security. There was goodness in this man, she knew. How deep her own feelings went she could not say, but when he lifted his head, she said, "I like that very much, Luke. Good night."

"Good night. I'll see you tomorrow."

Stepping into the house, Jenny found her father sitting in the parlor reading. It was late for him, and she said, "What are you doing up so late?"

"Waiting up for my daughter. Have to be sure she's all right." He rose and came over to her, putting his arm around her, and she kissed him on the cheek. "Are you serious about that young man?"

"We're just good friends, Dad."

"You look tired. Is something wrong?"

"I'm not getting the job done." She told him briefly of the attempted raid and of the failure it brought. "I just can't handle it."

"You haven't been at it long, Jenny. You're just tired. Go to bed now, and things'll look different in the morning."

"Maybe you're right. Good night, Dad. I'll see you tomorrow."

Twenty minutes later Jenny lay in bed, but she could not sleep. Over and over she explored various schemes to make her office more effective. Finally a plan began to form, and she thought for a long time and then, satisfied, rolled over and went to sleep.

CHAPTER TWELVE

THE RAID

★ ★ ★

Jenny did not say anything for over a week about her plan to go after the moonshiners of the county. She stayed awake at night thinking and planning, but it was not until the first of September that she called Moon aside and laid before him the results of her planning. The two of them had been patrolling along the county roads when Jenny turned and said, "Billy, I think it's time for us to make a dent in this awful moonshining business."

"It's a little hard. We found that out last time," Moon replied. His coppery skin glowed in the bright sunlight that filtered in from the open window beside him. He glanced quickly at Jenny, then asked, "What've you got in mind?"

"You've been talking about Al Jennings, and we know pretty well about that still of his. I think it's time to hit him, Billy."

"Jennings is a pretty tough customer, and he's sharp too."

"Well, we can't wait any longer, but this time I want us to do it differently."

"Different how, Sheriff?"

"I don't want anyone at the office to know about this raid."

"You've been thinking about that too, I see."

"I've got my suspicions and so have you, but we can't prove anything."

"Two of us won't be enough. We have to have more men."

"We can do it if we use Frank and Kermit."

"I don't know. They're pretty old guys. They were good men in their day, but this could get rough. I think we'd better get more people in on it."

"If we do that, then word can get out. You and I will plan this alone. Then, when we're ready to go, we'll let Frank and Kermit in on it. We don't tell anybody else anything and that way we can take Jennings off guard."

"I'd like to nail Jennings, but I still think we need more men."

"You know more than I do about this business, Billy, and I trust your judgment. But I need to make a showing. I haven't had a single important arrest since I've been in office, and the moonshine business is booming. We've got to make some sort of effort."

The two spoke of the possibilities for a time, and finally Billy said, "Okay, if that's what you want, Sheriff, we'll try it. But they're hard to sneak up on. I think they're making another run now. They'll be busy for at least another day or two."

"Then let's do it either first thing in the morning or this afternoon."

Moon was startled. "This afternoon! Without any planning?"

"Why not? We know where the still is. All we have to do is close in on them. If we can sneak up and catch them off guard, they won't have a chance."

Moon thought silently for a time. "Well, actually there are only three of them, sometimes only two. If we catch the old man Al and bust up that still, that'd put at least one moonshiner out of business. And a bad one too. Al's a pretty bad guy, Sheriff. He killed a man over in the next county. He got off, but everyone knew he was guilty. It won't be any play party, but we'll do it if you say."

Jenny hesitated, then nodded firmly. "All right, we'll do it, then. Shall it be this afternoon or in the morning?"

"Might as well make it now. We'll go by and see if we can catch Frank and Kermit."

★ ★ ★

Kermit Bing answered the door and was surprised to see Sheriff Winslow standing there. "Why, hello, Sheriff. Come on in."

"Thanks, Kermit." Jenny stepped inside and said quickly, "We've got a very important job right away. Can you come?"

"Why, sure. What's up?"

"We're going to raid Al Jennings's still."

"About time," Kermit nodded. "That man shouldn't be roaming around free, and his boys are just as bad."

"We're going over now to see if Frank's able to go. It'll be just the four of us. And, Kermit, don't tell anybody."

"Right, Sheriff. Where will I meet you?"

"Frank has the car. I'll have him come by and pick you up. We'll meet out of town in one hour out past the cotton gin."

"All right. I'll be ready when Frank comes."

"This could be pretty dangerous, Kermit. Billy says Al Jennings and his boys are killers."

"Everybody knows that," Kermit said. He smiled and said, "You're really getting into this sheriffing business, aren't you, Miss Jenny?"

For a moment Jenny hesitated. Bing suddenly looked old and tired. For one instant she was tempted to call the whole thing off, but she had convinced herself so thoroughly that all she could say was, "We'll be real careful about this, but there should be only three of them, maybe two. I'll have Frank bring the shotguns and rifles by."

"All right, Sheriff. I'll be ready." He stopped suddenly and snapped his fingers. "I'm supposed to be at the scout meeting tonight. My oldest grandson, he's getting his Eagle Scout badge."

"Well, that's wonderful! I know you're proud of him. What time will that be?"

"Not till seven o'clock."

"We'll be back in plenty of time for that. I'll go with you."

"Would you really, Sheriff?" Bing was pleased. "That'd mean a lot to Tim and to me too."

"I'll be sure to be there, then. Meanwhile, I'll see you out by the cotton gin."

Bing nodded and after he shut the door, he went over and looked at the picture of the two young boys on the wall. "An Eagle Scout. Just think of that," he said. Then he straightened up and moved toward the bedroom to put on his uniform. He dressed quickly and strapped on the thirty-eight he had carried all of his years as a deputy. At a knock on the door, he went to answer it and found Deputy Arlie Pender standing there. "Hello, Arlie, what's up?"

"I came by to see if you could take my duty tomorrow, Kermit. I got something I need to do."

"Why, I guess so."

"Appreciate it, Kermit." Pender left and strolled back to the car, but stopped suddenly and snapped his fingers. "I forgot to tell the old man I had the early shift." He wheeled and hurried back to the house, but as he stepped up on the porch, he stopped abruptly. Bing was on the phone, and Pender stood to listen.

". . . can't go hunting with you tomorrow, D.C. Got to work an extra shift. What? No, I can't go this afternoon. We're raiding a still, and tonight I've got to go to the awards for the scouts. Whose still? Well, it's Al Jennings's, but don't say a word, you hear me?"

Arlie Pender moved silently off the porch, then hastened to the car. He jumped in and said, "We got to get to Max, Merle."

Merle Arp turned and said, "What's wrong?"

"There's gonna be a raid on Al Jennings's still this afternoon. Max will want to know about it."

Merle Arp sent the car ahead with screeching wheels. "You're right about that," he said grimly. "He promised Al protection, and Al will come lookin' for him if he gets into trouble."

"We gotta hurry. It must be the sheriff, Moon, Frank, and Kermit."

"Why didn't they tell us about it?"

"Because they're not stupid. They suspect we've been tippin' off what's going on. Come on. Get some speed out of this rattletrap."

★　★　★

Conroy stared at the two deputies. "You sure about this, Arlie?"

"Yeah, old man Bing didn't know he was tippin' me off, but they're gonna hit Jennings all right."

"What are you gonna do, Max?"

Max Conroy laughed. "They're gonna find out they bit off more than they can chew."

"You gonna get 'em to move the still?"

"Not time for that," Max growled, "but there's time to put that sheriff away and Moon too. Killed in the line of duty. Maybe they'll even get a medal."

The two deputies stared at Conroy and did not speak for a time. "That's pretty crude, Max," Arlie Pender said. "Killin' a sheriff is bad business."

"You fellows get out of here. Make yourselves obvious. I want you to be able to account for your time." He turned and hurried away, and Merle Arp shook his head. "Come on, Arlie. I don't want any part of this. Somebody could go down for it."

★　★　★

Billy handed out the shotguns and saw that each of the other three had plenty of ammunition. "You'll have to be closer with these, and I'll take the rifle. One thing about a shotgun, it's hard to miss with it."

"What's the drill here, Billy?" Frank Eddings asked. He was a tall, lanky man, and his hair, at the age of sixty, was still

black. He had dark eyes and had been known as a tough officer all of his career. He held the shotgun loosely and stood
waiting, his eyes on Moon rather than Jenny.

"You all know where the still is. It's in the same place the
Fender brothers made moonshine."

"Kind of a hard place to sneak up on," Eddings murmured. "It's right out in the open."

"What's it like, Billy?" Jenny said nervously.

"Well, Frank's right. It is hard to sneak up on. It's an old
barn right out in the middle of an open field. The old house
burned down a long time ago, so the barn's just standing
there all by itself. Nobody lives there now, but Jennings has
been using it for a spell."

"Well, if it's out in the open, how do we get to it?"

"I'll work up to where I got a good view of the door. The
other three of you come at it from different angles. What I'm
hoping is that they're so busy makin' the shine that they
won't know until we open the door and throw down on 'em.
So, we'll come up as quiet as we can."

Jenny listened, and her hand tightened on the barrel of the
shotgun. Somehow she had to keep her fear from these men,
but it was difficult. She had read books about men going into
battle during war, and this was much the same. She listened
carefully to Billy as he went over the plan, and finally when
he said, "All right, any questions?" she did not say a word,
nor did the other two.

"It ought to go down pretty easy," Moon said. "They're not
lookin' for us, and I'll go in first."

"Better let me go with you, Billy," Eddings offered.

"No, I want you three outside to be sure they don't get
away. I don't think they'll argue with this thirty-thirty. They
know what it can do, and I can get off three shots quicker
than they can think."

"All right, Billy," Eddings said.

Bing spoke up and said, "Sheriff, why don't you stay back
out of this? It doesn't seem right for you to put yourself at
risk."

"It goes with the job, Bing. Thanks for thinking about me,

but this is something I agreed to do when I took the office. Let's go."

Jenny felt strangely numb as she got into the car with Billy. As he pulled out, she glanced back to see Eddings driving the other car close behind them. They drove for some fifteen minutes, then Moon pulled over and said, "We go in from here."

Jenny got out, and her mouth felt dry. She waited until the other two got out of the car and looked to Billy. She felt utterly helpless and knew that without Moon it would be a total washout.

"We can walk through the trees here. It's not more than an eighth of a mile. We'll go quiet, and when we get to the edge of the tree line, we stop and see how it looks. Come on."

The sun was moving westward in the sky, and Jenny looked at her watch and saw that it was five minutes until three. She gripped the stock of the rifle until her hand ached, and glancing around, she saw that the three men with her seemed to have little concern. They were all old hands at this, and she felt a sudden sense of shame at the fear that clutched at her.

As they moved along, a sudden rustling startled her, and she uttered a short, strangled cry and whirled quickly.

"Just a deer, sheriff," Kermit said. He had come up even with her and reached out and patted her shoulder. "Nothin' to be afraid of."

"Kermit, I hate to say this, but I . . . I'm scared spitless!"

"Nothin' wrong with that."

"Aren't you scared just a little bit, Kermit?"

"No, not anymore, but I was the first time I went on a job like this. I was no older than you, and it was a tough one. But then again, I got less reason to be afraid than you."

"Why, you're as likely to get shot as I am."

"Yes, but my life's mostly behind me. All the good things are gone. Since I lost Helen, why, nothin' seems to matter much. But you're young. You've got your life in front of you. That's why I wish you had stayed back, Miss Jenny."

"I can't do it, Kermit. Don't worry. I'll be all right."

They hurried and caught up with the other two, who had

reached the edge of the woods. "There it is. No sign of a car, but it could be inside. Don't see any smoke either, but that doesn't tell us anything," Moon said. "Well, we can do this slow or fast. I say we go fast. If they've got a lookout, the faster we go the better. You spread out now and let me take the door. Are you ready?"

Jenny nodded but could not say a word, and then Moon said, "All right, let's do it." She felt like a robot, but her legs obeyed her will. She checked the safety to be sure that it was off, and the four of them leaped out of the woods at a fast trot. Jenny moved out to Moon's right along with Kermit, and she saw that Frank had darted to the left. The four of them made a ragged line as they approached the front of the barn. She could hear the sound of the men's feet and her own pounding the dry earth and wished fervently she had never thought of such a thing. She also wished she had never decided to run for sheriff, for she knew now that this was beyond her.

Jenny was caught off guard, as were the others, when a shot rang out. Billy hollered, "Look for cover! They're waitin' for us!"

Then the air was filled with gunfire. She heard the boom of shotguns and the crack of Billy's rifle, and looking up, she saw a man, in the open window of the loft, suddenly disappear as if driven back by a fist. But she also saw the flickering of rifles or sidearms that filled the air with a rolling thunder.

"Get out of here!" Billy said. "There's too many of 'em!" He turned to one side, and Jenny saw blood on his neck.

"Billy, are you all right?"

"Yes, get out of here!" He was raking the barn with the thirty-thirty, the shots causing one continual roar. The other men were keeping up the fire as they backed away. They had almost reached the edge of the woods when Jenny heard a muffled cry. She turned to see Kermit as he fell back on the ground. She ran to him, crying out, "Billy—Kermit's been hit!"

She heard Billy say, "Keep firing! Give us cover, Frank." And then he was there with her. Jenny saw the spreading crimson on the front of Kermit's shirt, and her heart felt as if it were squeezed in a gigantic, freezing fist. "Kermit," she whispered. "Kermit . . ."

Billy picked the man up, threw him over his shoulder, and gasped, "Let's get out of here." He raised his voice, "Come on, Frank. Get away! Get out of this place!"

Jenny followed numbly as they dove past the tree line. A bullet clipped a branch off beside her head, and she saw the leaf fall to the ground. But then they were in the trees.

Billy was gasping for breath, and then Frank came up and said, "Let me help you with him, Billy."

"Put . . . me down."

The two men lowered the bulky form of Kermit to the ground, and Jenny saw a bloody hole on the back of his uniform. The bullet had gone all the way through. She knelt down and put her arms around him and whispered, "Kermit, oh, Kermit, don't die!"

She heard Kermit try to speak, and when she lifted her head, she saw through her tears that he was smiling at her! "Don't you cry, Miss Jenny." Blood bubbled up through his lips, but Kermit reached up and tried to touch her cheek. "I'll be seein' my Helen now. I wish . . ."

And then Kermit Bing suddenly stiffened—and then relaxed.

Jenny cried out weeping, and then she felt Billy's hand on her shoulder. "He's gone, Miss Jenny. We've got to get out of here."

Jenny Winslow clung to the body of the old man. Blood stained the front of her uniform and had gotten in her hair. The world seemed to be spinning, and she looked up and said, "Billy, he can't be dead!"

"He did the best he could," Billy Moon said softly. "He wouldn't want you to stay here in danger. Come on, me and Frank will carry him. You take the guns."

Jenny clung to Kermit for a moment longer, squeezing her eyes tightly shut. Then she touched his cheek a final time and got to her feet. As the men picked up the still body, she remembered something.

He won't be there to see his grandson get his Eagle badge.

She remembered the pride in Kermit's eyes when he had

told her of this, and the memory made his death seem more than ever like a terrible, terrible tragedy. Jenny's mind was numb, but as she followed the two men struggling with the old man, she knew that this moment would never pass away from her memory.

PART THREE

A Proposal

★ ★ ★

CHAPTER THIRTEEN

THE SIGN OF JONAH

★ ★ ★

For most of her nineteen years, Jenny Winslow had lived in a safe and secure cocoon. Her father's money and position had insulated her against many of the shocks and bruises that less fortunate young women encounter during their early years. Jenny had been born with a proverbial spoon in her mouth. Clothes, jewelry, travel—all that money could buy— had been available to her, and her parents had delighted in seeing that she had those things that made up what most would call the "good life." If the world outside was harsh and cruel, Jenny didn't know it. Even when her mother died, she'd had her friends and luxurious home and unlimited allowance to comfort her.

When the stock market had crashed, Jenny had crashed with it, but she had adjusted to a new life. Now, however, as she sat in the auditorium of Bethel Church, she had never known a more miserable time in her entire life. She had, of course, suffered when her mother died and when her family had been stripped of practically every possession and forced to leave the comforts of a wealthy world to take up residence in a backwater Georgia farmhouse. That had seemed hard, but none of these hardships had touched the deepest recesses of her spirit as had the death of Kermit Bing. For the first time in her life, she felt responsible for another person's death.

Ever since Jenny had held the dying man in her arms and watched the life fade away until Kermit lay with that awful stillness of the dead, she had been like one of the walking wounded on a battlefield. Some soldiers get frightfully wounded but keep going forward, doing their duty in spite of a life-threatening injury. In some respects Jennifer was like this. Since the death of Bing, she had spoken, had eaten, had slept, and had performed those things that had to be done— but they were all automatic, for her spirit seemed frozen and dead.

As the sound of a hymn interrupted Jenny's thoughts, she lifted her chin and forced herself to face forward, where the body of Kermit Bing lay in a bronzed coffin. The lid was open, and although she could not see the remains of the old man, an image of his face rose in her mind. The hymn "Rock of Ages," she knew, was Kermit's favorite song. He had often gone around humming it or whistling the tune. Now she listened to the words numbly as the congregation sang:

"Rock of Ages, cleft for me,
Let me hide myself in thee;
Let the water and the blood,
From thy wounded side which flowed,
Be of sin the double cure,
Save from wrath and make me pure."

The words brought her no comfort. Indeed, nothing about the funeral or anything else was able to bring comfort to Jenny. She sat stiffly, her hands clenched together unconsciously, deliberately turning her eyes away from the coffin at the front of the auditorium. As Reverend Devoe Crutchfield got up and read the obituary, her eyes moved without willing it to the family that sat in the front of the church. She was sitting on the left side of the auditorium and could see the faces of Kermit's family. She had gone to them and expressed her grief, but her lips had been numb, and she had been unable to say anything meaningful. Perhaps it was impossible to say anything at a time like this, but she had forced herself to go. Now she saw the profile of Kermit's grandson, whose Eagle Scout presentation he had missed, and Jenny saw tears rolling down the boy's cheeks. Quickly she looked down and bit her trembling lower lip. She did not watch Crutchfield as he read the obituary, but finally when he began to speak, she blinked back her tears and looked up. Luke Dixon was sitting beside her, and she felt a touch on her hand. She took his hand and squeezed it hard, and he returned the pressure as Crutchfield continued to speak.

"An evil and adulterous generation seeketh after a sign; and there shall no sign be given to it, but the sign of the prophet Jonas: for as Jonas was three days and three nights in the whale's belly; so shall the Son of man be three days and three nights in the heart of the earth."

Looking up out over the congregation, Crutchfield's voice was clear, although sadness marred his features. "We're all grieved," he said quietly, "as always when we lose a friend, but I would preface my remarks with this one. When you lose something, it's lost because you don't know where it is, but we do know where our brother Kermit is. He's in the presence of God. And since we know where he is, he is not really lost. What we are feeling is our own sorrow, because for the time being we cannot see Bing or talk with him or do any of those things that we do with friends or relatives. But I'm convinced that one day, no man knows how long, we will all see Bing again, those of us who know Christ Jesus."

The church was absolutely silent, and the smell of the banks of flowers came to Jennifer as Crutchfield spoke of the promises of the Bible. The vivid colors and the freshness of the flowers were counterpoint to the sorrow and the grief on the faces of those who sat in the pews. Jenny had attended other funerals in her life, but the loss of Bing was like a knife shoved through her heart.

"The Scripture says that there is one sign that Jesus was who He said He was. You will remember that He made no little claim for himself. He said He was the only way to heaven. He said this very clearly and very plainly. 'No man cometh unto the Father, but by me.' The world hates that sentence as it does no other statement in the Scripture. For the world insists that men and women can go to heaven if they are good people, no matter what religion they follow. Mohammed or Confucius, why, they're just as good as Jesus. But Mohammed is dead, and Confucius, his bones are somewhere in an obscure Chinese tomb, I suppose. Jesus said that no sign would be given but one, and that was that He would come out of the tomb after having died and would authenticate His claims to being the Son of God."

For some time Crutchfield spoke of Jesus and His resurrection. Then finally he said, "You do not have your Bibles with you, I'm sure, as you would in an ordinary service. But when you go home I would like you to turn to the book of First Corinthians, the fifteenth chapter, and read it word for word—and then read it again—and when you've done that, read it one more time. This will be difficult for some of you, for this is a long chapter. It takes up three pages in my Bible, fifty-eight verses. It's a tremendously important chapter, for the apostle Paul was chosen to explain Jesus to the world through his letters, and it was in this chapter he takes up this most important subject of all. And as we grieve here, I would like for us to take time to see the magnificence of our faith. Paul says, 'If Christ be not raised, your faith is vain; ye are yet in your sins. Then they also which are fallen asleep in Christ are perished. If in this life only we have hope in Christ, we are of all men most miserable. But now is Christ risen from the dead, and become the firstfruits of them that slept.'

"Very clearly, Paul says our hope of heaven stands on this one issue: did Jesus come forth from the grave? And in this whole chapter Paul triumphantly shouts, 'Yes, He is alive! He is risen!'"

Jenny had heard Crutchfield preach many times. She had thought for a while that she might be interested in him as a husband, but she had never found a love for him like that. As she listened, she realized that he was a bigger man than she had thought. He preached at a small, obscure rural church with no stained-glass windows, but he preached with such power that she was somewhat shocked. His expression was alive as he read verse after verse from Paul's letter, and finally he said, "Paul ends his argument with these ringing words,

'O death, where is thy sting? O grave, where is thy victory?'"

Closing his Bible, Devoe was silent for a moment. Then he said, "We are on this side of the river while our brother Kermit has passed to the other side. One day every one of us will have to cross that river, but as we cross it, Jesus will be there with us. And once we are across, we will be in the presence of the King, as our brother is right now. We weep for him, we feel our loss—but we celebrate the entrance of Kermit Bing into the presence of Jesus Christ and of His Father!"

Jenny could not keep the tears from flowing then. She knew that Luke beside her was aware of her grief, for he put his arm around her, and she turned and put her face against his shoulder. As a final hymn was sung, she felt the pressure of his arm pulling her to her feet. He led her into the aisle up toward the casket in the procession, and when she looked down on the still face, she felt as if she could not go on. She turned quickly, grateful for Luke's help, for she was blinded by her tears, and he guided her down the aisle and out of the church.

They stepped outside and Luke led her to the car. He opened the door; then she turned to face him. Looking up, she whispered, "I just don't know how I can stand it, Luke!"

Luke put his arms around her and held her for a moment. She leaned against him, surrendering almost her whole weight, and he whispered, "It's hard, but he was a Christian, and we will see him again."

★　★　★

Ruby French looked up from the ledger, laid her pen down, and flexed her fingers. Her eyes went to Jenny, who was standing by the window gazing out.

"You've been staring out that window for thirty minutes, Jenny. What's wrong? What do you see out there that's so important?"

"Oh, nothing. I guess I'm just too lazy to work."

Ruby studied her boss thoughtfully. Picking up the pen, she tapped the end of it on the desk and glanced at Billy

Moon, who was standing at the counter drinking a cup of coffee. Their eyes met for a moment, and Moon's obsidian eyes seemed to send a message. They both understood that this was not the same young woman who had come into the office with such high hopes.

Jennifer turned and saw the two looking at her. She lifted her chin and said, "I think I'll take a run down to the Williamson place."

"You want me to go with you?" Billy asked.

"No, somebody painted a few ugly words on their barn. Probably just kids. I can handle it alone. I'm sure you have plenty to do."

Moon turned and watched Jenny as she put her hat squarely on her head and left. When the door shut, he sipped the coffee and turned to face Ruby. "She's taken Kermit's death hard."

"Sure has. She's not tough enough for this kind of work."

Moon nodded, then came over and sat down across from Ruby. "You took it pretty hard yourself."

Ruby was surprised at the statement. She had always considered herself strong enough to handle anything, and somehow his remark seemed to question her inner toughness. "Guess I'm handling it as well as anybody else . . . except his family."

"No offense."

Moon's answer did not satisfy Ruby. She was a fiercely independent young woman, and now she faced the deputy and insisted, "I'm fine."

Moon put both his hands flat on the desk and pressed against it. He had rather small hands for a man his size, but they were thick, and Ruby knew that he had a grip like a vise. He could take Coca-Cola caps between his thumb and the tip of his forefinger and squeeze them until they doubled up. She did not know any other man who could do that. There was a strength and solidity to him that most men lacked, so that even when he stood beside larger men, he seemed somehow more substantial. "You've been down yourself, Ruby. I've noticed it."

"Well, Kermit was a good guy."

"Sure, but it's more than that."

Ruby tried to frown. "You've got nothing to do but go around watching women to see if they're depressed?"

Moon picked up the coffee, drained it, then put it on the table and shoved it to one side. "You need to get out more."

"And do what?"

Moon clasped his hands together and squeezed them. "What about Jack Edington? You used to go out with him once in a while."

"Not interested."

"And Ben Latimer. You went over to the state fair with him."

"Wasn't interested." Ruby got up, disturbed by the conversation. Walking over to the table that held the coffeepot, steaming atop a hot plate, she poured herself a cup of coffee. But when she turned, she was surprised to find that Billy was standing right behind her. He moved so softly for such a big man that she hadn't heard him approach. "Don't worry about me, Billy," she said.

"I do worry about you," Moon said. "And I know what could get rid of the blues for a woman like you."

Ruby stared at him skeptically. "What's that?" she demanded, leaning back against the table, effectively increasing the space between them.

"A hug."

Ruby had wondered for some time when this was coming. The other deputies had made passes at her, and she had cut them off frigidly. Now her eyes glinted. "Oh, and I suppose you're volunteering for the job."

"A man does what he's gotta do." Moon smiled suddenly, and humor gleamed in his dark eyes. "It's a man's duty to spread sunshine and cheer."

"I've had lots of volunteers for that."

"You think I'm kidding, but a hug will do wonders for you. I've been working on this theory a long time, and here's what I finally figured out, Ruby. Four hugs a day are necessary for survival."

"Only four?"

"Well, it takes eight for maintenance and twelve for growth."

Suddenly Ruby laughed. "You're a caution, Billy!"

"Listen, now, I worked hard on this theory. But I think it's important who you get the hug from. For example, a hug from a man's son would be worth about twenty from his mother-in-law, I figure. And I think it differs from area to area, depending on community standards."

When Ruby saw that Billy made no move toward her, she relaxed. A smile turned the corners of her lips upward, and she said, "And you've been administering some of those therapeutic hugs to Maisy down at the Elite Café."

"Well, it's a dirty job, but someone has to do it," Billy said and shrugged modestly. "I tell you what. Why don't we go out and eat tonight, and while we're eating, I'll explain my theory more fully."

Ruby considered this and for a moment was tempted to say yes. She was attracted to this man, but still she hesitated. It wasn't because Billy was Indian. She cared little about the opinion of some small-minded people in this town. No, her hesitancy had more to do with men in general. Ruby had survived a hard marriage and had built up a wall against men. She said, "I . . . I don't think so. Thanks for asking, but you know I'm suspicious of men."

"I noticed that," Billy said. "You just haven't known the right one." He turned and started for the door.

After he left the room, Ruby stood, still staring at the door. *He sounds all right, but he's a man, and he'll take advantage if he can.* Something about her thought displeased her, and she shook her head and went back to the ledger and began to write.

★   ★   ★

Jimmy Duo was playing solitaire with a greasy, worn deck of cards. One of the cards was missing, so he had made a three of diamonds out of a piece of cardboard. The sunshine streamed through the barred window like bars of pale gold, and Jimmy hummed under his breath, looking up only when he heard the outer door open and close. When Sheriff Winslow came to stand in front of his cell, he smiled and nodded. "Good morning, Sheriff. How be you this mornin'?"

"I be fine, Jimmy. Was breakfast good?"

"Best ever! If you don't do anything else as sheriff but hire a good cook to take keer of us, then I say you done good."

Jenny stood there smiling at Duo. He was a pitiful man to her but always cheerful, and she made it her business to stop by every day to give him a word of encouragement. The ravages of drink had lined his face, and he was thin almost to emaciation, for when he was not in jail he spent every dime on wine or alcohol in some form. He had even drunk wood alcohol, he had told her once, and it had nearly killed him.

"I wish you had a better life, Jimmy."

Duo looked up surprised. "Do you, Sheriff?"

"Yes, I do. You're not an old man. You've got a lot of years ahead of you."

"Not if I keep on drinkin' wood alcohol." Duo smiled cynically. "But I don't reckon I'll try that again."

"Do you have any family?"

"No, I ain't got nobody."

"Not even a cousin or an uncle? Someone like that?"

"Somebody put me on the porch of a Methodist orphanage in Cincinnati, Sheriff. No note or nothin'. Just left me there like I was a bottle of milk or somethin'."

"Was it hard in an orphanage? I've heard bad stories."

"Well, since I never knowed nothin' else, I couldn't say. They never beat me or nothin' like that. You know what I missed most when I was a kid?"

"What was that, Jimmy?"

"Nobody ever told me I done good. When I was a kid I used to work hard around the place, and all I wanted was for somebody to say, 'Good job, Jimmy.'"

"But nobody ever did? Not even one?"

"Well, they was a lady there that cooked. I carried the wood in for her stove and kept her box filled. She'd say, 'Thanks, Jimmy, you done good.' Made me feel just right."

The bleakness of his story saddened Jenny. "How'd you get the name Jimmy Duo?"

"I picked it out myself. They called me John Smith, and I didn't like that none. So when I got to be twelve years old, I was reading this here book about a detective. His name was Jimmy Duo. I don't even remember who wrote it now—but I liked it. It sounded good and tough and short and was easy to spell. So I called myself Jimmy Duo. That's what I've been ever since."

"I'd like to see you stop drinking. I know that might be hard for you."

"It ain't hard. It's impossible! You think I ain't tried, Sheriff? I tried lots of times, but it don't never work." A sad light touched Duo's eyes and he shook his head. "Reckon I got good intentions, but I always go back and start drinking again."

"Have you ever thought about becoming a Christian?"

"I don't see as how God needs no drunks in His church."

"But I think God could help you if you'd just trust Him. I've heard lots of men and women too testify about how they drank until they got converted, but then God took away the desire, or He helped them endure it."

Duo looked down at the cards before him. He put his forefinger on the three of diamonds and pushed it around slowly. He was silent for such a long time that Jennifer finally said, "What's the matter, Jimmy?"

"You see that card?" He held up the piece of cardboard. "That ain't no real card. All the rest of them, they're alike. But this one was missing, so I made one, but it's just kind of an imitation. I reckon that's what I am, Miss Jenny. Just kind of an imitation feller."

Sorrow filled Jenny then, and she realized that the world was full of people like this—with no purpose, no hope. Finally she said quietly, "I'd like to help you, Jimmy."

"You done helped me already, Sheriff, just showin' an interest and gettin' us a good cook. We all appreciate it."

Jenny wanted to say more, but she felt unable. She thought suddenly, *I've got to get someone here who can talk to Jimmy. Maybe Clint. I'll ask him to come by and visit and witness to this man.* Aloud she said, "Well, Jimmy, Noah's fixing up a good lunch. I'll come back and we can eat together."

"That'd be prime, Miss Jenny. You do it."

★   ★   ★

The sun had dipped beneath the western horizon, casting shadows that made the mountains look like humps of dusky elephants. Jenny glanced at them and then, on impulse, pulled off the main road, steering the car through the high, dead grasses that had grown up on the old logging road. Towering walnut trees rose on each side all the way down to the river, forming a canopy that shielded the earth from the September sun. The squad car bumped over the ruts that had been made during the previous winter and had baked over the summer into a surface almost as hard as concrete.

The road bent itself sharply around a group of tall river birch, and Jenny stopped the car, then shut off the engine. The silence seemed to fall upon her, and for a moment she simply sat there holding on to the steering wheel. Finally with a sigh she opened the door, got out, and walked toward the river. She remembered coming here for a late swim and the embarrassment that had followed when her picture had been taken by one of Al Deighton's reporters for *The Daily Standard.* It all seemed long ago, and as she walked slowly along the bank, the thought came to her that troubles were relative. At that time she had been so humiliated she could hardly bear to get out of bed and face the sly grins from the men of the county. Now the death of Kermit had made that seem small and insignificant.

The late afternoon sunlight filtered down through the tops of the birches, giving the place a cathedral atmosphere. A frog uttered something that sounded like *Yikes!* and wildly leaped into the river. Jenny caught a glimpse of him as he disappeared and sent concentric rings around the clear water that lapped the bank. She stood for a moment watching the rings until they were smoothed away by the slight current, then moved over and leaned against a tall water oak. The silence seemed to soak into her, and she watched the river for a while as it flowed by, its sibilant whisper the only sound.

The stillness was broken by a sharp chattering, and she looked up to see a dapper gray squirrel peering at her from around the edge of the oak. She smiled and murmured, "I didn't mean to invade your territory. You'd better start gathering nuts. It'll be winter soon, and you'll be hungry."

The squirrel gave a frisky twist of his tail, then made a wild run up the tree to disappear into the upper branches. Jenny thought how she had changed since coming to Georgia. She would never have talked aloud to herself in those days in the city. There were too many people around, and she would have felt embarrassed. Now, however, there was no sense of embarrassment, and she simply stood there, mostly thinking of Kermit. The time went by as slowly as the water flowed past her in the river, and she was startled when she heard her name being called. Quickly she moved away from the tree and turned to see Clay Varek walking along the side of the bank. He came up to her and smiled, then said, "I didn't expect to find you here."

"Oh, I just wanted to stop and unwind a bit."

"I saw you at the funeral, but it wasn't a time to speak."

"It hurt me bad, Clay." Just the memory of Kermit's face as she had seen it, still and without animation, swept over her. She turned away, unable to face him, then bent over and picked up a stick. She swished it through the air, then tossed it in the river and watched it float downstream.

"It gets to you. I felt the same way when my buddy died. There's nothing much to do for it except hurt."

"Why, that's the way it is!" Jenny said and turned to face him. "I cried like a baby after that funeral."

"I know. I saw you and Dixon leave. It was a hard thing."

"I went to the scout award ceremony where Bing's grandson got his Eagle Scout badge. Bing was looking forward to that . . . and so was his grandson."

"That must have been tough."

"All I could think of was if it weren't for me, Kermit would have been there. He was so proud of that boy! It was almost the last thing he said to me. So I felt I had to go."

"It's the kind of thing you'd do, Jenny."

When Jenny did not reply, Clay studied her. He noticed that her eyes were a deep green color that seemed to have no bottom. Her lips were pressed tightly together, but he noted that they were shapely. Her hair was pinned into some sort of tight knot, but the brightness of it, as always, drew his eyes. He had never seen such bright red hair in all of his life. Although he did not mean to do so, he glanced down and admired the clean-running physical lines, the lovely turn of her throat, and the curve of her shoulders and waist. Suddenly she turned and caught him looking at her, and he saw her lift one corner of her mouth in a humorless grin. Then he saw tears fill her eyes. For all of her inner strength, at that moment she seemed helpless, and as her tears spilled over, he murmured, "Maybe I can help." Stepping forward, he put his arms around her, and she simply leaned against him, putting her face against his neck. Her body trembled, and he heard the muted sobs, but she recovered quickly.

"I did the same thing," he said as she stepped back and pulled a handkerchief out, "when John Summers died. But you've got God, haven't you? I didn't even have that to hang on to."

Jenny was embarrassed. She thought, *That's two men I've cried all over and that's enough.* She put the handkerchief back, controlled herself, and asked, "Why haven't you ever found the Lord, Clay?"

"I guess it just wasn't in my family. None of them were Christians that I knew of."

Jenny, once again, felt her helplessness. She had felt it with Jimmy Duo, and although she wanted to say something about her faith, she found it very difficult. "Getting to know Jesus isn't a family affair, I don't think, although it helps to have believing family members. It's not too late."

Clay's face suddenly grew tight. "I think it is," he said. He turned and said, "I have to be getting back."

Jenny watched him as he disappeared and knew she had touched some part of him that had long been sealed. She slowly made her way back to the car, wondering why she seemed so incapable of communicating the Lord to anyone. When she started the car, she sat there for a moment, ruminating on the strangeness of Clay Varek, then shook her head and drove out of the shadows.

CHAPTER FOURTEEN

A NEW YORK YANKEE
BITES THE DUST

★ ★ ★

Somehow Jenny was able over the next week to put at least the most agonizing memories of Kermit Bing aside. Deep down she knew she would never forget him, but knowing that life must go on, she buried herself in her job and found solace in doing what many had said she could not. Being a sheriff was not what she had expected, but every day, almost every hour, she was learning. She had a quick, retentive mind, and once she learned something she held on to it as tenaciously as a snapping turtle.

One thing that helped her through was her attention to Jamie Varek. She had formed the habit of stopping by and often took her a small gift. Late one Thursday afternoon she stopped by on her way home. It was a lovely autumn day, and she had really no desire to go home and to sit staring at the walls.

"Jenny—Jenny, what'd you bring me?"

Jenny stopped and knelt down, laughing as the girl came sailing out of the house and down the porch, followed by Clay. She caught her up in a hug and said, "What makes you think I brought you anything?"

"You always do. What did you bring me?"

Clay had come to smile down at the pair. "That's not polite. You're not supposed to ask for presents."

Jamie looked up and frowned. "I want presents," she said distinctly.

"You're going to grow up into a modern woman, Jamie," Clay said, smiling. "Don't pay any attention to her, Sheriff."

"But I did bring her something. You'll like it too," she said, a mischievous light dancing in her eyes. She turned and went back to the car and came back with a paper sack. "Come on up on the porch, and I'll show you what I brought." She ascended the steps, followed by Clay, and all the time Jamie was demanding to know what was in the sack. Sitting down on the swing, she lifted Jamie up beside her while Clay stood watching, a smile on his lips.

Opening the sack, Jenny pulled out a book and said, "Look, do you know who this is?"

"No. Little girl."

"That's Shirley Temple. And this is a paper doll book."

"Pretty little girl."

"Yes, she is a pretty little girl. I'll take you to see her in a movie some time, but this is what's called a *paper doll*. See, here's Shirley and look at all these pages. They are different dresses and outfits you can put on her. You have to cut them out, and I brought you a special pair of scissors." Fishing down into the sack, she pulled forth a pair of scissors with rounded ends small enough to fit Jamie's hands. "Look, I'll show you how to cut one out. You must be very careful. You see these flaps? That's what holds them on."

Clay Varek stood watching as the two played with the dolls. He pulled up a cane-bottomed chair, sat down, and tilted it back. The sight pleased him, and he finally said, "I don't know what Jamie and I would do without you."

"Well, now you've got paper dolls to cut out."

"Me cut out dolls! I don't think so."

"That's what daddies have to do. My dad did when I was no bigger than Jamie here, and Hannah said he did it for her too."

Clay grinned broadly. "Well, if a medal-of-honor man can cut out a paper doll, I guess I can too." He looked up at the sky and said, "It's almost dark. I've cooked too much supper. Stay and eat with us."

"Oh, I'd better not."

"Well, I don't doubt you'd get better grub at home, but Jamie would like for you to stay. Wouldn't you, Jamie?"

Jamie reached up and caught at Jenny. "Yes, stay and we'll play dolls."

"Well, all right," Jenny said. "But I'll set the table and wash the dishes."

★   ★   ★

Jenny had intended to go home after the supper, which had been surprisingly good. Clay had fried pork chops and boiled potatoes and had made biscuits. Jenny had bragged on the food, and Clay had shook his head. "Well, it's all I know how. We eat a pretty steady diet of this."

"I'll come by and make you a squash pie," Jenny said and smiled. She gave in to Jamie when the little girl demanded that she cut out more paper dolls.

Finally the child's eyes grew heavy, and Clay said, "Time for you to go to bed. Come along."

"Oh, let me put her in bed!" Jenny offered. She rose up, lifted Jamie, and for the next thirty minutes had a wonderful time brushing the girl's shiny hair, putting her pajamas on, and plunking her into bed. When Jamie had demanded a story, Clay had come in and leaned in the door listening as Jenny told the story of the three bears. Finally Jamie dropped off to sleep, and the two left the room. Clay left the door slightly open, and the two went back into the kitchen. "How about a cup of coffee?"

"All right. Then let's get outside and sit on the porch."

They had their coffee, sat on the porch, and for a time they did not talk. Finally Clay said, "Let's go down to the pond. I want to show you something."

"All right."

The two made their way to the back of the house, where a rather large pond caught the moon that had risen, a huge silver disk in the sky. "Look, they're still out there."

Jenny looked out and saw a duck swimming across the pond followed by a flotilla of ducklings. "Oh, aren't they sweet!" she said.

"I bet they'd be delicious," Clay said with a straight face.

Jenny turned. "How can you say such a thing? They're so cute."

"A calf's cute too, but I haven't noticed you turning down any veal."

"That's different." They had had this argument before, Jenny protesting that she couldn't eat deer meat because deer were so beautiful.

They stood there for a moment and then a strange-looking bird came out. It made an odd cry, and Jenny said, "What in the world kind of bird is that?"

"Don't know. He comes out late in the afternoon or real early in the morning. Listen to him. It sounds like he's saying, 'Get out! Get out!' I just call him the 'Get Out Bird.'"

"I'll bet Clint would know what kind it is."

"Probably would. I think he knows every bird and animal in this country. Want to walk around the pond?"

"All right."

They moved around the pond, not getting far from the house in case Jamie woke up. Jenny finally turned to him and said, "I've got to get home."

"It's good you came by," Clay said. He hesitated, then said, "I know you still think about Kermit."

"Yes, besides my mother's death, it was one of the saddest things that ever happened to me."

The moonlight made a silver track on the pond, and it reflected on Clay's face. Jenny watched him as he grew thoughtful. "Sad things come to us. There's no avoiding them. I heard a preacher once quote a verse that said, 'Man's born to trouble as the sparks fly upward.'"

"Where's that in the Bible?"

"I don't know. It's true, though."

"I suppose it is."

"One time I was on a job back in Chicago. We were doing a stakeout in a rough part of town. I saw a note somebody had left under a rock outside of a tenement. I picked it up and read it. I've never forgotten it."

"What'd it say, Clay?"

"It said, 'I just couldn't come—I hope you will forgive me.'"

"That's all? No signature?"

"No. I've often thought about that note. Who wrote it? I've wondered if the two ever got together."

"It is sad. You feel sadness more than most people, Clay. I can sense it in you."

Clay tried to smile. "Well, I feel like an orphan. I'm too young to die and too old to play."

Jenny put her hand on his arm. "You're not too old to play. You're still a young man. You've got Jamie, and you can do many things."

Clay was very conscious of her hand on his arm. With his other hand, he put his hand over hers. Her hand was warm, and he squeezed it, saying, "You're a comfort, Jennifer."

Suddenly Jenny felt a discomfort. This man puzzled her. He was an enigma, and she could not understand her own feelings about him. "I've got to go," she said, pulling her hand away.

The two walked back to the house, and when she left, he called out, "As they say in these parts, don't be a stranger."

"I won't. Come to supper tomorrow night—it's my birthday—and bring Jamie."

"We'll be there."

★ ★ ★

By the time Jenny had gotten down to breakfast, the three babies were all crying as if their hearts would break. Missouri was trying to finish breakfast, and the others were trying to pacify the three.

"These are three of the stubbornest babies I ever saw in my life," Lewis said. He was holding Michael while Hannah held Samuel, and Clint was tossing Temple up in the air try-ing to catch his attention. All to no avail. "Stubborn as blue-nosed mules," Lewis said, shaking his head. He glanced slyly at Missouri, who was hurrying to put breakfast on the table. "That's the Ramey blood in them," he said, winking at Jenny. "All of us Winslows have been nice, easygoing folks. Never impatient like these monsters."

As he had known would happen, Missouri's eyes sud-denly flashed, and she came over and grabbed Lewis by the hair. "Don't you talk that way about these babies, poor little things! They're just hungry, and if I ever saw a stubborn man in my life, you're it! Now, you sit down and let me start feed-ing these three." She gathered up Temple and Michael and headed off for the living room, leaving Samuel behind. Jenny grabbed Sam and sat down and tucked the tip of her little finger in his mouth. He clamped down on it, and she laughed. "You bite like a turtle."

"Getting breakfast and keeping those three fed is more than any human should have to do," Clint said.

Kat came scurrying in and sat down, demanding food at once. Lewis asked the blessing; then Kat began peppering Hannah with questions. "What does it feel like to have a baby kicking around on the inside of you, Hannah?"

Hannah flushed and said crossly, "Don't talk about such things!"

Kat stuffed her mouth full with a huge bite of toast smeared with apple butter, chewed it, and mumbled, "Why not?"

"Because it's not proper."

"Well, how am I gonna know if you don't tell me any-thing?"

"You'll find out when you're older."

Kat glared at her. "That's what everybody always tells me. I'm old enough now!"

"Well, you wait until after breakfast at least, and then you can talk to me. Or better still, talk to Ma. She knows more about babies than anybody I know."

"Doris Hartman thinks the stork brings babies," Kat

scoffed. "I've tried to tell her different, but she doesn't want to listen."

"I think you ought to leave her alone," Hannah said quickly. "That's a family matter."

"She thinks the tooth fairy leaves money under your pillow. And she's twelve years old. She ought to know better than that. I've tried to tell her different, but she won't listen."

Jenny listened to Kat with amusement. She wondered what in the world the young girl would be like when she was completely grown if she continued to be so outspoken. She got up after finishing breakfast, kissed Samuel, and handed him to Hannah, then stopped long enough to smooth her father's hair back from his forehead. "I'll be in early tonight."

"Well, I hope so," Lewis smiled, "I know Missouri has a special birthday supper planned for you."

She looked back at Hannah, saying, "I asked Clay to bring Jamie over to supper tonight."

"Good," Hannah said. "I know he gets lonely. I don't see how a man can take care of a child like that all by himself."

"He seems to do very well. She's healthy and happy."

"Wonder why he don't get married? Then he'd have somebody to take care of Jamie," Kat spoke up. "I'll tell him tonight when he comes that's what he oughta do."

"You keep quiet, Kat!" Jenny snapped. "That's his business, not yours."

Leaving the house, Jenny drove to work, and as soon as she walked into the office, Ruby said, "Bad news." She held up a newspaper, and walking over, Jenny took it. It was a copy of *The Daily Standard*. The headline said blatantly, "Sheriff Brings Death To Deputy."

Anger flashed through Jenny, and she began to read the article. It basically said that she was responsible for Kermit Bing's death, and for nearly half a page went on talking about her inability to serve the county properly and calling for her resignation.

"Can't you sue that idiot?" Ruby demanded.

"I don't think so. There's no law against criticizing a public official." Jenny was humiliated by the article, but she had learned that *The Daily Standard* could be depended on to point out her faults and to invent them when they did not exist. Finally she merely said, "Well, you can't stop a dog from yapping, so let's get on with our work."

The two women started their day, and about ten o'clock the door opened and a small man walked in and said loudly, "I'm lookin' for Sheriff Winslow. I guess you're her."

The man had a northern accent, Jenny recognized at once. She had grown accustomed to the softness and the rather slow pace of southern speech, and this man's accent, as well as his clothes, identified him as being from the North. "I'm Sheriff Winslow."

"I'm Saul Greenberg, Sheriff. I'd like to have an interview with you. I'm with *The Chicago Tribune*."

"You came all the way from Chicago to interview me?"

Greenberg was a sharp-faced man with quick eyes that looked Jenny up and down before answering. He was one of those men, Jenny recognized, that barely ever looked higher than a woman's chin. She disliked him immediately but was determined to be polite. "Come back to my office."

"Right you are, Sheriff."

Jenny led him back to the office, and Greenberg took a seat as Jenny seated herself behind the desk. "I'm doing a series of articles about the South." He grinned rather unpleasantly. "I think a female sheriff's about as unusual as common sense around this place."

Jenny said, "You have five minutes, Mr. Greenberg."

Greenberg's eyes narrowed. "Five minutes! That's not much."

"It took you a few seconds to say that. You can subtract that from the five."

"Wait a minute, Sheriff. You're not being cooperative."

"Ask your questions."

Greenberg stared at her, antagonism plain on his face. "I read the article in the paper yesterday. It says you practically got one of your deputies killed through negligence. How do you answer that?"

"It's a lie."

Greenberg waited for her to go on, and when she did not, he snapped, "Well, you have to say more than that!"

"I don't argue with liars, Mr. Greenberg. If you want the facts, read the report. My clerk will give it to you."

Greenberg began to fire questions at her, and Jenny answered them. Finally he said, "Whatever made you think you could be a sheriff anyway? Women weren't made to do things like that. Why don't you get a husband? Be like the rest of these southern women—stay barefoot and pregnant."

Jenny angrily rose up. "I'll show you the door."

"Wait a minute—"

Jenny reached down and got the man's arm and pulled him to his feet. He was a very small man, and she saw his face flush with anger. Turning him around, she gave him a slight push and said, "Do you need help getting through that door?"

Greenberg began to shout, and at that moment Billy Moon appeared. "You need some help, Sheriff?"

"Show Mr. Greenberg out, Billy."

"Right this way, Mr. Greenberg." Billy reached out and clamped his meat hook of a hand on Greenberg's arm. He turned and towed the reporter away, and when Greenberg started shouting invectives, he simply increased the pressure on his arm.

"Ow, you're breaking my arm!"

"I know it's hard for you Yankees to be polite, but I'd suggest you lower your voice or I'll break more than your arm." He gave the arm an extra few pounds of pressure, and Greenberg turned pale and began to whimper. "You're hurting me!"

Billy ignored this. He took him to the door, opened it, and pushed him out, closing it behind him.

"Nice fellow," Ruby said. "You're going to get a bad story in his paper."

"I doubt if many people read that."

"Well, if you want some bad news, I just got word that the budget's been slashed again. The county commission had an uncalled meeting. That means they just got together, drank whiskey, and made decisions."

"What grounds did they have for slashing the budget?"

"They said you're not making any headway against the bootleggers."

Jenny sadly looked down. "Well, there's some truth to that."

"You haven't been in office very long. It'll come."

Jenny shook her head and made no answer. She said nothing for the rest of the day, except for remarks about official business, and at noon Luke Dixon came by. He took one look at her and said, "Come on, birthday girl, let me buy you lunch."

"I'm not hungry, Luke."

"Well, you can listen to me eat, then."

Jenny could not help but smile. "All right. I'll do that."

The two went to the Elite Café and sat down, and Jenny found out that she was hungry after all. "I can't eat much," she said. "Clay and his daughter are coming over for supper tonight. Missouri and Hannah will fix enough for an army. Why don't you come too, Luke?"

"Can't do it. I'm going out of town. Going to the capital."

"What for?"

"Meeting with the feds. See what's being done to eliminate the export of moonshine from our fair state. Maybe it will be helpful to you."

"I'm about to give up. It seems like I'm getting nowhere."

Dixon put his hand on her arm. "You know what? The sun came up again this morning."

Jennifer was surprised. "What do you mean?"

"Well, I was shocked. I took one look at it and said, 'You son of a gun, you did it again!'"

"You're crazy, Luke. The sun comes up every morning."

"That's right, and you've got a whole new day tomorrow that hasn't been touched yet."

"You're trying to cheer me up, aren't you?"

"That's what I'm trying to do." Luke talked for some time, and finally he said, "You know, Jenny, bad things happen to everybody. They happen to me, but I go back and try to think of some good things that God's done for me."

"I'm sure that you're better off."

Dixon sipped his coffee, then shook his head. "They say we're made of ninety-five percent water. It seems like we'd slosh when we walk, but that's wrong. I think we're ninety-five percent memories."

Jenny listened to Luke for another fifteen minutes and finally smiled. "You're good for what ails me, Luke, but really the problem won't go away. I've about decided to resign."

Luke stared at her with alarm. "You can't do that, Jenny!"

"I think it'd be better for everyone."

"Better for Judge Hightower and for his cronies. Better for the bootleggers. But the people that elected you—would it be better for them?"

"But I'm not doing any good."

"Promise me this," Luke said earnestly. "Don't do anything hastily."

"All right. I won't. Thanks for the lunch."

"Anytime." Luke took her hand. He held it for a moment, squeezing it slightly, then smiled. "You're on a low limb right now, but it'll get better."

★ ★ ★

"That was a fine supper, wasn't it?" Clay said. He had come over with Jamie, and the birthday supper had been outstanding. There wasn't much money for presents, but from her family there was a beautifully decorated chocolate cake and a matching muff and hat. Clay had given her a hand-carved nameplate for her desk, and Jamie had drawn a special birthday picture.

Afterward, Clay and Jenny had gone out to sit on the front porch, while Kat was inside playing house with Jamie. The crickets made a symphony circling the house, and overhead the full moon beamed down with silver rays. Jenny had said little during the meal, but now she knew she had to talk. "Clay, I'm thinking about resigning."

Clay did not answer for a time, and she finally asked rather sharply, "Did you hear what I said?"

"I don't think you mean that."

"But, Clay, I can't do it!"

"You're doing a good job. You're new is all."

Jenny was feeling rather sorry for herself. From time to time she fell into this mood, and she knew it and hated herself for it. It was a defensive mechanism, and finally she began saying angrily, "It's easy enough for you to talk! All you do is stay in the house and take care of one little girl! Anybody could do that! But this job is hard."

"It's not as hard as my job." He turned suddenly to face her and seized the edge of her chair and swung it around. "Listen to me. You can't quit." There was a hard edge to his voice, like a bell clanging out a deadly tiding, and Jenny could not move. She had never seen him like this. There was something almost dangerous about him. It was not that she was afraid for herself, but she saw that he was a man who could not be ignored. She listened as he told her almost roughly how she had a chance to do something good, and finally he said, "You told me once you thought God had put you in this. Have you asked Him about resigning?"

Instantly, Jenny lowered her head. "No, I haven't," she whispered.

"If He put you on the job, I think you'd better stay there. I don't know much about God myself, but I know if He gave me something to do, I'd stick with it until I couldn't move."

Jenny did not speak for a moment, and then finally she said, "Clay, I feel so helpless. You know all about this kind of thing. Will you help me? Will you put on a uniform and a badge?"

Clay hesitated, then shook his head. "No, I won't. My first priority is Jamie. I can't do both."

Jenny got up. She felt angry, and she did not know if it was at herself or at Clay Varek. "Good night, Clay," she said frostily. Turning, she went into the house and went straight up to her room. Varek stood on the porch, and for a moment he was tempted to call her back. But then he settled back and shook his head, his jaw clenched. "I've got all I can do to take care of Jamie. That's all there is to it."

CHAPTER FIFTEEN

KAT HAS HER SAY

★ ★ ★

The sun was high in the sky as Kat moved along the dusty road headed for home. In her left hand she carried an old flour sack bulging with crawdads, and, from time to time, she would pause, set the sack down, and glance inside.

"Oh, you're gonna be good eatin'!" Reaching inside, she picked up a large crawdad, more than four inches long, and held it by its hard shell. She put her forefinger carefully in front of him, and when he pinched her, she squealed and jerked away. "You're gonna be good eatin' tonight, so just make up your mind to that." Dropping the crustacean back into the bag, she tied a knot in the top and began to sing as she approached the house:

"Muskrat, muskrat, what makes your back so slick?
I've been livin' in the water all my life
There's no wonder I'm sick
I'm sick, I'm sick, I'm sick.

"Rooster, rooster, what makes your spurs so hard?
I've been scratchin' in the barnyard all my life
There's no wonder I'm tired
I'm tired, I'm tired, I'm tired.

"Jaybird, jaybird, what makes you fly so high?
Been eatin' these acorns all my life
It's a wonder I don't die
I don't die, I don't die, I don't die."

The song pleased her, and she sang it again as she skirted the side of the house and went around to the kitchen, where she found Hannah peeling potatoes on the back porch.

"Look what I got, Hannah." Untying the sack, she went over and pulled it open. "Ain't they fine?"

"Don't say *ain't*. Kat, your grammar has gotten terrible since we moved here." Hannah looked down at the crawdads, and then her mouth puckered as if she had bit into a green persimmon. "I don't see how anybody eats those nasty things!"

"Well, the way Clint fixes them, they're good," Kat said. "He calls it crawfish *étouffée*."

"Well, you and Clint will have to settle that. I'm not cooking a bunch of bugs."

"Okay. Me and Clint will do it." Turning, Kat left the porch, and going out to the spring house, she dumped the crawdads in a large bucket and poured some water in. "That'll keep you fresh," she said, nodding with satisfaction. "But I'm eatin' you for supper tonight and that's all she wrote."

She heard voices coming from the barn and knew that it was Jenny and her father. Kat had no scruples against eavesdropping, so she stepped up next to the barn and put her ear to the large crack between the boards to hear more easily. Jenny was upset. Kat could tell by the sound of her voice.

"I just can't do it any longer, Dad. I just can't!"

"I know it's hard, Jenny, but you knew it would be."

"I didn't know it would be *this* hard."

"You're just upset about losing Kermit."

"Well, I am, but it's more than that."

A silence followed for a moment, and then Kat heard her father say softly, "I know how tough it's been, but I've been so proud of you, daughter."

"Oh, Dad, I haven't really done anything except to get a man killed."

"You didn't get him killed. He was killed doing his duty, and that's something any officer faces. Why, you face it yourself, Jenny."

"It's different when it's somebody else."

"I remember during the war. We had an officer, a lieutenant, named Jamison. He had all kinds of courage himself, but he just couldn't order men to go in under fire. He finally had to be replaced. I think they made a clerk of him in the quartermaster department. He wasn't afraid of risking his own life, but he just couldn't do it to others."

"That's exactly the way I feel, Dad, and I know you're going to say that I ought to keep on. You never wanted me to quit at anything."

Kat remained absolutely silent listening as her father and Jenny spoke. She had been aware for some time that Jenny was acting strangely. Kat herself had thought it would be wonderful to be able to wear a uniform and a gun and drive around in a police car and make people do what you wanted. Now, however, she was seeing a side of Jenny she had not known existed. Jenny had always put up such a tough front that Kat had never suspected she had these fears, but as the conversation went on, she began to see that her sister was actually afraid and this disturbed her.

"If only I had someone I could really *trust*, Dad!"

"You've got Billy Moon."

"Yes, and Billy's great, but he's only one man. You know what I think?"

"What's that, Jenny?"

"If Clay would help I think I'd be all right. He's been on a big-time Chicago police force. He doesn't talk about it much, but I know he was a good policeman. When we went to pick up the votes during the election, there were some hard people there, but they just backed down when Clay stepped up."

"You talked to him about coming on as a deputy?"

"Yes, I have, but he says it's all he can do to take care of Jamie."

"I suppose that is a big job."

Kat heard no more, for she picked up her bucket of crawdads and tiptoed away, making as little sound as possible.

Stashing the bucket in the shade of the house, she trotted out of the yard, and as soon as she was out of sight of the house, she said aloud, "Well, Jenny needs help, and Clay is the one who can do it!"

* * *

Clay stepped through the gate inside the fenced coop he had built to keep the chickens in and looked over his small flock. They were not a very attractive bunch, for he had picked up odds and ends of different kinds. Some of the birds were white, others were black, and some were speckled. They clucked and gathered around him as he tossed some feed out and watched as they scrambled around clucking noisily. "Eat up! For one of you this is your last meal on the earth. Got to have supper tonight and fried chicken is *it*."

His attention was captured when he heard someone call his name, and he turned to see Kat Winslow trotting up to the house. She was wearing a pair of faded overalls with patches on the knees and was barefooted. A battered straw hat perched on her head rather precariously, and her tawny hair fell over her forehead when she yanked it off and came to stand before him. She had gray eyes that were almost green at times but now seemed almost blue. "Hello, Kat. What are you doing here?"

"I came to talk to you, Clay."

"That sounds serious."

"It is, but you go ahead and finish what you're doing."

Clay turned and glanced at the chickens. "It's a matter of life and death, Kat. Jamie and I are going to have chicken tonight, and I'm wondering which one of these to pick."

"Doesn't make any difference, does it, as long as they're fat enough."

"I guess it does to them, but they don't know that."

"You want me to pick one?"

"Sure. Go ahead."

"Then I pick that big white one right over there."

"All right. That's what I'll do. You want to stay and have supper with us?"

"No, I'll have to go home, but I want to talk to you."

Clay studied the young girl. She was, he knew, fourteen years old and was caught in that time of life when young girls go through the process of turning from gangly creatures into shapely young women. He had learned to like Kat, but he had told Jenny once, *"She's going to have to quit being a boy pretty soon. Put on a dress and start acting silly like a girl."* And now he stepped outside the chicken yard, fastened the door securely, and said, "Come on up on the porch. We'll talk."

"Where's Jamie?"

"She's taking a nap."

The two of them sat down on the porch, and Clay said, "You sit there, and I'll go get you something to drink. It won't be cold, but it'll be wet."

Five minutes later the two were sipping warm lemonade, and Kat asked suddenly, "Is it hard to raise a baby alone, you bein' a man and all?"

Clay was surprised by the question, but then he nodded. "Hardest thing I've ever done."

Kat gulped down the lemonade, then wiped her mouth with the back of her hand. "Well, why don't you get married, then?"

Clay shook his head and smiled. "That's not a very good reason to get married, to find a nursemaid."

"People do it, though. They get married for all kinds of reasons. You know old man Tatum down by the river in that old white house?"

"I know him. What about him?"

"Well, he's an old man. I mean really old. He must be . . . oh, I guess forty or fifty. That's pretty old. And he married Sarah Simington. She ain't no more than fifteen."

"That's just a year older than you are—and Jenny will skin you if you don't stop saying *ain't*."

"Well, he didn't care nothin' about her. He just wanted someone to keep house, cook, and wash his clothes."

"I'm surprised she married him."

"I told her she was crazy," Kat said, then paused to finish

off the lemonade. She set the glass down on the floor beside her and nodded. "She's not pretty, and I guess she figured if she was gonna have any kind of a home, that'd be her only chance. She won't like it, though."

"Not very romantic."

"Romantic! I reckon not."

Clay Varek sat listening as Kat rattled on. Finally she took a deep breath and said, "I came to talk to you about Jenny. You gotta help her, Clay."

"Help her. What's wrong with her?"

"Her job's getting her down. She's gonna quit if you don't do something."

Clay's eyes narrowed, and he studied the young woman. "I don't know what I can do."

"You can go to work for her. That's what. Get you a gun and catch those moonshiners. You've been a policeman, and you know how to do stuff like that."

"Did Jenny tell you to come here?"

"No, I listened while she was talking to Daddy. She told him she was going to quit, and she said that you could help, but you won't."

"Well, I'd like to help, but I can't."

"Why not?"

"Because I've got Jamie to take care of."

"We can take care of Jamie. I can watch her after school in the afternoons, and Hannah and Missouri Ann can watch her in the mornings. She's easy to take care of. She's such a good girl."

Clay sat silently rocking back and forth slightly, then shook his head. "That wouldn't be right, Kat. You see, when Jamie's daddy got killed, I promised myself that I'd take care of her."

Kat said sharply, "Nobody's arguing about that, but you could help Jenny and take care of Jamie too. All you need is a little help, and I'm telling you that you can leave her with us."

"Did you talk to your dad about this, or your ma?"

"No, but I will if you'll do it."

Clay Varek, in all truth, was tempted. His life had become very narrow, and he had had great difficulty in adjusting at first. But now he was getting bored. He admired Kat for coming. She was a forward young lady full of a thousand schemes, but there was a basic honesty in her that you could not find in many adults. "I'd like to help Jenny. Let me think about it, will you, Kat?"

"Sure." Kat rose and said, "Thanks for the lemonade. I've gotta get on home now."

"All right, Kat. I wouldn't say anything to Jenny about this if I were you."

"I won't, but I'm gonna ask God to let you come to work for her." She nodded confidently and said, "You'll do it. God will *make* you!" She turned and left the porch in a single leap and then trotted down the road, stirring up small clouds of dust as she ran.

Clay Varek watched and smiled, amused at the girl. But then he grew more sober. "Maybe I ought to do it." Clay leaned against the pillar that supported the porch roof and put his mind on the problem. He sat so still that a chipmunk streaked across the ground in front of him with the usual calamitous air of the small creatures. Clay watched as it stopped and sat up. It tucked its front legs tightly against its chest so that only its paws were visible. To Clay, the chipmunk looked somewhat like a man coming to ask for a favor and holding his hat. The two regarded each other and then, like a flash, the chipmunk scurried away and disappeared around the corner of the house.

"Maybe I oughta do it," Clay said again. "She needs help, and she's not likely to get a lot of that around here."

★ ★ ★

Lewis Winslow was somewhat surprised when Clay Varek turned up at his house. He had looked out the window and saw Clay get out of the truck and watched as he picked up Jamie and brought her up on the front porch. Lewis went out at once to meet him, but Hannah had beaten him to it. She was already reaching for Jamie, saying, "Come along. I've just got some gingerbread about ready to come out of the oven. I'll give you a piece of it."

"Be all right with me. Maybe I'll eat some myself later."

Lewis waited until Hannah had taken Jamie off, then he said, "Sit down, Clay."

"Oh, I can't stay long," Clay protested. But he sat down in one of the cane-bottom rockers, and for a time he spoke of common things. Clay said once, "Us Yankees have kind of a hard time here in the South, don't we?"

Lewis laughed. "Yes, we do. I didn't even know what grits were when I came down here, and now I have to have them every day or I think I've been cheated."

"One thing I can't get over," Clay said slowly, "is how friendly people are in this country. They always speak and nod even to strangers."

"Yes, they do. And you know they do another thing that never happens up North? Have you noticed, Clay, how when you're driving and you pass another car, whoever's driving usually waves at you?"

"That's right. They do."

"That never happened in New York, I don't think. Sometimes people around here just lift their fingers from the steering wheel, but they nearly always look at you and give you some kind of a sign. Even total strangers."

Varek nodded. "I think that's a good thing. I don't know why southerners are different, but they are."

"It may have something to do with the pace of life," Lewis mused. "Things are somehow slower around here, at least slower than they were in the middle of New York City."

The two men sat there talking idly, and finally Lewis said, "How are you getting along, Clay? I know it's been a hard adjustment for you to make leaving the big city and bringing Jamie here."

"It's been tough. I'm not sure I can do it for the next fifteen, sixteen years until Jamie's grown."

Lewis studied the face of Clay Varek. It was a strong face, not handsome but intensely masculine. His ears lay flat against his head, and his tawny hair needed cutting. There was a rough attractiveness to the man, but in his eyes, Lewis saw dissatisfaction. "I guess most of us are looking for something. As for me, when I lost all of my money and my home, I was just looking for anything. A place to get a roof over my head for me and my family."

"Well, you've made it here, Lewis. Your family's all settled in. You've got a nice place."

"We don't have any money and are not likely to. What are you looking for, Clay?"

A bleak look swept across Varek's face. "I don't know, Lewis."

The blankness of the answer gave Lewis an inclination to pursue the subject. "You know a friend of mine lost his leg going up San Juan Hill. We kept in touch, and years later he went back there. Of course he didn't find the thing he lost. I'm not sure we can do that."

"What are you saying, Lewis?"

"I'm saying most of us have lost something. Maybe not a leg like Charlie but *something*. And there's not much point in going back and trying to find it again. Usually we can't. I think you need to look for the right thing."

Clay straightened up and his eyes met those of Lewis Winslow. "And what is the right thing?"

"I guess you know what I'd say. I'd say that finding the Lord is the right thing."

Clay nodded. "I know that's what you feel. I wish I did sometimes."

"You will. You've got some folks praying for you, Clay." He smiled slightly. "We didn't wait to ask your permission."

Clay studied the man in front of him. He knew there was a rock-hard honesty in Lewis Winslow. The whole family had it, and Varek admired them all tremendously. "Maybe religion will come to me," he said.

"Plenty of religion about, but Jesus is more than that."

"What do you mean by that? I don't understand."

"Well, Jesus made one claim that stands out. He said, 'I am the way, the truth, and the life: no man cometh unto the Father, but by me.' So that's the difference between Jesus and everybody else. He said the only way to get to God was through Him."

"Pretty narrow door."

"Too narrow for most people. They want it to be broad. They think God should just take everybody, no matter what kind of religion they have. But there's one more verse in the Bible I wish you'd think on, Clay. It's in Hebrews. It says, 'Without shedding of blood there is no remission.'"

"I don't get it."

"You would if you read the Old Testament for a while. It's a bloody book. Once under Solomon's reign they sacrificed over a thousand animals in one day. Blood must have been everywhere, but all of those lambs that were slain didn't wash away any sins. That's why Jesus came to shed His blood because He had the only blood that could wash away sin."

For nearly twenty minutes Lewis spoke softly about his deepest beliefs. He spoke mostly of Jesus, how He came to save sinners. Finally he said, "That's what you need to be looking for. It's what *all* of us need to be looking for, Clay."

Clay's head was down. He had listened silently, and Lewis had no idea how he was taking all this. Perhaps he was angry, as some men get when they are confronted with Christ. Finally he looked up and nodded. "I'll think on it, Lewis."

"I wish you would."

"Did you know Kat came to see me?"

"That girl gets around everywhere."

"She overhead you and Jenny talking. She told me about it."

"Talking about what?"

"She said Jenny wanted to quit and that I ought to help her."

Instantly Lewis nodded. "If you would, it would be a comfort to me, Clay. She's afraid, and she's uncertain, and right now she's got more confusion than she needs."

"But I've got Jamie to take care of."

"Leave her with us while you're working."

Startled, Clay said, "That's what Kat told me. But I knew I had to talk to you."

"That girl's got a head full of sense along with some mighty wild ideas. Look, one more child won't matter around here. If you would help Jenny, it would be a big load off my mind, Clay."

"I'll go talk to her."

"Sure. You leave Jamie here, and I hope it works out."

★ ★ ★

"Hello, Ruby, is the sheriff here?"

"No, she's eating lunch down at the Elite Café."

"Thanks, Ruby."

Leaving the sheriff's office, Varek walked down the street. He turned into the Elite Café and saw Luke Dixon and Jenny sitting at a table together. He hesitated and almost turned to leave, but Dixon saw him and called out, "Hey, Clay, come on over and join us!"

Clay walked over and said, "Hello, Luke . . . Jenny, how are you?"

"Sit down, Clay. We're about through eating, but we're going to have dessert."

Clay hesitated, then sat down. When Jenny asked about Jamie, he smiled and said, "I left her at your house. Your dad said that with three babies around, one more child wouldn't matter."

"I think he's right about that, and Kat loves to play with Jamie. Treats her like a big doll."

The waitress came over and brought pie. Clay took a cup of coffee but no more. He listened as the two talked, saying little himself, and finally Dixon rose and said, "Well, I've got to get back to work. Good to see you, Clay."

"You too, Luke."

"That's a good man, Jenny," Varek said, watching the lawyer leave the café.

"Yes, he is."

Something in her tone caught Varek's attention. "You two going together—dating or anything like that?"

"We go out once in a while."

Varek sipped his coffee, considered that, and then he said, "Jenny, I've been thinking you might need some help. I'd be glad to fill in on a part-time basis."

Jenny's eyes flew open wide, and she could not speak for a moment. "Oh, Clay, it's what I've been hoping for!" She put her hand on his forearm and squeezed it. "You'll be so much help, and, to tell the truth, I've been downright discouraged."

"Well, I'm no magician, but I'll do what I can." Varek was highly aware of Jenny's touch, and wanting to prolong the moment, he said, "Maybe I'd better have a sandwich and a cream soda."

"It's on me." Jenny grew conscious of the hard muscle beneath her touch and, flustered, pulled her hand away. "Now, tell me how we can catch these moonshiners."

CHAPTER SIXTEEN

A MATTER OF KIN

★ ★ ★

Billy Moon came hurrying in, his dark eyes bright and a smile on his lips. "Well, it looks like the new man's going to work out."

Jenny and Ruby had been going over the new budget, trying to find a way to make it work. Both of them were surprised by Billy's abrupt entrance, and it was Ruby who said, "You talking about Clay?"

Moon came to stand in front of them, and he seemed more pleased than either of the women had ever seen him. "Arp and Pender aren't gonna like it. They wanted to see Clay fail ever since you took him on, Sheriff."

This was true enough. The two deputies had been sullen and resentful of Varek ever since Jenny had brought him into the office a few weeks ago. They had been free enough with their remarks that what was not needed in the sheriff's office was another Yankee! Clay had not responded to the two but had gone about his duties in a serious and professional way. He had been a great help already to Jenny, for he had a steady, confident way of doing things that pleased her. They had spent a great deal of time talking about the organization of the office. Jenny had waited for him to comment on Pender and Arp, but his only remark had been, *"You had to have some-body, and they know the country."*

"What did Clay do, Billy?" Jenny asked now.

"I don't guess you know Clyde Wiggins, do you?"

"No. Who is he?"

"Aw, he's a sorry fellow that lives over by Judkins Creek. Been in about almost every kind of trouble there is."

"That's right. He's a hard one," Ruby said, nodding. "He's been in jail more than once, but nobody's been able to pin anything serious on him. Did Clay have trouble with him?"

"No, I think he had trouble with Clay." Billy laughed softly and leaned forward, putting his fist on the desk. "I just stayed back. I really wanted to test him out. Wiggins is a tough one, and I wanted to see how Clay would handle him."

"What was the charge?"

"Oh, he was drunk, as usual. We caught him with two gallons of moonshine whiskey. He couldn't drink it all. He's bound to have been peddling it. We found him in Tal Holbert's place, the same place you got your famous black eye, Sheriff."

Jenny did not like to be reminded of that. "What happened?"

"Oh, Clay told him he was under arrest, and Wiggins pulled out that big pig sticker of a knife he always carries. He's cut more than one man open with it."

"What did Clay do?" Jenny demanded.

"Well, I couldn't really tell. He walked straight up to Clyde, and when Clyde pulled that knife back to cut Clay, things got sort of blurred."

"Blurred! What does that mean?" Ruby demanded.

"I don't know. It happened so fast. I tell you that Varek is quicker than greased lightning. All I know is one second Wiggins was standing on his feet trying to put that knife in Clay, and the next he's on the floor hollerin' and screamin' that his arm is broke. And it was too."

"Good!" Jenny said with intense satisfaction. "Where is he now?"

"Oh, Clay took him to Doc Peturis to get his arm set, but he'll be doin' some time for this one, I think."

"I doubt it," Ruby shook her head doubtfully. "He's one of Max's friends. I expect he'll get bailed out tomorrow."

"Maybe so, but he won't be goin' full speed. I put him in the backseat with Clay, and he got clear over on the far side of the car. He kept watchin' Clay like Clay was gonna eat his gizzard or somethin'. I hope we can put Wiggins away where the dogs won't bite him. Wiggins is meaner than a junkyard dog himself, and Clay sure took his measure. He's a nervy cuss, the kind that takes chances. Walked right up to Clyde like he was holdin' a broom straw instead of a razor-sharp knife."

Jenny said no more, for she was both pleased and worried. She could not help but think of Kermit Bing, and she was terrified that someone else would get killed and another death added to her conscience. Later when Clay came in, he acted as though nothing had happened, and when she asked him about Wiggins, he said merely, "Oh, he's not really rough. He just smells bad."

★　★　★

Clay had come to pick up Jamie and take her home, but the Winslows insisted that he stay for supper. The table was filled with heaping platters of fried fish, fried potatoes, and hushpuppies. There was also yellow squash, crunchy fried okra, purple-hulled peas, and fresh-baked bread.

"I caught most of these fish," Kat announced to Clay. She insisted on sitting next to him, and now she picked up one of the fish that had been fried whole. "Look, you hold the fish like this and you start at the front and you just pull this top fin out." She demonstrated how to eat the fish. The entire fin came out, exposing steaming-hot white meat.

"Now, you just put your teeth against the top. See, like eating corn on the cob. This way you don't get any bones in your throat."

Clay winked at Lewis before saying to Kat, "I guess you've mastered the art of eating fish."

Kat dominated the conversation. "Tell me about breakin' that old Clyde Wiggins's arm."

"Nothing much to tell," Clay said, helping himself to a fresh mound of hushpuppies. "These are good, Mrs. Winslow."

Missouri Ann beamed. She was holding one of the babies, as usual, and shifted him to her other arm before answering. "Anybody can make good hushpuppies."

"Hushpuppies aren't as good as these crawdads," Kat announced. "Try some of them. I caught 'em myself, Clay."

Clay eyed the crawdad étouffée. "I never ate crawdads before."

"You'll like 'em," Clint said. "I cooked 'em myself. I was a short-order cook one time on Bourbon Street in New Orleans. Maybe I'll go back there and become a famous chef."

Kat said, "No, you can't go back. You've got to stay here and take care of your family. You're going to have a baby."

The meal was delicious, and finally Lewis said, "I understand you're doing a fine job. We appreciate it, Clay."

"I was the one that made him become a deputy," Kat announced loudly.

"You are the one who eavesdropped on me and your sister—and stop bragging."

"It ain't braggin' if I can do it, Daddy. And I did it, didn't I, Clay?"

"I reckon you did."

Everyone was amused by Kat's pronouncement. The talk then went around to the problem with the bootleggers, and Jenny shook her head, a cloud coming into her eyes. "It's so hard to catch them, and when you catch one there's always another one to take his place."

Lewis smiled. "I remember a fellow once in our county. He was overrun with blackbirds, and he set out to shoot 'em. He killed three with a shotgun, and I asked him, 'You think that discourages 'em?' He looked right at me and said, 'It discouraged those three.'"

"I don't see why the federal officers can't help," Missouri Ann said. "It's really their job, isn't it? I mean it's a federal offense."

"There just aren't enough of them. They're overworked," Jenny said.

Clay chewed thoughtfully on a morsel of fish and swallowed it. "What we need is a good undercover agent. I had a good one in Chicago. He was right on the inside, knew every crook there. He'd tell us about a job that was gonna be pulled, and we'd be right there."

"Well, is he still there?" Lewis asked with interest.

"No," Clay said, and something came into his face. "They found out he was an undercover man, and we found him dead in an alley." He shook his head and added, "It's hard to find a good undercover man. The trouble is you have to find someone that the crooks trust—but who's honest. There aren't many like that."

"There must be someone around here that could do that," Missouri Ann said. "I'll pray on it."

Lewis reached over and squeezed Missouri Ann's neck. "I'll bet you will," he said, "and you'll probably get an answer."

After the dessert, which was an apple pie Hannah had made, Clint said, "Come on out. I want to show you one of my newest inventions."

Clay got up and walked outside. Clint led him around the house to the barn, and when they stepped inside, he said, "I'm not quite through with it yet, but I think it'll work."

Clay looked down at the invention, which he recognized at once. "Why, it's a three-seat baby carriage."

"Hard to go anywhere with three infants. I couldn't decide whether to make it where they'd all three lie next to each other or in tandem, so I finally compromised. Two in the back and one in the front. That makes it narrow enough to maneuver."

"Why, this is great! Where'd you get the parts?"

"Oh, buggies from the junkyard. There was an old one up in the loft somebody left. Anyway, it'll make life a little easier on Lewis and Missouri."

"That's a great job. They'll love it."

"Clay, do you reckon I could become an undercover agent?"

Quickly Clay looked up. "Not a chance in the world," he said. "Everybody knows you're tight with the sheriff. You wouldn't get anywhere. Neither would I. Nope, I respect Missouri's praying, but I doubt if it'll do any good. There aren't many people that can live that kind of life. You have to be one of them. That means doin' what criminals do on one side, and they do some pretty rough things. I couldn't handle it, I don't think."

"Well, don't put it by Missouri to pray one up. That woman is a powerful woman of prayer."

★ ★ ★

Lewis maneuvered the carriage down the sidewalk, conscious that everybody who passed stopped to stare.

"That's what I like, wife, everybody looking at me. I always like to be the center of attention."

"You do not! You hate it." Missouri walked alongside Lewis and took his arm. "Isn't the carriage wonderful?"

"It really is. That Clint's a wonder." He leaned forward and looked at the three infants—Temple in the front with Samuel and Michael in the back. "I don't know how that man does it, but it's easier than trying to carry them in your hip pocket."

"What did you think about what Clay said, about an undercover agent?"

"I don't think they'll find anybody. It's hard to sneak up on bootleggers. They're crafty, violent people and so are the men who traffic the stuff. As a matter of fact, I hear some racketeers are filtering in from the North to do just that."

The two walked along, stopping from time to time as people came over to look down into the carriage. Most of them smiled and reached in to touch the infants, and for once all three of them seemed happy and content.

Missouri watched Lewis's face as they walked along the street. Finally she said, "Lewis, you don't really mind having three babies, do you?"

"Mind! Why, I've never been so proud in my life."

"I was afraid you'd be upset."

"Not a bit of it! I wouldn't turn back the clock for anything." Lewis was very much aware that, although Missouri never mentioned it, she was intimidated by the thought of his first wife, who had been a cultured woman. Missouri was learning to speak with a little better grammar, but she still was not entirely secure.

"Nope, I wouldn't go back," Lewis said. "You can't live in the past. You can go back to a place you once knew, but all you can do is say, 'Oh yes, I know this place.' You may remember it, but it won't remember you. These boys, I want to pour my life into them." He turned to her and added, "And into you, wife." He saw tears come into her eyes and put his arm around her. "God has given us three wonderful children, and we're going to raise them and love each other, and I don't want to hear any more about it. Look, let's go into the sheriff's office and see how many criminals my daughter's caught."

The visit to the sheriff's office turned out to be a huge success. Ruby came over at once and stared down at the babies and then picked Temple up and cuddled him. Billy Moon was standing beside her. "You like babies?" he asked.

"I like to hold them and play with them, but I guess it's a little bit different from taking care of one full-time, isn't it, Mr. Winslow?"

"It sure is," Lewis said. "I'll be glad when the grandchildren come along. Then I can just spoil them and give them back to their mamas."

At that moment Jenny came out and greeted them. "What are you two up to?" she asked, smiling.

"I'm out showing off my sons. I bet there's not another man in the county who's got three sons like this."

"You're getting foolish, Dad."

Missouri watched as Jenny spoke to her father. As always, she admired the closeness between the two and was pleased with it. Finally she said, "Jenny, I've got a name for you."

"A name, Ma? What kind of a name?"

"For the kind of thing that Clay talked about. What did he call them?"

"An undercover agent?"

"Yes."

Jenny looked around. "Come on into the office." She led the way, and when the two women were alone, she said, "You really think you know a man who might do this work?"

"I prayed hard, and the answer came right sudden. I had a cousin named Maybelle Johnson and she married Chester Hagan. She married young, and she had one son, but she died when he was born. He kind of raised himself. His pap wasn't much good. He got kilt in a fight over at Bald Knob when the boy was only six or seven. He's been in a passel of trouble, but I think he's basically a good man. Anyhow, the Lord put his name in my heart, and I think you ought to go see him."

"What's his name, Ma?"

"Hooey Hagan. His real name is James, but nobody calls him anything but Hooey. He lives all by himself out in a little shack he built, and to tell the truth I know he's done some bad things. But I've been prayin' that he'll get saved, and maybe this is the way God will work it. If he can do this thing for you, it might make a difference."

"I'll go talk to him."

"Take Clay with you. He lives right in the heart of that bootleggin' country. Here, I drawed you a map." Reaching into her pocket, she pulled out a folded sheet of paper and said, "You just tell him that I sent you."

"All right, Ma. We'll go see him."

★　★　★

"I'm not sure this is a good idea, Jennifer." Clay stopped, and when Jenny turned to face him, he shook his head doubtfully. "We don't know anything about this fellow Hagan."

"But Missouri does. He's her nephew."

Clay and Jenny had made their way through the woods in the car until the road practically played out, and they were afraid to drive any farther. The road was a gauntlet of mud puddles left by recent rains, and Clay had warned, "If we get this car stuck here, we'll never get it out."

They had advanced on foot, pushing their way through

the thickest woods Jenny had ever seen, and now Clay said, "Wonder what makes her think this fellow Hagan will do it? An undercover man puts his life out on the line almost every hour."

Jenny hesitated. She knew Clay did not really believe in prayer, and she finally said, "Well, she thinks God gave her the name."

Clay Varek studied the young woman in front of him. Her face was flushed from the walk, but she still looked beautiful. Stubborn too. He saw it in the corners of her lips and the upward tilt of her chin. "I can't argue against that, but we'd better be careful. A lot of undercover men go bad. They take money from the law and get on the inside, and then they spill everything they know to the crooks."

"I never thought of that." Jenny's brow wrinkled, but then she shook her head. "Let's talk to him anyway."

The two followed the twisting, winding road, which evidently was the remains of an old logging road. Finally Clay said, "It ought to be right here, but I don't see anything."

At that instant a voice called out, "Hidee!"

Both Clay and Jenny whirled, for the voice had seemed to come from nowhere. They stared at the man who stood in the shadows of the trees, not paying so much attention to his features as to the rifle he held in his hand.

"You folks lost?"

"No," Jenny said rather breathlessly. "We're looking for James Hagan."

For a long moment the man did not say anything, and Jenny had a chance to examine him. He was small, not over five-six, and very lean. He wore a pair of worn khaki pants and a thin shirt that had lost all trace of color from many washings. He wore a floppy hat, and from beneath the band, cinnamon-colored hair escaped. He had the brightest blue eyes Jenny had ever seen and a droopy cavalry mustache that hid most of his mouth.

"That's my name," he said, "but most folks call me Hooey."

"I'm Sheriff Winslow and this is my deputy Clay Varek,"

Jenny said quickly. "Your aunt Missouri gave us your name, Mr. Hagan."

"Just Hooey's okay. You know Aunt Missouri?"

"Oh yes, she's my stepmother now. She married my father. Perhaps you'd heard."

"I did hear somethin' about that, but I wasn't sure if it was so." He turned to Clay and said, "I heard about your run-in with Clyde Wiggins. He's a pretty mean feller."

"Yes, I had to arrest him. He was selling moonshine liquor."

"He's a right touchy feller, and he'd steal flies from a blind spider, I reckon, but he's a tough one." His eyes came back, and he studied Jenny. "Never seen no woman sheriff, especially sech a purty one."

"Oh, not that pretty," Jenny protested.

"I reckon I know a purty gal when I see one, and you're prettier than a pair of green shoes with red laces! When I heered tell of a woman sheriff, I thought you must be too ugly to catch a man. You take my cousin Velma. She's so ugly she looks like she's been hit in the face with a dead squirrel. Reckon thet's what I was expectin'."

"Could we talk with you awhile, Hooey?"

"Shore. Come on up to the house. Maybe we could find somethin' to drink."

The two followed Hooey Hagan as he made his way down the road. He led them to a two-room shack, and when the two stepped inside they exchanged glances. It was much cleaner than they would have expected.

"How about a sawmill lunch?"

"What's that?" Jenny said.

"A can of sardines, a handful of crackers, and a bottle of soda pop. Or you could have some Arkansas chicken."

"What's that?" Clay said.

"I reckon you folks would call it bologna."

"We're really not hungry, Hooey. We came to talk business."

Hooey's bright eyes fastened on her. "Can't imagine what business a sheriff would have with a critter like me."

"Well, it's kind of a hard thing to say, Hooey. I'm the first woman sheriff in this county, and I'm having a difficult time of it."

"I reckon how that might be."

"We're trying to catch the bootleggers. That's the main problem, but we're just not getting anywhere with it."

Hooey Hagan put his rifle down, and reaching into his pocket, he bit off a huge bite from a plug of tobacco. He replaced the plug and chewed thoughtfully while Jenny went on to explain the problem.

"I knowed one of your deputies," he remarked. "The one that got kilt."

"You mean Kermit Bing?"

"That's the feller. I always liked Kermit. He plowed a straight furrow and went all the way to the end of the row. That other sheriff before you, Max Conroy—he ain't worth no more than a bucket under a bull."

Jenny was slightly amused by this but knew that somehow she had to convey the truth to this strange man. She decided there was no way to do that except to tell in plain words why they had come. "We need an undercover agent, Hooey."

"Whut's thet?"

Hooey listened as Jenny explained what an undercover agent was, and when she had finished, he said, "Whut in the blue-eyed world makes you think I'd do thet?"

"Mostly because Missouri said she prayed and God gave her your name."

Hooey grinned. "That woman's been prayin' for me for as long as I can remember. She tried to convert me since I could walk, but I reckon I jest ain't convertible." He turned to stare at Varek and said, "What you think about all this, Deputy?"

"I think it would be a dangerous job, Hooey." Clay went on to tell some of his experiences in Chicago, and Hooey listened without saying a word. Finally Clay said, "It doesn't pay much and it's dangerous."

Hooey was silent for a long time just studying the pair, and finally Jenny felt there was no point in staying any longer. "Well, you might want to think about it—"

"I liked that feller Kermit. He done me a turn once."

"What was that, Hooey?"

"He caught me red-handed. I ain't gonna tell you whut, but it would have been enough to send me away to jail fer a spell. I shore did dread goin' to the pen, but that feller Kermit, he gave me a second chance. He turned me loose and made me promise not to do—whut it was I was doin'."

"He was a good man," Jenny said. "I think about him every day."

Hooey Hagan stood quietly and then shrugged his thin shoulders. "I guess that made me turn the corner. I was pretty rough before that, but since then I've been walkin' a pretty straight line. I reckon I'd like to do somethin' to make it right with Kermit."

"You know who killed him?"

"I reckon I do, Sheriff, but I ain't got no proof. But I'll tell you what I do have. My own still. I been makin' shine, jes' fer my own personal libation, mind, but I could up my production and make like I want to sell it to some of them Yankees."

Jenny was stunned. "Does that mean you'll help us, Hooey?"

"I reckon as how I will."

Jenny suddenly felt that the load had left. "Here at least is a chance!"

Clay was staring at the small man. "It'll be dangerous."

"They shouldn't've killed Kermit. He was a good man," Hooey said. "Now, tell me one more time what in the cat hair it is I am."

"You're an undercover agent."

"Sounds important, don't it?" Hooey said with satisfaction. "Now, I get in with the fellers that are breakin' the law and make 'em think I'm one of 'em."

"That's right," Jenny said, nodding.

"Well, I reckon as how that would be right interestin'. Everything that goes around the door can't be Santa Claus, you know."

Jenny blinked. She had no idea what Hooey was talking about, but she put her hand out. "Thank you, Hooey. I'll tell your aunt that you're with us."

Hooey Hagan grinned, then sobered. "She'll be all over me to git religion, she purely will!"

CHAPTER SEVENTEEN

SETTING THE TRAP

★ ★ ★

When Clay Varek turned from the hallway and entered the large living room, he found Jenny sitting on the floor playing with Jamie. For a moment he stopped, and the fatigue that had settled over him after a hard day's work seemed to vanish. There was something about the picture of the red-haired sheriff sitting cross-legged and drinking tea out of a tiny cup across from Jamie that pleased him. He thought suddenly of how his life had changed since he had agreed to become a deputy. The arrangement had worked out so well with Jamie, and he knew that the child was much happier and contented staying with the Winslows during the day. She had told him over and over how much fun she had playing with Kat and how the women of the house always took care of her and made her good things to eat.

"It looks like a tea party to me," Clay said. "You mind if I join you?"

"I don't think we mind, do we, Jamie?"

"No," Jamie said. "Sit down, Daddy. We're playing house."

Clay sat down, crossed his legs, and took the small cup that Jamie handed him along with a matching saucer with a tiny piece of cake on it.

"Did you make this cake, sweetheart?"

"Yes."

Jenny winked at him. "I helped a little bit, but you'll have to brag on it a lot."

Indeed, Clay did brag on the cake and on the tea, which was really iced tea without the ice. This was a moment of intimacy for him, and he had spent so much time alone that it seemed to sink into his spirit. He watched Jamie as she served the tea out of a tiny teapot, managing to spill most of it, and dutifully drank it. Finally Jenny got up, saying, "Tea party's over."

Clay got to his feet. He picked up Jamie and hugged her. "Time to go home."

"Can I go to Sunday school?" Jamie asked suddenly. She reached up and put her hands on each side of Clay's face and seemed very serious. "Tomorrow is Sunday school day. I want to go."

"I'd love to take her, Clay, if you don't mind," Jenny said.

"That would be fine."

"Would you like to go with us?"

"Yes," Jamie cried, "you go, too, Daddy!"

For a moment Clay considered refusing, but Jamie was patting his cheeks and nodding her head up and down begging him. "All right," he said. "I'll go too."

Clay turned to Jenny and saw a smile on her face and knew he had pleased her. She had invited him to church many times, and he had always found some reason for not going. And even now he agreed reluctantly. He had not been to church in years and did not know what to expect.

"I'll come by and get you about nine-thirty," Jenny said.

"Should I wear my uniform?"

"No, not unless you want to. I'll have to because I'll be going on duty as soon as church is over." She came forward and hugged Jamie and, in doing so, managed to touch Clay. "I'll see you both tomorrow morning," she said.

As Clay left the house listening to Jamie patter about what she had been doing all day and about Sunday school, he thought, *I've got to watch myself. I'm getting pretty caught up with these Winslow folks.*

* * *

The next morning, Jenny drove Kat, Clay, and Jamie to church in her county car. Hannah, Clint, and her father were coming a bit later in the truck, and Missouri Ann was staying home with the babies, who were all three fussy with colds.

During the adult Sunday school class, Jenny noticed that Clay seemed quiet but attentive. Afterward she asked him, "Did you enjoy the Sunday school lesson?"

"As a matter of fact I did. You didn't tell me your father was the teacher."

"He's really become a student of the Bible over these last few years. I wish some of it would rub off on me."

"I think you do pretty well."

"Let's go by and be sure that Jamie's all right before the service starts." The two made their way down the hallway, which was crowded with people coming and going from Sunday school rooms to the main auditorium. There was a babble of voices, and when they got to the children's room, Clay stepped inside and saw Jamie sitting on a chair holding her doll Jemima, which she had insisted on bringing.

"Daddy, look. Jemima likes Sunday school."

Clay smiled. "How about you? Do you like it too?" He went and knelt down beside her and listened as she chattered on about the Sunday school time. Clay was fascinated at how quickly she was picking up words. It was almost like magic to him, and now he said, "Well, we're going to church. We'll be back soon."

"No, Jemima wants to go." She held up the doll and said earnestly, "We want to go with you, Daddy."

Clay hesitated, but Jenny said at once, "I'm sure she'd be very good. Some people take their two-year-olds into church. If you want to, I'll help take care of her."

"All right. If you're sure it'll be okay."

"It'll be fine. Come along. Bring Jemima, Jamie."

Clay picked Jamie up, and the two left the children's room. They made their way down the hallway and turned into the auditorium. It was filling up rapidly, and Jenny said, "Look, there are a couple of seats." She led the way down the aisle, turned in, and they took their seats. When Clay set Jamie down on the seat beside him, Jenny whispered, "I wanted us to get close to the side door."

"What for?"

"In case Jamie has to go to the bathroom."

"I hadn't thought of that, but I should have."

"It's all right. If she has to go, I'll take her."

The service began almost at once, and Clay felt awkward and out of place. The song leader was a tall, handsome man in his fifties and had a rousing tenor voice. He urged the congregation to sing vigorously, and he called, "Let's sing number eighty-two! You all know that one and it's a good one." Jenny handed Clay a hymnal.

"But you don't have one for yourself," he said.

"Oh, I know all the words to that one. It's one of my favorites."

The organist struck a chord and the pianist on the other side of the platform chimed in, and the congregation all stood at the song leader's signal and began to sing.

"Amazing grace! How sweet the sound—
That saved a wretch like me!
I once was lost but now am found,
Was blind but now I see."

"You have a good voice, Clay," Jenny leaned over and whispered.

"I used to sing in a quartet when I was a young fellow. I haven't done much singing lately."

"You ought to take it up again."

"You sing pretty well yourself." Clay looked down at the songbook and said, "You know all the songs in here?"

"Oh no, some of them we almost never sing. Some we sing almost every week."

The service continued with spirited singing, an offering was taken, and finally the minister rose. "He looks a little bit like Abraham Lincoln," Clay said.

"I always thought that. He's a wonderful preacher. I was

kind of sweet on him when we first moved here. He was such a help to us."

"He's married, isn't he?"

"His wife died not too long ago. He's trying to raise his two children by himself. All the women of the church are going crazy trying to find him a wife. Lots of candidates."

"But not you?"

Jenny turned and smiled at him. When she smiled her eyes crinkled, and she shook her head. "I'd be a terrible preacher's wife. Almost as bad as I am at being sheriff."

Devoe Crutchfield had a fine voice for preaching, and he obviously loved to preach. He looked out over the congregation, smiled, welcomed the visitors, then said, "This morning my message will be taken from the eighth chapter of Matthew. We'll read verses twenty-three to twenty-seven together."

Jenny leaned over with her Bible open to the place, and Clay mumbled along as they read together.

"And when he was entered into a ship, his disciples followed him.

"And behold, there arose a great tempest in the sea, insomuch that the ship was covered with the waves: but he was asleep.

"And his disciples came to him, and awoke him, saying, Lord, save us: we perish.

"And he saith unto them, Why are ye fearful, O ye of little faith? Then he arose, and rebuked the winds and the sea; and there was a great calm.

"But the men marvelled, saying, What manner of man is this, that even the winds and the sea obey him!"

Crutchfield looked out over the congregation and smiled, saying, "The subject of my message this morning is 'When Jesus Goes to Sleep.' I know that sounds like a strange sermon title, but obviously Jesus *did* sleep. There are two mistaken assumptions often made about Jesus—one that He is God only and not man at all. That error has been around the church for a long time. The other is looking only at the human side of Jesus and forgetting that He's the one who made the universe and is in charge of it."

Clay listened as Crutchfield went on. He had been expecting a dull sermon, but Crutchfield skillfully drew a picture of the storm that came. He was a good preacher, and he came at once to his point. "The disciples were probably just about folks like us. When they got caught in a storm they got panicky. And when people get panicky, they look outside themselves. And where did the disciples look? Up to the front of the boat where Jesus was asleep. Now, you must remember that they had seen Him feed five thousand people with just a few fish and a few loaves. They had seen Him lay His hand on a leper eaten up with that horrible disease, and the flesh had become as fresh as a newborn baby's. They had seen Him do miracles of all sorts, but now when their need was great, He was asleep."

Crutchfield leaned forward and looked out over the congregation. Suddenly Clay realized he was looking straight at him, or so it seemed, and he felt exposed. "Have you ever felt like that? You're caught in a storm, you can't help yourself, and after you've tried everything to get yourself out of it, you suddenly know that no one but God could do that. We've all been there, haven't we?"

Clay remembered back when Jamie's father had died, and he had felt exactly like that—alone, helpless. Crutchfield's next words struck at him.

"Most of us at one time or another have been caught in a tragedy, in a terrible problem, something we couldn't handle ourselves—and when we called to God, it felt as though there were no one there."

Why, that's exactly what happened to me, Varek thought. He glanced down at Jamie, who was coloring a sheet of paper with a blue crayon that she had brought from Sunday school and thought how desperate he had been to help this child. But at the time there seemed to be no one to help him, just as Crutchfield had said.

The sermon proceeded, and finally Crutchfield spoke of how many things can happen to destroy lives. "And it's natural for us to call upon God, and we get disturbed when God doesn't answer at once.

"I suppose the disciples must have been upset with Jesus.

They were in terrible trouble, and there He was sleeping. But however it seemed to them, they were in no danger, and I'll give you one good reason. There was no danger that that boat would sink because Jesus was in it. He had come to this world to die for the sins of every man and woman and child, and God the Father was not going to let Him perish in a storm until His mission was fulfilled. And I'd like to suggest to you this morning, friends, that it's a wise thing for you to ask Jesus into your boat. Sooner or later you're going to hit a storm, and you're going to face death and sickness and problems you can't handle. But if Jesus is in the boat with you, you can do what these disciples did. Look what the Scripture says. 'His disciples came to Him and awoke Him, saying, 'Lord, save us. We perish.'"

Crutchfield closed his Bible and looked out over the congregation. "Every sermon ends the same, in this church at least. You will notice that every time I preach I wind up at this point right here. All of us are helpless, and only Jesus can help. Some of you have had Jesus in the boat with you for fifty years or even longer. Some of you have had Him only a few weeks or months. Some of you," he said quietly, "don't have Jesus in your boat at all. He's not part of your life, and I would urge you to think of this. When the storm comes, what will you do then? The disciples woke Jesus, and the Scripture says He arose and He simply rebuked the waves, and the storm became a great calm. That's my message today," Crutchfield said, nodding. "And I'm going to give those of you who do not have Jesus in your boat—that is to say, in your life—a chance to get Him in there. He's waiting and always has been for you to invite Him in. We're going to stand together and sing 'Just As I Am,' and as we sing, I would urge you to come just as you are and let Jesus Christ be your savior."

By this time Jamie had gone to sleep in Clay's arms. He stood up carefully, and she snuggled next to him. He looked down at her face as the congregation began to sing, and the song moved him strangely.

"Just as I am without one plea,
But that thy blood was shed for me,
And that thou bidst me come to thee,
O Lamb of God, I come, I come!"

He noticed that three people went forward and that Crutchfield prayed with each of them. After the invitation was over, the minister said, "We're glad that these have found Christ and are coming to follow Him in baptism."

After a closing prayer, the congregation began to move out, and the murmuring sound of voices filled the auditorium. As they passed out the door, Jenny said to Reverend Crutchfield, "I don't know if you've met my new deputy, Brother Crutchfield. This is Clay Varek and his daughter, Jamie."

Varek shifted Jamie into one arm and took Crutchfield's hand, and the preacher's smile was warm. "Glad to have you with us. I hope you'll come back."

"I'll do that, Reverend."

Clay walked out to the squad car, opened the door, and got in, Jamie not stirring. Jenny started the car and pulled out from the curb. "Did you like the sermon?"

"Yes, I did. I liked the preacher too. He seems like an upfront guy."

"He really is. He's a good preacher, but he's a good pastor too. Every time there's trouble or sickness, you'll find him right there." Clay did not answer, and finally Jenny turned and glanced at him. "You never thought of giving your heart to the Lord Jesus?"

Clay found it difficult to respond. He had grown up with almost no Christian influence. His parents had never gone to church, and to him Christmas was simply a time when you decorated a tree and exchanged presents. Easter was the time for chocolate Easter eggs. He had known many who claimed to be Christian, and many of them had not been much in his estimation. Jenny's question bothered him, and he finally said, "No, I haven't."

Jenny swerved to avoid the body of a raccoon that had not made it. When she brought the car back on the right side of the road, she said, "You ought to do that, Clay."

Clay Varek could think of no answer. He had been moved by the sermon, and even the hymns had spoken to him. But he only said, "I don't think it would work, Jenny . . . not for me."

Jenny said no more, but when they reached Clay's house she said suddenly, "Look, there's Hooey."

"Wonder what he's doing here? I told him not to contact us in public."

Jenny stopped the car, and when they got out, Hooey came over to them. He was wearing overalls and a straw hat pulled down over his face. "Howdy," he said.

"Hooey, I told you not to come and not to be seen with us."

"Ain't nobody seen me, Sheriff, but I had to get word to you right now."

"What's going on?" Clay said quickly. Jamie was beginning to stir in his arms, and he shifted her while he watched the smaller man.

"Well, I been doin' a little tradin' with them Yankee fellows that came down to buy shine."

"You've actually met them?" Jenny said.

"Oh, they ain't hard to meet if you know where to look. They been tryin' to get me on their list for some time, but I didn't want to sell no shine myself. Just drink it a little bit. But I tell you what. They're a tough bunch, Sheriff. If you gonna hang their hide on the fence, you'd better be plumb careful."

"I will, but why'd you come, Hooey?"

Hooey laughed and pulled his hat off. "I come to tell you that your deputies come around after I sold the stuff and told me that I was gonna need some protection."

"Protection! From what?"

"From gettin' arrested, I expect. They come to tell me that I was gonna have to pay 'em off or they'd arrest me."

"They knew you had the moonshine?"

"Knowed it! I reckon they did. It didn't take long for 'em to get to me either, right after I sold the shine to them Yankee fellers. About as long as Pat stayed in the army, I reckon."

"Did you give them the money?" Jenny demanded, her eyes narrowing. She was angry clear through. From the beginning she had suspected Arp and Pender of being poor officers, but to think that they were actually joined with the people they were supposed to be arresting infuriated her.

"Nope, I told 'em I'd give it to 'em tomorrow."

"Where you gonna pay 'em off?"

"Why, they said they'd come back to my place. Ain't that a pretty come-off? Deputies takin' money from criminals like me! Wouldn't that cock your pistol?"

"We've got a lot to do before tomorrow," Clay said. "We've got to have hard evidence on them."

"You tell me what to do, Clay, and we'll do it."

"All right. We'll set it up. We'll set a trap for them."

"Well, we'd better be careful. They're sly as foxes, them two."

"There's a way"—Clay smiled grimly—"and I'll tell you what it is. . . ."

★   ★   ★

"You got the money, Hooey?"

Hooey had come outside of his house and was standing loose-jointed staring at the two deputies. He grinned and said, "And what if I don't pay you fellers off?"

"Aw, come on, you know what'd happen," Arp said. He pulled his belt up and touched his nightstick. "We'd have to whip you a bit and then take you in for sellin' illegal alcohol."

"Let's get this over with," Arlie Pender said. "Give us the money."

"Come on inside. Might even give you fellers a sample of my merchandise. I keep the money hid in there."

He turned and went into the shack, and Pender followed him. Hooey marched over to the table, which sat in the center of the room, and patted the jug. "This here's fine moonshine," he said. "Goes down right smooth." He found three glasses, filled them up, and handed one to each deputy. He picked up his own glass and said, "Here's to crime."

Pender laughed roughly. "I'll drink to that," he said. The three men drank, and Pender shuddered as the alcohol hit his stomach. "That ain't bad stuff," he said, "but I'll have to confiscate that jug."

"Now, give us the money."

Hooey shook his head. "You fellers are a caution. You makin' two livin's—one upholdin' the law and one breakin' it. I wish I could get in on that."

"This Prohibition ain't nothin' anyway," Arlie Pender snorted. "It'll be voted out pretty soon."

"Well, that'd put me out of work and a lot of other folks." Hooey went over to a battered chest of drawers, opened the bottom drawer, and fumbled through what seemed to be a rat's nest of old clothes. He came out with a tin box, turned to the two deputies, and opened it. "You fellers are hittin' me pretty hard," he said, getting out some bills. "Cain't you shave the price a little?"

"Come on, Hooey, give us the money," Pender snapped. He reached out, took the bills, divided them, and gave half to Arp. "We'll be comin' round to collect again pretty soon."

"Don't it hurt your feelin's takin' money for lookin' the other way while us criminals sell shine?" Hooey grinned.

"Well, not a bit. You have the money ready."

"What about that female sheriff? What if she takes a notion to raid me?"

"Don't worry about that. We know every time there's a raid gonna take place. We'll get word to you, and you can clear everything out," Arp said.

"Okay, be sure you do."

"Come on, let's go, Merle." Arlie Pender turned, and Merle Arp followed him. They stepped outside the door and headed down the road toward where they'd parked the squad car. They had not gone more than five steps, however, when a voice hit them hard. "Stop right where you are! Get your hands up!"

Both deputies whirled to see Billy Moon and Clay Varek both holding shotguns at ready position.

"Hey, what is this?" Pender said. "What are you guys doin'?"

"You're under arrest. Don't move your hands. Billy, take their weapons."

The two deputies began to sputter. "You gone crazy, Varek? You can't do this to officers of the law."

"Moon, take their billfolds. Shake them down."

"Be glad to, Deputy Varek." Moon grinned and pulled out the wallets of the two. He opened both of them up and said, "I didn't know you fellows were so rich. Look at this money."

"That's honest money. You can't prove a thing."

"I think we can. Step back inside both of you."

Pender and Arp began to curse, but they went back inside the shack with the pressure of the shotguns. As soon as they stepped in, Pender said, "You can't prove nothin'."

"I reckon as how they can with that money I give you," Hooey said, smiling.

"We'll fix you, Hooey. We'll put the word out that you're a stoolie."

"You'll have to do it from the jailhouse, I reckon." Hooey grinned broadly.

Merle Arp had been a bully all of his life. He turned his meanest scowl on Varek and said, "You can't prove a thing. Hooey here ain't nothin' but a moonshiner. No judge is gonna believe him."

"You think they'll believe me, Arp?"

Both Arp and Pender whirled to their right and saw Jenny Winslow step out of the bedroom door. She smiled when she saw the expressions on their faces. "I'll be the witness against you, and you're not going to make it."

"You can't prove we took money."

"I think we can," Clay nodded. "That was marked money you took. Look, you see this?" He pulled a bill from Arp's billfold and said, "See that little red dot right there in the corner? We marked that, and you've got it in your pocket."

"Well, ain't this fine, now!" Hooey laughed, his eyes bright with enjoyment. "After Judge Pender gets through with you two, you'll feel like you slid down a forty-foot razor blade into a vat of alcohol!"

CHAPTER EIGHTEEN

"TAKE HER OUT!"

★ ★ ★

The courtroom was packed for the trial of Merle Arp and Arlie Pender. The newspapers had carried the story of the arrest of the pair, and now that the time of judgment had come, it seemed that half the people in the county had tried to pack themselves into the relatively small courtroom. Judge O. C. Pender had kept a tight rein on both the district attorney and the lawyer for the defendants, a small dark-complected man with black hair. His name was Abe Goldman, and his reputation had preceded him. Clay had told Jenny, "He's the hottest criminal lawyer in Chicago, and I'm sure Pender and Arp didn't have the money to pay him, so the big boys in Chicago must have sent him down here."

Goldman had dominated the trial, but now it was time for Jenny to take the stand. When her name was called, she walked forward, raised her hand, and swore to tell the truth. As soon as she took her seat, the district attorney, Alex De-Rosa, came to stand before her. "You were at the home of Mr. James Hagan on September the twenty-fifth?"

"Yes, sir."

"What were you doing there, Sheriff?"

"We had been informed that there was going to be a pay-off of the two defendants."

"A payoff for what?"

"The informant told us that the defendants had agreed to let him sell illegal alcohol if he would pay them off."

"Objection! Hearsay," Goldman boomed.

"Overruled. Continue, Mr. DeRosa."

Alex DeRosa continued to lead Jenny through her testimony, which she gave simply and in a straightforward fashion. Finally DeRosa said, "I have no further questions."

"Your witness, Mr. Goldman," Pender said.

Goldman got to his feet and strolled across the room until he stood directly in front of Jenny. His black hair was pasted down with some sort of oil, and his eyes glittered as he began to speak. "You've had trouble with Mr. Arp and Mr. Pender in the past."

"No, sir, I have not."

"But when you took over as sheriff you began to freeze them out, isn't that true?"

"No, sir," Jenny said calmly. "That is not true. I had a meeting at which all of the department was present, and I told them at that time that we would start from the beginning."

Goldman began to try to punch holes in Jenny's story, but she remained calm. Clay had told her, *"He'll try to shake you. If he can make you mad, he wins. No matter what he says, don't get rattled and don't show any anger."*

It was Goldman, however, who grew angry. Unable to shake Jenny's story, he began to make personal illusions. "So you hired a moonshiner to be your informant, is that right?"

"He volunteered when he was presented with the problems. Besides, there's no evidence of him ever selling moonshine liquor to anyone before doing so as an undercover agent."

"Do you consider it proper for an elected official to deal with criminals?"

"Objection!" DeRosa said. "Calls for a conclusion."

"Sustained. Where are you going with this, Mr. Goldman?"

Goldman was angry and showed it. He began to fire questions at Jenny, but when she kept her calm, he finally whirled and said, "No further questions."

After that, the trial was rather short. When the jury filed out, Clay, who was sitting next to Jenny, said, "This won't take long."

"Are you sure, Clay?"

"I never saw such a clear-cut case."

Varek was correct, for in twenty minutes the jury came trooping out, and the foreman said, "We find the defendants guilty as charged."

Raymond Dent, the editor of *The Record*, let out a whoop and came over to put his hand out to Jenny. "Congratulations, Sheriff, you nailed those two!"

Jenny was pleased, and she accepted the congratulations of many who came by to speak to her.

Finally she saw Hooey talking with some of his friends and had said, "Excuse me. I have to go talk to Hooey." When she approached him, she said, "Can I speak to you a moment, Hooey?"

"Why, certainly you can." Hooey grinned.

He followed Jenny out into the hall, and she said at once, "Hooey, you're not going to be any good as an informant after this, but I need a new deputy. I'd like for you to take the job."

For once, words failed Hooey Hagan. He stared at her for a long moment and then shook his head. "You ain't thinkin' right, Sheriff. I'm a disreputable character. Ask anybody."

"I don't think you are so disreputable. You know these hills. You know every moonshiner in them. Clay says you're tough enough to lift perdition and put a chunk under it. His very words. So, I want you to think about it."

Hooey grinned broadly. "Well, that does take the rag off the bush! Me a deputy! I'll do her, Sheriff. When do I start?"

"We'll get you a uniform, and you can start tomorrow."

★　★　★

Vito Canelli stared at the two men across from him. He had come back a week after the trial, and Judge Hightower and Millington Wheeler had listened as he had started out in a deadly tone but now was shouting. "The supply's been shut off! Bootleggers are afraid to sell their product!"

"We'll take care of it, Vito," Judge Hightower said quickly. "Everybody's a little bit shook up after Arp and Pender got convicted but—"

"There'll be no buts to it! I put you two guys here, and we paid you good money and a bundle of it!"

Wheeler tried to pacify Vito by saying, "This'll pass away, Mr. Canelli."

"We're not waitin' for it to pass away. You don't have an inside man in the sheriff's office now, do you?"

"No, not really," Hightower admitted. "But we'll get somebody."

"I'm through waiting, and my boss tells me to crack down."

"What does that mean?" Wheeler said nervously. He was rather pale, because in all truth he was afraid of this man. He had gotten into this situation and now could see no way to back out. The minute he had taken money from Chicago he was trapped, and now he wished desperately he had never allowed himself to get involved.

Vito Canelli chewed on the stub of his cigar, then threw it on the floor and stomped on it. "I'm sendin' some men down. They'll know what to do. As for that sheriff, she's got to go."

"Well, she's got another two years to serve," Wheeler said tentatively.

"She gets out of the way or else."

"Or else what?" Wheeler said despite himself.

"Or else we'll take her out."

The rest of the meeting was a blank as far as Wheeler was concerned. He had found that his hands were shaking, and he put them in his pockets to keep the other two from seeing them. After Canelli left, he turned to the judge and said, "We're in trouble here, Dwight."

"No, we're not. You just keep your head, Wheeler, and we'll be all right."

"I wish I'd never gotten into this."

"Well, you are into it," Hightower said angrily. "So now you're going to stay in it!"

Wheeler left Hightower's house, and all the way home he was trying to think of a way to extricate himself from the situation. But he could think of nothing. When he got to his own house, he parked the car and went inside.

"Ellen and Andy are here," Helen said. "Where have you been?"

"Oh, I had a meeting."

"Well, they're waiting for you. Go on in and play with them until supper's ready."

Wheeler went into the parlor, where he found his two grandchildren working a jigsaw puzzle. They came to him at once, and he picked them up. Ellen was eight and Andy ten, and they were the pride of his life. "What are you doing?"

"We're working a jigsaw puzzle, Grandpa," Ellen piped up. "Come and help us."

"It's almost suppertime."

"Well, you can help a little bit. Look, I want that piece right there."

Wheeler sat down at the card table and for fifteen minutes had managed to put Vito Canelli out of his mind. He was, however, brought back to his problem when Andy said, "You gotta take me hunting, Grandpa. Deer hunting."

"Deer are out of season, Andy."

"Well, let's do it anyway."

"It's against the law," Wheeler said. "We'll have to wait until hunting season comes."

"Aw, what difference does it make? Just one deer."

Ellen was sitting on her grandpa Wheeler's lap. She reached up and patted his cheek. "Grandpa would never do anything wrong, Andy. You know that."

The child's words struck at Wheeler. He was like a man that had been hit by a bullet, and he said almost nothing until Helen came to call them to dinner. As they went into the dining room, he said, "I wish I were as good a man as they think I am."

"You are a good man," Helen said.

Wheeler had told his wife nothing about his dealings with the judge and Canelli. He had been struggling to pay off bills and make headway after losing large sums of money. Now he said quietly, "You know, sometimes I wish we were back in that little shotgun house we first lived in."

"That old thing! It was terrible."

"I know. We didn't have a dime, but we were happy."

"Aren't you happy now?" Helen said quickly.

Wheeler wanted to tell her what was happening to him, but she was part of the problem. She spent more money than necessary and liked to move up in society. For a moment he was on the brink of confiding in her, but then Andy said, "Come on, Grandpa, I'm hungry," and the moment passed.

★ ★ ★

"I didn't like that movie," Jenny said as Luke Dixon drove her home after taking her to see *Dr. Jekyll and Mr. Hyde.*

"Why, I thought it was pretty entertaining," Luke answered. The two of them climbed out of the car, and he walked her up to her house. When they stepped up onto the porch, he said, "Let's sit down for a bit."

"Sit down! It's cold out here."

"You're tough. You're a sheriff. Come on, we haven't had a chance to talk much."

"If you'd stop taking me to those awful movies, we'd have more chance to talk."

Luke pulled her down in the swing and put his arm around her. "All right, let's talk. You've gotten pretty good publicity lately. I think you're making headway."

"You mean people are ready to vote for me in the next election?"

"I'd vote for you. Prettiest sheriff in the whole world or anywhere else for that matter. Why, you're a regular sock-dologer, as Hooey puts it."

Dixon suddenly pulled her close and, turning her to face him, kissed her soundly. "There's your reward for being such a good sheriff."

Jenny said, "You want to watch that kissing, Luke. It's getting to be a habit."

Luke was quiet, but he released her, and he was so silent

she said, "What are you thinking about, Luke? It's not like you to be this quiet."

"I'm wondering," Dixon said in an odd tone of voice, "if you've ever thought of me as a man you might marry."

Dixon's words caught Jenny off guard, but she was honest. "I guess every woman wonders that about every man she goes out with."

Luke took her hand and held it in both of his. "Well, how do I rank?"

"I don't keep score."

"Maybe you'd better. I need to know when I'm winning and when I'm losing."

"It's not a matter of winning."

"I disagree"—Dixon shook his head—"with those people who say winning doesn't matter. If it doesn't matter, why do they keep score? Come on, give me a progress report."

Not sure that Dixon was entirely serious, Jenny smiled. "All right, on a scale of one to ten. Let me see. Well, personal appearance, seven."

"Oh, come on! I'm at least a nine. Look, see these teeth?"

"Well, maybe an eight."

"What about charm?"

"Oh, a nine at least."

"Right, and I can keep that up for at least forty years. How about wit and intelligence?"

"A ten!"

"A ten! Well, now we're getting somewhere. Financial ranking?"

"I'd say a two, if that high."

Luke squeezed her hand and then said, "But look at the future. After I'm a senator I'll be rich."

"You're too honest to be a senator."

Luke put his arms around her and looked into her face for a minute. He kissed her again, but this time his kiss was deep and passionate. When he pulled his head back, he asked thickly, "How did that rank, Sheriff?"

Jenny gently pushed him away and stood up. "I think I'd better go inside."

Dixon stood up too, and for a moment he simply stood

there, looking at her. "Think about it, Jenny."

Jenny realized then that Luke was serious. "Do you mean it, Luke?" she asked rather breathlessly.

"Wouldn't have said it if I didn't. You're so beautiful, Jenny," he said quietly. "And so fine. Everything you do is right and straight and true. It's not bad for you to be around a man that thinks that, is it?"

Jenny was moved, but something inside made her hesitate and she did not know how to answer him. "Good night, Luke," she whispered. "I'll see you tomorrow."

She stepped inside the door, and as she moved down the hall, she found Missouri rocking Michael. "How was your date?" Missouri asked.

"It was fine." Jenny hesitated, then turned and said, "Luke asked me to marry him."

"Are you going to?"

"I don't know, Missouri. How do you know when it's right?"

Missouri Ann smiled. "God told me to marry your daddy. That's a good way."

Jennifer Winslow hesitated. She bit her lower lip and shook her head. "Well, God hasn't told me anything, but I wish He would."

Missouri continued rocking after Jenny had left. She was troubled and did not know why. "Lord," she said, "you've got to help that girl. She really needs it."

PART FOUR

New Beginnings

★ ★ ★

CHAPTER NINETEEN

A MATTER OF GUILT

★ ★ ★

As Clay pulled up in front of the Winslow house, he saw that the old Studebaker truck bearing a trailer was backed up to the pen where Clara, the prize sow, was kept. "Looks like Clara's going off to market, Jamie."

"What does that mean, Daddy?"

"It means she's gotten big enough to sell and it's time to sell her. It looks like they're about ready to load her up." Getting out of the truck, Clay walked around and, opening the door, picked Jamie up. "You're getting big too," he said.

Jamie giggled and puffed her cheeks out. "I am big. See?"

The two crossed the front yard and moved around the side of the house. By the time Clay got to the pen, he could hear Kat's voice above everything else. As usual she was wearing ratty-looking overalls, and now she was standing in front of her father with a defiant look on her face.

"I don't want to sell Clara, Daddy!"

"Now, Kat," Lewis said patiently, "I've told you all the time you shouldn't make a pet out of Clara. We've got to sell her to have money to live on."

"But I love Clara!"

Lewis looked up and saw Clay standing there holding Jamie. "Hello, Clay."

"Hello, Lewis. A little disagreement here?"

"I told this child she shouldn't make a pet out of an animal that's going to be sold, but she's hardheaded. I think she gets it all from her mother's side."

"I am not either hardheaded!" Kat said loudly. She glanced over at Clint, who was grinning and said, "Clint, you don't want to sell Clara, do you?"

"Well, that's what we raised her for, Kat."

"But you like her, don't you?"

"I'm not overly fond of pigs," Clint said and shrugged. "I reckon you'll have to let her go."

Kat took one look at Clara, who had stuck her snout through the rail and was begging for sweets. Kat's face twisted, and without a word, she whirled and ran away, disappearing around the house.

"It's hard on the child," Lewis said, "but I warned her. She just wouldn't listen."

"I remember I had a speckled pup once, and my folks made me get rid of him," Clint said. "It still hurts even to this day."

"Well, that's a little different," Lewis said fretfully. "We've got to sell this hog. Come on. Let's get her loaded."

"That's a mighty big hog," Clay said, staring at the huge animal. "What if she doesn't want to get in that trailer?"

"Well, she's got to and that's all there is to it."

Lewis opened the gate to the hog pen and entered, his eyes wary. He lifted his arms and waved them wildly, yelling, "Get! Get on up in there, Clara!"

The sow, which weighed over five hundred pounds, stared at him. She had indeed become a pet, but only a pet of Kat's. The man waving his arms did not please her, and she moved to one side quickly. Lewis jumped in front of her and called out, "You get in that trailer! You hear me?"

"Maybe I'd better give you a hand," Clint said quickly.

And as Clint entered the hogpen, Clay put Jamie down and said, "You wait right here, honey. I'll help the men load the pig."

The three men formed a circle around Clara, who stared at them with her beady little eyes. She made a wild bolt, and

Clint, trying to bar her, was knocked off his feet. He rolled in the dust and yelled, "Cut her off, Clay!"

Dust arose as the three men tried desperately to put the hog up the chute into the bed of the trailer, but she was almost as big as all three of them put together and built low to the ground. Time and again she would simply brush against one or the other of them and knock them down.

"What in the world are you men trying to do?"

Lewis had gotten to his feet, a grim look on his face, and saw Jenny leaning over the fence, staring at him.

"We're trying to get this blasted animal into the trailer!"

Clay was dusting his uniform off, feeling rather foolish. "I didn't come out to wrestle hogs, but I was sort of conscripted."

Jenny looked at them with disdain. "Three grown men can't put one dumb pig into a trailer? You are so helpless!"

"Well, I'd like to see you try it!" Lewis said grimly.

"Okay, I will. You wait right there and don't bother Clara anymore. Get out of there and leave her alone."

"I guess we'd better mind her." Clint grinned. "When she gets her back up like that, it's hard to do anything with her. She's worse than Clara here for bein' stubborn."

The three men left the pen, Clint carefully locking the gate. "What do you reckon she's up to?" he asked.

He did not have to wonder long, for Jenny came back with a sack in her hand.

"What's in the sack?" Clint asked.

"Apples. Now, you three stay quiet. I'll take care of Clara."

Stepping inside the pen, Jenny said soothingly, "Now, Clara, I've got a nice apple for you here." She laid the apple on the ground, and Clara looked at her for a moment, then gave a series of oinks and came up. She chomped down on the apple and looked up eagerly for more. "Here's another one, Clara. Don't you like these nice apples?" Jenny laid the apple right at the base of the chute, and Clara at once came forward. She demolished this apple and oinked for more.

"All right. You can have this one." This time she held it in her hand while Clara took it and ate it hungrily.

"Now, one more time. This one you'll have to go after."

She held the apple up, and Clara moved to get it, but Jenny moved to stand beside the chute. "Here it is. Come and get it." She laid the apple right on the lip of the trailer bed, and when Clara went up, she adeptly gave it a touch that sent it rolling toward the front of the trailer. Without a moment's hesitation, Clara scrambled up the chute and entered the trailer, whereupon Clint, who was waiting, instantly closed the gate.

"I'd think that three grown men could outwit one pig," Jenny said. Her eyes were sparkling as she came out of the pigpen, and coming to stand before her father, she dusted him off. "The next time you have something difficult to do, come and get me, Daddy."

Lewis glared at her, then said, "I'm going to take all the money from this hog and buy myself something nice instead of buying you a present!" he said. Stiffly he walked around, got into the truck, accompanied by Clint, who grinned and waved. As the truck moved away with Clara rending the air with shrill piggish squeals, Clay shook his head with admiration. "That was slick, Sheriff. Next time I have a problem, I'll bring it right to you."

"Men always try to use brute force when a little sweetness would be a lot better."

"I'll remember that." Clay suddenly shook his head. "Kat's feeling bad. She's fond of the animal."

Biting her lip, Jenny's eyes clouded. "It'll be hard on her."

"Yep, growing up is hard. Are you ready to go?"

"All ready. Let me take Jamie in to Ma."

Clay kissed Jamie soundly and watched as Jenny carried her off into the house. He got behind the wheel, and when Jenny returned, he started the engine and pulled the squad car out of the yard. They had not gone far before they saw the truck and the trailer bearing Clara. "Think I'd better trail along in case Clara makes a break for it?"

"No, that's their problem. Let's go around them."

Clay honked the horn once and swung out. He waved at the pair and laughed as Clint waved back, but Lewis did not appear to have seen them. "You hurt your dad's feelings."

"I know. He doesn't like to think there's anything he can't do."

"Oh, by the way, there's something here I want to show you. I came across it in some old papers I was going through last night."

"What is it?" Jenny asked curiously.

"It's the rates that the mobsters charge for their services."

"Their services!"

"Sure, look at it."

Jenny looked down at the note, which was headed by the title *Rates for Crime*. It was in the form of a list, with an amount beside each item:

Punching $2.00
Both eyes black $4.00
Nose and jaw broke $10.00
Black jack $15.00
Ear chewed off $15.00
Leg, arm broke $19.00
Shot in the leg $25.00
Stabbed $25.00
Doing the Big Job $100.00

Jenny smiled slightly and shook her head. "This is a joke, isn't it?"

"Oh, the list is just made up, but, as a matter of fact, you can get any of those items done—sometimes a lot cheaper. Human life isn't held very highly in Chicago."

"Well, I think it's awful! Here."

Clay laughed, wadded the paper up, and stuck it in his pocket. He said nothing for a time, and then he asked, "What's new with you, Jenny?"

Jenny turned to face him. Two months had gone by, and they had had little success with putting bootlegging to a stop. They had made some minor arrests, but somehow they were never able to corner the worst of the bootleggers. Jenny did not have bootlegging on her mind at the moment, however, and suddenly, without meaning to, she blurted out, "Luke wants to marry me."

Clay took his eyes off the road and stared at Jenny for a

moment. He seemed troubled about this statement. "Are you going to?" he asked.

"I don't know."

"You must have some idea."

"Oh, I don't know what made me tell you that. Forget it, Clay."

Clay whistled a tune soundlessly as they moved along, then finally he said, "I guess you're hoping one day to get married and have children."

"Why, of course. I think every woman wants that."

"Well, it's good to have hopes, but they're pretty elusive."

"What do you mean?"

"Well, I've had a few hopes. Things I dreamed of. They'd come to me sometimes—kind of like sailors finding a new land. They stay for a while, then somehow, they just sail off."

CHAPTER TWENTY

"I'VE MISSED TOO MUCH!"

★ ★ ★

"One good thing about winter," Billy Moon said. "You don't have to fight the flies so much."

Ruby looked up from the work scattered on the desk in front of her and met Billy's eyes. He saw that her face was set in a tense sort of way and added, "But I guess flies are the least of my worries. How about a cup of coffee?"

"No. Thanks."

The brief monosyllables only added to Billy's impression that Ruby was, for some reason, in one of those moods that overtook her from time to time. He ambled over to the table and poured himself a cup of steaming coffee, black as tar. He came back, pulled the chair up, then sat down, holding the cup in both hands. He sipped the scalding beverage and said, "I never could stand to hear people talk about bad coffee. There's not any bad coffee. The worst cup I ever had was real good." He had hoped to amuse Ruby, and she sat there holding her pen so tightly that he could see her knuckles were white. "Somethin' wrong, Ruby?"

For a moment the woman did not answer, and then she shook her head. "Nothing you could fix, Billy."

"I'm a pretty good fixer. Give me a try."

"You can't fix things that went bad a long time ago."

Billy swirled the coffee around, stared for a moment into its depths as if seeking to find some answer, and when he did look up and speak, his voice was gentle. "You got a bad deal, but you can't live in a cave."

"You can't trust people either."

"You know better than that, Ruby. Some are no good. Some are."

"How am I supposed to tell good men from bad men?" With these words Ruby bit her lip, threw the pen down, and rose to her feet. She walked over, poured herself a cup of coffee in a large white mug, and then turned to stand staring out the window. Billy got up and walked over to her. He put his hand lightly on her shoulder and said, "Wish I could do something to help."

At his touch Ruby turned, and he saw the defense mechanism that seemed automatic with her. "You think I wouldn't like to trust people? I did once, and I found out what it's like when someone lets you down."

The two stood there, Billy's bulk making her seem small. "You know what the old poem says. Better to have loved and lost than never to have loved at all, or something like that."

"That's a crock of oatmeal!" Ruby said vehemently. She sipped the coffee and made a face. "This is terrible coffee— strong enough to take the enamel off your teeth! I don't care what you say." Her expression revealed something stirring within her, and she blurted out, "You know those little yappy ankle-biting dogs, Billy?"

"Sure. I can't stand 'em."

"Neither can I. I had a friend who had one once. I hated that beast. She put a muzzle on him so he couldn't bite anybody, but beneath the muzzle he was still that same ankle biter. You'd take the muzzle off, and he'd bite in a minute. That's what men are like."

"Come on, Ruby. You know some good men."

"I know some that look good and talk good, but you'd be surprised, Billy, how many men have come talking sweet and making promises, and the first thing I knew they were trying to crawl in bed with me."

The two stood there silently for a minute, and Billy saw the vulnerability in Ruby beneath her tough exterior. He had seen it before, and now it was very evident. There was a cry of some kind in her eyes. She was like a woman trapped inside a prison who couldn't get out, and he had a tremendous urge to take her in his arms. But he knew better than that. He smiled slightly and said, "You've been hurt pretty bad, Ruby, but you're young, and you've got a full life ahead of you. You can't go around keeping your heart in a box." He reached out and touched her face and saw the automatic shock register in her eyes. "Don't worry," he soothed. "It's just that you've got such smooth skin. You're such a fine-looking woman, Ruby. I hate to see you all alone."

Ruby stood absolutely still. His hand was on her cheek. Ordinarily she would have knocked it away, but a loneliness had welled up in her, and now she whispered, "I'm afraid I'll get hurt. I've been hurt too many times."

"Sure. Me too. Maybe not as bad as you, but all of us carry our scars around." He removed his hand then, ran it over his thick black hair, and shook his head. "You know, when I was a kid back on the farm we kept Brahma cattle. We had a bad freeze, and one of the calves got lost. I loved that calf, but when we found it, it was all stiff and wasn't breathing. Pa was going to bury it, but I begged him to bring it into the barn and see if it would come back to life. 'It's just a dead calf, Billy,' he said to me. 'You can't do anything about it.'"

Ruby listened carefully, her eyes fixed on Billy's face. "What happened?" she asked.

"We took him in the barn. I built a fire out of kindling and stuff and rubbed him down with sackcloth. He was pretty far gone, but I'd squeeze him to make him breathe. And you know what? He coughed and suddenly his eyes opened! I think that was the high point of my childhood. I nursed that calf back to health, and he followed me around like a pet. You know how big those things are, but he was as affectionate as a kitten. When I left home I hated to leave that Brahma bull. I missed that bull more than anything else."

"Why are you telling me this, Billy?"

"I'm telling you that you've been walking around like a

dead woman, and inside you there's a beautiful person just waiting to get loose. I'd like to see it happen, but you've got to trust somebody."

"How do I do that?"

"You just throw yourself off like you were on a cliff and trust that somebody will catch you."

The two stood there, and finally Ruby's lips softened and a humorous light touched her eyes. "Would you like to be the one to catch me, Billy?"

"I'm a pretty good catcher. Why don't we give it a try? Come out with me tonight. I'll let you carry my gun. If I get out of line, you can shoot me."

Ruby burst out laughing, and a good feeling coursed through her. "All right. We'll go to the winter carnival. We'll ride the merry-go-round. If you get fresh, I'll throw you out."

"Sounds like a winner to me."

★   ★   ★

Holding Jamie in one arm, Clay glanced around at the glaring lights of the carnival. The noise was almost deafening, and the air was cold, but the people didn't seem to mind. He stopped suddenly and said to Jenny, "Look at that." He motioned upward. "Billy and Ruby are up in that Ferris wheel."

Jenny looked up and laughed. "Ruby's terrified of heights. She told me so once. I'm surprised she's on that thing."

"I'm surprised she's with a man. She's a man-hater, isn't she?"

"She's been hurt pretty bad, Clay." Jenny laughed again. "Look at that. She's clinging to Billy."

"That's probably why he took her on the Ferris wheel in the first place. Smart man."

Jamie said, "Come on, Daddy. I want to ride the horse."

"All right, sweetheart. Here we go." They made their way to the merry-go-round, and Jenny watched as Clay bought a ticket, then carried the child onto the merry-go-round. He put Jamie on a horse, one that was rearing up with its hooves slashing out, and held on to the girl with one arm. When the merry-go-round started whirling to its cacophonous music, Jenny smiled at the pair. There was something about the innocence of Jamie and the absolute trust she gave to Clay that touched her. She knew he worried about being a good father, but now as the two went around and around, she felt a sense of pride in Clay. *He's doing what many real fathers won't do—investing his life in that child.* Finally the ride ended, and the two came back. Jamie's eyes were wide, and she talked incessantly, begging for another ride. Clay laughed and led her to another ride, this one consisting of child-sized cars that went around in an endless circle. He bought a ticket and put Jamie in the car.

"Watch me, Daddy!" she cried.

"I'm watching you." Clay stepped back to stand beside Jenny, and with a jolt the round platform began circling around. Every car contained a child, some two, and every time Jamie passed, she waved and called out, "Hello, Daddy! Watch me."

"She's a beautiful child, Clay."

"Yes, she is. Her mother was a beautiful woman."

"What happened to her? You never told me."

"She died when Jamie was born. When my friend was left alone, he had a hard time taking care of a baby by himself."

Jenny heard the sad note echoing in Clay's voice. She looked up at him and saw that he was moved, as always, when he spoke of his friend, who had later died himself. "You miss him, don't you?"

"He was the only real friend I had. The only one on the whole force I trusted to watch my back. The rest of them would have good days and bad, but Jamie's dad was like the Rock of Gibraltar. He never changed." Clay turned and suddenly asked, "Are you going to marry Luke?"

The change of subject, so abrupt and so sudden, startled Jenny. For a moment she could not answer, and she avoided it by waving and calling out to Kat. But when she turned back, she saw that Clay was waiting for an answer. "I don't know. He's a fine man."

"Yes, he is. I like him a lot."

"What about you? Are you ever going to get married?" Jenny had wondered many times about this, but she had never phrased the question.

"I doubt it. I made so many mistakes that I don't want to make another one."

His answer displeased Jenny. She shook her head, "Everybody makes mistakes, Clay."

"That's right. You know, I even know how to say that in Latin. *Errare humanum est.* To err is human," Clay said. "I know that. I've seen so many bad marriages I guess I'm gunshy."

"I've seen bad marriages too, but I've seen at least two good ones. My parents loved each other devotedly, and now that Mom is gone, Dad's found another woman to take her place. Not really take her place," she added quickly. "No one could do that. But Missouri and Dad are just like one person almost. They'll be together as long as they live."

"Good thing to be with someone like that."

"Why did you come to this part of the world, Clay? You're a city boy."

"I guess I had enough of the city. I thought if I got away," he said slowly and then paused to wave at Jamie and call out to her, "I could find a better life. Mostly for Jamie."

"But why here?"

He shrugged. "My grandmother grew up in Georgia. She used to talk about it a lot when I was a kid. She made it seem like such a peaceful, friendly place."

"Do you think place matters so much?"

"Well, downtown Chicago is a bad scene. Shootings all the time. Of course, if you're rich, you can avoid that by keeping a child in an expensive school. But I didn't have that kind of money."

The ride ceased, and Clay went to get Jamie. She squealed and begged for more, but he said, "No, we're going to have cotton candy now."

He led the way to the cotton-candy booth and soon all three of them were struggling to eat the pink, frothy mass.

"It melts, Daddy!" Jamie cried. "It melts right in your mouth!"

"That's the nature of cotton candy, sweetheart."

The three moved on, but Jenny's mind was still on what Clay had said in their conversation. "I don't think it matters so much where you live. You know you can be happy anywhere," she said.

"That may be so."

"I just read a book called *The Wonderful Wizard of Oz*," Jenny went on. "Kat loves it. She makes me read it to her as if she couldn't read herself. It's about this girl who lives on a dreary farm in Kansas. She gets carried away to some wonderland called Oz, but when she comes back after all her adventures, she finds out that she could still be happy on a farm in Kansas. She didn't have to have a magic place."

Clay smiled. "I think you'd be happy wherever you are. You've got that in you—happiness, I mean."

"I *am* happy, and I'd like for you to be, Clay."

"You're still thinking that I'm a heathen."

"Not that at all," Jenny said. Clay had continued to attend church with her family, and this pleased Jenny, but she knew he hadn't made a commitment. "I think you need to find the Lord just like everyone else."

"I've been thinking about what the preacher said last Sunday. You remember the sermon about Jacob wrestling with the angel all night long?"

"I remember."

"I never heard anything like it," Clay continued. "I didn't know that was in the Bible. Every night I think about that, and I guess you'd have to say I'm still wrestling with the angel."

His words warmed Jenny. She took his arm and whispered, "Keep on wrestling, Clay. You may limp when it's over as Jacob did, but you'll find Jesus. I know you will."

Clay turned to her, and for a moment all the noises of the crowd and of the ride seemed to fade, and everything except her face was out of focus. Her eyes were wide spaced and green as the sea, sparkling with some secret knowledge. He noted again the rich and self-possessed curve of her mouth and how the redness of her hair reflected the lights. She was shapely in a way that would strike any man, and now as he studied her, he said, "Don't give up on me."

She took his arm and squeezed it. "I'd never do that, Clay," she whispered. She wasn't smiling, but the hint of a smile played at the corner of her mouth and the tilt of her head. She was studying him in a way that was total and complete. He had noticed this before. When she put her attention on a person, it was focused and shut out everything else. And as he studied her, he was pleased that she cared enough about him to worry about intimate things like the matter of his soul. He was very conscious of the pressure of her fingers on his arm, and finally they turned and walked away, surrounded again by the laughter of the crowd.

★ ★ ★

The memory of Jenny at the carnival the previous night stayed with Clay Varek, filling his mind. After he had gotten home and put Jamie to bed, he had lain awake for a long time thinking of Jennifer Winslow. He had never known another woman like her, and as he rose the next morning and delivered Jamie to the Winslows, the sight of her brought the memories rushing back. He said nothing, but she smiled at him quickly, and he knew that she had not forgotten their conversation.

He dropped Jenny off at the station, and then he and Hooey went on a patrol. They attended to routine things until almost noon, and then Hooey stopped at a gas station to make a call. When he came back, he said, "Got us a chore, Clay."

"What is it?"

"The Jeters. They're gonna move a bunch of 'shine. A big truck's pulled in with Illinois plates."

"Let's go get 'em, Hooey."

"Reckon we ought to go get some help?"

"No time for that. You know how quick these things happen."

"Well, watch out for those Jeters. They're pretty mean. I heard once old Tom Jeter was struck five times by a rattlesnake and then the snake died."

"Well, come on." Clay smiled wryly, "There's two of us. We'll surround them."

The two wound their way around the country roads with Hooey directing. He spoke lightly of the danger, but he warned Clay more than once about how dangerous the Jeters were. "They're an ugly bunch. Ugly as a stump full of spiders, old Tom is! Don't let him get behind you."

"The same to you, Hooey. Watch out for yourself."

"Me! Why, I'll inundate them with bodily harm if they mess with me! Come on. Let's go show 'em where the bear sat in the buckwheat."

They drove down back roads and finally wound up on an old logging road when Hooey said, "Okay, we'll leave the car here. Be sure your gun is loaded. We'd better take these shotguns too."

Getting out of the car, the two men left, and Clay was amazed at how little sound Hooey made. The leaves were crisp, and he seemed to make an enormous amount of noise, but somehow Hooey walked lightly. He noted that the small deputy's eyes were constantly going from right to left, and more than once he seemed to see things that were invisible to Clay. *You have to be born in the woods to walk like that,* he thought.

Finally Hooey turned and said, "It's right over that rise. We gotta be careful, Clay. There's a cabin down in a little holler, and word I got was the truck's backed up there right now. I think old Jeter's been savin' his 'shine for a long time, and maybe that truck's got other calls to make. Maybe we ought to let the truck leave and see where they go next for a pickup."

Clay thought of this and then shook his head. "Nope, we'll take what we've got. Get the Jeters out of the way, at least."

"Well, we'd better get goin' before they absquatulate."

"Before they *what?*"

"Absquatulate. It means to take off—like Moody's goose, you know?"

Clay could not help smiling at the colorful language of the small man. "All right. Do we go together?"

"No, I'll go around the other side. You count to two

hundred real slow, and when you get there you come in. You'll be facin' the front of the cabin. I'll be around back, and I'll cover you. But don't walk out in the open."

"What do we do then?"

"I'll call out, and they'll come out shootin'. They ain't no other way, and them Jeters won't be took alive."

Clay nodded, and Hooey moved off, again making almost no sound. Slowly Clay tolled off the numbers, and when he reached two hundred, he lifted the shotgun into a ready position and moved through the woods. He climbed the slight rise and paused at the top. Down below in a valley an old weather-beaten house with a faded red barn in the back occupied a small clearing. Backed up to the barn was a truck, and Clay could see men moving things inside of it. Taking a deep breath, he started down the ridge, which was covered with second-growth timber. He was cautious, for he had learned his trade in a hard school. He would have felt safer in a big city with alleys and buildings somehow. Since he was not an outdoors man, he felt naked and exposed. Still, Hooey was there. He advanced down to the edge of the clearing and stood for a moment. Finally he saw movement, and then Hooey stepped out holding a shotgun. He waved Clay forward, and Clay at once advanced. As he walked, the truck seemed to grow larger, but his eyes were on the two men who stood alertly watching beside it. They were wearing suits and overcoats and fedoras. He had seen men like them often enough in Chicago.

"All right, you fellas, hold it right there or I'll salivate you!" Hooey shouted loudly.

Clay moved forward quickly and added his own call. "You're surrounded! Drop your guns, and nobody will get hurt!"

Even as he spoke, he saw the two men both reach inside their coats, and at once the air was filled with the explosions of the shots.

Clay heard a bullet strike a tree over to his right. Lifting the shotgun, he aimed it as well as he could and pulled the trigger. The gun had a terrific kick and stunned him, turning him half around. At the same time, while he was still half turned, he felt something strike his chest. It was like a giant had hit him with his fist, and he fell heavily to the ground. He was conscious of the sound of shotguns and pistol fire and of Hooey shouting and other men crying aloud. He reached up to touch his chest, and a terrific pain struck him. He looked down at the red blood on his hand, and he thought, *I'm dying, and I've missed too much!* It was his last conscious thought, and he slid into a darkness, profound and bottomless.

* * *

Jenny picked up the phone and said matter-of-factly, "Sheriff's office. This is the sheriff speaking."

"Sheriff, get an ambulance. Clay's been shot."

A coldness gripped Jenny as she heard Hooey's words. "Is he all right?"

"Bad hurt. He's at the Jeter place. Get Billy to come and bring the ambulance. He knows the Jeter place."

"I'll come right out."

"No, you go on to the hospital. We'll get Clay there as quick as we can."

The connection broke, and Jenny stood there gripping the receiver with all of her strength. Forcing herself to relax her hold, she put the phone down and then dashed out of her office. "Where's Billy?"

"He's at the city hall."

"Find him. Tell him to get an ambulance out to the Jeter place. Clay's been shot. I'm going right to the hospital."

Jenny left, and she felt numb, as if she herself had been shot. *How bad is he? He can't die*, she thought.

* * *

The hospital was small and not equipped in the manner of a big city. Jenny paced the floor of the rather dingy waiting room for what seemed like hours until finally she heard the sound of the ambulance. She ran outside as the ambulance pulled up with the squad car beside it. Billy came at once to her. "He's been shot in the chest. I don't know how bad."

"Is he conscious?"

"He come awake a little bit just as we put him in the ambulance, but then he passed out again."

And then the attendants were there, and Jenny stood aside as they wheeled out the still, limp body of Clay Varek. The front of his shirt was stained with blood, and her heart seemed to contract. She went to him at once and bent over. "Clay . . . Clay, do you hear me?"

"He's out," the ambulance driver said, nudging her aside. "We've got to get him into the operating room now, miss."

Jenny would have followed them into the operating room, but a heavyset nurse stopped her, saying, "You can't come in here. The doctor will come out as soon as he knows something."

Jenny went to the waiting room and found Billy there. "What happened, Billy?" she said.

"The way Hooey told it, they closed in on the Jeters. They had two men from Chicago there. They started shooting when Hooey and Clay closed in, and Clay got hit right off."

"What about Hooey?"

"Oh, he's fine. He put one of them Chicago fellows down for keeps, and the other one took a shotgun in his knee. He won't be running anywhere. He arrested three of the Jeters too."

The two sat there talking about the arrest, and finally Hooey came in and gave his story. Hooey made little of his part in the raid, and Jenny said only, "You should have come and got more help."

"I reckon you're right, Miss Jenny, but we thought we might lose 'em."

Jenny would much rather that they had missed an arrest, but she did not say so.

The three of them sat there for what seemed like a long time. Finally a tall man came out wearing hospital dress, the cloth mask dangling under his chin. Jenny rose at once. "How is he, Doctor?"

"He's a lucky man. The bullet took him in the side and glanced off his ribs. It was a heavy bullet. It tore up a lot of flesh going in but luckily hit bone instead of organs."

"Can I see him? Is he awake?"

"Still under sedation. You can sit with him, though. He might want somebody there when he comes around."

Jenny went at once to the room where Clay had been placed. Her heart skipped a beat when she saw his pale face, but the regular rise and fall of his chest reassured her. She went to stand beside the bed and put her hand on his hair. He looked so helpless she wanted to cry. He had always been so strong and able, and now he was totally weak.

For a long time she stood there smoothing his hair, and then she suddenly leaned over and kissed him on the lips. He did not respond, but when she straightened up she knew she felt something for this man that went beyond friendship. Laying her hand lightly on his chest, she whispered, "Wrestle with that angel, Clay. You've got to be all right. You've got to be!"

CHAPTER TWENTY-ONE

A CHANGED HEART

★ ★ ★

Clay watched out the window as the flakes of snow drifted out of a gray heaven to carpet the earth beneath. Snow had always been something to be endured in Chicago, part of the hardness and difficulty of winter in a big city. Somehow here in the hills of Georgia he found himself enjoying the sight. He had been at the Winslows for most of the morning and had watched the brown, dead earth transform into a glistening white world. The trees that had been bare and naked were now clothed with sparkling ermine, so it seemed, the sharp edges rounded and curved and beautiful. The hills were smoothly contoured and even the small lake had frozen over and now had its own coating of the snow that shone brightly under the December sun.

"It's your move, Mr. Clay."

Clay turned from the window and grinned across the table at Kat. The movement gave him a sharp stab, but the worst of the pain was over. He'd missed death by a fraction, and ever since getting wounded, he'd thought about what that meant. He had been playing checkers with Kat for over an hour and now he reached out and jumped one of her red pieces. It was obvious that he was stepping into a trap, but he enjoyed watching the youngster, who loved to win at anything.

"I'll take *this* and *this* and *this*!" Kat announced, slamming her checker down on the board as she made her jumps. She raked off Clay's black checkers and chortled. "There, I've got you beat now!"

"Not yet." Clay shook his head and frowned. "I've still got three pieces left."

"But I've got seven, and two of them are kings. You might as well give up."

"Not me. It's not my style." Clay moved around, avoiding defeat for a time, but inevitably Kat made the last jump again, shaking the table with the violence of her move.

"There!" she crowed. "That makes three games in a row I've beaten you."

"I can't understand it." Clay shook his head with mock solemnity. "I was one of the best checker players in Chicago, and here I'm letting a little kid beat me."

"I'm not a little kid!" Kat flared up. Indeed, at fourteen she was passing through the stage of coltish adolescence, but already the signs of beauty were on her. The same beauty that Clay saw in Jennifer and in Hannah. "I beg your pardon, Miss Winslow. I didn't mean to offend you." Clay caught Kat by the nose and squeezed it.

"Ow!" Kat slapped at him and jerked her head back. She glared at him, saying, "You're just mad because I won."

"I guess that's right."

"I just won't play with you anymore unless you can take losing a little bit better."

"I'll try," Clay said, making his face into a serious mask. "How's the Christmas pageant going?"

"Oh, fine! You're going to love it, Mr. Clay." All anger was erased from Kat's smooth face, and she beamed at him, smiling broadly. "I wanted to play one of the shepherds, but Mrs. Simmons wouldn't let me. She said shepherds were all men. I guess a girl could be a shepherd as good as a boy, don't you reckon?"

"I don't see why not. Maybe even better."

"So I have to be Mary."

"Why, that's wonderful, Kat. I'll bet you'll be a beautiful Mary."

Kat glowed, for Clay's praises always pleased her. She did not know how careful he had been to speak well of her when she did choose to dress up and retire her tattered overalls. Suddenly Stonewall rose up from where he had been dozing before the crackling fire in the huge fireplace and ambled over. He reared up, putting his paws on Kat's lap and licking her face.

"Get away, Stonewall!" She shoved the huge animal aside and said, "He wants to go outside."

"Well, let's go with him. Jamie's asleep. I like to make footprints in brand-new snow."

"So do I," Kat said. She jumped up, almost upsetting the table, and Clay rose to follow her. They plucked their heavy coats from the hall tree, and Kat pulled a toboggan cap down over her ears. Clay was wearing his uniform, so he simply put his deputy's hat on. "I wish I could wear a cap like that," he remarked.

"You can wear one of Daddy's. It's right there."

"No, it'd look kind of funny with a uniform. Come along."

The two left the house and walked down the snow-covered walk. The snow was still falling rather heavily. "I love snow," Kat said. She looked up and blinked. "It bites at your face when you look at it."

"Well, don't look at it."

"No, I like it," Kat said. She reached out and took Clay's hand, and the two left the yard and began walking toward the woods in the south. They reached the small lake, and Kat said, "I bet we could walk on it. It's covered with ice."

"Nothing doing. I don't want to have to save your life. Too cold to plunge into freezing water."

Kat grinned at him and pulled at his hand. "Come on. Let's go into the woods."

Clay allowed himself to be towed along, grimacing a bit at the mild pain in his side, and soon they were walking through the woods that bordered the fields of the farm. "It's so quiet in here," Kat said. "I come here sometimes and just lie down and look at the trees."

"I expect you've got a lot of deep thoughts to think. I did when I was fourteen."

The two walked on for twenty minutes and finally turned back slowly toward the house. Clay's face was stiff with the cold, and he saw that Kat's nose was reddened by the breeze. "Better go back," he said.

"I guess so. I'm getting cold."

They were less than halfway back to the house when Kat suddenly began firing questions at Clay, mostly about his past. She was as curious as a coon, always prying into everything, and he fended her questions off as well as he could. Finally she said, "Will you ever get married, Mr. Clay?"

"Hard to say. Maybe I'll wait until you grow up."

Kat gave him a startled glance and then said, "Let's see. When I'm eighteen you'll be thirty-five. No, you'll be too old for me, I expect."

"I expect so."

"Don't you ever want to get married?"

"Sometimes I think it would be nice to have a wife."

"You ought to," Kat said. "Get married, I mean. I mean, Jamie needs a mother. You're a good dad to her, but she really needs a mama. I couldn't stand it when my mom died, but when Dad married Missouri it was so wonderful. I can go to her now and tell her anything, and she always understands."

"I think that's fine, Kat."

"I've been thinking about this, and I've got three women that might be candidates."

"Who are they?" Clay asked, grinning at her.

"Well, there's Madine Thomas. She's kind of an old maid, but she's got lots of money, and she's got a brand-new Buick automobile."

"Well, that's certainly in her favor. Is she pretty?"

"Well, not really, but she's pleasant. And then another one I thought of is Helen Fritch. She's real pretty. She's twenty-two and had lots of chances to get married. Lots of men run after her. She doesn't have any money, though."

"Well, I'd have to balance that out, wouldn't I? Who's the other one?"

"Well, I thought for a while you might marry Agnes

Courtney, but she got engaged to John Franklin last week. Of course, if you went after her, you might win her from him. He's not much of a man, I don't think."

"Got it all planned out, have you?" Clay laid his hand on the girl's shoulder and looked down at her fondly. "Well, you keep on planning, and maybe you'll come up with the perfect wife for me."

"I'll do that. You really need a wife, and Jamie needs a mama."

★ ★ ★

Missouri Ann had fixed a big noon meal as she always did. The whole family was there, and Clint, as usual, sat close to Hannah. From time to time he would tease her about expecting a baby, but Jenny saw that her sister was happier than she had ever been in her life. She took Clint's mild teasing with a smile, and often she would reach over and touch him as if to reassure herself that he was real.

That's so sweet, Jenny thought. *Hannah never thought she'd have a husband, and now she's got such a fine one. I'm so happy for her.* Aloud she said, "Would you want your child to be a boy or a girl, Clint?"

Mischief lit up Clint's eyes, and he said with mock seriousness, "Why, it'd have to be, wouldn't it?"

Everyone laughed but Jenny most of all. "You are crazy, Clint Longstreet! I mean which *one* would you like?"

"I reckon I'd like for it to be a boy. Females are cantankerous." Clint shook his head solemnly but gave a sly wink to Lewis and Clay. "Always out to rob a man of his freedom. Why, you just look at me. Here I didn't have a care in the world, and now this woman's got me all tied down with a marriage license. And now she's started the first of what'll be a passel of young'uns. Why, I don't know if I can stand it."

"You look like you're handling it pretty well to me," Clay said, smiling. His ideas of marriage had changed greatly since he had come to know the Winslows. The marriage of Missouri and Lewis was so solid and real that it changed his mind about second marriages. He also had watched Hannah and Clint carefully. Clint, he knew, was a man somewhat like himself, tough and hard in a sense, but Clint Longstreet was obviously deeply in love with Hannah. His every gesture showed it, and he constantly brought small gifts to her. Not large things but just any kind of gift made Hannah's eyes glow.

Kat suddenly piped up. "I've been thinking of a wife for Clay."

Clay said quickly, "Now, Kat, that's just foolishness. We were just playing a game."

"Game, my foot!" Kat objected. Her lips tightened, and she stared at Clay. "Why, we already settled that!"

"Who are the candidates, Kat?" Lewis asked quickly, enjoying Clay's discomfort. He listened as Kat named them off, then said, "Well, that's a good start. Maybe the rest of us could help a bit. There's Mrs. Freeman. She's a widow with three children. The oldest just thirteen. That'd be a good deal for you, Clay. She's a very pleasant woman, and you got a family all made without the trouble that goes with it."

Missouri snorted. She was putting a huge dollop of mashed potatoes on Lewis's plate and shook the spoon under his nose. "Lewis Winslow, don't be foolish! Why, she wouldn't be a fit wife for Clay."

"Why not?" Lewis protested. "She's got that nice farm all paid for. Clay would just have to move in."

"Maybe she wouldn't have me," Clay said, grinning. "Is she particular?"

"Particular! Why, she's tried to get every man that came within a broomstick's length of her," Hannah snapped. "I wish you would leave Clay alone."

"Well, I'm just tryin' to help," Kat said. She bit off an enormous bite of fried chicken and began mumbling something.

"Don't try to talk with your mouth full."

Kat swallowed the chicken and then pointed the bone at Jenny. "I always wanted Mr. Clay to marry Jenny, but she's going to marry Luke."

Jenny's face grew red. "Kat, you close your mouth this instant! I am *not* engaged to Luke!"

"Well, you're just as good as. He asked you to marry him,

didn't he? And you didn't say no."

"Now, that's enough," Missouri said quickly, seeing Jenny's embarrassment. "There'll be no more talk like this."

A rather awkward silence fell about the table, and Jenny raised her head to look across at Clay and found him watching her. Ever since he had been shot and she had feared he might die, something stirred in her every time she looked at him. Even now as he held her gaze, she knew that soon she would have to either put him out of her mind or—quickly she shifted her thoughts, unwilling to finish them, and concentrated on the food. Throughout the rest of the meal, however, she felt Clay's eyes on her, and though she tried to avoid them, found herself looking back at him. The bullet wound had been painful but not critical. Now Clay's face had resumed its healthy coloring, and the masculine strength that glowed from him was as powerful as ever. She could not help thinking of how her heart had contracted and seemed to freeze when she had seen his face pale as old ivory and his chest bloody on the table in the hospital. Even now she knew that this man had entered her world and made an impression on her that she could not put aside.

Finally the meal was over, and Kat announced it was time to go to the pageant rehearsal.

"It's too cold for me to go out," Lewis said. "Clint, would you mind taking her?"

"Oh, I'll do it," Clay said quickly. "You'd like to see it, wouldn't you, Jenny?"

Jenny hesitated, then nodded. "Yes, you'll have to bundle Jamie up, though. It's cold, and the heater's not working right in the car."

"We'll make out," Clay said.

Missouri Ann Winslow watched the two. They seemed stiff and awkward around each other, but there was an insight in the woman that saw beneath the surface. She watched Clay as he helped Jenny on with her coat and noted that he half reached out to straighten her collar, then drew his hand back quickly when she turned her head. "You can stay as late as you please," Missouri said. "We'll wait up for you."

★ ★ ★

The air was freezing, and more snow was falling. It was one of the coldest Decembers that Millington Wheeler could remember, and as he stood outside the church, he stamped his feet to get some feeling back into them. He was wearing his heaviest overcoat, but the icy breath of the wind had numbed his ears. His wife had brought their two grandchildren to pageant practice at Bethel Church, but Millington had refused to go in with them. He had not, as a matter of fact, attended church for two weeks now. He had not been able to explain this to his wife, for he could not explain it to himself.

Now standing outside the church and listening to the muted singing, he tried to put the thoughts of his wrongdoing out of his mind, but it was there imbedded in him like a hook. He had not slept well recently, and he dreaded waking up in the morning, for even as he put on a mask and went about his work during the day, his heart was somehow dismal, and over all of it was laid a fear he had never known before.

"I've *got* to get out of this mess!" he muttered. The snow bit at his face as the wind carried it in a gust that dusted the lightest flakes against the heavier crust. "I can't go on with it anymore—but how can I do it? I'll be bankrupt. I'll lose the house and everything else—and I'm too old to start over again."

The sounds of singing came to him, and he made out the words, "O come, all ye faithful, joyous and triumphant..." The words seemed to pierce him, for he could not remember the last time he had been joyous. Looking back over his life as he stood in the numbing cold, he realized afresh that he was not a man who knew God. He had tried hard enough. He had prayed. He had joined the church. He had even become a deacon at the urging of the pastor. But all the years that had followed, he had felt somehow like an impostor. And even now the thought ran through him, *A man can learn how to play a part. He can even learn to say prayers out loud and to talk the talk, but there's something in other people that's not in me.* A cry seemed to rise up in him, and he was startled to find tears filling his eyes. He was not a man to weep, but this was not the first time in recent days that tears had overtaken him.

Finally the cold became unbearable, and Millington walked toward the church. He opened the door, stepped inside, and closed the door silently behind him. Then he stepped across the foyer. The church was dark except for the lights now over the scene that had been created for the pageant. He had seen it before many times, the fake trees and the manger, the shepherds in the field. He saw the young boys, most of them wearing bathrobes with towels wrapped around their heads and carrying crooks that had been made by Tim Sullivan, the carpenter. *They don't look much like Palestinian shepherds*, Millington thought, but then suddenly he heard a voice quoting from the Scripture. He had heard the Christmas story and read it so many times that it had become fixed in his memory, but somehow the words now seemed to pierce him:

> *"And there were in the same country shepherds abiding in the field, keeping watch over their flock by night.*
> *"And, lo, the angel of the Lord came upon them, and the glory of the Lord shone round about them: and they were sore afraid.*
> *"And the angel said unto them, fear not: for, behold, I bring you good tidings of great joy, which shall be to all people.*
> *"For unto you is born this day in the city of David a Saviour, which is Christ the Lord."*

At the instant the voice quoted the last verse, and the words "a Saviour, which is Christ the Lord" were spoken, Millington Wheeler experienced something he was never able to explain afterward. A terrible fear came upon him. He was not easily frightened, but suddenly he saw himself standing on the brink of an abyss about to be plunged down into infinite and eternal darkness. At that moment he believed the Scripture, and for the first time in his life, hell became absolutely real to him. "I'm lost—I'm lost!" he cried. Without another word he turned and blindly left the church. He hurried away, but the verse came to him again as clearly in his mind as if it were spoken aloud. *For unto you is born this day in the city of David a Saviour, which is Christ the Lord.* Wheeler was walking rapidly away from the church through the snowy fields and suddenly he could bear it no longer. He fell on his knees in the snow and cried out aloud with a voice filled with agony, "Oh, I have no savior! God Almighty, I throw myself on your mercy—I ask you to save me! Change my heart, and let that savior who was born in that stable be *my* savior!"

The whistling wind carried the words of the agonized Wheeler only a few feet as he knelt there pouring out his heart in the darkness. He never knew afterward how long he had knelt there, but he always knew one thing: at that moment in that snowstorm as he knelt on the hard crust of snow, something changed for him forever. He heard no voice. He had no vision. But into his heart there came a peace he had never known in all his life. He continued to kneel with his head bowed for some time. Then finally, knees shaking, he got up. He expected the peace to leave, but it seemed to glow within him, and despite the cold night air, he felt a great warmth in his spirit. He looked up into the heavens, and the snow bit at his face. Aloud he said, "Oh, God, I feel you've done something in my heart. You have saved me! And I will serve you and be obedient to you for the rest of my life!"

★   ★   ★

"Why, Millington, come in!" Judge Dwight Hightower stepped back and surprise washed over his face as Wheeler came inside. He closed the door, then said, "What brings you out on a night like this? Come on into my study."

"No need for that. I'll say what I have to say right here. It won't take long."

Hightower instantly narrowed his eyes and stared into Wheeler's face. He saw that the man's face was pale, but whether with cold or some other emotion he could not tell. "What's the matter, Wheeler?"

"I've come by to tell you that I'm out."

"What do you mean, you're out?"

"I mean, I'll have no more to do with Vito Canelli or with you, at least as far as this bootlegging thing is concerned."

Alarm ran through Hightower, for he saw trouble ahead as a man in the prow of a ship sees an iceberg looming unexpectedly. "Come on. We've got to talk about this. It's not that simple. You can't just back away from those boys in Chicago."

"You probably won't understand this, Judge, but I might as well tell you now. Something happened to me tonight, and I know only one thing. I'm not going to do anything that would displease God if I can possibly help it. I know that may sound odd to you after what I've been, but I'm going to be a different man from now on. I'll take no more money, and you can just cross my name off the list."

Judge Dwight Hightower was usually good with words, but at this moment he found himself speechless as Wheeler continued to talk. "I'm going to be God's man. I hope you will be someday too, Dwight. You're going down the wrong road just like I was, and there's but one end to it. I gave my heart to Jesus Christ tonight, and I urge you to do the same." Wheeler hesitated, then nodded with a "Good-night." He put his hat on, opened the door, and shut it firmly behind him.

Hightower stood as if stunned, and then thoughts began to race through his mind. He made his way back to his study, shaken by the encounter, and began to pace the floor. "He *can't* pull out! Canelli won't let him. Once you're in with those men the only way you leave is feet first."

For half an hour Hightower tried to think of a way out, but finally he sat down and picked up the phone. He waited for the operator, then said, "I want to call Chicago, and I want to speak to Vito Canelli."

CHAPTER TWENTY-TWO

THERE'S ALWAYS A HARVEST

★　★　★

Helen Wheeler looked up as her husband entered the room. She was embroidering a piece, but at the sight of his face she put the embroidery aside and asked, "What is it, Mill?" She was the only one who called him by this shortened version of his name, and now as she watched him, she was puzzled. "You've been so different the last two days."

"I guess I am different, Helen." Wheeler stood there for a moment, then came over and sat down beside her. He turned to her and said, "I've got a confession to make that I know is going to hurt you."

Helen Wheeler's first thought was *He's found somebody else!* She could not find words for a moment; then she said, "What is it? You've been so quiet the last two days. I know you've been thinking on something."

Wheeler had waited for two days, not speaking to anyone about the experience he had had outside the church when he knelt in the snow. He had gone to the office only rarely but had sought out solitude and had read the Scripture and prayed more than he had in his entire life. His great fear had been that he would lose the peace that had come to him when he had called upon God. But it had not gone away. He felt a joy that could not have been of this world, and the peace was something he had only heard about. He had underlined the Scripture where Jesus had said, *My peace I give unto you.* Now, after two days, he was convinced that he indeed had found the Lord, but as he sat looking into his wife's troubled eyes, he knew that hard things lay ahead. The thought came to him, *A man can be forgiven, but some of the results of his acts are still there. There's always a harvest.*

"Helen, I've done some wrong things in business."

Helen Wheeler gave a gasp of relief. "In business? I thought it was—"

"You thought it was what?"

"When a man comes in and tells his wife he has something to confess, it's almost always something about another woman."

"Oh no, not that! Not ever that, Helen! I've always loved you. There's never been anyone else."

Joy came then to Helen Wheeler, and as he reached over and pulled her close, she hugged him fiercely. And then when he released her, she said, "Whatever it is, we'll get through it together, Mill. Now, tell me." She listened quietly and intently as Wheeler began to speak. He did not spare himself but told her about his secret gambling when he had lost money that should have been hers and the children's. Then he told her how he had fallen in with Hightower and Vito Canelli. Tears came into his eyes and said, "That's the bad news, Helen. I've been nothing but a criminal."

Helen reached over and took his hand and held it up against her cheek. "But you can get out of it, Mill. You can leave."

"You don't hate me?"

"No. How could I do that?"

Millington Wheeler took a deep breath. "I don't see why you don't. I hated myself. But let me tell you what happened two days ago."

Once again Helen Wheeler listened as her husband told her about his experience with God. He spoke slowly, and she could see a light in his eyes she had never seen before. And finally he said, ". . . and so, Helen, that was two days ago, and

I've been praying and waiting to see if it was real. And it *is* real, my dear. I know that I belong to God now."

"Oh, I'm so happy, Mill! I'm so happy for you!"

The two embraced, and then Wheeler shook his head. "I thought I was a Christian. I tried to be, but I was wrong. I'll have to go before the church."

"People will understand. You're not the first person to make this mistake, but now it's all right."

"No, my soul's all right, but we're going to have a hard time. I've got to let the sheriff know what I did, and it may mean—" He broke off and looked at her straight on. "I may even have to go to prison."

"Surely not if you get out, and you tell them what's happened."

"That's called turning state's evidence." A grim expression swept across Wheeler's face. "I don't want to involve anybody if I can help it, especially Hightower. I've thought of him as a friend. He's a hard man and shrewd, and he was the one who got me involved, but still I don't see how I can confess his crime."

"You'll have to do as you think right, Mill."

"Yes, and the first thing I've got to do is call the sheriff and tell her what's happened."

★ ★ ★

When the phone rang, Jenny picked it up. "Sheriff's office. Sheriff Winslow speaking."

"Sheriff, this is Millington Wheeler."

"Why, hello, Mr. Wheeler. What can I do for you?"

"Could you come out to my house, Sheriff? I have ... I have something you need to hear."

"Why, of course, Mr. Wheeler. I'll be right out."

Putting the phone down, Jenny turned to Ruby and said, "I've got to make a run. I'll probably be back in thirty minutes."

"Where you going in case I need to find you?"

"Millington Wheeler just called. He wants to talk to me."

Ruby stared at her employer thoughtfully. "I wonder what he wants."

"Somebody's probably on his property or something."

"You know where he lives? It's out in the country."

"Yes, I know his place. I'll be back soon."

Leaving the office, Jenny pulled her coat tightly around her and pulled her hat brim down over her face. The wind had died down, and the sun was shining, making the snow that still lay on the ground glisten so brightly it hurt her eyes. Getting into the car, she put on a pair of sunglasses plucked from her pocket and left town.

The Wheeler place was only fifteen minutes away, but it was part of a large farm that had belonged to Wheeler's family. Most of it he had sold off, but he had kept thirty acres and his home, a tall two-story place with four huge white pillars in front. It reminded Jenny somewhat of her own house, though Wheeler's was larger and more grand. She pulled up in front of the house, got out, and mounted the steps. She was stamping her feet preparing to ring the bell when the door opened, and she found Wheeler standing there. "Hello, Mr. Wheeler."

"Come in, Sheriff."

Jenny entered and scraped her feet on the rug. "Hard to go anywhere without making a mess with all this snow."

"That doesn't matter. Here, let me hang up your coat and hat."

Jenny handed them to Wheeler; then when he motioned to her, she followed him down a polished oak hallway and turned off to the left. She had never been in the house and was impressed at the size of the parlor. A huge fireplace made of native stone dominated one end. A bright fire crackled and popped in the fireplace, and one wall was nothing but windows, allowing the sunshine to come in. Helen Wheeler got up, and Jenny greeted her. "Hello, Mrs. Wheeler."

"Hello, Sheriff."

Something about the woman's air touched off an alarm in Jenny, and she sat down at Wheeler's word, but he did not take a seat. He went over to stand before the fireplace and looked down at it for a moment, saying nothing. Jenny looked at Helen Wheeler and saw that she was looking down at her hands, which were not entirely steady. "Is there something I can do for you, Mr. Wheeler?"

Turning from the fireplace, Wheeler came over and stopped in the middle of the room. He said, "Sheriff, I'm going to have to confess that I've been involved in criminal activities."

The alarm that had touched Jenny now increased. "Do you want to have a lawyer with you? You're entitled to one."

"No. I want to tell you, and then you can tell me what comes next."

"All right, Mr. Wheeler. Go ahead." Jenny sat there listening as Wheeler began to speak. She had never admired Wheeler, for he had seemed rather cold, but now as she listened, she saw that there was a brokenness in him that had not been there before. She listened alertly, shocked by what she heard. Wheeler was a deacon in his church and a leader in the community, yet by his own admission, he had engaged in activities that were disgraceful and illegal. Much as her own brother, Josh, had, she realized.

Finally Wheeler threw his hands up in a defeated gesture and said, "That's what I have done. Now you'll have to tell me what's going to happen."

"Tell her the rest of it, Mill," Helen Wheeler said quickly. She turned to face Jenny with tears in her eyes. "He's a different man, Sheriff. You must believe what he says."

Jenny turned to face Wheeler and got to her feet. "What is it?" she asked quietly. She listened as Wheeler told her about his experience outside the church, and finally he shrugged and said, "I hear there's such a thing as jailhouse religion. That criminals often pretend to have religion in order to get special favors. I wouldn't blame you if you thought the same of me."

That thought had been lurking in Jenny's mind, but she took one look into Wheeler's face and saw something that had never been there before. Something in his eyes and the simplicity with which he spoke, making no claims for himself at all, and indeed suggesting that what he was doing seemed suspicious. For some reason Jenny, who did not often make snap decisions, knew the conversion of this man was a fact. She stepped forward and put her hand out, and he took it with surprise. "I'm so happy for you, Mr. Wheeler. It came late, but it *has* come."

"You believe, then, that I'm telling the truth?"

"Of course I do. Others may not, but I do."

Tears filled Wheeler's eyes, and he turned away, muttering huskily, "Don't know what's the matter with me. I haven't cried since I was six years old, and now I'm nothing but a . . ." He did not finish, for his wife came over and put her arm around him. The two embraced, and then they turned to face Jenny.

"What's going to happen to him, Sheriff Winslow?" Helen Wheeler asked.

"It's not going to be pleasant, but the fact that he's come forward and confessed voluntarily helps. And if you'll cooperate, I think the worst thing that can happen to you would be a suspended sentence."

Wheeler studied her for a moment, then nodded. "I'll do anything I can. I hate to involve anyone else, but I'll tell you all I know, and you can do with it what you will."

"I think it would be best if we went down to my office, Mr. Wheeler."

"Of course."

"This isn't an arrest," Jenny said quickly. "But I need to get this down on paper." She hesitated, then said, "It's going to be hard on you, I know."

"Not as hard as what I was facing without God," Wheeler said and found a smile. "Helen is with me, and I'm determined to do whatever I can to make restitution."

"I think you can do a great deal," Jenny said. "This won't take long. Perhaps an hour or two until I get all the facts. Then you can come home."

"You're not going to arrest me?"

"Not now, though I may have to later. But you'll be a material witness in the case that'll follow."

Wheeler turned and embraced his wife again. She kissed him and said, "Hurry home, dear. I'll be waiting."

"I will. I'll be right home as soon as I can."

Jenny watched the scene between the two and felt a sense of gladness. She was sorry that Wheeler had stepped outside the law and had betrayed his profession as a Christian, but she believed firmly in his conversion, and as the two left the house, she said with reassurance, "It'll be all right, Mr. Wheeler. You wait and see."

The two got into the car, and Jenny started the engine. She pulled out and took one last look at the house, where she saw Helen Wheeler standing on the front porch. "Wave good-bye to her."

Wheeler waved and turned to Jenny. "Not every woman would have been as understanding."

"I'm glad you realize that."

They had not gone more than a quarter of a mile, barely off of the man's property onto the county road which was unpaved, when suddenly they saw a car slanted across the road and two men beside it, waving at them. "I guess they slid off the road and can't get going," Millington said. "You got a rope or a cable? Maybe we can pull them around."

"Yes, in the trunk." She stopped the car, and the two got out. "Having a little trouble?" she said cheerfully.

The two men were both wearing long, dark overcoats and fedora hats. They were large men, one of them with a sharp face like a ferret, the other blunt and battered, obviously an ex-prizefighter. The sharp-faced man suddenly pulled his glove off, reached inside his coat, and came out with a gun. "Hello, Sheriff, we've been waiting for you. Take her gun, Ollie."

The blunt-faced man called Ollie moved toward Jenny, who stood absolutely still. She did not even glance back at Wheeler, who had gotten out of the car. She felt the gun leave her holster and saw it stuffed into the side pocket of Ollie, then Ollie turned and said, "What about the guy, Mikey?"

The thin man smiled unpleasantly. "Just frisk him. He's probably not carrying, but we wanta make sure."

Jenny kept her eyes fixed on the tall man called Mikey. "What do you want?" she said.

"Why, we want you, Sheriff. You and Mr. Wheeler there. Come along. Put 'em in the car, Ollie."

Jenny turned to see the thickset man seize Wheeler by the arm and pull him along. Wheeler's face was pale, but he did not say a word. Jenny's own arm was seized then, and she was hustled to the car, a long black limousine. Mikey opened the door, and Ollie shoved them in. The two men got in the front, Mikey driving and Ollie turning in the seat, holding a pistol on them. "You be nice," he said, "and maybe you'll live a little longer."

"What do you want?" Wheeler said, staring at the driver.

"Like I said. We want you and the sheriff. You've been givin' us some problems, so we came down from Chi-Town to take care of it."

Instantly the situation was clear to Jenny. She had known for some time that she was the target of the criminal element, and now she suddenly turned and said, "Did you tell anyone what you told me—besides your wife, I mean?"

Wheeler's face was set in shock. "Yes. I told one person."

"And I guess that one person made a call, so here you two are," Ollie said. "Now, sit back and don't try nothin' funny."

Jenny watched the road, but they made so many turns she was lost. Finally they pulled up in front of an old house that looked abandoned. As they got out, she heard the sound of running water, and looking to her right, saw a small waterfall not over six or eight feet high, but the water made a loud gushing sound as it fell.

"This is the old Franklin place," Wheeler said suddenly. "It hasn't been lived in for years."

"That's enough talk. You two get in the house!" Mikey snapped.

He nodded to Ollie, saying, "Lock 'em up good, Ollie, and if they try anything funny, put 'em down."

Ollie was holding the pistol in his right hand. He tapped it against the palm of his left and grinned. "A pretty thing like that? It'd be a shame. She could be a lot of fun."

"You do what I'm tellin' you, Ollie. I'll be back as soon as I go use the phone."

Ollie then shrugged and waved the pistol at the front door. "Come on. No funny stuff, or you'll be sorry for it."

Jenny stepped up on the porch and walked inside, followed by Wheeler.

"You can cook up some grub. I'm hungry. You make a fire in that wood stove."

Jenny gave a cautioning look to Wheeler and said, "All right," knowing that only God could save them now. The two men were obviously killers, and she had no doubt, nor had Millington Wheeler, that they would be victims unless God intervened.

CHAPTER TWENTY-THREE

CLAY FINDS THE WAY

★ ★ ★

Raymond Briggs did not look like an FBI man—at least not the way most people envision agents of the bureau. He was small, not over five-six, had a pale bland face, nondescript brown hair, gold-rimmed glasses, and was mild mannered. When he had first appeared, Clay had instantly judged him to be incompetent. He was more accustomed to big men with a decisive manner, and he had been so buried in his own misery that he made a snap judgment. Now as he sat across from Briggs, he squeezed his hands together and tried to concentrate on what the man was saying. "You've got to remember, Deputy Varek, kidnapping carries a death penalty. The kidnappers wouldn't have anything to lose if they killed the captives."

"I know that!" Clay snapped. "What I want to know is why they kidnapped them in the first place."

"It's not local, I don't think," Briggs said mildly. He had a pen in his hand and from time to time would look down at a sheet of paper in front of him. His writing was meticulous and so small it was almost microscopic. He studied the paper for a time and finally looked up. "I understand you are very close to Sheriff Winslow."

"What's that supposed to mean?"

"Why, it just means that when we're too close to a problem we can't see it clearly."

Clay Varek knew that Briggs was right. He shook his head and said quietly, "I haven't been able to think straight, Mr. Briggs, and you're right. We are very close."

"We've gone over all the possibilities of local people being behind this, but I don't think that's the case. Mrs. Wheeler has told us that her husband made a full confession of his part in criminal activities, and we've had reports that Vito Canelli has been in the area a number of times recently. And I can tell you for certain that Canelli is totally bloodthirsty. He'll kill without a qualm. You know him from your Chicago days, you say?"

"I met him a couple of times. We almost got him once on a bust, but he was too clever. He was Al Capone's right-hand man before Capone was sent to prison—although we've never been able to literally prove that."

"You know what kind of people we're dealing with, then."

"I keep waiting for the phone to ring for them to make some kind of a demand."

Briggs took off his glasses, removed a handkerchief from his pocket, and began polishing them, letting the silence run across the room. The clock on the wall was ticking loudly, and from outside the office there was the sound of cars passing on the street. Finally Briggs said softly, "I don't think there's going to be a call. Most kidnappers want money, but in this case I think they want to get Wheeler out of the way. They're afraid of his testimony."

"What about the sheriff?"

"Well, she's been an aggravation to the bootleggers and the mob knows it. You know how they look on things like that."

Clay did not answer. He felt strangely inept and unable to think. Usually his mind was clear and sharp, and he could make decisions instantly, but since Jenny had gone missing, he had been like a man in a fog. He looked up now, and Briggs could see the misery in Varek's eyes. "I'm afraid," he said simply.

Briggs held Varek's glance for a moment and then nodded,

"I can understand that. I've got every man available out searching, and I'm sure you do too, but it's like finding a needle in a haystack."

"We've got to find them, Briggs, we've just got to!"

Briggs hooked his glasses behind his ears and rose to his feet. "I don't know this country. All we can do is look. We don't even have a description of the car. From the tire tracks we know it was a big, heavy car, but that's not much to go on."

"Some of the known bootleggers must be in on this. Why don't we pull them in and make them tell us what they know."

Briggs shook his head. "That's the kind of shortcut that will get us into trouble." He hesitated, then said, "I'm sorry, Mr. Varek. We mustn't give up hope."

Clay looked up and saw that the words did not agree with the expression of Agent Briggs. He well understood that Briggs had already given up hope and was convinced that Wheeler and Jenny were already dead. Clay rose to his feet and said, "I can't sit here. I've got to do something."

"Keep in touch," Briggs called out as Clay left the office. Clay did not turn, and Agent Briggs shook his head. "Too bad. It's just too bad. They wouldn't have any reason for keeping those two alive. I'm afraid Varek's going to take it hard."

★　★　★

Clay approached the cabin with his gun pulled, but when he entered he found that it was abandoned. It was a shack they had been keeping their eye on because there had been bootlegging activity there in times past. He knew that the Cundiffs had used it and the Skinners also, but there was no sign of recent habitation. A heaviness descended on him as he holstered his gun. He walked out of the cabin and then headed down the road to where he had parked his car half a mile away. The snow had almost disappeared under the heat of the previous day, leaving behind mushy, muddy ground. Overhead the skies were blue, and as Clay trudged along, a mockingbird flew past him, warbling a loud song. Clay paid no attention, and all the way back to the car he tried desperately to think of some way to save Jenny and Wheeler. He reached the car and got in, but when he started to turn the key, despair deeper than any he had ever known welled up in him. He placed his hands on the steering wheel and leaned forward, putting his forehead against the wheel. He remained there for a long time, but time had ceased to mean anything to him except that it was fleeing by, and every second meant that there was less chance that Jenny was alive.

She can't die! God, you can't let her die!

The cry burst out of the deepest part of Clay Varek's being, and it rose to his lips so that he knew he was crying out aloud, something he could not remember ever having done. The coldness of the wheel seemed to burn into his forehead, and he gripped it with every bit of strength, as if he could rip the truth out of it.

Clay Varek had known helplessness before. When his partner had died in his arms, there was no way he could keep the life in the man, and he felt exactly like that now. But he felt even more than that. He suddenly had a picture in his mind of Jenny's face and could see the vitality and the sweetness that had attracted him from the first. He could almost hear her easy laugh and see her eyes sparkle. Grief and fear so mingled in his breast that he could only hang on to the wheel as if it were a life preserver and he were a drowning man.

Finally he drew a deep breath, and the quietness of the country about him surrounded him. He looked out the window at the trees, the sky, and the earth. Blindly he searched as if he might find Jenny simply by looking, and then in despair he closed his eyes and sat there gripping the wheel. Slowly the silence entered into him, and yet in that silence there was a grief that he could not contain. He was shocked to find tears rolling down his cheeks, and he did not wipe them away.

Finally he spoke aloud and began a prayer. It was not eloquent, and his voice was broken. "God," he said, "I've left you out of my life, and now I'm in such trouble. God, you know I haven't followed your laws, and I don't know how to pray.

But I pray anyway. I pray for Jenny and for Wheeler. That you would save them from death." He prayed for a long time, stopping from time to time, and finally as he sat there, he began to remember verses of Scripture. He had heard more sermons recently than he had in his whole life, and he remembered vividly one text that Brother Crutchfield had preached on the previous Sunday. *Whosoever shall call upon the name of the Lord shall be saved.*

Those words seemed to come to him in a powerful way, and as Clay Varek sat there, he knew that God was somehow dealing with him. He kept his eyes closed and finally put his hands over his face. "Oh, God, I've heard that Jesus is the Son of God, and I believe that. I know I can't make bargains with you, but I need you. I've needed you for a long time. You've said that anyone who would call upon you would be saved, so, Lord, I'm calling on you right now. I ask you to save me in the name of Jesus."

This was not the end of his prayer. It seemed to go on for some time, for Clay Varek remembered his past, which had not always been good. But finally he finished confessing to God his grief at the life he had led and said in an exhausted voice, "I can't do anything to help myself. If I get any help, Jesus, it'll have to come from you!"

★　★　★

Missouri Ann Winslow had been listening to Clay for fifteen minutes. He had come to the house exhausted but determined. When she had let him in and led him to the living room, she was glad that, for once, all three of the babies were asleep. She herself had slept little, for she had stayed awake fasting and praying for Jenny and for Millington Wheeler. In fact, Clint and Lewis were out searching for them right now. Clay would not sit down, so Missouri stood with him, watching and listening carefully as he told of his misery.

"... and so I found out that I loved Jenny, Mrs. Winslow, and I sat in that car, and I begged God to save her. And Wheeler too, but the prayer that I finally prayed was for God to save me. I'd never prayed like that before, and I still don't know whether I'm saved or not."

Missouri quickly nodded. "You're saved, Clay. I can sense it in you, and Jesus never refused anyone who came to Him."

Clay shrugged his shoulders but managed a smile. "I don't feel like asking any favors, but I'd like for us to pray together that Jenny would be found safe."

"We'll do that, but I want to tell about a dream I had last night."

"A dream?"

"You'll find out if you serve God long enough that He uses dreams." Missouri nodded firmly. "It was very brief. I could hear Jenny calling to me. Her voice was clear, and I knew it at once. But the other thing I heard was the sound of water."

"Water? You mean like the surf?"

"I've never heard the sea. No, this sounded like a water-fall."

"What else was there?"

"That was all. Just Jenny's voice calling and the sound of a waterfall."

Clay Varek stared at the woman in front of him and said, "I don't know what that means."

"Neither do I, but it's from God."

"I can't stay here, Missouri. But before I go, I want you to pray for Jenny and for me and for Wheeler too."

The two bowed their heads, and Missouri Ann Winslow prayed a prayer that was so passionate it was almost violent. Finally she looked up through tearstained eyes and said, "I don't know what to tell you, Clay, but God will not abandon us."

★ ★ ★

As Clay parked the car in front of the sheriff's office, Hooey Hagan was standing on the sidewalk. He came at once, and Clay demanded, "Any news, Hooey?"

"Not a thing," Hagan said. "It's plumb discouraging."

"Let me tell you this, Hooey. I've been talking with

Missouri Ann, and she told me a dream she had. I can't make any sense out of it." He repeated what Missouri had told him, and Hooey blinked his eyes. "Well, I swan! There's only one place I can think of that there's a waterfall loud enough to make lots of racket."

"Where is it?" Clay demanded. "Are there many waterfalls around here?"

"As far as I know there's just this one."

"Come on. Show me."

★ ★ ★

"That's the old Franklin place. And look, there's a car out in front. Can you see the license?"

"Yes," Clay said harshly. "It's an Illinois plate."

"Well, I'll be dipped!" Hooey breathed. He turned his electric blue eyes on Clay and said, "Let's go get 'em. They've gotta be in there."

"We need help on this. You take the car and go back. Get Briggs and bring what help you can. Don't let 'em go bustin' in there. Sneak up on 'em. I'll be right here. In case they try to leave, I'll stop 'em."

"You sure you can handle it all alone?"

"Do it, Hooey."

Clay watched as Hooey ran back through the woods toward the grove where they had parked the car. He stood concealed by the thick foliage of the trees, never taking his eyes off the house. Hope had risen in him. He wanted to get closer, and he worked his way along, crawling on his stomach most of the way, getting mud all over the front of his uniform. Finally he reached the edge of the clearing in front of the house and, crouching behind an old barrel, scanned the house. For a long time he could see nothing. And then finally, on the second floor, he saw a face, and his heart seemed to stop.

"It's Jenny!" he breathed. "It's Jenny, and she's alive! Thank you, God." He fell to his knees, exultant, and said, "God, let me get Jenny out alive and Wheeler too. If you can do this, I want to serve you the rest of my life. But this one thing I ask of you right now."

★ ★ ★

Briggs shook his head and insisted, "We've got enough men here to take the place, Varek."

"And what's the first thing they'll do when we go in shooting? They'll kill Jenny and Wheeler."

Briggs had brought fifteen men with him: two other FBI agents, the rest of the deputies, and some city policemen. They had crept in slowly and now stood waiting for the decision.

"The longer we wait," Briggs said, "the more chance there is to lose them. You sure you saw Sheriff Winslow in the window?"

"Yes, she's alive, and we've got to get her out. But we can't go charging in there, Briggs, you know that as well as I."

"We can't afford to wait until dark and sneak up."

"There's another way. I don't know how many are in there. One man I didn't know came out to the car, but I'd suspect there are two or three more."

"Yes, I think you're right, but we can't wait. As I've told you, they have no reason for keeping the two alive."

"They're on the second floor, and I've seen other movement down on the first floor. I think they've got them locked in a room up there."

"That's just a guess. You don't know that."

"I know Jenny's there," Clay said, biting off the words. "Look, there's a shed roof covering the porch. If I can get up on that roof and get to the window, I can get inside. Then you can make your play. I'll be there if anyone comes upstairs to harm Jenny or Wheeler."

"It's broad-open daylight!" Hooey protested. "How you gonna get there?"

"I've circled the house. The other side's only got one window on the first floor. Unless somebody's looking, I can sneak around to the back and crawl in underneath that window to the front. Then I can climb up on the roof and get to that window and into that room."

Briggs stared at Varek for a long time, then finally said, "If they see you, you're a dead man. But if you want to try it, it's as good a plan as any."

Clay nodded. "When I get up there and inside the room, I'll give you a signal. That means I can take care of anybody coming from downstairs. You make your rush as soon as I give the signal."

"All right, Varek." Briggs nodded his agreement. "It might work."

Clay turned, pulled his gun, and checked it. Holding it in his right hand, he moved down through the trees and disappeared.

"Do you think he can do it?" Briggs asked Hooey.

"Why, that Clay Varek's all kinds of a feller! I'd trust him with a key to the smokehouse."

Briggs shook his head. "I don't think it'll work, but it's the only game in town. All right, you men. Get ready. When we go in, we go in with a rush. I'll take the front door. Hooey, you go cover the back. If the rats come out that way, stomp 'em!"

★　★　★

Jenny was sitting in a chair at a table staring at her hands. Wheeler was lying on one of the two cots. They had been kept without food and only with a gallon jug of water. Neither of them had slept much the previous night. Wheeler had surprised Jenny. He had been calm, and the only remark he had made had been, "It's all my doing that you're here, Sheriff. I deserve what's going to happen, but you don't."

Jenny now looked over at Wheeler's face and saw that his eyes were closed. His face was drawn, and his hands were folded over his chest.

Jenny watched him for a moment, then got up and walked back and forth. There was no doubt in her mind that the gangsters were going to kill her and Wheeler. She had not told Wheeler this, for he still had hopes that they were being held for ransom. Jenny knew that no ransom would satisfy Vito Canelli. She and Wheeler were in the way, pawns to be knocked off the board without a moment's compunction.

As Jenny walked, she realized with a start that the fear she had felt at first had, for the most part, vanished. She found herself thinking of the things she would miss in the world if she did not live through this experience. She thought of her family, of course, and how they would miss her. She herself would be with the Lord, so that part did not trouble her.

The one thought that troubled her most was the fact that she would lose out on what she had hoped for in her life. She had always, like most young women, wanted a husband and a family, and now it did not look at all likely that she would have either one. One thing became brilliantly clear. She knew she was not in love with Luke Dixon. The man that occupied her thoughts was Clay Varek. As she paced, she shook her head in wonder. *I wonder how long I've been in love with him. I do love him. I know that now.*

She knew Clay had strong feelings for her. Perhaps he loved her too. He had been held back by personal matters, but Jenny remembered the light in his eyes whenever he looked at her, and now she thought, *If I get out of this alive, I'm not going to wait. I'm going to tell him I care for him. That's not the way it happens in the romance books, but I don't care.*

It was in the midst of this that she suddenly heard a sound. At first she thought it was outside the door, and she steeled herself for one of the assassins coming in to put a bullet in her and end it all. Then she realized the noise she heard was not outside in the hall but outside the window. She whirled and stood watching as the faint scrambling noise continued. She glanced at Wheeler, but he was asleep. Finally she took a step forward and then halted when she saw a man there. She was confused and could not imagine one of the criminals being outside her window—and then she saw that it was Clay.

A glad cry came to her lips, but she withheld it. She moved quickly to the window. She had tried to raise it before, hoping to escape, but though she could see no lock, the window refused to budge. She guessed an old coat of heavy paint had sealed it shut. Clay tried to lift as well, then she watched as he pulled out a pocketknife and worked it along the frame. Finally, together, they raised the window, careful to make no noise. She stepped back as Clay climbed in. His eyes were blazing, and he suddenly reached out, and she fell into his arms. She held to him tightly and murmured, "Clay, you came!"

Clay held Jenny for just a moment. When she looked up, her lips were parted. He bent forward and kissed her and said, "I have to tell you that I love you."

"I was going to tell you if you hadn't," Jenny said. "I found that out."

Suddenly Wheeler snorted, rolled out, and swung his feet over the cot. He stared at Clay Varek in confusion and then got to his feet. He opened his mouth to speak, but Clay held up his hand. "Get over in the corner, both of you. Jenny, you get over there." He waited until they were in opposite corners and then nodded. "I'm going to give a signal, and when I do, there's going to be some shooting." He pulled his revolver from his holster and said, "I'll handle anyone that comes through the door, but you stay back." Moving to the window, he leaned out and made a fist and pulled it down three times as if he were pulling the whistle on a locomotive. He waited until he saw movement and then turned quickly and said, "They're coming." He quickly placed one of the chairs under the handle of the door and then moved back to one side so he would not be standing directly in front of it.

From below there rose the sound of alarm, followed by a single shot. A barrage of shots then occurred, and Clay stood tensely, his gun held out in front of him. The shooting seemed to go on for a long time amid cries, and finally they heard a crashing sound.

Footsteps coming up the stairs were plain enough, and Clay raised the gun. But then a voice cried, "Hey, don't shoot! It's me—Hooey!"

Clay grinned and removed the chair from the door. He opened it, and Hooey stepped in, followed by Briggs.

"It worked slicker than goose grease," Hooey beamed. "Of

course, them fellers didn't give up. One of them gonna be pushin' up daisies right soon. But the other one's talkin' right now about who hired him."

Briggs came in and looked around. "Are you all right, Sheriff?"

"Yes, I'm fine."

"I'm Briggs—FBI. And your name is Wheeler?"

"Yes, Mr. Briggs."

Briggs looked at the two and said, "Well, it's all over. One man dead, and one of our men got nicked but nothing serious. I guess you'd like to get home to your families."

"Yes," Wheeler said quickly. "I know Helen must be nearly crazy."

"Come along, then," Briggs said.

Hooey watched the two men leave and then turned to face Clay and Jenny. "I always did like a happy ending," he said, grinning. He saw that the two were staring at each other and hadn't heard a thing he'd said, so he left without another word.

Clay took Jenny in his arms and kissed her, and when he raised his head, she whispered, "I love you, Clay, and somehow I knew you'd come."

"I've got a lot to tell you. Things have changed, Jenny. I've changed. Come on. I'll tell you on the way."

CHAPTER TWENTY-FOUR

A CHRISTMAS LOVE

★ ★ ★

Christmas Eve brought to Georgia, and to the entire country, the usual activities—tree decorating and gift wrapping and church pageants. Kat had starred glowingly in the role of Mary and announced that she would become an actress.

Two weeks had passed since the rescue of Jenny and Millington Wheeler from the Chicago gang. The FBI and the sheriff's department worked together and dealt what amounted to practically a death blow to the moonshine industry in the county. Vito Canelli had been implicated by his underlings, and he awaited trial in Chicago.

Millington Wheeler had been given a suspended sentence, and had confessed his wrong to the church. He had been forced to put his house up for sale, but this had been as nothing to him and his wife. "I've found Jesus," he had smiled, "and what's a house compared to that?"

As for Judge Hightower, he had mysteriously disappeared, and it was rumored that he had been knocked off by Vito's men in retribution.

The last two weeks had brought a peace to the hearts of

both Clay and Jenny. Clay had been baptized, and Jenny had stood beside him proudly afterward, her eyes glowing with joy. Luke had attended the baptism as well and now shook hands with Clay, telling him how happy he was that he had found the Lord. Then Luke turned to Jenny and held out his hand to her too. Jenny took it and held it in silent farewell. Luke smiled at her, but Jenny saw unmistakable sadness in his eyes. It was clear Luke understood that while they might remain friends, their relationship would never be the same.

The Christmas party at the sheriff's office that afternoon was a light affair but with a big surprise. Billy and Ruby announced that they would marry, and the news caught many people off guard. They all knew Ruby had always been hard in her estimate of men, but Billy grinned as he told everyone, "She just hasn't had a man to love her like I plan to."

Jenny and Clay were enthusiastic in their congratulations, and after they left the party and were on the way home Clay asked, "Do you think they've got a chance to make it?"

"Of course they do. They're going to get married and live happily ever after."

Clay laughed, put his arm around her shoulder, and drew her close. "Do you really believe in that?"

"Yes, and it's what we're going to do too. Get married and live happily ever after."

"I'll vote for that." Clay kept his arm around her shoulders, and when they reached the Winslow home, Lewis greeted them warmly.

"You're just in time for supper. We're going to eat and then sing carols around the fireplace, and I may preach a sermon."

Laughingly Jenny went to her father and hugged him. "You've had all the Christmas you need. I think three fine boys is enough."

"You're right about that," Lewis said as he released her. He grinned a self-deprecating grin and shook his head. "What I like about having three sons all the same age is you don't have to worry about making plans."

"What does that mean?" Clay asked curiously.

"Well, it means I know what I'll be doing for a long time.

Changing diapers and holding babies, and then when they can walk, I'll be chasing them down. Later on I'll be teaching them how to fish and become good men."

"It sounds like a winner to me, Lewis," Clay smiled. He looked over at Jenny and winked. "Maybe we'll have triplets. Three more boys. Then we'd have enough for a basketball team."

"And if Hannah comes through"—Lewis laughed—"maybe we can get a baseball team together."

★ ★ ★

The meal that night was a triumph—a golden-roasted turkey with corn-bread dressing and cranberry sauce, peas, and fresh-baked rolls, and to finish it off, pecan and pumpkin pies.

Before they began eating, Lewis rapped on his glass and said, "Before I carve this bird I want us to thank God. He's been good to us. He's given me a fine wife and three fine sons. He's given Hannah a good husband and a child to come. And He's given Jenny a man strong enough to sit on her when she needs it."

"Here, here," Clay agreed, winking at Jenny.

"And He's given Jamie a good mom," Kat piped up.

"And what's He given you, Kat?" Lewis smiled fondly at his youngest daughter.

"The best family in the whole world! And God bless us every one!"

They all echoed that sentiment and fell to eating with all their might.

Afterward they sang carols around the fire, admiring the tree Clint had cut down and they had all helped to decorate.

Finally, despite Kat's protests, everyone went to bed. The three youngest Winslows went peaceably for once, and finally Clay and Jenny were alone. They sat on the couch in front of the fire, and for a long time they were silent. Jenny felt safe and secure with Clay's arm around her. From time to time they would speak, but the solitude and the warmth of the crackling fire and the joy they both felt seemed to be all that was needed.

Finally Clay said, "I'm a little bit scared, Jenny."

"You were never afraid of anything."

"Yes, I was. Lots of times." Clay looked at the fire and murmured, "I want to serve God, but I really don't know how. And I want us to marry. It's going to be a bit of a problem, though."

"Why?"

"Well, I never believed in a man working for his wife, and that's what I'll be doing."

"No, you won't." Jenny reached up and put her fingers under Clay's chin, gently turning his face toward her own. "I had a meeting with the commissioner yesterday. I told him I wanted to resign."

Clay blinked with surprise. "You told him what?"

"Yes. And it's what I want, Clay. I never wanted to be sheriff anyway. Maybe God put me in office for a while, but now I think it's time for me to step down."

"But what about the job?"

Jenny leaned forward and kissed him soundly. "We're going to have a great new sheriff."

"You mean Hooey?"

"No, of course not Hooey." She took Clay's hand and held it up against her cheek. "*You'll* be the new sheriff. You'll fill out my term, and then you'll have to run for election. But you'll make it. I think you'll be sheriff for a long, long time. And I'll stay home and be a wife and make you happy."

Clay shook his head. "I'll never be able to keep up with what's going on inside that head of yours, Jennifer Winslow. But that's good. I'd hate to be married to a woman with no surprises—and with you I don't have to worry."

He pulled her close, and her lips were soft and yielding under his own. The fire snapped and popped, and the grandfather clock ticked solemnly.

Stonewall, lying by the fire, lifted his head and watched the couple curiously, then yawned and went back to sleep.